INFERNO

The Seventh

Kelly Turnbull Novel

INFERNO

By

Kurt Schlichter

Paperback Edition ISBN: 978-1-7341993-5-2

INFERNO - Kurt Schlichter - Hardcover - 101122 – Final v81

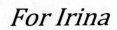

For Irina

ACKNOWLEDGEMENTS

I think my acknowledgements are getting repetitive yet redundant. So many of the same people help me out with each new one that I could just write "Ditto last time" and get it mostly right. But that would miss the point, which is to thank those who have made the Kelly Turnbull series possible. So, here we go again...

First, as always, is my hot wife, Irina Moises. Once again, she was there every step of the way, reading and critiquing the multiple drafts and insisting that we do just one more read to purge it of the hated scourge of typos.

Lots of other folks contributed and supported this series. I can't list them all, but I'll try to name a few...

Thanks to friends and supporters like Drew Matich, Matthew Betley, Larry O'Connor, Cam Edwards, Glenn Reynolds, Chris Stigall, Tom Sauer, Hugh Hewitt, Duane Patterson, Pat and Robert O'Brien, Seb Gorka, Dan Bongino, Ned Ryun, Christian Collins, WarrenPeas64, Big Pete, Tim Pool, Josh Steinman, Jim Hanson, Nick Searcy, Dana and Chris Loesch, and many more. And to those I can't name because I'm so controversial, or they are so shy, thanks!

Thanks to gun guru Bill Wilson of Wilson Combat for his advice and technical expertise.

Thanks to Adam Kissel, who always volunteers for a detailed copyedit that inevitably finds a bunch of typos that Irina and I missed. He's remarkable!

My cover artist, J.R. Hawthorne *aka* Salty Hollywood, crushed it yet again with this cover.

Thanks to everyone who has followed me on Twitter and GETTR, all the Gladiators at *The Schlichter Arena* on Locals.com, and everyone who reads my stuff at Townhall.com – you guys are great!

And I must, of course, thank the hundreds of thousands of readers who have followed this story from beginning to end!

Finally, I would also like to thank the Bulwark staffers' pool boys for picking up the slack with their wives. Just kidding. Or not.

And, finally, I always thank Andrew Breitbart, because without him, these books (and more) would never be!

KAS, October 2022

PREFACE

This is the seventh novel in the Kelly Turnbull series. Wow.

Yeah, these books jump around. I did not write them in chronological order and probably would not have even if I had imagined we'd be here now, closer to ten volumes than to one.

The last two books, *Crisis* and *The Split*, covered the beginning of the national divorce that provides the background of the story. *Inferno* returns to the other end of the story arc, and picks up after *Collapse* as United States forces have invaded and occupied part of the formerly blue West Coast. But all is not well – as you shall see.

If you care about years, this takes place in the mid-2030s. If you are picky, you'll notice that real life has disrupted the Kelly Turnbull canon. All those black swans have come back to roost in my timeline. You need to ignore the nagging memory that in some earlier book I referred to some lib hack who did not become president, or overlooked some lib hack who did. Lighten up. This isn't *Star Trek* and you aren't some virgin nerd with nothing in his life but trivia like Captain Kirk's zodiac symbol and Sulu's favorite color.

Somebody reading this is, right now, thinking, "Uh, James T. Kirk is an Aries." I had to Google it, and I'm still a little weirded out that someone spent time figuring that out and putting it on the web.

Anyway, if the canon consistency is imperfect, just go with it. After all, it's just a story. It couldn't happen in real life, right?

Right?

Well, a lot of people tell me that they originally thought my depiction of the future was crazy, but now it seems to be coming true. And I am not thrilled with that.

I don't want this to come true. This is not a template for my preferred future. It's a warning.

I write that in the prefaces of all of these books, but that never, ever stops the liars and/or morons from ignoring it. Let them run their lying pieholes. They mean nothing. I am talking to you, the loyal reader.

Part of why I have written these novels is because of what I fear might happen if we let people like them win. Like its six companion volumes, *Inferno* is a warning, not a road map.

I just hope you find it entertaining and as much fun to read as it was to write.

Regardless, my message to you is this: Do what needs to be done to ensure that these books never come true.

When you pass through the waters, I will be with you; and through the rivers, they shall not overwhelm you; when you walk through fire you shall not be burned, and the flame shall not consume you.

Isaiah 43:2

BOOK ONE

1.

"Hey, I don't believe in guns," Kelly Turnbull lied.

His black Wilson Combat CQB, basically the ultimate version of the classic .45 caliber M1911A1 pistol, was nestled in the small of his back, out of view of the two dirty men standing to his front on the forest road with pump-action shotguns leveled at his guts.

He wore a short-sleeve, tan button-up shirt that said "United States Forest Service."

"I'm just a ranger, guys," Turnbull said calmly. That statement was true, but not how the other gentlemen thought.

The guy on the left had a beat-up Mossberg 500 with a pistol grip and a sawed-off stock. Under his flannel shirt was, improbably, an ancient Molly Hatchet concert tee. His running buddy on the right sported a droopy black moustache and a Remington 870. That was a classic scattergun too, and at this range it was more than capable of effectively tearing Turnbull in half with a swarm of double-aught buckshot.

The sky above glowed a dreary orange.

The acrid smell of smoke had hit Turnbull about twenty miles earlier as he had entered the back country in his F-150. Now ashes floated down on the trio, carried by the wind from the forest fire raging a few miles north near what had been Lassen Volcanic National Park. Before Mt. St. Helens detonated in 1980 with the power of a score of hydrogen bombs, Mt. Lassen's 1915 eruption had been the last one to happen within the old continental United States. Another was coming due, but today the disaster *du jour* in Northern California was the conflagration within the forest that the old People's Republic and the pre-Split California state government had both studiously refused to manage.

The guy with the Remington took his hand off the pump action to brush the white/grey ashes off his moustache. The Molly Hatchet fan spoke.

"Who the hell told you that you could even come up here, Smokey the Bear?"

Moustache guy thought this was funny and grinned.

"It's kind of my job. This is a forest, right?" said Turnbull.

"Yeah, but it's *our* forest," said the Hatchetman. "NorCal Cartel, bitch."

"NorCal for life," 'Stache added for emphasis.

Turnbull's Forest Service Ford truck idled behind him, parked where they stopped him. The beat-up white Dodge pick-up the dope growers drove was parked across the road perpendicular to the blacktop to his front, their rear. On the north side, the road gave way to a deep ravine with a stream at the bottom that you could glimpse between the pines.

They were standing on old California State Route 32 about ten miles from where the little town of Chester was supposed to be to the east. Whether it was still there after over a decade of being in the blue was unclear. From the potholes, and the fact that these dirtbags were feeling free to stop traffic venturing into the wilderness, it was clear the blues did not spend much time asserting their dominance up here. Nor had the red forces that had recently fought their way north through California gotten around to clearing this wilderness.

Northeast California was failed state territory, at least for the time being.

"You guys know about the war, right?" Turnbull asked.

"Yeah, so what?" asked 'Stache. Like his buddy, his eyes were bloodshot. It was pretty clear that these guys had broken up the monotony of guard duty with several bong hits.

Turnbull answered his own question.

"So, the United States is back in charge in California, which means we rangers are coming back to work. This is a national forest, and the US federal government kind of wants its woods back."

"What if we don't feel like giving them up?" asked 'Stache.

"That might be a problem."

"I think *you* got a problem, ranger."

"Look guys, you can grow all the dope you want for all I care. Live and let live. Just let me get back in my truck and do what I gotta do here and we're cool."

"Oh, we ain't cool," Hatchetman said. "You brought us gas and a nice pick-up truck. Besides, you think the Cartel is just going to let a cop leave?"

"I'm a ranger, not a cop. My business isn't with you or your cartel. You get back in your truck, I'll get back in mine, and I'll be on my way."

More ash fell.

"Fire's coming closer." Turnbull observed. "And I don't think anyone's trying to put it out. You sure you boys want to stick around guarding the road and dealing with me?"

"Don't worry about us, ranger," said Hatchetman. "Worry about yourself."

"You're lucky we caught you, ranger," 'Stache said. "We'll just shoot you. Those 'Nihilists, they'll keep you alive for a long time."

"'Nihilists?" asked Turnbull. "What, like Kraftwerk fans?"

"Annihilationists," Hatchetman said, pronouncing it slowly as if Turnbull was the idiot. "They think the world's better off with everyone dead, so they want to kill everyone. That's their thing. Tommy Doom."

"What's a Tommy Doom?"

"Their head honcho," Hatchetman replied, again slowly, again as if Turnbull was the dumb one.

"I like the name. Evocative. I am wondering, though, why these Annihilationists haven't killed you yet?"

"Because we'd kill *them* if they stepped to us. We ain't afraid of them, so they respect us. We got a truce. We trade with them. We got some stuff they want, and they got stuff we want."

"I can guess what stuff you guys got. What stuff do they got that you want?"

"Girls," Hatchetman said. "They got lots of girls, and the girls don't care. They're planning on dying as soon as they kill everyone else anyway."

"That's some commitment to their cult, I guess. So, where are these Annihilationists?"

"Out in the woods past Chester, but that don't matter to you," said 'Stache. "Because we got orders about what to do with trespassers."

"What, you're supposed to kill rangers who try to come in here?"

"We're supposed to kill anybody who tries to come in here. So, if you're a praying man, now's the time."

"And you think you can take out a ranger?"

The pair laughed.

"What are you going to do?" scoffed 'Stache. "Tell us that only we can prevent forest fires?"

Hatchetman giggled.

"Oh," Turnbull said. "I think there's been a misunderstanding."

"Yeah, there has been, forest ranger."

"I mean by you. See, I'm not *that* kind of ranger."

Hatchetman stepped forward, his Mossberg at waist level pointed at Turnbull.

"Oh yeah? So, what kind of ranger are you?"

"The airborne kind."

"Huh?"

Turnbull leapt forward, his left hand grabbing the shotgun and forcing its muzzle to the side. His right hand went behind him fast, his hand gripping and drawing out the Wilson .45 in a move he had practiced thousands of times for just such an occasion.

Hatchetman had the presence of mind to pull the trigger, and the double-00 buckshot pellets tore out into the trees. 'Stache, however, hesitated, validating the ancient doper wisdom that one should not get high on his own supply.

Turnbull brought up the Wilson and fired two Federal Hydra-Shok hollow points into 'Stache's chest. The doper sprawled on the blacktop and the Remington clattered across it.

Turnbull whipped the pistol around and aimed it squarely at Hatchetman's face.

"Let go the shotgun," Turnbull said patiently, holding the scattergun by the barrel. The man swallowed, then released his grip. Turnbull took the weapon and set it on the ground, the barrel of his pistol dropping slightly but never leaving center mass of the ferocious barbarian depicted on Hatchetman's t-shirt.

Turnbull stood erect again.

"Now, tell me more about these Annihilationists."

"They, uh, they get these kids in from the cities. Talk them into coming here. They live in the woods and raid where they can. They're crazy. They think they need to save the earth by killing everyone else. This Tommy Doom guy calls himself The Last."

"The Last? Like Last comma The?"

"Yeah," Hatchetman said, shaking.

Turnbull shook his head and sighed. It was never uncomplicated.

"Just an easy extraction," Clay Deeds had said. "No big deal. Come on Kelly, it's important."

Deeds, assuming that was his real name, had been Turnbull's handler for the last dozen years. He had the bearing of a particularly cunning Roman senator of the late Republic, and the viciousness to survive where a mistake could get you dead. He had his tentacles at the heights of power, and could probably get the President on the phone. It was Clay Deeds who came up with the operations and vectored Turnbull and his other operatives in to do the wet work. For Deeds, Kelly Turnbull was where the rubber met the road.

Turnbull realized that this made him the tire in that metaphor.

Deeds would inevitably wheedle him into a mission, and it would inevitably turn into a bloodbath. Now Turnbull felt like kicking himself for falling for it yet again. He returned to the matter at hand.

"Now, where are your cartel's farms?"

"I'm not saying shit about the NorCal Cartel."

"Okay, now you're flirtin' with disaster," Turnbull said, lifting the muzzle to the man's face.

Blank stare.

"That's a Molly Hatchet joke," Turnbull said. "But really, it's not a joke because if you don't tell me where the farms are I'm going to shoot you."

"*They'll* kill me."

"So, you have a dilemma."

"Eat sh-" Hatchetman began but the hollow-point interrupted him in mid-vulgarity. The ejected shell clinked on the asphalt.

Turnbull took the shotguns and gathered up about 50 shells from the pair and put it all on his front seat. Then he loaded the two dead dopers in the back of their truck, went into the cab and put it in neutral. With some effort, he pushed it forward and got up enough momentum to carry it off the side and down into the ravine. It crashed and trashed its way downward about halfway until it smashed into a tree.

Then Turnbull got back into his United States Forest Service truck, put it in gear, and headed toward Chester.

The ash was coming down harder now as Turnbull drove east on SR 36. The sky was overcast and there was an eerie orange glow. Before he left the town of Red Bluff on I-5, he had figured he had about 12 hours to get in and out before the fire got here. Whether that was still a good estimate or not was unclear.

Except for the dusting of ash, which gave the appearance of dirty snow flurries, it was a pretty drive. Tall pines rose on each side of the road, but even from the highway Turnbull could see the undergrowth was thick and tangled. Forests needed to be managed or burned, but very similar people had been in charge in both Old California and in what had been the western half of the People's Republic. The rulers were city people whose knowledge of the wilderness consisted of knowing it looked pretty, and they had opted out of managing the forest. The fuel on the ground had built up to a critical mass. It was going to burn, and burn bad.

This current fire was totally out of control. The red forces that had invaded and conquered much of the western half of the People's Republic months before had not yet even tried to occupy the northeastern corner of California. There was no way they could contain this mammoth blaze. The fire was going to burn until it burned itself out. It might be weeks.

The shotguns lay next to him on the passenger's seat. He scanned for threats ahead and off-road as he drove. But the biggest threat might well have been the road itself. The decade of People's Republic rule was evident in the condition of the highway. He frequently swerved to avoid potholes and more than once a swathe of asphalt had simply fallen away in a landslide, leaving only a narrow strip to maneuver across to continue his journey.

He passed something called "Butt Mountain" and continued on. The town of Chester was supposed to be ahead. He had read what he could about it in preparation for this mission. When the Split happened, it had a population of about 2,100 and had largely relied on tourism and forestry. Chuck Norris, now a revered congressman back home, used to have a vacation house there.

What it was like now was anyone's guess. Deeds had only been able to get him some old satellite imagery from a couple weeks before, and it told him nothing more than that there was still a town there.

A hand-painted sign appeared on his left. It was a wood sheet with red lettering: "YOU'RE DOOM AWAITS."

Another improvised billboard a few hundred meters further down the road read "YOU'RE DUTY IS TO DIE."

Evidently, the malicious Annihilationists hated proper English as much as they hated all human life.

He drove on and suddenly the trees disappeared – there was a large, empty field where forest had been extending off the road in both directions. Then there was another sign, this one an official one, albeit old and peppered with rust-fringed shotgun pellet holes.

"CHESTER POP. 2,207."

The town was still there, with more activity than he expected. People were in the streets, mostly with tools like shovels, picks, and chainsaws, dressed to work. They all stopped and stared at the "US FOREST SERVICE" emblem on his doors when he slowed down and rolled into town, but no one tried to stop him as he passed.

Some of the stores seemed to be open, though more were shut down. There were few vehicles moving, but plenty were parked along the sidewalks. Many of those had obviously not moved in a while.

One thing caught Turnbull's attention or, rather, the lack of something caught it. There was none of the kind of awkward propaganda signage he was used to seeing in the blue. Nothing about warning the subjects to turn in racists, transphobes, and other enemies of the state to People's Security. No crowing about how the PR supplies all material needs, and how it was owed commensurate gratitude. And there were no ever-morphing multi-colored flags.

He passed four men and a woman in work clothes pushing a wheelbarrow loaded with tools. They stared at him as if he was riding in on a unicorn.

There was a diner ahead, and it was open – a pair of men were coming out as he pulled up to it and parked. They did not seem obviously hostile, but Turnbull always erred on the side of firepower.

He stepped out of the pick-up with the Mossberg 500 in hand. The smell of smoke was even stronger outside the cab, but oddly, it seemed to have a tinge of roasted coffee.

The pair was not panicked by the sight of the shotgun, and they stopped in front of him.

"You a forest ranger?" one asked, curiously, not hostilely.

"That's what the shirt says," Turnbull replied.

"It's been years," said the other.

"There's been a change in management in California," Turnbull said. "The US is back."

"Well, are you feds going to help us with this fire?" the man asked. Ashes fell between them, more than before out on the road.

"You look like you're doing what you need to, but I'll do what I can."

"Are you all they're sending?"

"One fire, one ranger."

The men grunted and moved on. A big rig tanker with "WATER" painted on the side roared past. Dripping hoses were hanging off the sides.

"Slow down!" someone shouted. The truck kept going.

Turnbull went up the steps into the diner. He pushed open the door and a little bell rang. All eyes came his way.

The establishment had probably been old-school even back when old-school was merely school. The walls were decorated with yellowing photos of loggers, fishermen, and local high school sports teams. An autographed portrait of Chuck Norris smiled down on the patrons. It was probably from the aughts, but the icon hadn't changed much.

There was a row of booths across the front, and a long counter. Several booths and seats were occupied. In back was a kitchen where a couple men were cooking. A pair of waitresses were up front. They did not wear uniforms or even name tags, nor did they need to. Everyone here knew everyone.

The place went quiet when Turnbull entered, the shotgun pointed at the floor.

"Holy shit," the older waitress said. "Never thought I'd see you guys come back."

"Here I am," Turnbull replied.

"Well, take a booth. I'll get you a cup of coffee on the house."

"Coffee?" Turnbull asked as he slid into a booth facing the door. "Must be extremely responsible coffee by now."

The waitress laughed as she poured a cup. "Damn blues and their watered-down responsible coffee. We barely got anything up here before the war and we haven't seen real coffee in months. No, this is our own special brew – coffeeberry and chicory. We roast it out back." She put the cup down on the table in front of him.

Turnbull eyed the dark brew suspiciously. "There's such thing as coffeeberry?"

"Yep. Also called 'buckthorn.' Try it. It won't kill ya. If it was poisonous, we'd all be dead."

Turnbull took the cup and put it to his lips. It was hot. He carefully took a sip. It was horrendous, only distantly related to coffee, and a step down even from the PR's infamous responsible coffee.

"It's good," Turnbull said, memories of lying about many atrocious meals eaten as a guest of Arab and Afghan village elders flooding back from his Special Forces days.

"Bullshit," the waitress laughed. "We all know it's awful. But I appreciate the gesture."

The bell on the door jingled as it pushed open and an older man stepped in. Turnbull's hand had reflexively gone to his shotgun, and the waitress noticed.

"Ranger, huh?" she said dismissively. The older man approached and sat down across from Turnbull, looking him in the eyes.

"This is Mayor Pete," the waitress said. "Not to be confused with that other one." She returned to the counter.

"Welcome to Chester," Mayor Pete said. "I guess the federal government is back."

"Yeah. You probably heard that the PR is under new management. I'm here to look around."

"Horse shit," said the mayor. "I don't know what you're here for, but that 12-gauge says it's not just to count trees. Now, I got to get out there and organize these folks to cut back the forest and wet down roofs enough so that the fire that's coming doesn't wipe us out, so I don't have a lot of time to waste. Why are you here?"

Turnbull sized him up. The mayor, like the others, had no apparent fear of him or his weapon. That meant they were either stupid – and stupid people would probably not survive long surrounded by crazed death cultists and drug cartels – or someone had a deer rifle scope's crosshairs resting on his temple. These folks probably did not have a lot of bullets left, but they only needed one to punch through the window and ruin his day.

"I'm here to bring someone out. Not one of yours. Someone I think is wrapped up with this Tommy Doom character. I just need some information and I will be on my way."

The mayor nodded. "I thought it would be something like that. If you want my advice, you'll turn around and get out of Dodge before the fire gets here."

"I don't want your advice. Just some information."

"Then we'll trade, information for information. You first. We know there was a war and the United States took out the People's Republic. That true?"

"Partly. The eastern PR is still pretty much intact. The US invaded the western People's Republic and it's occupying most of California and some of southern Oregon. Washington is partly deep blue. The rest of the Beaver State and Washington are unoccupied, like this area. Anyway, the Chinese tried to land in California, but we stopped that. They did land in Panama and took the west side of the canal. We may get invaded from Mexico, if the Chi Coms can get the Mexicans to cooperate. So, it's a mess."

"Yeah," the mayor replied. "We used to send people out to Red Bluff and Redding to trade and get gas and coffee and the like, and news too, but that ended when the war started. We're kind of in the dark. All we get are rumors, like that they blew up the Golden Gate Bridge. Crazy nonsense like that."

"No, we blew that up." He used the "we" specifically.

"You're kidding me."

"Nope," Turnbull said. He noticed a man pay for his meal with six chicken eggs and then leave.

"Can I get some scrambled eggs?" Turnbull asked the waitress, who nodded.

"So, when are the reds going to come out here and bring some law and order?" asked the mayor. Turnbull was still old enough that referring to the good guys as "reds" was jarring.

"Good question. It's one thing to take territory. It's another to control it. There is a lot of land and the red soldiers are citizens who mostly want to go home instead of stay here on occupation duty. The provisionals – well, some are okay and some you don't want around."

"Why the hell did you reds invade if you aren't going to keep order?"

KURT SCHLICHTER | 13

"I'll ask General Karl Martin Scott next time I see him. He's the new commander on the West Coast. Now, my turn. Why aren't you all dead?"

"What do you mean?"

"Well, you have the NorCal Cartel in the area and they are bad dudes. And then you have the Annihilationists around too, and they want everyone dead. So, why haven't they killed you?"

"Well, because they need us, I guess. We have a doctor, mechanics, and such. At least until the war, we used to go get things from civilization. It's easier to trade with us than fight us, so we live and let live with the dopers. Same with the Annihilationists, though our deal with them is not quite as good."

"What do you mean?"

"Well, they agreed that they would kill pretty much everyone else before they got around to us."

"That's a kind of deal. I'm not sure it's the good kind."

"I think they have the same deal with the Cartel. So, we get along for now. Every once in a while, lowlanders would come up here from the blue to hike or whatever and they'd sometimes disappear. Or they would go raid in the Central Valley or up in Oregon. They used to recruit at the universities and their new recruits would pass through. I just remember their eyes."

"Their eyes?" asked Turnbull.

"Yeah," said the mayor. "Their dead eyes."

"Well, I'm looking for one of those. Girl, about 20. Was at Berkeley. After the invasion, they tried to find her at the university. Her friends said she came up here just before."

"There are lots of girls. Just because Tommy Doom doesn't like babies doesn't mean he doesn't enjoy the process of making them."

Turnbull had a photo of Caitlin Bowers in his pocket. He pulled it out. The mayor glanced at the pretty, smiling redhead. She was in her Young Antiracist Pioneer overalls with a rainbow scarf. On the right side were her merit badges, on the left her privilege demerit badges. She had one Turnbull recognized for "Cisgenderism."

"Like I said, there are lots of girls."

"How many total Annihilationists are there?"

"I dunno. Under fifty."

"Weapons?"

"Some guns, but mostly axes and knives. The Last – that's what Tommy Doom calls himself – says it's better for Mother Earth to kill with blades than bullets. Something about lead poisoning the earth."

"Now, where are they?"

"Well," the mayor said. "Here's the thing. If you go there – and you strike me as the kind of guy who will – and you get caught, then you'll tell them we told you where to find them and maybe there goes our truce."

"Do I look like the kind of guy who would talk?"

"Mr. Ranger, with what we hear those psychopaths do to people, everyone will eventually talk."

"As long as they aren't cannibals," Turnbull said. "Been there, done that."

"They make a big deal of being vegan," the mayor said. "Except for that. They call it 'recycling.'"

"Not cannibals. I really hate cannibals." Turnbull said, shaking his head. "Still, I need to know. Where are they?"

The mayor sighed. "If they get you, you did not hear it from us. Anyway, this fire may make it all moot. About ten miles north of here is an old Boy Scout camp. The blues used it for one year for their All-Identities Scouts and renamed it 'Camp Lia,' but we still call it by its old name, Camp Fleischmann."

The waitress walked over and put down a plate of scrambled eggs. "This ain't on the house," she said.

"Here," Turnbull said, handing over the Mossberg. The waitress took it and smiled.

"I'll get you some bacon too."

The mayor spoke. "I got to get back to work. We figured this fire was coming one day, so we've been cutting back the forest away from town for years. We got to set some backfires and clear out some brush in and around the town, and wet down buildings with our water tanker. With a little luck, the fire will burn around us. I don't know what the Cartel and the Annihilationists are going to do."

"The Cartel guys do not strike me as the thinking ahead type," Turnbull said. "And maybe the Annihilationists will be into it."

The mayor stood.

"We can only hope. Good luck."

"You too," Turnbull said. The mayor pulled open the door, and as he stepped through the diner was again filled with the smell of smoke.

Turnbull dug into his eggs.

Camp Fleischmann was situated around two small lakes nearly directly north of the town. There was an unguarded gate two miles up where the road went private. The lock was fused with rust. A sign hanging on the bar read "WELCOM DEATH."

Turnbull parked off the road and left the key wedged in the visor. Taking the 12-gauge Remington, he started north between the trees. The trees were not thick, and there was considerable grass between them. Dry grass. The place was a literal tinderbox. And on the horizon, the coming firestorm cast an eerie glow against the low clouds.

He made his way upward on a low grade, the smoke burning his nose and the ashes falling like snowflakes. It was hot, though only partly cloudy. He had done worse marches, but this still sucked. The two dozen shotgun shells in his pockets jingled against his pocketknife and his pair of handcuffs as he walked.

The road was fifty meters to his right. It appeared little used but he did not want to take the chance that it was being watched.

At the moment, he had no real plan. Whatever he did would be improvised. It was not the technique he preferred, but in his line of work it was the one he usually ended up going with.

"Freaking Deeds," he muttered, still wondering how he had gotten talked into this.

"It's critical, Kelly," Clay Deeds had told him. "Garrett Bowers is very connected, very influential. His daughter-in-law left his son and stayed in California after the Split. The son was killed in the fighting and this girl is all the family Bowers has. Now, her classmates say she ran off in the boonies of California to join some weird cult. If we can get his granddaughter back for him…"

"We?" Turnbull had replied.

"You," Deeds conceded. "You're not a politician, Kelly. But politics didn't just end when the Split happened. Bowers is an important man with influence we need to be able to leverage."

"Which *you* need to be able to leverage."

"That's right," Deeds said. "And I make no apologies. There is a lot going on under the surface in the red. The war is not over and it is not clear what the next step for the United States is, where we go from here."

"I hate politics," Turnbull had said.

"You have the luxury to," Deeds said. "I don't. I need Caitlin Bowers out. It's important."

And Turnbull had bought it.

A bramble snagged his jeans and Turnbull swore, but not too loudly. He could not believe he had said "Yes" to Deeds yet again.

Turnbull estimated he was within a mile of the old Boy Scout camp when he passed a sign lying on the grass. It was professionally done, but old. He could make out what was a smiling little boy in a uniform skirt and beret. It read, "ALL GENDER SCOUTS," and a talk bubble from the transvestite kid's mouth said, "My penis does not make me a boy!"

Turnbull continued on, scanning the horizon for Annihilationists. He saw no one and wondered where they all were.

There was a scream far ahead, a male. He went to a knee and listened. More ash fell and he brushed it from his nose.

No more screaming. He surmised that whatever had happened was over.

He slowed his pace, taking cover behind successive trees, and he inched forward toward the camp. Up ahead, he saw a dilapidated building, maybe a sleeping cabin in better days, and three people. They were dirty, with raggedy clothes, and they were young, probably early twenties. Two of them seemed to be vigorously hoeing the earth.

Turnbull crept closer, the shotgun ready. There were a male and two females, neither one Caitlin Bowers. They were in the midst of a patch of dirt tending to what looked like potatoes. The image of Brian Stelter came to mind for a moment, but these young people were thin, very thin, and even from a distance it was clear that their hands were neither soft nor girlish.

One of the girls was filling a basket with the small tubers.

"Gotta hurry," instructed the man. He looked back toward the smoke. The fire was getting close. "Gotta go soon."

The girl said nothing and continued loading the cargo. None of the trio had weapons, other than the hoes.

Turnbull got to the last tree at the edge of the plot unseen and made his plan. It was not what he thought was a particularly good plan, but the oncoming fire was limiting his options.

"Don't any of you move!" he commanded, stepping out from behind the trunk and aiming the shotgun directly at the wide-eyed male.

The girl with the hoe promptly dropped the implement in the dirt and ran off screaming "Breeder!" at the top of her lungs. The other two froze, holding absolutely still.

Turnbull was relieved that apparently the fear of death still worked, at least for the moment.

He walked into the plot through the plowed earth, gun on the male.

"Stand up," he ordered the girl, who did, spilling her tater trove.

"You should not have come here, breeder," she said.

"Stop talking," Turnbull snapped. "Either of you know a Caitlin Bowers?"

"We give up our breeder names when we come here," the male said.

"Of course you do. It's never simple. Okay, well you know Tommy Doom?"

"The Last," said the girl, reverently.

"Yeah, let's all go see him."

But the girl turned and ran, screaming a warning. The male remained frozen. Turnbull kept the gun on him as the girl fled.

"*You* I *will* shoot if you run," he promised. "Now, take me to your leader."

The male was shaking. Apparently talking about death was one thing but facing it was another. He turned and walked forward, Turnbull's left hand on his shoulder and his right holding the scattergun.

The ash was getting heavier.

"You know there's a fire coming, right?" Turnbull asked as they headed toward the main encampment. More buildings appeared, but they were obscured by ash. The smoke was getting thick and the sunlight was diffused by it.

"We're going to leave," the male said unsteadily as he walked. "That's why we were digging up the food. And that's why they were recycling."

"I thought you wanted to die."

"I do. All human life is a blight on the earth."

"Then why not stay and fry?"

"Because then who will kill all the rest of you?"

"Okay, you stop talking too," Turnbull directed.

There was a crowd ahead in what had probably been the parade field for the old Boy Scout camp. The open area was surrounded by buildings and the grass was gone – it was all dirt.

There were several log Xs to one side, and there were humanish figures tied onto them. None were moving, and none were whole.

Recycling.

There had to be three dozen people gathered there, all dirty, all lean, most with some kind of tool or axe or knife, all in a semi-circle awaiting him.

They did not move toward him. They only stared.

Turnbull walked forward. He was committed to what he was now assessing as a sub-optimal plan.

Oh well, he thought.

Turnbull stopped inside the semi-circle, twenty feet from the nearest cultist, and pushed the male forward to return to his friends. Brandishing the shotgun – he saw no firearms among the cultists – he looked them over. Lots of very red eyes. What kind of smoke caused it – kush or brush, or maybe both – was unclear. But there was more going on – they all seemed vaguely unstable, with wide eyes and open mouths. Drugs, hunger, indoctrination – the perfect storm of group insanity.

Yeah, this was a bad plan. But there was no real option but to make the best of it.

"So, where's this Tommy Doom guy?" Turnbull called out.

"The Last!" hissed an angry harpy with a sickle.

"Where is he?" Turnbull asked. "Fire's coming, and we don't have a lot of time to waste."

A male with a shovel took a step forward, and Turnbull's barrel was now on him.

"One more step and you get your death wish," Turnbull snarled, and the man stepped back into the crowd. "Now, where's this Last guy?"

"I'm here," said a tall and stout man with a beard, perhaps in his mid-thirties, pushing his way through the crowd. The man smiled, and there was crazy in his eyes. The ashes landed and collected on his brown beard.

This guy is not missing too many meals, Turnbull thought as he shifted his aim to center mass on this new target.

"I am The Last," The Last announced.

"Any of this crew decides to get salty and you'll be The First. You read me?"

"We don't fear death," The Last said. "We embrace it. We owe the Earth our doom."

"Yeah, that's great," Turnbull said. "But it seems to me we don't have a lot of time to discuss your personal philosophy. Fire's coming, and if you really want to kill everyone on Earth you need to roll pronto."

"Oh, there is always time to talk about the truth," The Last said. "Like how Nathan here seems to lack commitment." He looked at the unfortunate male Turnbull had taken captive in the potato plot.

Nathan seemed very upset, panicked even, and because he was staring at The Last he did not see the male walk up behind him and draw a buck knife across his throat.

Blood spurted out and Nathan fell to his knees surprised, holding himself upright for a moment as his shock turned to...was it joy? He smiled and fell forward into the dirt.

"The Earth Mother's will is done!" The Last shouted.

"All hail the Earth Mother!" the assembly shouted.

"He's free now," The Last told Turnbull. "We will free all the world." He lifted his arms upwards as ash rained down on them. The fire was getting close.

"I'm not here to talk crackpot theology, Tommy," Turnbull said. "I want Caitlin Bowers, and if I don't get her, I'm spraying you and this crowd's guts with buckshot and I guarantee your trip to the Earth Mom's lovin' embrace will be long, hard, and unpleasant."

The Last laughed, then the whole group joined in, a twisted, tweaked laugh that belonged to a comic book villain.

"There is no Caitlin here," The Last said. "But there is a Sunflower."

"Really?" Turnbull hissed.

Sunflower stepped forward, rail thin and grimy, her eyes wide and unfocused. Turnbull recognized Caitlin Bowers underneath the exterior, which was a sad simulacrum of the cute co-ed she had been at Berkeley.

"You want me?" she asked Turnbull.

"Come here," Turnbull said. "And the rest of you just stand there. I'm taking her, and you can get back to whatever the hell you're doing."

The Last laughed.

"Go with him, child," he instructed her, and she stepped forward.

Turnbull saw the glint of the blade in her right hand as she approached, a wide smile across her face. She never got it back for a swing because Turnbull thrust the shotgun barrel hard into her solar plexus and she went right down, the Swiss Army Knife dropping in the dirt as she collapsed.

The guy who offed Nathan lunged first. He got three steps before Turnbull blew a hole in his stomach and he flew backwards with a crimson splash.

Turnbull pumped out the empty and racked in another shell, searching for The Last, but he was gone. Turnbull began blasting away at waist level into the crowd.

It was pandemonium as some fell, others tripped, and many ran. Their lizard brains largely took over, detecting the threat and carrying them away before their addled conscious minds could recover control and force them to seek death instead of fly from it.

The shotgun clicked empty and Turnbull reloaded with red shells from his pocket, pausing to blast a whole in the chest of a cultist making a charge with a shovel. The others were scattered for the moment, but how long that would last before they reorganized was uncertain.

Time to get the hell out of Dodge.

"Get up," Turnbull said, yanking Sunflower to her bare feet. She yelped.

Turnbull pulled her along, and she staggered. Turnbull's hand locked on her wrist and twisted. She howled but came along.

They ran south, passing the ring of buildings surrounding the parade field and heading out past the potato patch. Sunflower stumbled, but Turnbull was not having any passive resistance and bent her wrist hard every time she hesitated.

Her grandaddy might get Caitlin back broken, but he would get her back.

They made it to the woods, going south hard the same way he came up. Turnbull did not like going out the way he had come in one bit, but there was no time for subtlety. If these lunatic cultists did not get them, the fire would.

The forest fire was much closer now, as Turnbull confirmed when he turned to look behind them for pursuers. The flames might even be at the camp by now.

"They will come for me," Sunflower/Caitlin said smugly as Turnbull dragged her along. "They will kill you. Or the fire that climate changed spawned will."

"We'll see," Turnbull replied, adding, "Stop talking."

It was slower going than he liked. She periodically resisted, and her bare feet – only just starting to callous over after her dispensing with footwear upon her arrival from college – made it hard going. Her soles were bloody. But that was damage Turnbull would accept.

The ash was falling harder now, and he could hear a roar in the distance behind them. The fire? If thousands of acres of trees in the woods burn, do they make a sound?

And shouts.

They were coming, and faster than he and his captive were going.

"I'm here!" Sunflower screamed. Turnbull jerked her hard and she grabbed a tree. He pulled her off it, but it was clear this was not going to work.

Time for a new plan.

"They will carve on you all night," Sunflower gibbered, apparently forgetting that in the not-too-distant future everything within their sight was going to be a blackened wasteland.

Turnbull spotted what he was looking for, a branch of a certain width about six feet above the ground. He pulled her underneath and lay the Remington against the trunk and fished out his set of handcuffs. He snapped one end around Sunflower's left wrist and then snapped the other around the branch. It took a moment for her to realize her predicament, and then she began to curse him in the vilest series of obscenities he had heard since the last time he drank with sailors.

"I'm here, here!" she shouted to her fellow cultists when she finished cursing him. "I'm here!"

"Keep yelling," Turnbull said, grabbing up the shotgun and disappearing into the brush.

He swung out far to the west, below the crest of the ridge, then moved back north. Turnbull rushed from tree to tree, pausing to look ahead. No one yet, but the fire was coming. Ash dropped lazily from the sky, and he had to suppress his cough when he breathed some in. Behind him, Sunflower or whatever she was calling herself was screaming.

They would converge on her, and he would hit them from the flank.

Turnbull moved east again, heading upwards toward the crest of the ridge, moving more slowly now, watching for targets.

It appeared they did have some guns, because one of the pursuers came into view carrying some old bolt-action hunting rifle. His finger was hooked inside the trigger, and if his buddies were around there is little doubt he would be flagging them. Handing a gun to a zonked-out college student was sub-optimal, but Turnbull took no chances. The pursuer stumbled past him heading south, toward the howling captive, and Turnbull opened his pocketknife and lay down the shotgun.

The man never turned around, being fixated on going toward the screaming girl, and when Turnbull caught him and threw his arm around his neck, he was shocked. That lasted until the blade went in the base of his neck. His legs buckled and Turnbull let him drop to the grass. A quick glance confirmed he had no use for the old rifle, and then Turnbull sprinted back for his Remington.

It was unclear how many more there were coming to get them. Maybe the whole cult was coming. That would be a problem.

The fire was coming too, and the sky was a smoky orange. It was all he could do to keep from coughing. The girl was still shouting, but now there were other voices, males trying to organize their sweep south.

They had no idea their quarry was behind them, hunting them.

A pair walking a few yards apart were ahead. One yelled to some others out of sight to the east. It was easy to be out of sight – the smoke was growing thicker. Turnbull followed them for a moment, making his plan.

It was pretty simple. He shot the first one in the back and had racked out the empty and in the fresh shell by the time the other turned to look at him, perplexed.

Turnbull dropped the other one next, and pumped the shotgun again.

More yelling, including the girl. They were calling out for their missing comrades, and it was a confused mess. How many were there? At least three, judging by the voices.

"The Last! Thank you!" he heard Sunflower shout in the smudgy distance. Turnbull moved that way.

Turnbull did not see the wild-eyed cultist until his attacker was out of the brush with an old .38 revolver firing as fast as he could pull the trigger. He was close, ten feet or so, but the first round was still high. The second was center mass, but Turnbull was pulling the 12-gauge up for a shot when the round slammed into the shotgun's action. Turnbull's hands felt like they had been hit with an electric shock from the impact. He knew without pulling the trigger that the shotgun was useless as a firearm, so he used it as a missile, heaving it at the shooter.

The cultist was drawing a bead on Turnbull when the black scattergun flew toward him, and he flinched. His round went wide.

Turnbull's Wilson Combat was out now, and he fired two .45 slugs into the skinny gunman. The target fell back into the brush, and Turnbull rushed onward toward where he had left Caitlin Bowers hanging by her arm from a tree limb.

There were two shapes in the clearing where the girl was tethered, one with a double-barreled shotgun.

Turnbull engaged him first, putting three into him. He staggered backwards, then fell on his ass, discharging both barrels into the sky, then tumbling face-forward into the dirt.

Turnbull saw movement toward the girl and shifted his aim.

"Stop," he told The Last.

The cult leader had a buck knife and was making for Sunflower, but he froze in Turnbull's sight picture.

"Free me!" she screamed, but it was obvious that she did not mean freeing her from the tree but from this mortal coil.

"Let's see how much you really love death," Turnbull hissed. "Take a step. Move an inch. Come on, Last, don't you want to see what all the fuss is about?"

"I can't die," The Last said. "Not yet. Not until my work is done."

"Kill me!" Sunflower pleaded. "Let him kill me!"

"Go on," Turnbull said.

The Last smiled and tossed away his blade.

"You're not going to kill me," he announced.

"You're right," Turnbull said. Ashes descended on them, heavier now. The smoke burned his nose and throat.

He dropped his aim and blew out The Last's right knee cap.

"The fire's going to kill you," Turnbull said, sliding his weapon back in his belt.

The Last groaned and rolled on the ground clutching his ruined leg as Turnbull stepped past him, pausing to pick up the knife. There would be no easy exit for this bastard.

"No!" Sunflower shrieked as Turnbull took her down. "You can't leave him!"

"Sure I can," Turnbull said, clicking the lock open and pulling her away, leaving the cuffs hanging from the branch.

"Die!" The Last shouted at Sunflower through gritted teeth. "Die for the Earth Mother!"

"Yes!" Sunflower screamed back as Turnbull dragged her along.

"Die, die!" The Last shouted as they faded from view. The fire was coming.

"You first, Last," muttered Turnbull as he pulled his captive along.

They got to the truck and Turnbull threw Sunflower/Caitlin inside the cab, then slid in himself. He regretted not taking the extra time to retrieve the cuffs, but while she was still crying, she was visibly calmer now as he took the keys from the visor and slid them into the ignition. Orange sparks alighted on the windshield. The fire was nearly there – it must be moving ten miles an hour.

The engine roared to life, and Turnbull turned around and headed back down the road. His rearview was entirely orange.

The Last was no doubt now The Crisp.

"Why won't you let me die?" she asked him placidly.

"You're going back to your grandfather," Turnbull said. "And he's going to get you the help you need to forget all this Annihilationist bullshit."

"Our species is a virus. I am a virus."

"Hey, your barbecued shaman back there was just using you people. Can't you see that?"

"You are the one who can't see," she said, her face shorn of any affect.

Turnbull shook his head. This girl was going to occupy all the headshrinkers her granddaddy's dollars could buy.

The people of Chester were just as shocked to see Turnbull roll in the second time as they were the first, though with the fire maybe a half-hour behind him this entry was significantly more dramatic.

Everyone was running around with shovels or axes. They had done a good job cutting back the forest, but now they would need to tamp out whatever blazes the rain of sparks ignited.

He stopped the truck near the diner, which seemed to be the informal command post. Mayor Pete was there on the sidewalk, giving orders.

"They are all going to burn," Caitlin said blankly.

Turnbull ignored her and turned to look out of his window. She looked out the window of the cab with dead eyes.

"Get that tanker to the west side now! We gotta wet down the old Norris place! It's a piece of history," the mayor shouted into his walkie-talkie. Whoever was on the other end said, "10-4." The mayor pivoted toward Turnbull.

"You got her back?" he asked, incredulous.

"I got her," Turnbull said, nodding his head at his captive.

"Well, I lost that bet."

"How are the roads?"

"No way. The fire will catch you for sure. But you're welcome to stay here and help us."

"Doesn't look like I have a choice."

"How is she?" the mayor said, gesturing toward the girl.

"A basket case," Turnbull said. "She's...they really broke her. You got someplace I can lock her up until..."

Then he heard the passenger door open.

"Get back here!" he yelled, pivoting and lunging to grab her, but she slipped out onto the pavement.

Turnbull saw she was grinning as she backed up, and then he saw why. The tanker truck was hauling up the road.

"Caitlin!" Turnbull shouted.

She smiled, an insane smile of joy and fulfilment.

Turnbull bolted across the cab, but he was too far away.

She was still smiling as she stepped into the road in front of the truck and disappeared in a spray of pink mist.

2.

"The blues are even worse than other people realize," Kelly Turnbull said. "People who weren't inside it, like us, they don't get it. They break people's minds. And their souls."

There was silence, broken only by a far-off whistle. It was probably an oriole. And then there was barking.

"How many dogs do you have anyway, Kelly?" Ernie Smith asked, his BAR slung over his shoulder. Pensive Kelly was the worst Kelly. Smith wanted to change the subject, and Turnbull was fine with that.

"More than five. I'm infantry, so I can't count past the number of fingers on one hand," Turnbull replied, cradling his lever-action rifle. He was looking across a grassy field and surveying the darkening wood line that ran east-west to their front.

There were dogs all over the field, a half-dozen rambunctious golden retriever puppies now pushing a year-old and not realizing that they were supposed to be hunting and not playing. Mama Dog was there, watching over them. Old Jeff, his original mutt, and a fellow grizzled vet of the Indiana insurgency, was taking it all very seriously. A boar had got him once – *once* – and after that close encounter of the tusk kind he was all-business whenever he went out stalking the Texas brush with his master.

"I'd have put a night vision scope on that weapon if I knew you were going to drag me into the damn woods this evening,"

Smith said. "You invited me to come all the way out here and I didn't expect to have to kill my own dinner."

"It'll be *my* dinner next week. Lorna's doing steaks back at the house." Turnbull paused and held his brand-new jet-black Henry Big Boy X Model lever action muzzle up. It was light yet solid, and, but for the suppressor, it would have been shorter than many other long guns. It bore some modern touches, like a red-dot optic on a rail mounted above the action, but its Wild West heritage still shone through. He had fired a few rounds earlier at a stump – the action was silky smooth, and with the suppressor the gun was relatively quiet. Its .44 Magnum round would take down a wild pig with no problem.

"Oh, I have a history with this model," Turnbull had said, admiring his gift earlier back on his porch.

"You have a history with pretty much every gun," Smith observed. Turnbull had smiled a rare smile and motioned his friend along.

"You knew I'd have to give it a test run," Turnbull said as they tramped through the brush. "You bring me a present and you know I'm going to have to unwrap it."

"I figured," Smith said. "If we see a pig, you take care of it. If it gets close, I'll take care of it. This here is a Marine's gun – the Pacific, Korea, Vietnam. It's got a history too."

Ernie held a refurbished, nearly century-old M1918A2 Browning Automatic Rifle, the legendary BAR that American soldiers had used to eliminate enemies around the world, that is, before America itself was torn in two. He had found it lurking in the back of the armory he oversaw back at headquarters in Dallas and he had carefully brought it back to life, then borrowed it for his visit to the hinterlands where his friend lived nearly off the grid. The weapon was heavy and old, but it would still knock the hell out of anyone unlucky enough to get in the way of its .30-06 rounds. Ernie Smith, the gun guru, loved the hefty solidity of it as well as the history behind it.

"Didn't they smoke Bonnie and Clyde with a BAR?" Turnbull asked.

"Well, there's some controversy about that," Smith replied, his voice low and his eyes still scanning. "Clyde was a fan. His gang robbed National Guard armories and took some BARs for themselves. They outgunned most of the cops they met up with. But the posse that ambushed them had a Colt Monitor, which is a spin-off of the BAR – it had a pistol grip and was shorter – and a Remington Model 8 in .35 caliber. The posse may have had an actual BAR too – there's debate."

"No debate about what happened to Bonnie and Clyde."

"None whatsoever. They got messed up real good, just like in that old movie."

"Didn't Warren Beatty become a senator or something over in the blue?" wondered Turnbull.

"Yeah," Ernie replied. "But I remember reading that he got arrested for something, maybe felony cisgenderness or the like."

"He had to be 90 years old. Gotta respect his commitment to his craft. Anyway, if we do see a boar, I'll try this Henry out on it before those .30-06 rounds turn it into ground pork."

"Well, I don't see any pigs, and your lovely fiancée is going to wonder why we're late for dinner."

"I don't see any either," Turnbull said. He considered this for a moment. Tonight his ranch, despite his yeoman efforts, was rarely hog-free.

"Shooting boars beats shooting blues. Pigs don't shoot back."

"But both can ruin your day, if you're not careful," Turnbull said quietly, watching Jeff. The old dog was uneasy, walking back and forth instead of probing ahead, like he usually did.

"True," Ernie said, and then after a moment, he asked: "So, did you think about Clay's offer?"

"I gave it all the thought it deserved," Turnbull said, his boots making almost no sound as he approached the trees. "All none of it."

"So, I'm supposed to tell Clay you want him to pound sand?"

"I'd be more colorful, but 'pound sand' will do. You know what happened in NorCal."

"I do. What a mess. But the war ain't over, Kelly. The blues still hold part of Washington on the West Coast. The Russians are in New England, helping the blues hold it and trying to suppress the Maple Syrup Rebellion." A shadowy figure led the long-simmering red insurrection in the woods of Maine, and the rumor was that this guerilla leader was Tucker Carlson.

"OGP," Turnbull replied.

"OGP?" Ernie wondered. "Are you quoting Naughty By Nature?"

"That's OPP. OGP. Other guy's problems."

"They can still make it *your* problem by re-activating you, colonel. And they need you. Nobody knows the blue like you. Not even me, and I lived there for nearly 15 years."

"And I've been fighting for nearly 20, before, during, and after the Split. If I was a cat, I'd be on life negative six. But now I got my fiancée, I got my dogs, I got my ranch, and I got my money. I got my retirement coming to me. It's over for me."

"It ain't over until the fat lady sings, not that I want to be fatist or assume anyone's gender," Ernie said.

"That's also ableist because you assume xe can sing," Turnbull said absently, still focused ahead of them. Jeff was even more agitated now, and the Mama Golden was frozen, watching, ears up.

"Where are the pigs, Ernie?" Turnbull asked.

"Don't look at me. I'm a city mouse."

"There's a dry creek bed in that tree line. They come up that way every dusk to feed near the house."

"Maybe the hogs figured out your ambush position."

"Maybe." Turnbull did not sound convinced.

Jeff lowered himself, growling, watching the tree line. Mama Dog turned and growled, and then she tore away back toward the main house several hundred yards west. The puppies, initially confused, followed her.

"Your dogs don't like boars."

"No, they *love* boars," Turnbull said, kneeling and motioning Ernie down into the tall grass too. "They survived dodging blue patrols back in Cali. What they *don't* love are strangers with guns."

"Shit," hissed Ernie.

"The creek bed runs straight up to the house. That's the approach I'd take if I was coming in."

"How many you think there are?"

"Probably a lot."

"You better call Lorna," Ernie said, the BAR ready.

Turnbull took out his cell with his left hand, his right inside the loop lever of his new rifle. He shielded the light, then put it away.

"No signal."

"That a surprise? You live way the hell out here in Bumfuck, Egypt."

"I lease a cell tower plot to US-AT&T. There should be plenty of signal."

"Killing cell sigs is pretty advanced tech."

"Yeah," Turnbull said. "Seems like our blue buddies are getting pretty ambitious."

"If there's anyone they would want payback on, it's you."

"Coming on my land with ill intent is a really bad idea."

"Oh, I know," Ernie said. "But remember, we haven't actually seen anyone. This is all speculation."

"True. But I've never not had the worst-case scenario happen."

"Well, you are Kelly Turnbull, and how long has it been since you killed anyone?"

"Few months, probably." Who was that last one? A bunch in NorCal. Then before that, he remembered, his old frenemy Martin Rios-Parkinson, who he shot off the Doran Bridge in San Mateo, California, just before the collapse of the western half of the People's Republic of North America.

"Well, a few months is a record for you. You're overdue. Okay, how do we do this?"

"If they really are in that creek bed then they are focused on the house. They'll maneuver on that. We can swing in behind them, take them from the rear before they get there."

"Lorna?"

"If they surprise her, she's got a problem. If she surprises them, *they've* got a problem," Turnbull said. "I'll lead, and let me deal since I'm quieter with this suppressed Henry."

"Roger."

Turnbull rose and moved low and quietly across the field toward the tree line that pointed toward his house like an arrow. Ernie followed, the heavy BAR in his hands. Jeff the Dog saw Turnbull coming and went ahead, carefully entering the tree line and then disappearing inside.

It was becoming darker by the moment as the sun disappeared completely. Turnbull and Smith moved slowly and deliberately, approaching the woods and the creek bed axis of advance within it. It was utterly still.

Turnbull entered the tree line, his Henry rifle up and ready. Smith followed, the BAR primed for full auto. He was a Marine; Turnbull did not have to tell him that the machine gun's purpose would be to suppress whoever they encountered. And when it kicked live, everyone within five miles would know it.

The parched creek bed was a few meters inside the woods running perpendicular to their approach. There was still enough light to see it, a white scar wending its way between the trees.

Jeff the Dog went into the sandy depression without hesitation, and Turnbull eased up a bit. Clearly the dog, with his superior hearing and smell, sensed no one right there. The mutt was now sniffing the sandy bottom and Turnbull stepped down into the dry creek bed, covering west toward the house while Ernie pulled out the bipod legs at the front end of the BAR and covered east.

The dog's nose was hovering over boot prints.

"Psst," Turnbull whispered. Ernie looked over and Turnbull pointed out the prints. The toes were aimed toward the house.

More boot prints came into view, leading off ahead. Ernie nodded. The dog started up the creek bed in pursuit. Turnbull followed, rifle ready. But he also double-checked the Gerber Mark II knife he carried on his left hip, and the jet-black Wilson Combat CQB .45 that was holstered on his right thigh.

Ripples of light, shadows, the call of either a dove or an owl – Turnbull took it all in as he moved forward. The dog was ahead a few yards, his head low. They were both hunting. And in the distance, he could make out the lights of his ranch house.

The dog stopped. He stared ahead, though Turnbull could not see exactly what the dog was looking at. He was silent, without even a growl.

Turnbull looked down – sandy creek bed ahead, and no stray twigs or branches to snap. He raised his left hand in a fist and sunk to his haunches, turning to the squatting Ernie and pointing ahead.

"We'll take him and find out what's up," Turnbull whispered.

Ernie nodded.

Turnbull had the rifle ready, one finger on the trigger and the rest in the loop, and led with it as he moved forward. Ernie followed, BAR ready.

The dog stopped up ahead, eyes fixed. Turnbull paused. He let his own eyes adjust.

A man.

A dark blob in a black uniform, and he looked bumpy, definitely pouches and web gear. He was prone on the ground, looking through the trees toward the house, pointed that way, lying on his stomach behind a gun. In the low light, it seemed to be an MRAD – a Barrett Multi-Role Adaptive Design bolt-action rifle, which sort of looked like a souped-up M4 in 7.62mm. But it could reach out and touch someone with the hitting power, accuracy, and at a range, that an M4 could only dream about.

Nice gun, Turnbull thought. Where the hell did the blues get one of those?

It was an obvious overwatch position. From there, the sniper could cover the east face of the house and the approach of what had to be his buddies up ahead.

The house itself seemed sedate, with lights in the windows. They had not hit it yet.

The red dot danced on the sniper's back as Turnbull approached, one slow and deliberate step at a time.

"Nothing yet," whispered the sniper. He had a radio. Turnbull licked his lips.

It took 60 long seconds to reach the man's boots, and Turnbull paused for a moment before tapping them.

"Don't you...," he began, but the man was spinning onto his back grabbing at the HK USP in his shoulder holster.

Turnbull fired, sending a .44 Magnum slug dead center into the sniper's ceramic chest plate. There was almost no sound expect for the impact, a dull thud, and then the cycling of the lever action as Turnbull pumped in another round.

He was still moving. The intruder's hand was around the German automatic and pulling it out of its holster.

The second .44 slug went in through his forehead. The darkness covered up the less than aesthetically pleasing consequences of the huge bullet.

"So much for taking him and finding out what's up," Ernie said, eyeing the twitching corpse.

"I know what's up," Turnbull said, jacking in another round, then pausing to feed two rounds into the side gate. "You set up right here. Cover across there," he continued, gesturing with his left hand.

"And you?"

"I'm attacking," Turnbull said, rushing forward.

Ernie lay down next to the MRAD and placed the BAR on its bipod so it could cover the whole open area in front of the house. To the right was the stable, and his Dodge sedan and Turnbull's classic Ford pick-up truck were parked on the driveway to the left.

The only thing moving was Turnbull. Ernie paused to look at the MRAD. His own armory back in Dallas issued them, so these bastards clearly had good taste.

The radio on the dead man crackled.

"Overwatch, status? Overwatch?"

"Oh shit," Ernie said, and then he turned back to his front and waited.

Turnbull moved fast, but ready, rifle up and assessing.

Where would they assault the house from? They would want to minimize the approach across open ground, so it would probably be from the stable. They would be on the far side, screened from view of the house, but how many? The Henry did not have a 30-round mag like his usual assault rifle did. Each shot would have to count, but then a .44 Magnum round counted twice.

Movement by the barn, two shapes, 50 meters away, armed with tricked-out M4 family weapons. Turnbull realized he was in the open in a field, with foot-high grass, and they might have night vision. They definitely had body armor.

Screw it.

He raised the rifle and aimed low, then fired at the lead target's leg. The *pfft* of the suppressed round was not as loud as the man's scream as his femur snapped.

No sense wasting shots on chest plates.

The other one pivoted and sprayed wildly on suppressed auto. His rounds went high – Turnbull could hear them crack over his head. He aimed. The red dot landed on the second man's thigh and Turnbull squeezed.

The target went down, his leg bent at a disturbing and impossible angle, and Turnbull charged.

The first guy had recovered enough to raise his rifle just as Turnbull closed to 25 meters, and Turnbull's next shot took him through the right eye. His partner took the next one straight through his left eye.

Turnbull jacked out the empty round as the wooden wall of the stable exploded outward in a silent string of rounds fired from the other side. He dropped to his belly, racking another magnum round into the chamber.

Two shapes, moving fast from the other side of the stable, cut across the front of the house toward the vehicles. Turnbull raised up to fire and then dropped back down – they were spraying his way suppressed and silent, but on full auto.

Ernie had to see them, Turnbull thought, and Ernie did, but the ranch house was in his background and there was no way he was unleashing a storm of .30-06 rounds into a dwelling housing Lorna.

Their suppressive firing slowed and before they disappeared, Turnbull got off one shot, which must have missed because no one dropped. The pair was now behind his vintage 2021 Ford Bronco truck.

And the Bronco was off-set from the house.

One of the reasons lawmen and outlaws in the 1930s liked the BAR so much – even more than the famous .45 Thompson submachine gun – was that the big .30-06 slugs would tear right through an engine block.

The Ford's sheet metal body was not even a consideration.

"Sorry about your ride, Kelly," the ex-Marine whispered to himself.

Ernie opened fire on the truck, blowing off all twenty rounds from the century-old mag. The hail of bullets blew out both facing tires and the windshield, and the shredded truck collapsed on its rims.

"Damn it," muttered Turnbull as he watched his beloved Ford disintegrate. It was a classic, but not anymore.

There was a pause as Ernie reloaded another magazine, and Turnbull got up and charged, the .44 Henry ready.

One of the black-clad intruders came out from the rear of the truck, firing full auto. Ernie cranked up on him and Turnbull unleashed a flurry of rapid shots.

Even as the rounds tore into the first shooter, there was a black motion from the front of the vehicle. Turnbull pivoted to jack the lever as the second man hit the stairs up to the porch, spraying the front door with suppressed automatic fire.

Turnbull had the rifle moving up but there was no way he was going to make the shot before the attacker smashed through the door into the house. That did not stop Turnbull from trying, and it was over the top of his rising rifle that he saw the lower panel of the door blow outward and the intruder fly backward off the porch and sprawl onto the grass.

Turnbull was at a run now. There was no movement in the house, and the wounded attacker was lying on his back, his upper legs and groin a shredded mess.

Lorna had remembered the Remington 870 loaded with double aught Turnbull kept by the front door. And she remembered to shoot low if the target was in body armor.

The man's M4 rifle had landed several yards away, and his helmet had come off. Turnbull slowed with the Henry up, looking and aiming, but not quite believing.

The injured man groaned and said, "Shit!"

Turnbull stopped, looming above his quarry, the weapon aimed at the attacker's face.

"Lorna!" he shouted. Nothing. "Lorna!"

"I'm in here," she yelled back from behind the door. "I'm hit."

"Bad?"

"You ever been shot good?" she bellowed.

"Put pressure on it," Turnbull directed. He kept looking at the wounded man clad in black fatigues lying at his feet.

"Schiller?" he said, baffled.

"Hey Kelly," the man replied, grimacing.

"You have some explaining to do, Joe," Turnbull said coldly. In the distance, he could see Ernie and his BAR moving up to confirm the kill on the other guy who had been lurking behind his ruined Bronco.

Joe Schiller laughed bitterly. He lifted his head up to look at the wreckage of his lower abdomen below his tactical belt and the holstered HK USP pistol, then collapsed back into the grass, expelling a groan.

"Yeah, you're a mess. I think your Tinder cred just dropped precipitously," Turnbull observed. "But maybe you'll find someone in SuperMax who'll love you just the way you are. You know, penis-free."

"You were always an asshole, Kelly." He groaned again.

"Yeah, I didn't much like you either, but was our little personality clash enough for you and your pals to try to kill me? How did the blues turn you?"

"Blues?" Schiller laughed, even though it hurt. "You have no idea what this is about, do you?"

"I figure you'll tell me," Turnbull said. Ernie trotted up.

"This one's running buddy is slab-ready. Where's Lorna?"

"Hit, inside. Go help her. If the comms are still out, we'll need to drive her to the medics." Ernie nodded, and Turnbull looked straight at Schiller.

"I figure you are going to be begging to tell me what this is all about."

"No, Kelly, not me. Your bitch kind of made it all not worth it from here on out."

"You should watch your mouth before it ends up like your junk."

"The thing about having nothing to lose," Schiller said with difficulty. "Is that you have nothing to lose."

"What is this about?" Turnbull hissed.

"The future," Schiller said, amused at Turnbull's bewilderment.

"What the hell are you talking about?"

"You or me, Kelly," Schiller said, smiling grimly. "Choose."

"Don't you..."

"Choose!" Schiller's hand went for the HK USP at his side and Turnbull instinctively blew the back of Schiller's head apart with a round through the bridge of the wounded man's nose.

"Shit!" Turnbull said, jacking out the empty round. The shell case flipped away into the grass.

He stared at the dead man for a moment. Jeff the Dog came up and sniffed, then trotted away, unimpressed.

"I think he took out a kidney," Ernie yelled from inside. "She's bleeding bad. We need to evac her now."

Turnbull stepped toward the stairs to the porch and then paused.

So did the dog.

A noise.

Distant.

But closing.

A helicopter.

Two helicopters.

"Choppers inbound, Ernie," Turnbull said.

Ernie was helping Lorna hold the red dishrag over the hole in her right side.

"Coming to finish the job?" he asked.

"Don't know."

"Keep the pressure on," Ernie told her, and she nodded. He picked up the BAR and joined Turnbull.

"If they're bad guys, I'm going to kill them all," Turnbull said evenly.

The Blackhawks were military – door gunners with rotary cannons each leaned out the sides. But they did not open fire. Instead, they swung in and landed in the grass, kicking up a storm of dust.

Turnbull didn't move – he just stood ready with his rifle.

A half-dozen operators, dressed and equipped identically to the intruders, poured out of the craft and took up defensive positions in a perimeter around the landing zone.

And then out came a civilian.

"Looks like I'm late," the man said.

"Clay?" Turnbull said when the man finally reached him, accompanied by two troopers.

"You okay, Kelly?"

"Lorna's inside, hit bad."

Clay Deeds turned to the troopers flanking him. "Evac her, now!" They ran inside.

"What the hell is going on?"

"Kelly, the whole of old Task Force Zulu – it's gone. Almost everyone. All tonight. Synchronized hits. Except you and a couple others."

"Like you?"

"Obviously, I'm here, but not for lack of trying. They blew up my house."

"Your family okay?"

"You're my only family, as far as anyone knows."

"Well," said Turnbull, "You can put Joe Schiller in the dead column." He gestured to the hunk of twitchy meat on the dirt.

"I don't understand," Deeds said, staring. Schiller had been part of Task Force Zulu.

"Schiller led the kill team. There are four more stiffs. I'm betting they were all operatives."

"I thought…"

"You thought it was the blues?"

Clay Deeds nodded. "Revenge is a dish best served cold and all that."

"Well, they'd have good cause for what we did to them during the Split and since. But it was red secret squirrel types, just like us."

"Bought off by the blues?"

"That's a lot of buying off for a country busy falling apart," Turnbull replied. "He denied it before he went for his piece. Said it was about the future."

The troopers were helping Lorna out to the helicopter.

"Don't let the rib-eyes burn," she said. Then they moved her off to the aircraft. Ernie stayed behind.

"There are only a few of us Zealots left," Deeds said.

"Zealots?" Ernie said.

"Task Force Zulu," Turnbull said. "We called ourselves 'the Zealots.' We did missions up to and during the Split."

"What kind of missions?"

"If I told you, I suspect these assholes would have to kill you too," Turnbull said. He was serious.

"After we get her to the hospital, we need to find out what the hell is going on," Deeds said.

"Oh," Turnbull said. "I'm finding out. You can count on that. And after I do, I'm going to get even and then some."

"Well," said Ernie, leaning on the BAR. "I better bring you some guns and ammunition."

Turnbull glanced at the Blackhawk with his fiancée preparing to take off, and then looked at the dead man at his feet. Then he looked at his friend and spoke before ducking low to run into the waiting helicopter.

"You better bring it all."

3.

When Turnbull awoke and looked out his hotel window, Dallas seemed perfectly normal, bright and bustling, but totally indifferent to what had occurred the night before miles outside town in the country.

Kelly Turnbull sighed. Where to begin?

The prior evening, Deeds had elaborated about the situation during the chopper ride into the city. The engine was roaring. They both wore headphones and spoke on the intercom. Deeds assured him the crew was good to go.

"Old Task Force Zulu would be combat ineffective if it was still a going concern. Of those still alive a decade later, counting Schiller, ten are dead, two unaccounted for, and two are us."

"Schiller said this was about the future," Turnbull said. "What the hell does that mean? We worked together over ten years ago. I expect most of us Zealots were retired, out of the game."

Deeds shrugged. "Cole Suthern was running fishing excursions in Key West. Wes Albert was 250 pounds and had a cake shop in Dothan, Alabama. Their only future was melanoma and diabetes. Why kill them?"

"It doesn't make any sense," Turnbull said. "Unless it's blues, but how the hell would they even know about us? The point of a secret unit is to be secret. And how would they turn Schiller and other operators? Schiller was a tool, but he hated the blues."

"That someone got inside the US intelligence community is the issue. Maybe our old friend Harrington and the Chi Coms are behind it. We know he got to China after you took down the Golden Gate," said Deeds.

"Maybe it's some blues mad because we stopped them from nuking the summit at St. Louis," Turnbull said, going off his mic and shouting it to Deeds over the sound of the rotors. "Except I think we killed all the blues involved in the plot."

"If that bomb had gone off, the Split would have been a lot bloodier than it was," Deeds said, also off the intercom. "That episode is the biggest secret there is."

"Did they kill Casey too?" Turnbull asked after a moment, replacing his headphones.

"Casey Warner?" asked Deeds.

"Yeah, the computer guy with the Twitter account and elfs."

"Elves, I think, is the plural. He was my only operative who ever played *Dungeons & Dragons*. No, Kelly, he's one of the unaccounted-for ones. We don't know where he is. His house got hit but he was gone. I do know that he was still on the job, though."

"Working for you?"

"No," Deeds said, considering. "He went to another unit. I can't tell you what his unit does, but I don't see a connection."

The chopper slid over the airfield and landed. They spilled out and walked low under the rotors until they were clear. There were five government sedans waiting.

"I need a car. I'll go get a room," Turnbull said. "Best we split up."

"You got ID?" asked Deeds.

"I have a bug-out stash in town. New identity, credit cards. A new cell too." Turnbull had tossed his own phone out of the chopper on the way in from the ranch. It only had a dozen numbers and he had memorized them all, so no great loss.

"You sure it's not blown?" asked Deeds. "I'm not sure what we can be sure of right now."

"I think it's good. I didn't get it through channels. I know a guy," Turnbull said, suddenly realizing that he might have a lead. He continued. "We need to talk to Casey. And we need to follow up on Schiller and his team of stiffs."

"Call my secure number when you're set up, Kelly. I'll tell you what I find out," Deeds said. The spymaster gestured to one of the drivers, who handed his keys to Turnbull. "You sure you don't want to stick with me and my security?"

Deeds had about a dozen men with him, all aggressively surveying the surroundings.

"Nah," Turnbull replied. "All this heat might scare them off, and I want them to come."

Turnbull sat down on the mattress in the hotel room rented to one Richard Edward Rude. His pistol was on the nightstand, and the identity documents he had retrieved from a Wells Fargo USA safe deposit box were spread out on the sheet. There were four stacks of US currency, hundreds and twenties totaling $7,500 each. Now he used his new cell to dial the secure number for Clay Deeds. It rang once before Deeds picked up.

"Lorna's stable," Deeds said.

"Good," Turnbull replied.

"She protected?"

"I have my guys on her."

"What do you got?" Turnbull asked.

"Casey is definitely in the wind. I talked to the head of his unit. Had to twist his arm but I got the info. Casey is off the grid completely. And he left just before the hits."

"He knew," Turnbull said. "He's a weird guy, but he's cunning. He's not the type to do this, and he thought Schiller was a schmuck. He must have gotten wind of it and jammed."

"As for Schiller and the four other corpses, no records."

"Of course not," said Turnbull.

"Schiller went back into the military ops side when Task Force Zulu wound down after St. Louis. He popped up in the regular

Army like you did for a while, then poof. After that it's a dead end. The others have a couple military tatts between them, but no records."

"Deniability," Turnbull said, gazing out the window. The Hilton Hotel Anatole overlooked the freeway and, in the distance, the new US Capitol. He had a 20th-floor room at the end of the hall.

"Where are you going to start?"

"I guess I need to find Casey Warner," Turnbull said. "I'll check out his place."

"I'll get you his address. Just stay in one piece, Kelly."

"You too."

Turnbull hung up and looked at his iPhone. What was the name of the big Twitter account Casey had? He was so damn proud of all his followers.

Turnbull remembered.

@FullAutoGalt.

Turnbull downloaded the Twitter app and created his own account using a dummy email - @TwitterIsDumb76748. Then he took a look at the @FullAutoGalt timeline.

It said the account had 213,211 followers. Turnbull shook his head – 213,211 people who wanted to listen to Casey's babbling?

Unbelievable.

He skimmed down the timeline. The last entry was three days ago and it was a meme of General Karl Martin Scott, except the general's head was – wait, was that...?

A male organ, with a little army hat.

Subtle. Apparently, Casey Warner was not a big fan of the savior of the Republic either. But to be fair, Turnbull hated all generals equally.

He closed the app and put his Wilson .45 in his holster. From habit, he confirmed there was a round in the chamber. He carried his Gerber knife as well. There was a citizen pin on his shirt – not that he wanted to make a deal about it but some people sometimes got in the face of slackers and he had no time for nonsense.

There was a Starburns coffee stand downstairs in the cavernous lobby and convention complex, with the cream counter lying beneath a poster of an elderly Lee Greenwood attesting that "I'm proud to be an Americano drinker!" Maybe a half-dozen people stood in line, a couple of them with long weapons and a couple more open-carrying pistols. A single harried employee was taking orders and trying to make the brews. She seemed to have a Walther PPK tucked in her apron. There was grumbling.

"Is there a freaking single place where there's not a line anymore?" one middle-aged woman asked. She had a pink CZ75 in a Fendi shoulder rig. It had rhinestones.

Turnbull waited, taking the time to think about his next steps. His anger had cooled somewhat, in the sense that he was now entering the cold fury phase.

What the hell was going on? Schiller was a jerk, sure, but lots of people were jerks and most of them didn't try to kill him.

The sparkly lady finally got her big half-caf, half-decaf with two pumps of sweetener. "Venti" and "grande" had been replaced by "big" and "bigger" when Starburns replaced Starbucks after the Split.

"Coffee," Turnbull said to the harried barista. She had a citizenship pin on her blouse, meaning she had served.

"What kind?" she asked, exhausted.

"Coffee coffee. Like in the Army."

"We don't have that. We only have good stuff."

"Then give me the closest to it. Black."

She went to get it, then brought him back a cup and put it on the Formica counter.

"Eight twenty."

"That's pricey," Turnbull said, handing over a ten. "For that, they can afford to get you some help."

"Where would we get them with the war on? Most people who're citizens or who want to be are still on active duty. They're calling me back again in two weeks for six months."

"Stay safe," Turnbull said, declining his change.

"If I don't get killed rescuing the blues from socialism, then I still miss out on half my twenties. And for what?"

"Thanks for the joe," Turnbull said, walking outside.

The G-ride provided by Deeds was a 2033 Ford Fusion. Like it, most of the cars still ran on gas, but Texan Elon Musk's Tesla Motors had made significant inroads into the market and offered several models of electric vehicles, powered by the dozens of new nuclear plants springing up all over the red states. Musk had pulled out of the blue completely before the Split while the Big Three automakers had tried to operate in both new countries. Their blue facilities had gotten nationalized for their trouble, then shut down because of climate change. But they had prospered in the red.

Turnbull got on the freeway. The ubiquitous lawyer billboards that had once dominated the landscape were gone. Now, he passed mostly commercial ones, and the occasional ones with slogans like "SERVICE MEANS CITIZENSHIP." It annoyed him – too much like the propaganda in the blue for his taste. But here, you could dissent. A billboard with the face of General Karl Martin Scott – obviously the work of fans since a serving officer could not have sponsored it, read: "WE NEED REAL LEADERSHIP TO WIN THE VICTORY AND BRING OUR CITIZEN SOLDIERS HOME." It was attributed to "The Committee to Draft General Scott."

President Karl Martin Scott?

"Pompous ass," Turnbull muttered. His short time in Scott's company was plenty. The soldier's growing popularity was inexplicable to Turnbull. There was even talk the general might resign his command of the West Coast theater of operations and then lead a third party to challenge the Republican and

Conservative parties for the New White House. Of course, Scott never said anything about that. On the rare instances Turnbull watched the news, the general would scoff at the idea and reiterate that he had come back to active duty to fix the mess in California and the rest of the Pacific Coast theater and that was his total focus.

He never came out and said it directly – he knew what Harry Truman did to Douglas MacArthur when the general got involved in politics – but it was pretty clear that General Scott's plan was total war to total victory regardless of the cost. Anything was better than this stalemate. And Turnbull, despite his feelings toward the general himself, was not unsympathetic to the policy.

There was little traffic in Dallas that morning; the town seemed a bit empty, like back during the beginning of the Chinese COVID pandemic well over a decade before. But the missing people were not sick. They were deployed. If you were a citizen, you served, and Uncle Sam needed every swinging Richard right about now. The northeastern border could go hot any time. The Chinese were lurking south of Mexico, and Washington and Oregon remained to be pacified. America had been on war footing for nearly a year, since the invasion of California, and it was starting to hurt.

There was no end in sight, either.

Turnbull drove through town toward an address Deeds had given him. It was Casey's house.

"They may be watching it in case he comes back," Deeds warned him.

"Hope so," Turnbull said. "I'd like to meet a live one and discuss the situation with him in depth."

"I'll bet you would," Deeds replied. Turnbull hung up.

He took 75 north and got off and headed east into a residential neighborhood of low, modest homes. Kids played on the lawns and rode bikes – the videogame laws banned children's games in order to ensure they did not spend their childhoods staring at screens.

There were lots of flags, not just the (fewer) stars and stripes – there was idle talk of adding Nevada and California back as stars someday – but also blue-star flags representing deployed family members. There were occasional gold-star flags as well.

Casey Warner's house was in a leafy cul-de-sac. Turnbull drove by the intersection twice, looking for occupied vehicles that might contain people surveilling the house, but he did not see any. The third time, he turned and drove down the dead-end street. From his car, Turnbull could see there was yellow and black police tape on the door, which had been broken down and was now sort of leaned up against the open entryway. Turnbull parked and got out, walking up the front sidewalk.

"Hey, that's a crime scene," called out the next-door neighbor who stood by the hedge with a deer rifle. The man was bald and wore glasses along with a t-shirt reading "U.S. Navy – Ahoy!" It featured a picture of an aircraft carrier manned by a pirate, and the planes were parrots.

"It's okay. I'm with the government," Turnbull said, not slowing.

"Well, you got credentials?" asked the man.

"Yes," Turnbull replied, not breaking stride.

He stepped onto the porch and pulled out his Gerber Mark II knife. He sliced through the tape, slipped the blade back in its scabbard, and went inside with his hand on his holstered .45.

It was a one-story ranch style. There was a long hallway stretching to the back of the house, where the living room and kitchen were. At the end, the kitchen was on the right and beyond that another hallway probably leading to the bedrooms. There were glass windows and a sliding glass door straight ahead, and beyond them the backyard with a grill and some patio chairs.

The house showed little evidence of damage, and if they tossed the place they did not do much of a job. It was clear from the décor that Casey liked comic books and conservatism. There were Marvel movie posters on the wall, including one for *Avengers: The Next Generation*, where the heroes fought a villain called The Pinko, a mutated college professor who wanted to impose world socialism. He was played by a 'roid-buffed Michael Cera.

There was a Dell computer at a desk in the living room –*Star Trek* action figures lined a shelf above it – but the hard drive was gone. Whether Casey took it or the bad guys did was anyone's guess.

And there was a bookshelf which was a shrine to Casey's favorite conservative authors – Loesch, Levin, Katz, Hunter, Kelly, another Kelly, Edwards, Stigall, Sexton, Bongino, Wright, Sheld, Shapiro, and Limbaugh (both Rush and David) were all represented. Casey even had a copy of each of radio legend Larry O'Connor's books, including his bestselling unauthorized biography of Val Kilmer, *Hollywood Superjerk*.

And then there was a signed copy of Teddy King's bestseller *Listen Up, Dummies*. It was on a little stand, in a place of honor. Turnbull had spent some time with the radio host long ago; now King was bigger than ever, holding forth across the country for three hours a day starting at noon Central.

Turnbull was not a listener. And Casey had been green with envy when Turnbull had mentioned that he and Teddy had once shared an adventure following the Split and the unpleasantness in St. Louis.

There was a sound from the front of the house, and Turnbull's .45 was out. Someone was coming. Turnbull moved to the doorway of the living room. The steps kept coming, and a shape emerged.

Turnbull moved, pressing the gun to the man's bald pate and he pushed him against the wall. The deer rifle dropped to the floor. It was the neighbor.

"I could have shot you," Turnbull said, not moving his gun.

"You shouldn't be in here," the neighbor said.

"I told you. I'm with the government."

"You and everyone else."

Turnbull lowered his .45.

"Everyone else who?"

The neighbor turned to face him, less scared than annoyed.

"A bunch of guys rolled up and rushed the house. We thought it was a police raid, you know, to bust lib terrorists or something, but that didn't make sense because Casey was no commie. But they went in and when they didn't find Casey they just left. Then we called the cops after we secured the scene. The cops looked around, probably took a report, and put up the tape. Then some more folks showed up later. And they showed credentials."

"What kind of credentials?"

"Well, I didn't study their credentials, you know. They spent some time inside and left. I put the tape back up on the door."

"Very neighborly. Did you know Casey?"

"Sure. Nice guy. A citizen. He worked in computers. A little weird, but easy to underestimate. One time a neighbor's boyfriend came over and started getting rough with her. Casey told him to move on and the guy took a swing and in a flash Casey had him on the ground with a broken arm and that HK P30 Casey carried was stuck in his mouth."

"Interesting," Turnbull said. Casey was definitely a dork, but that boyfriend was lucky to have limped away alive.

"I saw him leave. Fast too. I said 'Hi' and he just got in his car and got out of here. Hasn't been back."

"What time did he go?"

"Yesterday, like three." A couple hours before the visitors to the Turnbull ranch showed up.

A noise.

Turnbull froze.

"You hear that?"

The neighbor squinted.

"Someone's coming," the neighbor said.

"Get out the back."

"I'm not going anywhere. This is my neighborhood." He reached down and picked up the deer rifle. It was bolt action, some Remington model with a scope.

Turnbull stepped out of sight at the end of the hall and gestured for the neighbor to move back from it as well. The neighbor complied. They heard footsteps on the other side of the hallway wall. Then the wall splintered and erupted as one of the intruders opened up with what sounded like an M4 on full auto.

Turnbull dropped to Casey's hardwood floor as the rounds tore over him, blasting back through the divider wall with the .45 in the general direction of the shooter.

The neighbor scrambled with his rifle toward the hallway leading to the bedrooms as Turnbull dropped the mag and reloaded with another eight-rounder.

No yells, no moans.

No hits.

Turnbull heard a second empty mag drop to the hallway floor.

There were muffled shouts and Turnbull heard what was definitely a bolt slamming shut.

"Cover the back window," Turnbull whispered to the neighbor. The neighbor pointed the deer rifle toward the sliding glass doors and the backyard.

"You're oh and two," Turnbull yelled at the shooter, scrambling backwards across the wood floor.

The firing started again, this time angled downward, through the wall from the entry hallway. Rounds erupted across the hardwood. Turnbull lunged forward into the entryway, landing on the floor with the Wilson up.

The intruder had a plate carrier over his polo shirt, and dark shades. He saw Turnbull from the corner of his eye just as he ran dry again.

Turnbull fired two-handed four times, twice into each femur. The man fell shouting.

Behind him, the glass doors shattered and rounds ripped into the walls around him. Turnbull twisted around as the second shooter in the backyard on the patio walked his stream of bullets toward him.

There was a roar like a thunderclap and the shooter in the backyard flew backwards from the impact of the .30-06 round the neighbor had planted in his skull. His M4 clattered on the cement and came to rest against Casey's Weber grill.

It was messy. No need to check that guy to ensure he was dead.

The wounded man to his front groaned. Turnbull leapt up and forward and took the shooter's SIG Sauer M17 from its holster and tossed it away. This time, the shooter was going to live and to talk.

"Is that all of them?" the neighbor asked, opening and closing his bolt. Turnbull did not answer immediately. He moved to the front door and surveyed the area outside. There was a late-model sedan double parked – they must have driven by and seen Turnbull's ride out front. There were no other operators in sight.

"Looks like it was just them," he announced.

There was a siren in the distance. Other neighbors were coming outside, most with rifles of their own.

Turnbull pivoted back to the wounded intruder, who was bleeding profusely.

"If I don't put tourniquets on those soon, you'll bleed out," Turnbull said. "So, incentivize me to help you."

"Kiss my ass, traitor," the wounded operator hissed through clenched teeth.

"Where did you get 'traitor'? Who sent you?"

"We'll get you," he managed to say. Blood was pooling under his legs.

"Crap," Turnbull said. He looked at the neighbor. "Go in Casey's bedroom closet. Get me some belts. We gotta stop the bleeding."

The neighbor nodded and disappeared. The injured man jerked and twisted.

"Yeah, that looks really painful," Turnbull said. "I'm only keeping you alive so we can continue our little chat."

The neighbor returned with two belts, which Turnbull set to work wrapping around the injured man's legs. He was finishing the second when the first police officer got to the door, Glock out.

Turnbull's pistol was holstered. He lifted up his bloody palms.

"I'm a federal agent undercover. Don't shoot me."

"We'll redirect the shooter's ambulance to our facility," Deeds said on the phone. "And I've already contacted the Dallas police chief. They'll let you go and forget about this whole thing."

"We need to talk," Turnbull said, standing in the kitchen. Cops milled about and EMTs worked on the wounded man. The neighbor was giving a statement.

"About Casey Warner's new job," Turnbull continued.

"I think you're right. But not at the facility. You're too hot. We'll meet. I'll text you where we can meet."

"When?"

"Tonight. Try not to shoot anyone until then, all right, Kelly?"

"No promises."

"Looks like you're making up for lost time, killing-wise," Ernie Smith said. They were in an Americamart parking lot, at the far corner, away from most shoppers but very hard to approach without being seen. Americamart had taken over for Walmart in the red as most of Walmart's major shareholders were family members who embraced leftist politics and migrated to the blue. For their trouble, they got nationalized without compensation. One former billionaire made it back to the red and found work as an Americamart greeter.

"I'm going to need some enhanced firepower," Turnbull said.

"Step into my office," Ernie replied, walking to the back of his Explorer.

When the rear door lifted, Turnbull saw a tarp covering the floor of the cargo area. Ernie pulled it off.

"That's a lot of guns," Turnbull marveled.

"I wanted to give you options," the armorer said. "First up, are you sticking with the Wilson CQB as your primary?"

"Yep," Turnbull said. Ernie passed him an OD green canvas duffel.

"I thought so but I wanted to check. You'll need these."

"What's this?" Turnbull said, looking inside the bag and opening up one of the boxes of .45 bullets.

"Those are 135 grain Lehigh Defense XD rounds."

Turnbull examined the copper tip of the round. It looked almost like the tip of a Phillips head screwdriver.

"Not a hollow point?"

"Nope," Ernie said. "The advanced nose design is the key. They go 1250 feet per second and punch through barriers, then on the other side it creates massive tissue damage equal to a big hollow point. It has to do with the hydraulic flow through the tissue. Cavitation, enhanced energy distribution – technical details. The bottom line is that this is one deadly bullet that doesn't care if it has to shoot through heavy clothing, windshield, or car door to get to the bad guy. It's still going to put him down."

"Sweet," Turnbull said, dropping the box back in the bag.

Next, Ernie picked up a dozen metallic M1911 mags. "Wilsons, eight shots. A couple ten shots in there too. You're probably running low."

"Nice," Turnbull said, putting the magazines in the bag with the super bullets.

"You'll need a rifle," Ernie said. "You'll probably want to carry more ammo, so 5.56 instead of 7.62?"

"Yeah."

Ernie picked up a rifle that looked much like an M4, but smaller and with a telescopic stock. "Heckler & Koch HK416C. Compact carbine. Nice optic. You want anything else on it?"

Turnbull took it and checked the action. "This will work." He slid it into the bag along with ten 5.56mm magazines.

"Now, you want a backup pistol?"

"Yeah. You got a Wilson Compact CQB?"

"No, I don't have a Wilson Compact CQB," Ernie said, annoyed. "I work for the government, man."

"What do you got?"

"How about a Springfield XD-S 4.0? Nine-millimeter. Five and one in the pipe."

Turnbull examined the small automatic. "Sold."

"Now," Ernie said. "I don't know if you need it, but in case you have a hankering for a scattergun, I do have this."

The armorer picked up what looked like a fairly short, black pump shotgun with no stock, just a grip, and a rail on over the receiver.

"Mossberg 590 Shockwave SPX."

"Okay. You got double aught?"

"Oh yeah," Ernie said, handing over several boxes. They all went in the duffel.

"Slugs?"

"You hunting elephants?"

"I want what I shoot to go down."

Ernie handed him a box of Winchester PDX1 12-Gauge Defender Segmented Rifled Slug Shotshells. "They will not get back up." Turnbull eagerly stuffed the box into his duffel.

There were several other weapons laid out on the floor of the cargo area, plus more ammo.

"That it?" asked Ernie as Turnbull surveyed them.

"For now."

"You got any leads?"

Turnbull shook his head.

"Well, I got one for you. That MRAD sniper rifle from the guy by the creek? I ran the serial number. I thought it was familiar. It was from my own damn armory."

"No shit," Turnbull said. "Who signed it out?"

"No one. And no one else has access to that arms room but me."

"I guess someone else does."

"You know, Kelly," Ernie said, shutting the rear door of his SUV. "I survived a long time in the blue by watching and keeping out of politics. But I am getting the same kind of vibes here. This is something bigger than some assholes with a vendetta. There are powerful people in our US government and they want you dead for some reason."

"Ernie," Turnbull said, hefting the duffel bag over his shoulder. "We were supposed to be better than the blues. This politics stuff is just not right."

"You know, Kelly," Ernie said. "You are a tough cat, but you are naive. You think there are no politics anymore just because this country decided to take the Constitution seriously? You think there can't be bad guys? It's human nature, man. Power. Money. That didn't get repealed when the country split."

"I gotta go find Casey Warner."

"You keep safe, Kelly. You still owe me a rib-eye."

Turnbull nodded and headed to his car.

The sun was going down over Dallas. He drove into the downtown, passing the place where Oswald made his shot, and heading toward a district of bars and restaurants. Lots of small businesses were shut down. He had not noticed so many closed-up shops the last time he came to the city.

And then he hit the brakes.

A protest or something was up ahead. The traffic was all stopped on the street while farther up ahead, hundreds of people were shouting as they paraded across the road.

Turnbull got out, joining others who stepped out of their cars to watch too.

This was not a common occurrence, and the Dallas cops observing it seemed baffled about what to do.

They had flags, lots of US flags, and signs too. One had General Scott's face on it.

And they were chanting. "Justice for citizens, no free ride for slackers!"

It was the best-dressed protest Turnbull had ever seen –
mostly what looked like regular people instead of the motley
collections of losers that made up the constant protests in the
blue. Even from a distance, he could see every one of them
seemed to have a citizenship pin. There were a few wheelchairs
rolling along – wounded vets?

"We served, they slacked, why should we be under attack!"
someone shouted into a bullhorn.

Turnbull grimaced. They needed some chant practice, but
their hearts seemed to be in the right place. Except for the
General Scott part.

"Get out of the road," a guy yelled from next to his Porsche. He
had a sports jacket on that probably cost a couple grand, and his
date was likewise dolled-up. No citizenship pins.

"Shut the hell up, slacker!" shouted a man whose beat-up
Chevy was idling next to the sports car. He was middle aged and
he did have a pin. "They fought for this country. Let them
march!"

"Hey, you can have your pin and drive a shit box, pal. So I
don't get to vote? Aw shucks. I just gotta make do with her and a
whole shit-ton of money."

The guy in the Chevy unleashed a torrent of obscenities and
the slacker flipped him the bird. The marchers cleared the road
ahead.

"Gotta go, Army boy!" The slacker said, sliding back into the
driver's seat.

Turnbull watched this go down and suppressed his desire to
ram his Fusion into the Carrera. About half the population of the
new United States were residents, not citizens. They could not
vote, or run for office, or sit on a jury. But they could spend all
their time getting rich, while citizens were getting dragged off to
serve their military commitments.

A year ago, it would have been unthinkable for a slacker to
have attitude with a citizen. But after a year of full-scale
mobilization, that had changed. With wages up because of the

worker shortage, the slackers were doing fine while citizens called to duty again and again were at risk of losing jobs, farms, and homes.

"Citizens first!" the marchers shouted. The parade had passed by but Turnbull still heard them shouting. He slid back into the driver's seat and traffic began to move. His mind went back to one of the books he had read long ago, one on ancient Rome. In the early Republic, only citizens could serve, and for the masses of citizens this led to them becoming impoverished when they spent years on campaign. Eventually, uprooted from their land, they flooded into Rome and became the infamous mob. The resulting instability turned the Republic into the Empire.

He hit the gas and accelerated with the traffic, and to his right the guy in the Porsche and his escort were laughing – probably at the suckers who served.

He again suppressed the urge to ram his car into them and went to find someplace to eat. His destination would not be up and running for a few hours.

4.

The bouncer looked to be about three hundred pounds.

"You've grown, Jeb," Turnbull observed. "Like, fatter."

Jeb laughed. He wore a dark suit and had a wireless earphone. It looked like he was packing a Desert Eagle .50, probably less for its effectiveness at blowing large holes in people than as a field expedient club.

"It's all muscle, Kelly," the bouncer replied. He was probably right – the man was a tank. He was stationed by the velvet rope at Chrome, a nightclub with a long line to get in. And he was picky. If he had not served with Turnbull years before, Turnbull would have never gotten in the door.

Jeb did not bother searching Turnbull for weapons. Most people were packing. They were just expected to act like adults and to suffer the consequences if they failed to.

"How have you been doing?" Turnbull asked.

"Stressed. People are getting dumb. Drinking too much, acting the fool. Lots of citizens fighting slackers. Wait, I'm not supposed to call slackers 'slackers.' Anyway, Senator Nick Searcy was in here drinking Pappy and someone got in his face for being in the Conservative Party and Matthew Marsden – you know, the new James Bond? – breaks a chair over the Republican guy's head. Had to drag that Republican jerk out to the sidewalk – he mouthed off, so he was wrong. Republicans are soft. Anyway, sorry for getting political."

"Sounds like a fun night, though. He here?"

"He is," Jeb said. "He's in his office in back. Hey, if you got something going, I'm open. I hate this job. I should have stayed in."

"I know where to find you." They shook hands.

"You might want to take off that citizen pin if you want to lay low, Kelly," Jeb said, serious. Turnbull noticed Jeb was not wearing his.

"Nah. I'm good," he replied. Jeb lifted the velvet rope and Turnbull walked past. A gaggle of young men, soft ones in nice clothing, stared.

"Why are you letting this rag bag in before us?" one inquired of Jeb. Turnbull stopped and sized the man up.

"Kid, you need to be silent now," Jeb said.

"Or what?"

"Or I will introduce your face to that brick wall," Turnbull said.

The young man was silent. Turnbull went inside.

Inside, the old Cher song "Do You Believe in Love" was playing loudly. The elderly leftist had been one of the most vocal celebrity supporters of The Split until two years in when she was arrested and imprisoned in a reconditioning camp for "racism, slut shaming, and degrading justice-involved individuals" decades before in her hit song "Gypsies, Tramps and Thieves."

Cher's fellow progressive chanteuse Bette Midler fared even worse. She decided that she would personally resist the red invasion of blue California and attacked an infantryman from the 1st Cavalry Division who was standing guard on Rodeo Drive, swinging a diamond studded Hermes purse while shouting "Stop murdering our democracy!" The young man, baffled, pushed her down with his rifle, breaking her hip. He then reported to his sergeant that he had been forced to butt-stroke Joy Behar.

The crowd was young and well-dressed, a real contrast from outside in the real world. There were a few citizen pins, but fewer than he would expect – about half the population were citizens and the rest residents. He was unsure if it was because folks were taking Jeb's advice, or just because most of the citizens in this demographic were off on the front lines.

"Shiner Bock," he said, leaning over the bar. The bartender nodded and filled a glass.

"Twenty," he said, putting it down.

Turnbull sighed and handed over a $20 bill. It had the face of Ronald Reagan on it.

Turnbull took his beer and walked toward the back. The people were partying like there was no war on, and for most of them that was an accurate statement. It grated on him.

A champagne cork popped and Turnbull's hand nearly went for his gun. Luckily, he did not spill his beer. The people with the bubbly laughed and poured.

There was another bouncer in the rear near the office door. He surveyed Turnbull as he approached, but was not hostile – he figured Turnbull had business.

"Tell him Kelly Turnbull is here." The man nodded, spoke into his mic, waited for an answer over his earpiece, then nodded again and opened the door. Turnbull went in.

"Kelly Freakin' Turnbull!" Liam Queenan shouted, getting up from his desk, his bright blue sport coat flapping as he came around to greet his visitor.

"How you been?" Turnbull asked, shaking hands.

"Look at my place – you tell me."

"Very fancy. Not quite my crowd though."

"Yeah, because they are other people and you hate those."

"Pretty much," admitted Turnbull. "I need some help, Liam."

"Well, it can't be my contacts on the West Coast because the freaking government messed that all up by reconquering it."

"Yeah, you made a lot of money helping me when I was bringing folks out. Now I guess you'll have to do some honest work," Turnbull said.

Liam shook his head. "Not me, man. This joint is about as close to honest as I'll ever get."

"Like I said Liam, I need something."

"So, you need a new identity? I can do you up."

"I'm good, identity-wise. No, I need someone else's."

"I don't get it."

"Casey Warner. I introduced you."

"I know Casey," Liam said, now dead serious.

"I'm thinking you just did a rush job for him."

"Kelly, you know I love ya," Liam said. "But I can't..."

"You can. I'm not out to hurt him. I'm out to help him. Look, there are some bad folks after him. You probably figured that out. And they are associated with our government. You probably figured that out too because he came to you instead of getting his creds from the spooks. Well, those same guys are after me. I need to find him to find out why."

"You're asking me to break my code, Kelly," Liam said, despondent.

"You're a criminal, Liam. There's no code."

"I have a code," insisted Liam.

"Well, break it, because I need to find this guy and to do that, I need to know where he's at."

Liam sighed.

"I could lose my reputation doing this, Kelly."

"I promise not to tell the other criminal forgers and fixers that you helped me out. First, who is he?"

"Justin Pope."

"What?"

"That's the name. Justin Something Pope."

"Okay, you got copies of the credentials?"

Liam furrowed his brows.

"No, I don't have copies, Kelly. That kind of defeats the purpose. If I get busted and the cops search my stuff, they find all the fake identities I set up, including yours, and my customers would be mighty pissed."

"All you remember is the name?"

"Yeah, Pope, because I'm Catholic. I go to mass and everything."

"Is there anything else, Liam, anything at all that might help?"

"Well yeah, one thing." Liam paused.

"Okay, what is it?" demanded Turnbull.

"The whole package, the whole identity. It was blue."

"Blue?"

"Yeah, it was for the blue. A blue identity, just like I used to set you up with back in the day."

"Not red, blue?"

"Yeah, blue. People's Republic of North America. Privilege card – I think I gave him a Level 8."

"What state? Probably New York."

"No, Washington. Of course, they don't call it that anymore since Washington was racist or something."

"You mean DC?"

"They don't call it DC either, but no. The state. You know, next to Canada. They call it Hillaryia now, I think. Maybe it changed again."

"What the hell is he going to Washington for?" Turnbull asked impatiently.

"Search me. I figured he was doing what you do – going in to get someone out."

Turnbull sighed, his mind working on the puzzle. "Do you know where in what used to be Washington state he was going?"

"No, not a clue. He has a Seattle address on his creds. Doesn't mean he's going there, though."

"Did you put him in touch with anyone?"

"No, all my blue contacts went radio silent once the war started."

"So, maybe, Casey's heading to Washington state."

"Hillaryia."

"Whatever. The point is, how can I find him?"

"I didn't give him a cell, so I really don't know how." Liam shrugged. "Sorry."

"No, you were a big help. Thanks."

"You want a drink or something, Kelly?"

"Gotta roll. Thanks."

"Don't mention it. I mean literally. Don't tell anyone I told you nothing."

Turnbull nodded and did an about-face to the door.

He moved toward the front of the place, past the partying people. Out there in the world, people were fighting. In here, they were slurping Negronis.

Targets to his front.

The four guys from outside were blocking his path. Turnbull knew the look.

"You really don't want to do this," he said flatly.

"Oh yeah we do," their leader said.

"This is such a cliché," Turnbull said.

"I don't know what that is," replied the leader.

"It's like a thing that happens a lot in movies, like four dumbasses deciding to take on a guy who is going to wreck them, and then he wrecks them."

"I don't think you're so tough with your fat ass bouncer buddy protecting you," the mouthy one said.

"He was protecting *you*," Turnbull said. "Can we not do this?"

"Guns out," the man said, laying a chrome Beretta on the bar. The others started laying out their own.

Turnbull sighed. He pulled the Wilson Combat CQB from its holster and placed it on the bar.

"Okay, asshole...," the mouthy one began. He closed to about 18 inches away.

"Hold on," Turnbull chided his opponent. He reached down into his pocket and withdrew the Springfield XD-S 4.0. It went on the bar. Then the Gerber came out and went on the bar next to the hold-out piece.

"Now?" the punk said.

"Wait," Turnbull said. He reached back under his jacket and took out the Shockwave 12-gauge. The man's eyes got wider as Turnbull held it.

"You got anything else?" the mouthy one asked.

"No," Turnbull said, slamming the scattergun's handgrip into the punk's throat. The man gasped, clutching at his bruised windpipe, as Turnbull brought the shotgun hard across the temple of the next one. The second victim staggered and fell.

"That's bullshit, man!" one of the two unscathed ones blurted out. But neither of them made a move as their friends writhed on the floor.

"I don't fight fair because it's not a game to me," Turnbull said. "Are we doing this or are you going away?"

They chose going away, leaving their guns on the bar and their friends on the floor.

Jeb came up to Turnbull as he slipped the Springfield back into his pocket.

"A shotgun too? You expecting trouble, Kelly?"

"Always." On the ground between them, the bigmouth was still gagging.

"Sorry about the mess," Turnbull said as he walked out.

"The pair you capped today were operators," Clay Deeds said. They were standing on the infamous grassy knoll in Dealey Plaza. The old Texas School Book Depository loomed over them against the clear night sky. No better place to meet to talk about a conspiracy.

"What agency?"

"Probably military. The live one's not talking, mostly since he's in a coma. But he said that you were a traitor before he went out."

"They try to kill me and my fiancée and then they talk shit about me. I'm getting kind of annoyed with these folks, Clay."

"The point is some of these guys think they are doing God's work."

"That's the story whoever is sending them is telling them. But Schiller knew better."

Deeds nodded. "It's been a decade since Task Force Zulu disbanded and went our separate ways after St. Louis. Somebody is holding a grudge."

"Maybe he's Irish," speculated Turnbull. "I've had experience with that. Anyway, Merrick Crane III can't be behind it."

"No, because you stuck a thermite grenade in his tighty-whiteys and melted him onto a dance floor, as I recall from your debrief."

"In my defense, he was an asshole."

"A crispy one."

"True. I'm pretty sure all the blues associated with the plan to nuke the summit in St. Louis are dead. And now, most of the reds are as well."

"The attempt to wipe out the red and blue leadership is still deeply classified, Kelly. Very few people even know it happened. Very few, like six or seven outside of us. And there were some changes put into effect after that."

"You mean after they managed to steal a nuke from the Air Force and tried to blow up the future blue and red governments? I kind of hope so."

"It was a pretty traumatic experience for our own government. They took steps to avoid a repeat."

"So, it won't happen again. Good. But what's that have to do with the problem at hand, which is finding Casey Warner and then finding the bastards who keep trying to kill us?"

"I'm not sure, but I do find interesting what Casey has been doing the last couple years."

"What?" asked Turnbull.

"This is top secret, Kelly. Very close hold."

"I'm reliable, I think."

"Well, if this would get out it would have pretty major implications. I mean geopolitical level."

"You've built up your suspense. Now spill."

"After Crane stole the cruise missile warhead from Minot Air Force Base, he managed to take it to Canada and then smuggle it back into the US in a truck."

"I recall. And we'd both be a lot crispier if the tech he brought along had not messed with the timer."

"We could not let that happen again. The powers that be started a project. It's called Project Inferno. It went online a year ago – it took a decade of work. On the QT and very hush-hush."

"Okay."

"INFERNO is a satellite system that tracks nuclear warheads. *Every* nuclear warhead. Each nuke is essentially hand-made, so each is minutely different. INFERNO uses AI to identify individual nuclear weapons. And it can see them through anything."

"Except lead."

"No, Kelly, that's the thing. It's so sensitive and smart it can pick up enough to detect them through lead. And water."

"And water?" Turnbull said, his mind racing. "A lot of water?"

"Yeah, a lot of water. You know what that means?"

"It means we can see every Chinese and Russian boomer," Turnbull said, using the nickname for nuclear ballistic missile submarines.

"Yep. That's the big secret. With INFERNO, we made a system to make sure we never got surprised by some schmuck driving a nuke around in the US of A, and we accidentally found ourselves with tech that essentially eliminates the effectiveness of the sea leg of our enemies' nuclear triad."

Turnbull smiled. "Well, that's pretty great."

"It kind of is," Deeds agreed. "Obviously, this is the closest of close holds. Barely anyone in our own government knows about it."

"You do."

"Yeah, but it's my job to know stuff."

"So how does Casey fit in?"

"Well, a small team has to operate INFERNO. You want super-reliable guys. Guys with some relevant experience. And you want operators who can act on the info. For instance, if a nuke gets loose, these guys go find the bad guys and eliminate them and get the nuke back."

"Has that happened, besides St. Louis?"

"Nope. The main threat is terrorists stealing another or smuggling one in. The blues gave their nukes up to China, so INFERNO just watches the United States 24/7 and confirms that all our nukes are where they are supposed to be and there are no extras. Kind of a boring job. Lots of time for Casey to beep."

"I think you mean 'tweet.' Still, I don't see a connection to this," Turnbull observed. "Except that Casey somehow knew the killers were coming."

"I am drawing a blank too. I spoke to his boss to see if there was anything unusual going on with him at work. Nothing."

"I need to talk to Casey, but to do that, I have to find him. And he's heading to the blue West Coast."

"Somewhere in Washington state?" Deeds asked. "That's a big state."

"I think they call it Hillaryia now," Turnbull grumbled. He looked across Elm Street toward the folks gathered around the flagpole at the JFK Memorial. They had clearly been part of the march from earlier, and there were several signs lying against the monument.

"You ready to go back into the blue?"

"Nope. But until I get to the bottom of this, Lorna is in danger."

"And you too."

"Oh, I'm not the one in danger, Clay," Turnbull said. "Anyway, the answer is in the blue, or heading there, so that's where I'm going."

"It's a mess there," Deeds said. "But I'm more worried about what's happening here. We're standing in the right place to be discussing this."

"By the way, since you know everything, who really killed Kennedy?"

"Oswald. Alone. Remember, conspiracies are hard."

"But not impossible, or I'd be at home with my dogs drinking Shiner Bock."

"This unrest is getting worse here," Deeds said. "I'm worried about our country for the first time since the Split. Citizens are getting sick of carrying the entire burden for the war."

"The politicians could drop the citizenship through service idea, or they could draft everyone. Then everyone is a citizen."

"That's the problem," Clay said. "Then everyone votes and that changes the electorate – radically. We based citizenship on service for a reason – to avoid allowing the kind of people who caused the Split in the first place to be able to do that again here. And without The People's Republic for those people to go to, that means the electorate would get much more leftist if they could all vote by dint of merely having been born."

"General Scott thinks he's got a solution," Turnbull said.

"He thinks he's Caesar. If you are going to Washington…"

"Hillaryia."

"If you are going there, you'll have to go through his territory. He's trying to let citizen-soldiers come home and he's making it up with the provisional units that he's raising. You don't see much about it in the news because it's subject to military censorship, but what I hear is that it's getting pretty harsh."

"The people like him, though," Turnbull said. "Especially ones who never met him. Not me."

"In fairness, you don't like anyone. But this guy is ambitious and he's building a political powerbase here in the red – not directly, but through catspaws. And he's got the West Coast command answerable only to him."

"Sounds like Caesar."

"Or Sulla," said Deeds. "Just remember that they both marched on Rome."

5.

The idea hit him just as his head hit the pillow.

"Of course," Turnbull thought, but he knew carrying out his plan was going to be a pain.

He glanced at the bedside table. The .45 lay there, ready with an extra mag by its side.

Then he shut his eyes and went to sleep.

The freeway was pretty clear, with light traffic for late morning on a Wednesday. Turnbull turned on the radio and fiddled with the dial, passing news, religion, and right-wing talk – lots of right-wing talk, as left-wing talk would not have been allowed even if anyone had wanted to hear it since barring dissent in the media outside of narrow limits had come back into vogue before the Split. He finally found a familiar voice.

"Teddy King, the King of Conservative radio on the Eagle Radio Network! Jeff from Dothan, Alabama, you have an audience with the King."

Turnbull rolled his eyes.

"Uh, long-time listener, first-time caller, your majesty," Jeff from Dothan said. "I just want to tell y'all that I am a citizen and I am trying to figure out why the hell I am a second-class citizen in a country I fought for. I think a lot of us are."

"Jeff, that's a great point. We citizens served, and we deserve better from the damn Republicans and yes, from some of the soft Conservatives too! Didn't we split the country to get away from establishment shills?"

Turnbull sighed. Teddy had earned his citizenship after Turnbull had debriefed the authorities on the radio host's help during a classified operation well over a decade ago. Teddy had milked it ever since.

"I had to leave my farm for six months, Teddy," Jeff from Dothan continued. "I had to go sit on the border of Virginia with my armor unit and I'm still digging my butt out of debt. But the slackers who never did nothing are doing fine. Is that right?"

"It is not, and thank you, Jeff," Teddy King said, uttering the secret signal to his producer to end the call. He continued with a monologue.

"What's the answer, citizens? How long will this go on? Our citizens serve and suffer, and the free riders ride for free. We should have learned the lesson about endless wars. We're in a stalemate now, and it's killing us. Who the hell is going to win this war for us? Well, I have an idea, citizens. I know who can do it and how. General Karl Martin Scott. All we need to do is untie his hands and let him take care of business and we can get back to normal. No more mobilizations. No more war taxes. No more People's Republic! I am your King of Conservatism, Teddy King, standing athwart history yelling 'Attack!' Now, do you need a good night's sleep? The answer is My Pillow – use promo code 'KING' to get a..."

Turnbull flicked it off and took the next exit on the Stemmons Freeway. It was marked "NEW CAPITAL."

Turnbull drove into the New Capital complex built on what had been Love Field. It had been the only real open space left in Dallas, and the new United States needed a replacement Capitol after America split into two countries and the People's Republic kept Washington, DC. The new USA had not resisted that division during the negotiations, not at all. The Swamp was always blue, and the blue could have it.

The new American government closed the airfield, sending Southwest Airlines packing to DFW, and within two years had converted the land into a new nerve center for the new country. The new United States built the new Clarence Thomas Supreme Court Building, and a new White House too, along with a bunch of other key buildings. All of them were smaller than their predecessors, reflecting that this government was going to be smaller, as it was originally envisioned by the Framers. And the new capital city did not need all the myriad building complexes that the old capital had to support its various cabinet departments. The new agencies were parceled out to the states. The Department of Agriculture, for instance, was located in Omaha, Nebraska – it never made much sense to have the USDA located a hundred miles away from the nearest tractor.

The buildings themselves were all otherwise nearly visually identical to their analogues back in Washington, DC, but they were improved upon. The original buildings were very old and modern technical innovations had to be awkwardly grafted onto them. The new buildings were more accessible and were wired for 21st-century technology. Plus, they were updated with statues of important historical figures, like Ronald Reagan, Donald Trump, and Ron DeSantis, as well as many statues liberated from storage after being hidden away during the 2020 George Floyd riots.

Each of the buildings sat at the point of an equilateral triangle, with a grassy mall and reflecting pool in the midst. Various memorials and such were planted throughout. The peak of the New Washington Monument rose high above it all, set in the precise center of the triangle. It was different in that it was taller than the original; it loomed 100 feet higher than the old one, which had been re-named the "Victory Over Racism and Cisnormativity Monument." But the name change from that of the Founding Father had not fully purged all of the macroaggression represented by the monolith. It was declared "offensively phallocentric" by the People's Committee for Visual Justice, and the mere sight of it erect and proud was found by many experts in the People's Republic to cause trauma and make people feel unsafe. A proposal to actually dig out a pit in its place "to celebrate the Eternal Vulva" was carefully studied, but had not yet been acted on. Instead, they recently tore down the obelisk and its ruins simply lay there on the overgrown Mall.

In contrast to the grime and destruction of old Washington, DC, the New Capital gleamed. People wandered about gawking and open-carrying their weapons. Crime, unlike in the old District of Columbia, was almost non-existent. That included petty crime – it was perfectly legal to use deadly force in defense of one's property. After a gentleman had been hit by 13 rounds fired by the proprietor and various customers while stealing a red "Keep America Great" cap from a tourist vendor, one of the liberal Republican Party representatives had tried to make that a political issue. He dropped his crusade after the overwhelming response from the general public was, essentially, "Well, don't steal if you don't want to get shot."

Turnbull's destination was outside of the Mall, along a street full of offices and restaurants. He passed a Mobil station – $1.92 per gallon for regular. Turnbull shook his head at the figure. Prices were going up, even with the government's "Drill and Pump Everywhere" policy.

He found a parking spot not far from where he was going. He backed into the space – the better to get out fast, if need be – and walked down the sidewalk, checking for tails as he had done during the drive in as well.

Several of the storefronts were closed down, with the windows blocked off. It had not been that way the last time he was here. And the people seemed sullener than before – not overtly, but he felt it. And it occurred to him that if someone with his level of sensitivity sensed it, it must be real.

He came to a dark, modern building and checked up and down the sidewalk for tails. Nothing. He ignored the buzzer adjacent to the sign reading "Eagle Radio Network." If he used it, they would think he was a nut. Instead, he got out his phone and dialed the number he had memorized a decade ago but never had to use.

"This is the King. Leave a message."

"It's your friend from Boston. We need to talk. Now. Call me back."

Turnbull hung up and jaywalked across the street to the Starburns where he bought a lemonade drink called a "Gork-Ade." A picture of the smiling Seb Gorka, a Kahr KT9093 pistol in his shoulder holster, hoisting the tangy beverage was mounted on the wall. The doctor's drink was as good as Turnbull knew his shooting to be. Next to it on the wall was an ad with Dana Loesch enjoying a blueberry scone. She had an M4 strapped to her back. The tagline was, "This Starburns scone blue me away!" That was good enough for Turnbull. Lorna loved her hit sitcom "Full Mag," where she starred as Maggie, the matriarch of a heavily-armed family that had wacky adventures. He bought one of the scones too and waited.

He sat down facing the door, back to the wall, and waited for six minutes until the phone rang. Turnbull was pleasantly surprised – he had been wargaming various options to get inside the studio if he had not heard back within a half-hour.

"This who I think it is?" Teddy King asked.

"A voice from the past," Turnbull replied. "You've gotten awfully big since our little Beantown adventure."

"I'm on the air in two minutes twenty – what can I do for you?" He was not abrupt; he was genuinely curious.

"Let me in."

"In? What, are you here?"

"Across the street."

"This is trouble, isn't it?"

"Not for you, not if you let me in."

"They'll buzz you in and bring you up."

A flunky ushered Turnbull into the control room. Inside the studio, Teddy King sat behind the mic commiserating with Jon from Phoenix about the perfidy of politicians, especially the comparatively liberal Republican ones. Their eyes met and Teddy finished up with the caller.

"And remember, I need your input. My Red Twitter direct messages are always open for friends and communists too, though I will abuse you. My handle is @TeddyTheKing, that's @TeddyTheKing." He went to break. The minion ushered him into the studio and left them alone. Teddy killed his mic.

"Long time," Teddy said. "You haven't changed."

"You've gained weight," Turnbull observed.

"It's muscle," King insisted. "So, I'm guessing you don't want an autograph. Why are you here?"

"I need your help with a fan."

"One of your fans? Stalking you? Why don't you just shoot him. Or her?"

"Not one of my fans. One of yours."

"I have lots of fans."

"I'm only interested in one."

Teddy looked at him. The engineer broke in.

"One minute thirty seconds." The ad was playing through the monitor at a low volume, but Mike Lindell was selling a pillow.

"You have a huge fan who I need to reach."

"Why not just call him?"

"If I could I wouldn't be here. Look, I need you to tell him to contact me without actually using his or my names. There are folks looking for both of us."

"Are you crazy?" asked Teddy.

"You know the answer to that," Turnbull replied.

"Yeah, I do," the host answered. "You know, I have this great story about our Boston adventure and I can't say a word about it or they'll lock me up."

"Are you going to help me?"

"Yeah, but let me think. You sure he's listening?"

"No, but I bet he is. He's leaving for a while and if he's not gone already, maybe he is giving you one last listen before he goes."

"And you won't tell me where he's going, right?"

Turnbull shook his head.

"Well, I can guess," Teddy King said. "Is he engaged online?"

"He tweets. @FullMetalGalt."

"I know that guy!" Teddy King said. "He's great."

"They'll be looking for that name thing..."

"Username."

"Whatever. You can't say it. Or his real fake name. But I need him to reach out to me so I can get in contact with him."

"Thirty seconds," advised the engineer.

"Oh, well this will make for some compelling radio."

"Will you do it?"

"Sure, I guess I owe you. I'll try at least. Now, are the people looking for you two going to come at me if they figure out I'm helping?"

"Definitely."

"Oh great," Teddy said, leaning forward to his mic. The theme music came up, a kind of soft jazzy riff that made Turnbull cringe. After it played for a while, Teddy leaned into the mic.

"And you're back in the court of the King of Conservatism, Teddy King, here on the Eagle Radio Network. Now citizens, I have a very special message for a very special fan. There's a big, scary mutual acquaintance here who needs to chat with you. I'm not even sure of his real name, but I'm pretty sure that if he told it to me he'd have to kill me. Hell, he might just do that anyway. So, if you are full of metal and you are going Galt, get in touch with me with your contact info at @TeddyTheKing, that's @TeddyTheKing. Now citizens, are you tired of ammo that just doesn't make it happen penetration-wise?"

Teddy finished his ad and looked up at Turnbull.

"Subtle," Turnbull said.

"It's a fine line between subtle and incomprehensible. Give me a phone number. I'll pass on anything I get that's not insane. But it's mostly going to be insane."

"No, don't call me," Turnbull said. Turnbull saw a pad on the console and wrote out his Twitter username, @TwitterIsDumb76748. If the bad guys heard the show and figured it out, they could break into their Twitter direct messages. But hopefully Turnbull could make contact before then.

"I'll check it every twelve hours starting at midnight," Turnbull said. "I appreciate the help."

"No problem. I mean, fifty thousand people probably tuned out because that was boring, but that's cool."

"I appreciate the sacrifice," Turnbull said, turning to go.

"Hey," Teddy yelled.

Turnbull pivoted and looked back.

"Are you ever going to tell me your real name?" he asked.

"No," Turnbull said, turning back to the exit and leaving.

Turnbull used a VPN masking app to safeguard his location information and signed into his fake Twitter account. It took him a few moments to figure out where the direct messages were. When he did, he found there were two, one from @TeddyTheKing and one from @HotNHornELady6969. From her avatar, she appeared bountiful.

He read Teddy's message.

"Hey, I got a bunch of contacts and most were insane like I told you. Two seemed less insane. Good luck."

The messages had two phone numbers. Turnbull called the first one. It was a woman who told him "You sounded sexy and I wanted to meet you. I was married to a Democrat before the Split and it's time for me to get back in the game!"

Turnbull hung up. She called back and he blocked her number. He dialed the second number.

"Hey," said a male voice at the other end. It sounded like Casey.

"This you?" Turnbull asked.

"Didn't we hang out in some place in the tropics?"

"Cuba," Turnbull said.

"What's your piece?"

"Wilson Combat CQB in .45."

"Kelly, good to hear you aren't capped."

"Same with you. This line secure?"

"Secure enough. They haven't found me yet, but I've been moving."

"I think I know where. Why the blue?"

"It's the only safe place. Or at least safer."

"What did you stumble into, Casey?"

"These phones aren't that secure. Face to face, Kelly."

"Okay, where?"

"In the blue. I am out of here. Next Friday, noon, Space Needle."

"Seattle?" Turnbull said incredulously.

"Yeah. I can't change my out. It's all set up. Seattle. Five days."

The line went dead.

"Crap," said Turnbull.

He went back to Chrome, Liam Queenan's club, later that evening, and after assuring Jeb the bouncer that he did not intend to smash up any more customers, he started a rush job for his blue ID documents.

"How are you getting in?" Liam asked him as they waited. "I can't set anything up to get you inside in your time frame." In another room, his skilled forgers were putting the documents together – not perfect ones, and no linkage to the People's Republic computer systems, but ones that would pass the smell test if some People's Security Forces flunky rousted him.

"I figure I'll go up through occupied California and figure out the best way north from there," Turnbull said. "They have to be running ops north into Washington state."

"Hillaryia," said Liam. "Gotta call it by its new name. That's how they catch you. Oh, did you pick your pronouns?"

"I told your guys to go with the default," Turnbull snarled.

"You better make sure. The current default is zmer/zmim."

"They have an army to their south and the PR is still concerned about pronouns," Turnbull observed. He shook his head.

"Yeah, they are nuts," Liam agreed.

"No, it's worse than nuts. They break people's minds. There was..." He stopped.

"There was what?" asked Liam.

"Nothing," Turnbull said, but he remembered the pink mist where Caitlin Bowers had been before the tanker truck vaporized her.

"How long?" Turnbull asked.

"For you, fast."

Turnbull was on I-35 eastbound heading back to the Hilton Hotel Anatole in light traffic. It was dark; the new capital city gleamed. A billboard flashed by: "SCOTT: VICTORY AND RESPECT FOR CITIZENS - COMMITTEE TO DRAFT GENERAL SCOTT."

No general should ever be a president, excepting Ike and George Washington, he thought. *Or Jackson and that Tippecanoe guy.*

But then, the civilian government was messing up big time. Not a surprise that people would look for an answer – and a leader – in a respected institution.

Another billboard flashed by. "JIM HANSON'S PRIME AGED STEAKS – STEAK EATERS, TAKE IT FROM A SNAKE EATER!" The picture of the beef tycoon – he had his own show on The Food Network called "Man Meat" – had him standing by his Weber in a green beret wearing an apron that said, "I'D KILL FOR AN AGED JIM HANSON RIB-EYE!"

Great, now I'm hungry, Turnbull thought.

His phone rang. Turnbull put it on the vehicle Bluetooth speaker.

"Kelly," said Deeds. "They've made our cars."

"How do you know?"

"Because they just blew up the one that they thought I was in."

Turnbull knew there were trackers in all government vehicles. All they needed to do was know which cars to look for.

"You need to ditch your ride," Deeds said. "Pronto."

Turnbull scanned the freeway ahead for an exit.

"That might be a challenge," he said. He glanced at the mirror. There were several cars behind him, but that was not exactly unusual for an interstate.

He reached behind his seat to the duffel on the back seat and pulled it into the passenger seat. The 12-gauge was already there, as it was too uncomfortable to drive with it lodged in the small of his back. With one hand, he worked out the HK416C as he talked. A freeway sign warned of an exit two miles ahead.

"There's something else," Turnbull said, leaving the carbine on the seat and placing his right hand back on the wheel.

"In addition to highly trained killers probably closing in on you?"

"Yeah, in addition to that. If I live, I'm going into the blue. I got a meet with Casey Warner."

"You found him?"

"I had a brief chat with him, enough to set up a lunch date in Seattle."

"You're going to Hillaryia?"

"If I live," Turnbull said. He saw a car accelerating behind him. Maybe the black Ford sedan was in a hurry. But then, who besides undertakers and government flunkies drove black Ford sedans?

His left hand covered the buttons that dropped his four windows and he pressed. Warm air flooded the cabin.

In the mirror, the black Ford was still gaining.

"Clay, you may hear some loud noise in a moment," Turnbull advised. The Ford was coming fast on his driver's side.

"What?"

Turnbull slammed the brakes when the Ford was one length back. The anti-lock brakes did not lock up, but the sedan shot past and there were three men inside – three at least, and they reacted as Turnbull dropped behind them and then hit the gas and fell in directly to their rear.

The three dudes in the Ford were moving around with a purpose. Turnbull's right hand found and rested on the German-made carbine.

Maybe it was just a poor driver.

Nope – that was a rifle in the Ford. It was not so much that they had a rifle – lots of people had rifles in their cars in the new United States. It was that the one in the backseat was maneuvering it so he could fire out the rear window.

Turnbull hefted his own weapon to rest on the dash and used his thumb to click the selector switch to "AUTO."

The windshield exploded outward as Turnbull squeezed off the first burst. No visible damage to the car ahead.

He fired again, the brass clinking and clacking off the dashboard. This time, the rear windshield of the sedan shattered and the Ford swerved. He caught a glimpse of the front windshield splattered with something dark. It looked like the driver was out of the game.

The black Ford went hard left into the Jersey barrier dividing east from west-bound and threw up a shower of sparks as it slowed and finally stopped. Turnbull braked and came to a stop parallel to the Ford. The guy in the front seat was bringing up a black handgun. Turnbull brought his HK416C over to the driver's side window as the passenger popped off two rounds, one of which cracked as it passed through the window above his backseat.

Turnbull squeezed his trigger and emptied the mag into the passenger side of the idling vehicle. The sheet metal and glass erupted as the 5.56mm rounds punched into the side of the car. The shooter twitched and fell back, his handgun clattering on the asphalt after he dropped it out the window. A tire blew out.

No movement. Turnbull watched even as he dropped and replaced his mag. There was an orange glow. The car was catching fire.

"So much for a prisoner," Turnbull said as he hit the gas.

"You still alive, Kelly?" Deeds asked over the speakers.

"Well, I am. Them, not so much."

"Yeah, Kelly, I think you're right," Deeds said. "I think you need to get the hell out of Dodge."

6.

The C-17 landed at San Francisco International at about noon. Turnbull sat on one of the canvas seats in the back, near the ramp, wearing civilian clothes. He was surrounded by troops, none of whom spoke to the unshaven civilian with the rucksack and the Wilson .45.

They had flown out of what had once been called by the unwieldy name "Naval Air Station Joint Reserve Base Fort Worth" but was now known as "Maness Air Force Base," named after one of the Air Force generals called back to active duty following the Split when the new United States was putting together its armed forces. It was a major transportation hub for deploying soldiers, and across the airfield one could see the white and light blue 787 that served as Air Force One, as well as the Marine helicopters that carted the president around.

Deeds had set it up, of course. California was a military zone, restricted, so it was not like Turnbull could have jumped on a Southwestern or, better yet, Braniff, flight into 'Frisco. Braniff, the recently-resurrected old-school airline with brightly colored aircraft, was known for its attractive stewardesses and their miniskirts. If the new United States was anything, it was comfortable with traditional cisgender notions of beauty.

Turnbull had laid low at a Holiday Inn in Fort Worth the prior evening after the imbroglio on the freeway – it made the news and was attributed to terrorists. But first, he had to go back to the Hilton Hotel Anatole to get his few possessions, especially the cash. Money was bulky but it was the best tool of his trade. There were no killers there waiting for him, which was a nice change.

Still, he did not have everything he needed for his trip. He shopped for what he lacked – mostly functional civilian clothing, and a few other odds and ends, like a light sleeping bag – then stuffed it all into a brown tactical backpack he picked up for cash at a surplus store outside the base gate. Troops flying home would often sell the gear that they had bought themselves to these establishments, though with the repeated mobilizations for citizens they would often end up buying it back at those same stores at a generous mark-up on their way out again a few months later.

He stuffed the Mossberg in there along with his extra mags.

Turnbull had showed up at the base gate about an hour before the flight in an SUV he ordered through Ober, the successor app to Uber that dominated the US rideshare market. Uber had gone with the People's Republic after the Split, having loudly refused "to operate in sexist and racist states that make war upon womxn and minoritx bodies." It survived about as long as the term "minoritx," which lasted a year until it fell into disuse for "assuming numerical supremacy." Uber failed because the long list of requirements imposed on it by the new blue government made it impossible to operate at a profit. When it went bankrupt, the management was prosecuted for "wrecking, greed, and gouging."

Turnbull told the sergeant at the front gate that his name was Jones, Johnny J., and he was admitted without showing any identification – that was good, since he did not have any ID with that name. Apparently, Deeds had gotten the word out effectively because no one asked him for orders even as he stepped onto the aircraft for the daily milk run into SFO. He had no idea how, or even if, he was carried on the flight manifest, but it was clear this was not the first time that a passenger who did not exist was being whisked across the continent to the Bay Area.

In the departure lounge, where nervous soldiers sat in industrial black chairs or lay about on the linoleum floor with their heads on their duffels and their M4s close at hand, Turnbull grabbed a glazed doughnut and a little plastic bottle of orange juice, as well as a paperback to keep him occupied during the four-hour flight. He found himself reading something called *The Halfling Mage Saga: The Elf-Curse of Uhtred's Wand*. A wand was not all the hero was wielding; the paperback featured an astonishingly graphic sexual encounter between the Halfling wizard and a horny elf maiden. Still, it was not obscene enough to run afoul of the anti-pornography laws implemented in the US after it became clear that the rampant onanism promoted by the boundless smut that was readily available pre-Split was keeping young men from entering into normal relationships and cutting into the birthrate. You could still find dirty pictures on the net or in hard copy, but you had to work for it like you were a teen back in the 1970s.

Turnbull stepped out into the sun and made his way to the terminal. Around him, the soldiers were coming off the plane and lining up in formation. He ignored the shouts of the sergeants and headed across the tarmac to the terminal. Above him, from the control tower, a huge American flag flapped in the light breeze. It had a lot fewer stars than it did when he was growing up in Cali.

SFO was an almost entirely military airport now, with military flights plus commercial aircraft flying contract runs of soldiers or cargo in and out. But what was most noticeable were the civilian aircraft from the People's Republic days. Dozens of moldering jets in various livery were parked off on the side in large open fields, left to rot. They were not carcasses destroyed during the invasion – the actual battle damage to the airfield, the buildings, and to jets hit by airstrikes and artillery had been repaired. This was damage caused by the PR's own failed system. Planes stopped working, and there was no one to fix them – highly skilled technicians and mechanics were primo candidates to move to the red early on – and when the big machines stopped working they were simply towed to the edge of the airfield and left there. After over a decade, there were many more aircraft in the boneyard than actually flying. Of course, this was the fault of the looters and the wreckers.

The People's Republic had lived for years off the corpse of old America, and there was nothing left but bones to pick over by the time the United States invaded California to stop the PR's Chi Com allies from establishing a colony on the continent.

Beyond the airport, he could see South San Francisco and San Bruno, and the great bulk of San Bruno Mountain to the northeast blocking his view of San Francisco on the other side. On the southern face of the mountain were large white letters. Pre-Split, they read "SOUTH SAN FRANCISCO THE INDUSTRIAL CITY," having been placed there in a bout of civic boosterism a century before. After the Split, it was changed to "SOUTH SAN FRANCISCO APOLOGIZES FOR ITS EARTH-RAPE." A battalion of combat engineers had recently revised it yet again to "SOUTH SAN FRANCISCO GOD BLESS AMERICA." There had been some vandalism early on by the resistance; that ended when an ambush by security forces left five of the leftist vandals dead. Now the sign loomed over the Peninsula, a reminder that the blue had lost, and lost hard.

The leftist resistance itself had been largely crushed.

Turnbull drew a Chevy Blazer from the motor pool. The master sergeant in charge did not like it one bit, but he had gotten the word and handed over the keys grudgingly.

"Don't park it somewhere dark or out of sight," the sergeant said. "I don't want it back keyed or with slashed tires. And they'll steal your gas if they can."

"You see that a lot?" Turnbull asked.

"Not a lot, but once in a while. Just low-grade stuff like that. The blues collected all the guns so they can't really fight back any other way," the NCO replied. "Plus, the provos keep a pretty tight lid on any bullshit."

"Provos?"

"Provisional units. Not quite Army, not quite civilians. They play by their own rules and they don't take any shit from the blues. They can get out of hand, but what are you going to do?"

"Thanks," Turnbull said. Turnbull left without signing for the SUV, though he made sure to have the proper papers in case some MP pulled him over.

Turnbull pulled out of the airport motor pool onto South McDonnell Road, which ran parallel to the east of the nearly deserted Bayshore Freeway. The traffic was mostly military, including Hummers and other military transports. There were very few civilian vehicles. Only a small number of the locals were authorized a personally-owned vehicle in the occupied areas. There were some civilian-type government vehicles. You knew they were US government because, like Turnbull's Blazer, they were late-model American cars and SUVs. And there were buses, lots of diesel-belching buses carrying blue civilians to their assigned work locations. The smoke must have struck the climate cultists among them as blasphemy, but as the losers in the war their views were utterly irrelevant.

There were civilian trucks too, lots of them, mostly from the red, and most hauling food into the City. The United States had conquered blue California fairly easily, though with thousands of casualties, but it soon realized that it had taken on the task of feeding tens of millions of conquered residents. Thousands upon thousands had been assigned to farm labor crews, and the water that had been cut off from the Central Valley farms to save esoteric fish species had been turned back on, but it still took thousands of trucks to feed the Golden State.

And there were SUVs and pick-up trucks, mismatched but all marked with a black ∧ spray-painted on the doors.

Provisionals.

Many had unit flags waving. The provos themselves looked more like civilians in battle rattle, and ranged from STRAC to slack. A trio of them passed him on the road and gave him the stink eye. They seemed to have mostly AKs – probably from the PR weapons stores.

Turnbull was on edge and pulled to the side of the road to ponder his next move. It was not so much about how he would get north – he would figure that out and, worst case scenario, could drive up to the front lines in northern California and infiltrate. No, it was something else.

Would he take a detour to go by his brother Jim's house in Daly City?

He recalled what had happened there the last time he came through. He had left his brother and sister-in-law tied up so that the blues might not think they were collaborators sheltering Turnbull and his team. And his friend Tommy Quayle, wounded, had shot himself in their house rather than be taken alive and betray the mission.

But he could not stop thinking about his nephew Billy, and what his mother was doing to him, how she was trying to make him into a little girl to satisfy her own bizarre narcissism. Turnbull had warned her: If Billy was still "Cindy" next time he came through, Turnbull would keep his promise and she would regret it for the rest of her short life. He hit the gas, headed to Daly City, about five miles to the west.

His brother's house was a burnt-out husk. There had been a few ruined homes here and there on the way in from the I-280 freeway, but the other houses on the residential street were still intact. Still, the neighborhood seemed even dingier than it had when he came through a year or so before. The grass was overgrown everywhere, and leaves and cobwebs collected around the cars in the driveways. Broken windows were repaired with cardboard sheets taped up over the holes.

What had happened?

It was not artillery. None of the other houses were demolished. No, Turnbull concluded, their house was selected for destruction. The hog-tying scam had failed. When the

People's Security Force showed up, they saw through the deception and took their vengeance on the collaborators. Ironic that, since Jim and his wife Tiana were loyal blues who had tried to betray Turnbull and his team.

Served them right, he thought. But what about Billy?

There was a face in the window across the street, and it vanished behind a curtain the second Turnbull made eye contact. There was one on every street, a watcher and informer who kept an eye on things for the PSF when the blues were in power. Turnbull got out of the Blazer with his carbine and walked up to the front door.

He banged on it. Nothing. He banged again.

"Open up or I kick it in."

The door opened a crack. It was an elderly man with rheumy eyes wearing a dirty wifebeater and running shorts, though he had not run in a long, long time. He wore white athletic socks with several holes in each.

He said nothing. He just stood there staring as if he expected to endure some new hardship from the big stranger on the porch, so Turnbull spoke.

"You're the neighborhood snitch, aren't you?"

The man's eyes went to the ground.

"Am I right?"

"I was the local community coordinator," he said. "I helped keep us safe."

"You were the snitch. Okay, open up." Turnbull pushed open the door, and the stale air from inside flowed out. It smelled like wet basset hound and disinfectant. The place was dark too, with one weak light bulb working. At least under occupation, they got power.

Turnbull stepped inside, but did not shut the door. He wanted the fresh air.

"You knew the people across the street?"

The man seemed to be thinking about it.

"Jim Turnbull. Wife Tiana. A little boy, Billy," Turnbull said.

"He transitioned to a little girl. I think Cindy..."

The man stopped, because Turnbull's face indicated that it was a bad idea to go on.

"I never liked the transitioning," the man said, but quietly. "I was always against it. Always."

It was clear the old man was scared. Turnbull figured that he had that effect on people.

"There was a shootout. Then the People's Security Force took them all away and burned the place down, right? Did the Turnbulls ever come back?"

He knew the answer. He just needed confirmation to move on, confirmation that his family had been added to the long list of people disappeared by the PR regime.

"No," the old man said, confused. "That's not it at all."

"What do you mean?"

"They were heroes," the old man said. "I mean, to the blues they were heroes. But they were really...." He paused, not sure how to say what Turnbull wanted to hear.

"The PSF did *not* take them away? It did *not* burn down the house?"

"Oh no. They were on the news even as all the fighting was happening. Heroes of the resistance. It didn't last long because the USA beat the PR, and I was always for the USA, always loyal."

"Then what happened to the family?"

The man swallowed.

"I wanted to help. I volunteered to help. I was on the neighborhood watch for the reds when they took over."

"So, you snitched for the reds once you couldn't snitch for the blues anymore." Turnbull understood that locals aiding the occupation got an increased food ration, just like they had under the blues. He could see the dinner table in the kitchen and there were several ration pack wrappers strewn on it.

"But I didn't report the Turnbulls. I don't know why they came for them."

"Who came for them?" asked Turnbull.

The man swallowed again. He spoke very quietly even though they were alone.

"The Mutilated."

"The what?"

"The Mutilated," the man said, this time more urgently. He looked at Turnbull's eyes, silently imploring him to understand and not make him say it again.

"I have no clue what the hell you are talking about."

"I don't know how they found out about Cindy. Maybe doctor records? I know I didn't say anything. He was a boy again after the shootout. He was a boy again!"

"When was this?"

"A few months ago. They came and got them and they burned the house and took them away."

"Did you call the security forces?"

The man looked at him uncomprehending.

"Did you call 911 or whatever you have here?"

Nothing. Turnbull tried again.

"Did you call the security forces?"

"They *are* the security forces," the old man said, puzzled that this all made no sense to Turnbull.

"Did the family ever come back?" Turnbull asked.

"They don't ever come back," the old man said.

Turnbull left the man and walked across the street and into his brother's yard. The house was a charred shell, and it was pretty clear that the ruins had been picked over. Turnbull poked through it, not sure what he was looking for.

An air horn went off down the street – he had heard several blasts in the distance earlier – and people began coming outside and walking up the street. At the intersection, there was a truck. A pair of men were throwing ration boxes down off the back end. The old man came back with more of them than anyone else and stared at Turnbull as he turned into his house.

There was nothing to be found in the wreckage. Turnbull crossed back over to the Blazer and drove off. He headed back to the 280 on-ramp.

The vehicles appeared quickly, four of them, a couple of old SUVs and a couple pick-ups rigged as technicals with machine guns mounted in back. All of them were marked with the Λ symbol.

They flew flags off the back of the vehicles and they were odd, with black field and what looked like a red scalpel. The vehicles were coming fast, and it was clear that they were not passing him.

They were after him.

The old man had made a call.

Turnbull assessed the odds and slid the Wilson .45 between his legs, then pulled over slowly and deliberately. No sudden moves, at least not yet.

The vehicles came to a stop around him, and at least a dozen of the provos jumped out. They mostly had AKs with an occasional pump shotgun among them.

There was something odd about them. They had the usual tacti-cool gear he expected from provos, but they looked strange to him and he could not place why. Not just one of them – all of them. They all seemed odd even under sunglasses and with their scowls.

They circled him, weapons up and pointed at him as if he was some dangerous beast. Turnbull deliberately placed his hands on the top of the steering wheel as the leader approached without a rifle but with an M9 in a holster. The battered Beretta was likely from some blue armory captured by the reds and opened to the provisional volunteers.

Turnbull figured the leader was a man in his mid-twenties, but the leader was offputtingly girlish with incongruously soft features.

Maybe it's not a man, Turnbull reflected as the leader stopped at the window. In the end, it wasn't relevant. Turnbull consciously suppressed his blue territory habit of asking his interlocutor's pronouns.

"Who are you?" the leader demanded. The leader's voice was higher than it should have been.

"I'm a US Army colonel," Turnbull said. "Who the hell are you?"

The provisional leader seemed nonplussed for a moment, pausing to assess.

"Why are you and your pals interfering with my mission?" Turnbull demanded.

"What mission?"

"The one that's none of your concern."

"Show me some ID," the leader demanded. The nametape on the brown plate carrier vest the leader wore read "DUGAN."

"No," Turnbull said.

"What do you mean 'No'?" Dugan demanded.

"You have trouble with English? It means I don't answer to whoever you are."

"You better get out of that vehicle," Dugan sputtered.

Turnbull did, after slipping his pistol back into his holster. Standing on the street, he loomed over Dugan and most of the rest. He got a better look at them now, and Dugan was not the only one whose gender he had difficulty picking up on. All of them seemed...off. And they all seemed very agitated.

"This is our area of responsibility, our zone, and if you really are a colonel you would have liaisoned through HQ to operate here."

"I liaison with soldiers," Turnbull sneered. "Not with scraggly amateurs."

"You think we aren't soldiers?" Dugan asked, his high voice breaking. "You think we can't fight?"

"I think you're out of your lane," Turnbull replied.

"Do you know who we are?"

"Not a clue."

"We're the Mutilated." Dugan let that hang in the air for a moment, as if it was supposed to impress him.

"Congratulations."

"General Scott personally chartered us. We run this area. No resistance here, no way. We don't tolerate it. And we deal with the butchers wherever they are – we have authorization to cross territories to deal with them. *That's* who we are."

There was a muffled shout, like someone calling for help, and it was coming from the back of one of the Mutilated's SUVs. Turnbull saw a shape in the backseat, obviously gagged, thrashing about.

"That's a butcher," Dugan said.

"Maybe you need to explain it to me," Turnbull said. "Slowly. Pretend like I'm the dumb one in this conversation."

"You're from the red," Dugan said before pointing back to their struggling prisoner. "That is a butcher. And he is going to pay. They all will."

"Who, exactly, did he butcher?" Turnbull asked.

Dugan breathed hard, eyes locked on Turnbull's.

"Who did he butcher?" Dugan shouted. "Us! All of us!"

Dugan pointed at the assembled provos, at least a dozen, who were nodding and muttering.

"He and his accomplices, they mutilated us! Doctors, they called themselves. Gender-affirming surgery! They cut off her breasts, and they sliced out his Adam's apple. And they castrated me!" Dugan shouted, pointing to his troop, then himself.

"Him?" was all Turnbull could say.

"Him. Or another one. They are all the same. All butchers," Dugan said. "They cut us to pieces. They lied to us. They collaborated with the blues. In the People's Republic, they encouraged it. I was fifteen. Fifteen!"

There were tears in his eyes.

"They can't escape justice now. Not the gender identity counselors. Not the transition surgeons. Not the so-called parents who let it happen to their kids. To their *kids*!"

The rest of the Mutilated mumbled in agreement.

"What will you do to him?" Turnbull asked.

"Justice," Dugan said.

"Does General Scott know you're doing this?"

"Like I said, he chartered us. He gave us our dignity. He gave us justice. And for the MAPs too."

"MAPs?"

"Minor attracted people," Dugan spit, as if the words burned his tongue. "They were an important community in the PR, legitimate, affirmed. And they kept records, so we and others could track them down after liberation. We've dealt with most of them already."

"What do you mean 'dealt with'?"

"I mean dealt with."

"You took a family from near here several months ago. A little boy. They had not cut him yet."

Dugan shrugged. "We rescued a lot of kids."

"Billy Turnbull."

"I don't know who that is. But if we rescued him, he's safe, being fostered with parents who won't hurt him. We've rescued hundreds of kids since liberation."

"And what about his parents?"

"Justice," Dugan said.

"You need to do better than that."

"I don't need to do anything," Dugan said. "I don't think you're a colonel. I don't think you are authorized to be here at all."

"Then let's go see your pal."

"My pal?"

"General Karl Martin Scott. You're tight with the general, so let's go see him."

"I think we ought to deal with you now. Right here." Dugan's hand went to the butt of his handgun.

"If you cap me and I am who I say I am, you're screwed," Turnbull said. "But if you take me to headquarters either I am who I say I am, at worst you're doing your job sweeping up suspicious types, and at best you caught yourself a spy or terrorist. Either way, you are looking good to the general."

Dugan considered.

"I'll call it in. What's your name?"

"No names," Turnbull said. Besides the tactical concern that people were looking for him and they might even have people this far afield, he simply did not feel like obeying the gender dysphoric unit commander.

"You need to take me in," Turnbull continued. He had planned to stop at Occupation headquarters anyway to get himself a situation report on the frontier he would have to cross to get to Seattle, Hillaryia.

Dugan looked him over, considering. "Give me your piece."

"Try and take it."

Dugan hesitated, but thought better of creating a situation that might get out of control. If this guy was lying, they would find out soon enough. And the hero notion appealed to him.

"You ride with us."

"What about my ride?"

"It's safe. These cows know not to resist in the Mutilated area of operations."

Turnbull considered, then nodded.

"Bring his gear," Dugan ordered one of his troops, a squat likely female with a masculine jawline and residual facial hair. Those that were not surgically altered had received hormones for free in the old PR, but even after stopping the injections, their bodies were still changed forever.

"We don't have room," a tall, slender male with a falsetto said.

Dugan walked to the SUV and opened the door. It revealed the prisoner, who was ball-gagged and gibbering.

"Out, doctor," Dugan said, pulling the tied man onto his feet on the street. The doctor was trying to speak.

"He was a Pediatric Transition Specialist," Dugan said to Turnbull. "In the People's Republic, he was elite. He probably even had a car. And he hid out for a year after the PR fell and thought he was beyond justice. And if there truly were justice, we would have carved him up like he carved up our brothers and sisters. But it's his good luck you came along."

Dugan drew his Beretta from his holster and shot the prisoner in the forehead. The man fell back and twitched on the street, blood erupting from the wound.

"Justice," muttered the provos together.

Turnbull said nothing, but he wondered if that had been the fate of his brother and sister-in-law. As for the dead surgeon, he was indifferent.

You reaped what you sowed.

How could anyone have imagined it would not come to this after the last two decades?

Turnbull stepped over the quivering body and got into the Mutilated militia's vehicle. One of the provos brought along Turnbull's gear and stowed it in the now-empty back.

Dugan got in the front seat and closed the door. The slender provo was sitting next to Turnbull.

"Let's go," Dugan said and the little convoy pulled off, leaving the dead doctor to bleed into the gutter.

They got onto Interstate 280 to head into the City. Dugan was on the radio frequently as they drove. It was evident that the Mutilated were more than just these four vehicles.

"How big is your unit?" Turnbull asked.

Dugan wheeled around in his seat, his face red, and Turnbull realized that his unit was a sensitive subject. He pivoted to dial-down the awkwardness.

"Your forces. How many troops do you have?"

Dugan was satisfied by the clarification. "Over four hundred," he said. "There could be tens of thousands of us if we enlisted everybody they mutilated during the PR years and before. They mutilated anyone and everyone who they could manipulate into thinking they were a man when they were a woman, or vice versa. They never had enough food but always enough hormones. You couldn't get an appendectomy, but there was never a wait to get gender affirmation surgery."

"It's illegal now in the red," Turnbull said. He was not sure what else to say. "We don't cut people to conform to delusions."

"We needed help. They ruined our lives," Dugan said bitterly. "Making it illegal is just the start. We will make it right."

"Justice," the slender man next to Turnbull added.

Turnbull was not sure how he felt about his brother and sister-in-law, except vaguely nauseated. But if the roles were reversed, he had no doubt they would be celebrating whatever cruel fate the PR had for him.

7.

The main command post for United States Pacific Coast Occupation Forces Command ("USPCOFC," pronounced "Use-Pock-Offk") and its subordinate land component command, Army Force West (which had attracted the less-than-optimal pronunciation of "Arf-West"), was at the Presidio, which had been a US Army base for over a century before it was given to the City of San Francisco prior to the Split and converted into a park. Post-Split, it had been repurposed as a reeducation camp under the People's Republic, a particularly infamous one originally designed to hold the few remaining California conservatives. When the number of potential inmates turned out to be minuscule, it was expanded to confine anyone the regime felt needed to conform, or to be conformed – the religious, the dissenting, the ones who demanded their rights.

The Presidio had been reclaimed by the US Army after the final surrender of blue forces in the City – for some reason, San Franciscans always refers to the city as "the City." But to get there through San Francisco was problematic.

"Vendrel's Raiders territory," the slender paramilitary warned Dugan as they drove north. He clutched his AK.

"Competitors?" Turnbull asked.

"They run the Parkside," Dugan said. "A bunch of assholes."

"How beefy is your beef with them?" Turnbull inquired. "Are we going to get into a rumble for crossing their turf?"

Dugan turned and glared, irritated.

"Nobody screws with the Mutilated. We are General Scott's own."

"Aren't all the provisionals his own? He did let them organize. Probably gave you your weapons."

"We do special tasks," Dugan said. "Important ones. Cleaning out the blues, stopping resistance, bringing justice."

"Do you actually arrest people and prosecute them?" Turnbull asked. "Or do you just kill them?"

Dugan ignored his passenger and kept scanning the road ahead.

"Not that I really mind killing bad people," Turnbull said.

Dugan's eyes were on the road ahead.

"Technical. Vendrel's," he said. The pick-up had a Λ painted on the side.

"Do you want me to stop, turn around, what?" asked the nervous driver. She seemed to be female. Her chest was absolutely flat under her vest. There was a wisp of a moustache on her upper lip.

"Just keep going. They can see we're heading to the Presidio."

The convoy could not keep going. The Vendrel's Raiders – their flag was blue with a red sword held aloft by a black fist – had set up a roadblock, but there were few regular cars on the road. The guards' focus seemed to be on the buses that came through with local workers.

"Are they checking for weapons?" Turnbull said. "Where would people get them? The blues confiscated them all."

"Checking for money," said the slender paramilitary.

"They're shaking down the locals?" Turnbull.

"Taxing the cows," Dugan said. "Security isn't free."

"So you do it too?" Turnbull said.

Dugan turned back around to face Turnbull as the SUV came to a halt at the roadblock. "We have to live. We can't work while we're doing our duty to keep the peace, now can we?"

"What about the locals?" Turnbull asked. "How are they supposed to live?"

"I guess they'll figure it out," Dugan said. "They're blues, you know? They did this. They brought this on, not us. And if someone has to pay, we vote they do."

Turnbull found it hard to defeat that logic. It was still obnoxious.

The Mutilated convoy slowed, and one of the Vendrel's Raiders approached the driver's window. The paramilitary was a tough-looking guy, probably in his late-forties, without the kind of softness you usually saw among the blue state city-dwellers.

"Where do you think you're going, freaks?" he asked.

Dugan seethed. "Get out of our way. Army business."

"Army," the Raider snorted. "The Army is guys who fly in for six months then fly out again. I've been fighting blues from here to the Sierras for a decade while you were getting your nuts snipped off."

Dugan put his hand on his Beretta, but Turnbull put a beefy hand on his shoulder.

"Chill," he commanded. Outside, a half dozen Raiders were hefting their AKs.

"I'm not interested in getting capped in a turf war," Turnbull said through his window to the Raider.

"Who the hell are you? You look like a man, so you're not with these freaks."

"Not your concern. Let us through."

"Well, I think you should pay your toll."

"We aren't paying you shit," Dugan exploded. "We work for General Scott!"

"We all do, girly-man," laughed the Raider.

"We're not paying or explaining," Turnbull said calmly. "And if you don't get out of our way and back to shaking down civilians, you're going to have a very short but intense problem."

"Short?"

"Yes, because I'll kill you first. And if your pals manage to kill me, the rest of my guys will find them and they'll die too. I'm not a provisional. I'm Army. And I'm not doing this dick dance with you anymore. So, get the hell out of our way."

It had been a while since someone talked to the Raider that way. Almost exclusively, Vendrel's Raiders heard various versions of "Yes, sir" from those they hassled. But this guy looked serious, and the Raider had been in the game long enough to know the difference.

"Next time, coordinate clearance to pass through Raider territory," the provisional instructed them. Dugan raised his middle finger as the convoy accelerated past.

Turnbull watched a bunch of workers lined up outside the buses handing over bills.

"Gotta milk the cows," Dugan said flatly.

They continued north on what had been Nineteenth Avenue, then was renamed El Camino de Kamala, and was now Main Supply Route Dodge, toward Golden Gate Park.

There were still a few battle-damaged buildings on the way, mostly from artillery strikes as the surviving People's Republic and Chinese ground forces had withdrawn instead of shooting it out in the Sunset District. With the Golden Gate Bridge blown, there was no escape. They had surrendered instead of being killed. But the place was still run-down. And something was missing.

"Where are the hobos?" asked Turnbull.

"Gone," Dugan replied. "They aren't allowed."

"They aren't allowed in the red either. Rehab, jail, or the loony bin. Where are yours?" Turnbull asked.

"They aren't allowed," Dugan repeated.

Golden Gate Park, now clear of druggies, criminals, and degenerates, was an idyllic urban retreat once again. Soldiers walked down the paths with their M4s over their backs, usually with attentive civilians. It seemed the local talent was making plays for the folks with the steady paychecks and the ability to buy in the PXs. Everything outside of the bases on the economy was rationed; most people still lived on aid packages and even a private E-1 was a catch since he could show up with a pack of steaks and real beer that wasn't brewed in some Tenderloin basement. It was good duty for the single guys, or the functionally single. Very good duty.

They got into the Presidio through the main gate but had to go around the long way past Chrissy Field, where the PR's prison camp had been converted into a US Army prison camp. The gun towers loomed over the barbed wire fences and they stole glances at the inmates in orange jumpsuits wandering across the exercise yard.

Beyond the prison camp, looming high over the Bay, were the rust-orange towers jutting up above the remnants of the Golden Gate Bridge. The bridge's roadbed was gone, though twisted wreckage could still be seen poking through the waves. Cranes, mounted on each end of the bridge and on barges in-between, were at work on the repairs.

"I never get used to that," Dugan said. "I wonder how the hell they managed to knock it down, and on top of a Chi Com cruiser."

Turnbull did not tell him. But he did mutter a quick prayer for his lost comrades.

Headquarters, USPCOFC and Arf-West, was within the main post section of the base. A sign, brown wood with yellow engraved lettering, announced "COMMANDER: GEN KARL MARTIN SCOTT" and "CSM LOUIS Z. LIGHTFOOT." Turnbull smiled. He knew Command Sergeant Major Lightfoot from Iraq back before the Split. He took no crap and would gladly close the office door and give even the famous O-10 a profane piece of his mind.

New, functional, and ugly office buildings had been thrown up quickly to house the offices for the huge numbers of both military personnel and civil workers required to run the reconquered California and Nevada. They were jarring compared to the classical, red-roofed buildings of the Presidio, but function trumped form.

They passed several military police checkpoints, and Turnbull was a bit surprised that these Mutilated characters had the juice to pass through them with minimal hassle. Turnbull was a bit impressed that the provisionals were not just dismissed out of hand. Maybe they had some heat, if not blazing heat.

Soldiers, along with sailors and airmen, moved about carrying out their duties. They were all armed. There were a significant number of provos around as well, each in slightly different uniforms. Some even had their own patches on their shoulders.

The convoy parked. Dugan, the slender provo, and Turnbull walked toward the headquarters building with Turnbull carrying his backpack.

The master sergeant at the desk at the bottom floor of the main command building did not seem impressed.

"What do I tell his adjutant?" the sergeant said, visibly annoyed. "A provo has a guy who wants to see the gen-gen?"

"We're the Mutilated!" Dugan said.

"Not me," said Turnbull. "I'm uncut."

"You can wait," the sergeant said. "Maybe he'll see you."

"Have the general's minion tell him that the guy who gave him a tour of Gettysburg is here, and that he ought to talk to me," Turnbull said. "Do it."

The sergeant looked at him skeptically, but picked up the receiver and dialed. After a moment, he spoke into it and then paused.

"It'll be a second," the sergeant said. He put the receiver back to his ear. After a moment, his eyes widened.

"You can go up," the sergeant said. He seemed a bit surprised. The NCO looked to a specialist sitting nearby and nodded.

"Take them to the CP." He handed them visitor badges that said "ACCESS LEVEL BRAVO."

They went up three flights and the E-4 ushered them through another MP checkpoint before they entered the command post.

It was a large room, with lots of tables packed with computer monitors and phones.

The CP was also packed with troops from lots of different branches, not just Army soldiers, though as co-headquarters with Arf-West, the majority of the staff were from the Army. USPCOFC was a joint command – General Scott commanded all the forces, land, sea and air. There were blue-clad zoomies from the Air Force, a sprinkling of jarheads from the Marine Corps, some Navy folk plus a few Coast Guardsmen. There was even one baffled-looking member of the Space Force who probably had a job related to satellites. He wore thick black glasses and had forgotten to tie his left boot.

On the wall were a dozen big Vizio video monitors, one of them running Fox News with closed captions. Others showed graphics representing various battalion readiness levels, running from green down to black, which was combat ineffective. Most were yellow and a few were red.

The biggest screen displayed the situation map, with battalion-level unit symbols for both red and blue forces. The number of US forces seemed low for the size of the battlespace. Each front-line unit had a wide frontage – wider than doctrine allowed.

There was a lot more land than soldiers.

The forward line of enemy troops was farther back to the north than Turnbull had expected, much farther, with the enemy units mostly surrounding Seattle. There were no blue units in contact with red forces. In fact, they were well back from along the southern and eastern Washington border – the state was not denominated "Hillaryia" on the American battle map.

In between the forces, some of northeast California, all of Oregon, and most of Washington, were displayed as gray. No one controlled it. It was a failed state on the US mainland.

The Gray Zone.

Another screen showed the same terrain with conical overlays in blue from the north facing south, and similar ones in red from the south aiming north. Air defense coverage. It blanketed the whole Gray Zone, with what seemed to be Chinese ground-to-air missiles on the PR side and American coverage from an air defense artillery brigade arrayed across Northern California. The missiles were probably supplemented by combat air patrols by both sides, controlled by airborne warning and control systems (AWACS).

If it flies over the Gray Zone, it dies.

"I remember you," said a familiar voice, though Turnbull had only heard it on television, albeit often, since their one meeting a decade ago.

"General Scott," Turnbull said. He did not salute, since they were indoors and regardless, his own military status was iffy at the moment. Behind the generals were three hard men, clearly his personal security detail. They carried tricked M4 rifles, kept back, and watched, quiet but alert.

"Proud to present you this individual, sir," Dugan said in his odd voice. The general turned to the provo and smiled.

"Captain Dugan, you have continued to serve loyally and I know that I can count on you whenever I have a vital mission," he said. Dugan beamed. "I'd like to talk to this man alone, if you will excuse us. Operational security. But please stay close. I need your help."

"Yes, sir," Dugan said. He was overflowing with pride.

The general nodded for Turnbull to follow and he did. There was a doorway with a sign that read, "ACCESS LEVEL DELTA."

"I'm granting you DELTA access," the general said, leading him into a room off the command post floor. "I expect I can trust you with secrets."

The door shut behind them and Turnbull saw that there were a dozen hard-looking men sitting facing the front. They had top-shelf weapons and wore their gear like they knew how. A couple had "EOD" patches on their shoulders.

There was also a dog, a Belgian Malinois with a muzzle who was staring at Turnbull like he was a Milk-Bone. Several staff officers had been briefing the assembly. On the wall was another situation map. There were a number of marks in the gray part of the map, but the screen flicked off before Turnbull got a good look.

"This Operational Detachment - Alpha team was just spinning up for an operation," General Scott said. The team captain and his warrant officer – Turnbull did not know either one – were staring at him. The captain glanced at the general and then back to Turnbull, seemingly confused.

"He will *not* be joining you, gentlemen," Scott told them. "Focus on your mission."

The Green Berets stood up and gathered their gear. The captain approached the general.

"Sir," he began, but Scott cut him off.

"It's all right. Carry on. And good luck."

Turnbull said nothing. He did not know any of these men, and he appreciated that they were probably not thrilled to have some stranger walk into a mission brief.

The operators began to file out. They all looked like special forces operators – they had that way about them – but perhaps their cold reception was because Turnbull failed to subtly acknowledge their badassary. He admitted to himself that he probably would have acted the very same when he was an ODA detachment commander a dozen years ago. He did not take it personally, though he found it a bit tiresome.

A nose was at his crotch.

It was the dog, which was sniffing him and staring up with intelligent eyes. The beast wore a black rig and had a nametape that said "GIBSON" in yellow block letters. Turnbull wondered if that muzzle was keeping him from a messier version of Dugan's fate.

"I guess I'm a dog person," he said to the handler, who merely grunted.

"Is he named after Gibson the Mel?" Mel Gibson had just released the controversial *Lethal Weapon 8: Death to Heretics*.

Sadly, Danny Glover, famously liberal, was not aboard for the last few rounds. He had stayed in the blue and been exiled from movies over controversial statements he made when accepting the People's Republic's "Best Cis-Gender Male-Identifying Acting Person of Color Oscar" in 2027 for his role in *Antifa: The Musical*. Glover, who had just been handed the statue, said, "Wow, like I said on screen years ago, I'm too old for this shit!" The entire auditorium had frozen at his blatant ageism, and he never worked again in Hollywood.

"Gibson the drink," said the dog handler, and he left without another word, dragging the dog with him.

"Looks like you made a friend," Scott said.

"I'm not usually a dog person," Turnbull replied.

"Kelly!" said a booming voice. Coming into the room as the last Green Beret left was Sergeant Major Lightfoot. "How are you doing!"

"Hey, ix-nay on the ames-nay," Turnbull said.

The sergeant major laughed. "Sure, why not? I got excited to see my old battle buddy from Baghdad. Probably why I wasn't allowed in this mission brief."

"We're keeping this mission strictly need to know," said the general. "No offense."

"None taken, sir," Lightfoot replied, but Turnbull was pretty sure there was a little bit of offense taken. A primary NCO skill set was letting officers know they had ticked off their sergeant without actually saying it.

"I need to talk to him alone," the general said. "Can you and the staff give us the room?"

Lightfoot nodded and turned to Turnbull.

"Find me before you go."

"Roger, sergeant major," Turnbull said. The CSM and the staff officers filed out, leaving Turnbull and General Scott alone.

"I have to admit I'm a little surprised to see you here," Scott said. "Kelly Turnbull, ex-Task Force Zulu."

"Did I ever tell you my name? And I don't know what any Task Force Zulu is."

The general laughed a little bit, amused.

"I know a lot of things. I have a wide network, here and back home."

"I'll keep that in mind," Turnbull said.

"But I did not know about this visit. You are operating in my area of operations without me knowing about it, much less approving whatever you intend to do here."

"No time to coordinate," Turnbull said. "And I'm just passing through."

"You're going into the blue?"

"I'm going somewhere, general. It will not have any effect on your ops. And I'm operating on a need to know too."

"You don't think the commanding general of the West Coast has a need to know by definition?"

"No, sir."

Scott looked him over, hiding whatever annoyance he undoubtedly felt from Turnbull's studied insolence.

"So, what can I do for you to facilitate whatever operation you're planning?"

"I wouldn't mind some transport north. I'll infiltrate in. And while I'm here, I'd like your Mutilated militia off my back."

"The Mutilated have done great services for the United States. So have most of the provisionals. We could not maintain order without them."

"I saw the ops maps. You're short of troops. That's why you have not moved north and liberated Oregon and Washington. You don't have the forces to take them, much less hold them."

"You're right. Our service for citizenship rule means citizens have to keep serving over and over. It ruins their civilian careers, much like it did in the Roman Republic. A citizen would be called to the colors, then come home and find his farm bankrupt and sold off to some rich senator. Maybe his wife and kids too. Bad policy. And in the United States, it's the slackers who are prospering. Too many have decided not being able to vote or be on juries is a small price to pay for their lives not being upended by never-ending wars that no one is willing to win. And our political leaders cannot see a way out of it."

"But you do."

General Scott smiled. "We can win the war decisively. And we can deal with the slackers. The politicians simply do not have the stomach to do what must be done."

"I thought that when we split we were supposed to move past political nonsense."

"No, not as long as weak men run our government. But that's echelons above our respective pay grades."

"You know, your Mutilated provos shot a prisoner in the head in front of me today."

The general paused. "I expect they had a good reason."

"They said he was a gender transition surgeon for the blue."

"Then it seems that they did have a good reason. Don't tell me you've never killed anyone."

"I try to kill only bad people," Turnbull said.

"What do you call someone who chops up little kids?"

"He's bad people," Turnbull said.

"And? The blues committed enormous crimes. The provisionals were here and endured them. They want justice. MAPs, secret policemen, gender butchers. They made their choices. They can live with the consequences."

"Or not," Turnbull said.

"I'm not going to judge them on how they judge their tormentors," the general said. "Are you?"

Turnbull considered the question. He would not be judging them.

"I don't think there are a lot of folks with more reason to want some payback from the blues than me," Turnbull said. "And I'm not going to hesitate to do what I need to do. But guys like me are the exception, break glass in case of war kind of people. It seems like this is standard operating procedure here. The Constitution – is it ever going to come back here?"

"I have 33 million people to rule over in California. At least it's not 40 million – the other seven million went to the red or are illegal aliens in Mexico, or who died. So, we have to be firm. Here and back home."

"Are we planning on ever integrating California and the rest of the blue back into the USA sometime, or will we keep them as a permanent colony?"

Scott laughed a bitter little laugh. "Do you want 33 million new leftist voters? They had their chance to choose freedom. They chose the People's Republic. They chose serfdom. And they can now be our serfs. In a couple years they will be feeding themselves, and then they'll be extracting resources for us."

"A colony."

"A colony. Correct. Do you have a better idea? You want them back in a country with us? Haven't you fought them long enough to know what they are?"

"I know what they are. Better than most," Turnbull said. He had the sense he was being tested, and he was not clear if he had passed, or even if he wanted to pass. And it annoyed him.

"Enough about the big picture," the general said. "Let's focus on you. I will have my people arrange transport and have our Mutilated friends take you to quarters beyond prying eyes to prepare. Good?"

"Thank you, sir."

"You know, I thought you would be more focused on what needs to be done."

"Don't underestimate my focus, sir," Turnbull said.

The general smiled coldly then walked to the door and through it. The sergeant major came inside.

"Kelly, are you here for good?"

"Passing through. Your boss is an interesting cat."

"The general has a vision, and I'm not a big part of it. He has irons in the fire I know nothing about, and then there's the political shit with him back home. I handle our troops. He spends a lot of his time with the damn provos. He keeps expanding them and the problem is that some are disciplined and STRAC, but others are armed gangs in 'ed-up uniforms."

"Not sure of his options," Turnbull said. "I saw a lot of unrest back home among the citizens. Too many deployments."

"That's for sure. Our citizen-soldiers are burning out. And the more they burn out, the more the general builds up his private army to pick up the slack."

"I don't envy you, sergeant major," Turnbull said. "I gotta go."

The sergeant major extended his hand. "Be careful, Kelly. This occupation shit – I'd rather be in a straight-up fight than this. It's a hall of mirrors here."

Turnbull walked out back into the command post. The general was off to the side – his security detail nearby but unobtrusive – talking to Dugan, who was nodding and looking very serious. A four-star giving direction to a paramilitary captain – odd at the very least.

Turnbull did not like it. He was not sure why, but his senses were tingling.

Scott left the CP with his posse. Dugan approached Turnbull with the slender guy.

"Time to roll," the captain said.

"Where to?"

"Safe house. We're supposed to watch you, make sure you get out safely."

"How do I go north?"

"To be determined. For now, you come with us and wait."

Turnbull nodded. "I need to hit the head first."

Dugan was annoyed, but Turnbull did not wait for permission. He headed down the aisle toward the head, snatching a roll of masking tape off a table next to an unattended monitor. In the latrine, he went into a stall and closed the door. He taped his Gerber Mark II knife around his left forearm and the Springfield XD-S 4.0 he had in a pocket to his stomach. He released the mag and ejected the round out of the pipe of his Wilson. He dropped the hammer and slid the mag back in. Pulling out his shirt so it was baggy over the Springfield, he exited after flushing.

They made their way downstairs and left the building, walking outside to the little convoy as dusk approached. Turnbull tossed his backpack into the rear again, then slid into his backseat position. The slender guy slid into his seat and Dugan took shotgun. Turnbull yawned as the vehicles pulled out and exited the Presidio. It was a cool day and the air from the open windows was pleasant. In other circumstances, he might have napped.

They entered Golden Gate Park from the north heading south. No one said much, so Turnbull broke the ice.

"Where are we headed, anyway?" he said.

"Safe house," Dugan said, not looking back. "It's good and remote."

There were wooded areas to both sides of the road. It was a bit crowded, with what passed for rush hour beginning, and the two Mutilated pick-ups were behind them with a couple vehicles in-between. They were doing about 15 miles an hour.

"You know," Turnbull said. "Thanks, but I'll do this on my own. Pull over and let me out here."

Slenderman flushed and looked at Dugan, then hefted up his AK, aiming it at Turnbull's ribs.

"Give me your .45," Dugan said calmly.

"Didn't the general tell you to treat me nice?" Turnbull said with an edge of mockery.

"We're going to treat you real nice. The .45. Slow, two fingers on the grip."

Slenderman watched Turnbull intently as he slowly withdrew the weapon from his holster.

"That's a Wilson Combat CQB," Turnbull said, passing it to Dugan in the front seat. "It's worth more than your life."

"Nice piece," Dugan said, admiring it.

As Turnbull had expected, Slenderman glanced over to admire it too.

The blade was out of the sleeve and into Slenderman's neck before the provisional realized it. The tip punched between two vertebrae and severed the spinal cord; Slenderman's finger did not even twitch, though Turnbull pushed the barrel away anyway to be safe.

Dugan fumbled with the Wilson, managing to pull back the hammer and get his finger on the trigger then squeeze. The hammer fell with a click as Turnbull ripped the Springfield taped to his stomach out and shot the driver through the head below the ear, splattering brains out the open driver's side window. The vehicle swerved but Turnbull had the gun in Dugan's face.

"Why?" he demanded.

"I don't know," Dugan sputtered.

Turnbull shot him through the forehead. The round punched through the windshield and painted the inside with Dugan's cerebellum.

The SUV bounced off the road and slowed enough that the impact with a pine tree that finally stopped it did not even deploy the airbags.

Turnbull rolled out with Slenderman's AK and an extra mag from the dead man's rig. The second Mutilated SUV was confused and had slowed to a stop in the street. Turnbull opened fire on the windows. The driver twitched and jerked under the impact of the 7.62mm rounds. Turnbull could not see any of the other occupants, but he emptied the mag and dropped it to reload. Then he emptied the second 30-round magazine into the two Mutilated technicals in the distance.

No time to sort out who was dead, who was wounded and who was hunched up on the floor in a fetal position as the rounds ripped through. It was enough that no one was moving in the punctured, smoking vehicles.

Turnbull jogged back to his own SUV, got his backpack out of the rear, and retrieved his own rifle and his .45. Racking it, he slid the weapon back into his holster, and darted into the woods.

8.

Turnbull trundled along through Golden Gate Park, seeking to put as much distance between himself and the surviving Mutilated who would no doubt be looking for him. There were a few casual walkers on the paths, something unimaginable before the United States had imposed martial law. Under the blues – and even before the Split – all of San Francisco was a festering abscess of social pathologies. The park was a literal jungle, full of predators.

No more.

Turnbull drew a few puzzled looks as he ran through, but no one interfered with him.

He passed the former California Academy of Sciences, which had been converted into the "California Institution of Celebrating Indigenous Ways of Knowing," science having gone from a cudgel to use to beat the proles into submission pre-Split into a racist construct that colonized various "alleged" means of understanding. The formerly impressive buildings were broken and vandalized, and the occupation had not yet gotten around to repairing them.

Ahead was the Haight-Ashbury, the former hippie district that became a seedy den of crime and decay long before even the Crisis, much like the rest of the City outside of the walled-off secure areas where the elite had lived after the Split. It was not exactly charming now, but there were no low-lifes in sight and Turnbull did not need to watch each step to avoid being impaled by a syringe or stepping into a pile of someone's previous evening's meal.

As he had hoped, much of the neighborhood was abandoned. One house in three seemed to be empty. While the sun set and it grew darker – only one streetlight in five seemed to be casting even the most tentative light – Turnbull looked for the right place to hole-up. He found it on the 1100 block of Haight, a row of seedy, two-story townhouses sporting bay windows that were mostly covered with salvaged plywood.

Turnbull got a few glimpses of pale, frightened faces peering out from the uncovered windows. Would they narc out a stranger? Most of these were blues – they would not be looking to interact with either occupation forces or the provisionals. He would roll the dice on them pulling a Sergeant Schultz and seeing nothing.

Turnbull finally spotted a likely house – it showed some minor fire damage but was otherwise relatively intact. There was a gate at the side that went back to a small yard. He went in, hand hovering over his pistol – which he had racked after retrieving it from the twitching Dugan.

The neighborhood was quiet. The curfew was in effect, so the roads were clear of civilians.

But they were not entirely clear of traffic. A trio of Humvees growled by. Provisionals, and they were looking for something. He ducked down, out of sight as they passed. It was some new group with what looked like the Grateful Dead bear on their flag and painted, poorly, on the side of their vehicles. The provos themselves sported rifles as well as long, graying hair and more beards than usual. Were they some sort of militant deadheads? Turnbull was eager to forgo finding out, and the trio of trucks kept on truckin'.

The back door came open easily, and Turnbull cleared the townhouse room by room. If it had been before the Occupation, an unoccupied townhouse would have been a squatters' paradise, and this clearly had been in the past. But it was empty now, though the pungent scent of its previous occupants' liquid waste lingered behind. Turnbull went up to a bedroom on the top floor and decided that it would be his crash pad.

Outside, through the dirty window, he saw a two-Hummer military police patrol go by – actual US troops. They vanished down the road.

He dragged a foul mattress from another room into his lair and put the more appalling side to the floor. There were some sheets that did not seem too horrible, and he covered the mattress with them. It being San Francisco, it would get cold, and he had only the light fart-sack he picked up at the surplus store jammed down inside his ruck. He set out his sports bottle filled with water and took out a couple of the two dozen Quest energy bars he had bought back in Dallas. He also opened up a bottle of pills and popped in a tab of Cipro, an antibiotic to help ward off infection.

He went back downstairs and closed the back door. It was shaky and would not keep anyone out, but he needed it to be secure enough that it would take some battering to break through and give him a few moments to prepare a reception for any intruders.

Upstairs, under the pale green glow from a light stick, he reassembled and cleaned his HK416C. Satisfied, he inserted a magazine and charged it. Next, he examined the Mossberg shotgun and emptied it, cleaned it, and reloaded it with shells. That would be his primary weapon if there were intruders in his redoubt.

He paused as yet another provisional patrol passed by. There were a lot of them rolling that evening. They were looking for something, and he was pretty certain he knew what.

Now he had time to think.

General Scott had tried to off him. Why?

It was pretty clear he did not want anyone official to know about it. Scott could have arrested him right there in the CP, but he didn't. Of course, Lightfoot and others might have raised a stink. So he told Task Force Eunuch to do it. They would have taken his gun and left the cannoli, if their cannoli had not been taken long ago.

Again, why?

Was Scott in on the conspiracy? Maybe. But why the hell would he care about Kelly Turnbull and the rest of the Zombies of Task Force Zulu? They had actually rescued the general and kept him from being arrested by the blues a decade before.

Nothing made any sense.

Last, Turnbull broke down and cleaned the Wilson. It was tight and it took a little work to get the slide off. As he wiped the components, he tried to come up with a plan.

He had nothing.

After eating a protein bar, he put his ruck at the end of the mattress to use as a pillow and went to sleep.

Noise.

Not the door, but out in the backyard. At least a couple voices.

By now it was dark outside. Turnbull took up the Mossberg and did a quiet chamber check though he had loaded it after he cleaned it. A 12-gauge double-aught shell was seated in the chamber.

Carefully, he pushed himself up to look out the window toward the street. There were two trucks out there, definitely provisionals. A couple of the provos – these did not look particularly bizarre – stood guard with different weapons, one with an AR and the other an FAL. The AR guy was sitting in the cab and the FAL guy was looking at his smartphone.

Turnbull could just make out the Λ symbol that denoted an officially recognized paramilitary unit vehicle and the block letters spelling out "Ron's Rangers."

Turnbull did not recognize the symbol painted on each door, which appeared to be a rendering of a friendly-looking older man. The caricature did not look like Ronald Reagan to him, but then maybe these guys were terrible artists.

From the noise, it was clear others were messing about in the townhouse's backyard. But what he found interesting was the guards up front did not seem particularly tactical, as one might expect if they were looking for a fight.

Someone knocked on the backdoor downstairs.

Knocked.

Turnbull considered his options. Going downstairs was out, unless he wanted to risk a firefight. But the guards out front were not particularly attentive.

Turnbull made a 60% plan and resolved to violently execute it. He carefully lifted the front window open, and was deeply grateful that it slid up nearly silently. In any case, the guards did not notice. A few feet below the bay window was a shingled overhang, and ten feet below that a patch of dirt where a lawn had once been. The two guards were adjacent to it along the sidewalk.

Down below, at the back door, the knocking stopped. Turnbull could hear someone yelling.

"Please open the door. We respect your rights and want to talk."

Turnbull expected they would respect him right into a shallow grave down in the Crystal Springs watershed given the chance. With few options that did not involve going out in a blaze of glory, Turnbull went through the window, landed on the overhang, and jumped down to the dirt.

The guards heard him crash onto the shingles, and what they saw – a large blur dropping onto the ground a few feet away – did not register.

For his part, Turnbull's instincts took over and prevented him from shattering his ankles. Instead, he hit the ground with a perfect parachute landing fall, accomplishing the PLF with such smoothness that even the blackhats back at Fort Benning's jump school would have grudgingly approved.

Turnbull let his ankle collapse as the balls of his feet made contact. He then fell to his right, feet and knees together, taking the brunt of the impact on his calf and thigh and then his fourth point of contact. As he rolled through hitting his ass, he took the remaining impact in his lats, his fifth point of contact. Unburdened by a parachute, he rolled up to his feet, the cut-down shotgun up and pointed directly in the face of the stunned guard with the smartphone.

"Do not move," Turnbull growled, adding "You either" for the benefit of the other one.

They froze, eyes wide, staring at the shotgun.

They did not strike Turnbull as particularly hard men, both being in their mid-twenties, thin and a bit pasty, but their rifles were hardcore and that was sufficient reason to treat them as threats.

"I'm taking your ride," Turnbull said, moving forward on them with the hog's leg up and aimed. "Keys, now."

"I don't have them," the smartphone guard said.

"Kyle has them," said the other.

"Kyle is the executive until next week," said smartphone. "Until a week from Thursday."

"You better shit me some keys, boy," Turnbull growled.

"I can't. Kyle has them!"

"Excuse me!" came a voice from behind him. Turnbull spun.

There were another four provisionals, all armed with different weapons – one had a crossbow instead of a firearm – and they were coming around the side from the backyard.

Turnbull held his fire, but aimed his weapon at the leader, presumably this Kyle fellow.

"What is this?" Turnbull said.

"It's okay," Kyle replied. He was young too, maybe thirty. He had a scruffy and short beard. "We respect your rights. We can reason together."

"You not giving me the keys is giving me a reason to pull this trigger."

"Now, hold on. These vehicles are our property and we need you to respect that," Kyle said. A couple of the others nodded.

"We were looking for you because we heard the be-on-the-lookout alert and what happened with the Mutilated and we figured you were being oppressed."

"Oppressed?" asked Turnbull, baffled.

"Oppressed. The violation of one's rights is a violation of all of our rights. We figured you had to use your right to self-defense to protect yourself and then we got the alert that you were some sort of blue agent. We did not buy that. Too convenient. One of our sources told us they saw you come here. Lots of the people help us because they know Ron's Rangers respect their rights."

"What do you want?" Turnbull asked.

"Like I said, the violation of one man's rights is the violation of all of our rights. So we help the oppressed. Now, we probably need to go. This is more visible than I wanted and not everyone talks to us. The Mutilated and all the other provos want you bad. They can be dangerous, and they don't always respect due process. Do you wish to go with us?"

"Do I have a choice?" Turnbull asked, lowering the shotgun.

"Of course," Kyle answered with absolute sincerity. "Choice is the essence of liberty."

There was a cackle on the radio in one of the trucks. The guard who had been sitting in the cab spoke up.

"Looks like they know something is up here. We don't have long."

"You are welcome to come with us," Kyle said to Turnbull. "If you choose. You do have to pay your way, though – we eschew banal altruism."

"I have no idea what that means. Who the hell are you people?"

"Us? Well, we're a non-hierarchical, radical pro-liberty provisional force, small but dedicated. They call us 'Ron's Rangers.'"

"Ron Reagan?"

"No," Kyle said, a bit annoyed. "Ron Paul."

"You're libertarians?"

"Yes," Kyle said proudly. "Hardcore libertarians."

"Then you must be for real," Turnbull said. "Nobody would ever call himself a 'libertarian' if he really wasn't one."

The Ron's Rangers had perhaps forty men and women, and a dozen vehicles. They occupied the abandoned Grattan Elementary School nearby. The flagpole was empty.

"We have not been able to agree on a proper flag," Kyle told Turnbull as they walked in. "We disagree on a lot."

"Like on those restrictive age of consent laws?"

"Those are *Arizona* libertarians," Kyle sniffed, mildly offended. "I hate Arizona libertarians."

Turnbull wore the rucksack that he had retrieved from his room before they departed his hideout. He was given a cot and directed to find a place of his choosing in the school building. He took an abandoned classroom with good fields of fire outside through the windows and a couple of solid escape routes. Then he returned to the command post in the old cafeteria.

"I am the rotating executive until next week," Kyle told him as they sat down for breakfast. They were not communists, several of the provos emphasized. Everyone paid for his own food, usually in US script.

"We don't like it because it's fiat money," Kyle said, looking at a US twenty-dollar bill with Reagan's face smiling back. "At least the US is talking about going back on the gold standard. It was much worse when the People's Republic was in charge. Money was meaningless because they continually devalued it."

"How the hell did you people survive under the blues?" Turnbull asked. "You'd think they'd have hunted you down." He took a bite of his biscuit. It was not bad – perhaps being paid for their work inspired the cooks to do a good job.

"We were outlaws. They were hunting us," Kyle said with a hint of pride. "I was a student at Berkeley, privilege level 6, and I bought into all the collectivist crap I had been spoon fed through grade school to high school. Then I got to Berkeley and it was a hotbed of dissent. There was this underground of free thinkers. I knew it was illegal, but maybe that was why I was attracted to it. After a while hanging out with the radicals, I guess they trusted me enough and gave me something that changed my life. Something banned."

"Oh no, tell me it's not what I think it is."

"There was this old, beat-up, marked-up copy of *Atlas Shrugged.* Kyle's face bore a beatific smile.

Turnbull sighed.

"You read it?" Kyle asked eagerly.

"Not by choice."

"It really did change my life. I saw there was another way. I wouldn't say I was an Objectivist – though we do have a lot of those here – but I definitely incorporate Ayn Rand thought into my overall personal world view."

"So, you are fighting for a libertarian future?" Turnbull asked. He'd known some libertarians in school and warned them not to try to hang around with him.

"Absolutely," Kyle said, brightening at what he mistook for interest. "It is clearly the way forward for the occupied blue zone, and eventually red America too. Not right away, of course. I mean, we do have to play the long game."

"Yeah, you're libertarians. It's all long game for you guys."

"We built up a pretty big network at various campuses under the blues, but the People's Bureau of Investigation eventually infiltrated us and a lot of us were arrested or even killed. I had to go into the libertarian underground, but there wasn't much of one outside of academia. The PR was pretty friendly toward pot, so a lot of libertarians kind of lost their motivation for the cause."

"And what do you do here post-liberation?"

"Try to agitate for liberty. Help folks who get sideways with the authorities, like you."

"And you formed a little libertarian militia. It's kind of adorable," Turnbull said.

"We're one of the hundreds of recognized provisional units under the occupation government, but we have a real ideology. The vast majority of the provisional don't."

"I met the Mutilated. Charming, though I get why they're pissed. And some others who seemed interested in squeezing the locals for pennies."

"We're fighting for something besides revenge or the ability to shake down the blues."

"I appreciate you helping me out."

"I'm going to need some money, though," Kyle said. "Altruism is a trap."

"I'll give you some now. I'll give you more later – a lot more. You probably realize I'm not operating on my own."

"I figure you're backed. Some now, a lot more later."

"Agreed."

"But it's not all about money," Kyle said.

"But it's never not at all about money."

"We really do want to make a free country here."

"Good luck. California is broken, maybe forever."

"We're not a big provisional unit, but we have a reputation. Everyone trusts us. The thing is that the Mutilated have a reputation too, but it's a reputation for not only hunting down transition doctors and parents and MAPs but of doing the dirty work for the occupation forces. It's one of the militias that has no real belief system except hate, not that I really blame them. There were other groups that were dedicated to hunting down MAPs. They kind of fell apart when they finished off the last of the groomers. But we don't think that's how we should rebuild California and the rest of the occupied zone. We have an opportunity to make a paradise here based on liberty, but that doesn't seem to be General Scott's vision."

"What do you know about him?" asked Turnbull. "What's he doing with these militias?"

"I know he's gaining the personal loyalty of all the provisional units, and the provos far outnumber even the active-duty US forces in California. He doesn't care for due process or freedom or rights at all. If you play along with him, you stay recognized as a paramilitary organization – if you aren't recognized by the Occupation Authority, you become illegal and that's not good. He gives you guns and money and a free hand."

"But you Rand fans are recognized."

"Sure, but we try to do our work and avoid getting sucked into Occupation politics. And we are true to ourselves. Most provisional units all use AKs, because that's what the Occupation gives out. We give our people the choice of their weapons. Liberty."

"I'm all for firearm diversity," Turnbull said.

"So," asked Kyle. "What about you?"

"I need to get out of here," Turnbull told him.

"I figured that," Kyle said.

"You have not asked much about me," Turnbull said.

"I figured you would tell me if you chose to. I just figured you were in trouble with the authorities, seeing as they want you so badly."

"I'm from the red. But I need to get to the blue."

"North? We've helped people get out before."

It rubbed Turnbull wrong that people would need to escape from the red, but he put it aside.

"Washington state," Turnbull said.

"Hillaryia," Kyle replied, nodding as he considered it. "That's hard. You would have to pass through red lines and then cross the Gray Zone, and then cross through blue lines."

"That's a lot of lines," Turnbull conceded.

"Unless you go around them.

"Around?"

"We believe in an individual's right to pharmaceutical autonomy," Kyle began. "We have certain connections to persons who are entrepreneurs who might be able to avoid unpleasant interactions while traveling into the blue."

"Drug smugglers?"

"Yes," Kyle said. "Though the smuggling is into occupied California from their sources in the blue up north."

"I thought there was no more drug use in the Occupation," Turnbull said. Kyle snorted.

"There is a lot of illegal stuff in the Occupation. You can't defeat the free market, and drugs are the ultimate in capitalism. Sure, there are still users here. It's just there are a lot fewer. They stay real low key and under the radar. They saw most addicts get taken away by Scott's minions, supposedly to rehab camps. Except, we tried to locate those rehabilitation camps and have not been able to."

"A lot of people seem to have disappeared from here both before and after the blue got thrown out."

"We know what liberty looks like, and the Occupation is not much freer than the People's Republic, though I don't miss the PR's woke crap. But our goal is liberty. We've been fighting for it for years. If we are ever going to create a nation based on libertarianism, we need to do it here and now."

Turnbull was eager to redirect the conversation before Kyle got totally spun up.

"Your smuggler buddies – will you make the introduction?"

"They'll want money. They don't believe in altruism either."

"Make the introduction. I'll make it worth their while."

9.

Two shapes hung off the pedestrian overpass as the Ron's Rangers convoy of two SUVs passed underneath. Above them, on the cyclone fence that enclosed the walkway, someone had affixed a sign that read, "FREAKS DIE." Turnbull squinted. Below, swinging from ropes was one form he could not make out, though it was pink, and another that was blue and was easier to discern.

"Is that a cartoon fox?" asked Turnbull.

"Yeah, executed furries," Kyle said. "The MAPs I understood, though I didn't agree. The gender re-assigners too. But they are almost all gone, so now it's open season on mere weirdos. They gotta be very careful now."

"Who did it? The Mutilated?" Turnbull asked as they headed east toward the Bay.

"No, this is not Mutilated territory. Someone else did it. Vikings Militia, the Flaming Sword. Maybe Church Militant – those provos are hardcore. Usually, they sign their names when they leave bodies out to send a message. They make sure that the blues know that someone is evening up the score on all the favored groups under the PR."

"Payback is a bitch," Turnbull said.

"Yeah. See that vacant lot?"

Turnbull turned his eyes to a fenced-in area at the street corner. There was a pile of charred wreckage in the center. Some wilted flowers were stuck into the fence. He nodded.

"Glory Baptist," Kyle said. "A licensed church that ran its own school. The Blossom League demanded access to it. That was the MAP group – they liked the kids blossoming, see? It was dialed in, part of the PR. The Blossom League said it wanted to give those kids the options they were being denied. You can guess what that meant – the fact the kids were Christian probably turned them on even more. Anyway, the parents refused to give up their kids and holed up inside with the kids. They got some guns somewhere. The People's Security Force came and, long story short, the siege ended up with the church burning down. Everyone died singing hymns – men, women, kids. Dozens. I remember the media crowing about how the insurrectionists had been suppressed. Then, after liberation, some provos raided the Blossom League offices, got their membership list, rounded up a couple dozen members who were too dumb to have got out of Dodge before liberation, dragged them here, and shot them all."

Turnbull shrugged.

"There's no law anymore," Kyle said. "The MAPs are monsters, but what about the law?"

"The law was there to protect them, and they and their pals decided to get rid of it," said Turnbull bitterly. "I just hope those flowers were for the parishioners. But who the hell knows? Maybe they're for the perverts. Everything went upside down, off the rails. And they started it."

"It isn't right," Kyle said. "None of this is right."

"It's not about right and wrong," Turnbull said. "It's about decades of hatred building up and suddenly getting released. If you get rid of the rules, don't cry when they aren't there to protect you. And I have seen too many dead innocent people to shed any tears over some dead pedophiles or some dead butchers."

Kyle regarded him, and his eyes registered a lack of understanding. But how could this kid understand?

"You're too young to remember before," Turnbull said.

"Before the Split?" Kyle asked.

"Before the Split, before the Crisis. Before America went insane. The last days of the normal."

"That was before I was born. But you lived through it."

"Yeah, I lived through it all, fought through it all," Turnbull said, his mind wandering. He pulled it back to the present, in that SUV, in San Francisco, heading toward a meeting with his transport.

"Well," Kyle said. "I hope furries don't bother you."

"No, they bother me," Turnbull said.

"Oh," Kyle said. "Then tonight might be difficult for you."

The warehouse just south of what the PR-era sign still called "Fisherperson's Wharf" – "Persons and Otherkins of Fishing Wharf" had been considered and rejected as the new name for the tourist attraction only because all the words would not fit on the sign – jutted out over the Bay in the shadow of the dark and largely empty Bay Bridge that stretched out to Treasure Island. In front of the building was a motley group of civilians, most carrying plastic trash bags. It was not clear what these contained. There were also lots of provisionals out front, along with their vehicles. The Ron's Rangers mini-convoy pulled up and stopped, getting the stink eye from several of their competitors in the militia game but Turnbull was not tingling with any sense of a threat. He stepped out of the SUV and stopped. Kyle stepped out too, and Turnbull turned to him.

"Is that music?" Turnbull asked.

Kyle smiled. "Welcome to the underground."

They walked past the bouncers into the warehouse. The music, some old Britney Spears song from back when she was a girl bopper and not yet the wife of the United States Secretary of Transportation and the queen of the Dallas social scene, pounded at eardrum-rupture level. To his right, Turnbull learned what the trash bags were for – clothes. People were changing from street duds into their party gear. Inside here, protected, they were safe to let their freak flags fly. Some partygoers were simply ridiculous, others scandalous. A woman in a purple sparkling thong was having pasties applied to her ample breasts by a dwarf in a little tuxedo. There was a guy in drag who looked like Whoopi Goldberg – that, Turnbull decided, was a kink too far.

And it got worse. One fat boy was affixing a plush aardvark head onto his shoulders.

"Furries," Turnbull hissed.

None of the partygoers paid any attention to Turnbull or Kyle. The dancing, cavorting mass of humanity – there were hundreds of people inside the big, open cement floor dancing, writhing, and occasionally shaking their groove things – seemed to willfully ignore them, as if to acknowledge them would be to acknowledge the reality that existed in the Occupation just outside the warehouse walls.

"Welcome to Bosch," Kyle said. "The Occupation pretends this club doesn't exist, and the club pretends the Occupation doesn't exist, at least inside this warehouse. Bosch is the outlet for some of the vice that would otherwise be uncontrolled and therefore dangerous to the new establishment. It is the happening spot in red San Francisco."

Turnbull looked around at the degeneracy. "I'd hate to see what the happening spot in blue San Francisco was like."

"Yes," Kyle said, suddenly serious. "You probably would."

Turnbull followed Kyle through the crowd, which generally parted for them except for one middle-aged man dressed as an ostrich who jumped in their path and twerked lasciviously, for his trouble getting a boot in his ass that pushed him out of the way.

"Was that really necessary?" Kyle said as the ridiculous man sprawled on the floor, his beak bent.

"Yes," Turnbull said.

The DJ – DJ PeechFu$$, according to his banner – was spinning some high-pitched EDM nonsense that scrambled Turnbull's thought on every beat.

"Where are we going?" Turnbull demanded as they waded deeper into the rave.

"Our friend is in here," Kyle assured him. Turnbull grunted.

Toward the back was a VIP area, and there was the proverbial velvet rope between the masses and the players seated at various tables awaiting their bottle service. There were no shortages here, but from the piles of bills being handed over, the abundance would cost you.

The bouncers made no attempt to stop Kyle and Turnbull from entering the VIP zone. Turnbull figured, correctly, that whoever was throwing this party relied on the provos for security and discretion.

Kyle led Turnbull past the healthiest, best-dressed people he had seen since landing in occupied California. There was champagne, or rather the Napa Valley equivalent, and even some steaks. The Occupation was good for business, at least for some folks.

A wiry little man with small, round glasses and a white suit sat with his back to the wall at the rear of the VIP section. A plate with a half-eaten lobster was in front of him, and a large glass of something white and fizzy was in his hand. A couple of women, clearly interchangeable, fawned over him. Three very large men in suits – suits with bulges – hovered nearby.

Kyle stopped in front of him and he ceased cavorting and looked up.

"Kyle," he said, with an excess of enthusiasm.

"Jorge Adelante, meet my friend," Kyle said, gesturing to Turnbull. Turnbull caught a whiff of something that smelled like a cross between Axe Body Spray and hobo piss. It was coming off their host.

"Does your friend have a name?" Adelante asked.

"Yes," Turnbull answered.

Adelante waited for a beat, then fell back against the seat laughing.

"Your friend's funny," Adelante said to Kyle, grinning either from the humor or his psychopathy.

"Yeah, he's a barrel of laughs," Kyle said.

"Welcome to Bosch!"

"This is your shindig?" Turnbull asked.

"Shindig," giggled Adelante. "That's a great word. No, I'm just a guest. But I kind of keep the party going."

"So, you're the drug dealer."

Adelante's smile vanished.

"Why do you gotta be like that, No-Name?"

Turnbull saw – or rather, sensed – hands moving on Adelante's thugs and without consciously considering his course of action his Wilson Combat was out, skeletonized hammer back, pointed at the weird medallion lying on the black hair of Jorge Adelante's chest between the open sides of his white shirt.

"Gentlemen," Turnbull said to the three gunsels, all of whom had their paws on their gats inside their coats. "I'll blow his sternum out his back and take off one of your heads before the other two get their pieces out, so maybe just chill."

The ebbing beats of the electronic dance tune faded away as everyone stayed perfectly still. Turnbull locked his eyes on Adelante's.

"You know," Adelante said, "I would like the next song to be some new K-pop tune, but there's no more K anymore." He began laughing again.

Soon after the Split, North Korea, aided by Red China, had invaded and erased South Korea. An army of spoiled boy-band fans without US backup turned out to be no match for an army of communist robots who had grown up thinking boiled rat was a delicacy. Who would have thought it?

"It's okay," Adelante said. "Sit down, let's talk."

Kyle and Turnbull pulled out chairs and took them, but Turnbull's gun remained out and on the table. The thugs relaxed and, at a gesture from their boss, withdrew. The girls sat quietly. Eminem's new song, a rap meditation on aging called "Crusty AF," started up. The rapper had gone over to the red immediately upon the Split, famously stating, "I ain't giving up my bullion like a bitch."

"I don't think you are here to buy molly," Adelante said.

"No," Kyle said.

The song pounded out over the speakers.

I am old
I've been told
You been sold
I put death on hold.

"This new song is not good," Adelante observed. "So, you don't want molly and probably not coke or smack, so how can I be of assistance?"

"You are the most accommodating drug dealer I've ever met," Turnbull said.

"It is important to maintain good relations with my friends in the provisional forces."

"So they will let you do business?"

"Obviously, Mr. No-Name."

Kyle spoke up.

"My friend here needs transport north."

"North? How north?"

"Hillaryia. Seattle."

"Washington?" Adelante turned to Turnbull. "Why do you want to go there? It's even worse there than it is here."

"Well," Turnbull said. "See, some people tried to shoot me and shot my fiancée and I need to get to Washington or Hillaryia, whatever, to find out who it was so I can kill them and everyone else they ever met."

"Okay," Adelante said. "I get it. You cannot let people screw you and just walk away or you get nothing but screwed. That is the real law of the jungle."

"Can you help us?" Kyle asked.

"I can. It costs money though. If it was you, it would be a gift because you help me stay out of the spotlight. But No-Name here, he needs to pay. I'll make a call. In the meantime, you want?" Adelante gestured at the girls. "Guaranteed no monkeypox. I have them checked."

"Pass," said Turnbull.

Adelante went off for a moment and made a call. Turnbull watched him talk into his phone, then wait for about two minutes, then say a few words before hanging up and returning to the table.

"Can you go now?" he said after sliding back into his seat.

"Nothing keeping me."

"If you go now, you miss the party," Adelante said.

"And all the STDs too," replied Turnbull as he watched a man dressed as a panda do the Twist.

"I need something else besides a ride," Turnbull told Kyle as they drove through San Francisco's mostly dark streets. The Occupation had still not fixed the twenty years of pre- and post-Split abuse of the California power grid by the powers that be, or at least the powers that had been. Turnbull still smelled hints of Adelante's aftershave on his clothes.

"You need a lot of things," Kyle replied.

"Sat phone. Got one, or access to one?"

Kyle sighed.

"Commo is tight here. They monitor calls in and out, just like the PR did."

"Can you get me one, preferably with a digital scrambler? Tonight? Now?"

"I can get you anything if you have money. Do you have enough money for all this?"

"Yeah. Now get me the phone."

It was thirty minutes later when their contact came up to them as they sat parked adjacent to the intersection of Market Street and Jones in what had been the infamous Tenderloin.

Before the Split, and after, it was an open-air drug market where they would have been molested or robbed by the armies of dope-addled derelicts who infested the neighborhood. But now, thanks to General Scott's militias, they were perfectly safe and would have been even without their weapons.

You can't paint Scott all black, Turnbull noted uneasily. He did not allow himself to consider where all that human flotsam and jetsam had been relocated.

A man came to Kyle's window and they spoke briefly and familiarly – the libertarian provisional seemed to know everyone. Money was exchanged and the man handed him a sat phone. The vendor walked a few feet away and leaned against a boarded-up building, waiting for his customer to finish.

"Everyone out," Turnbull told his hosts. "I need some privacy."

"No more than sixty seconds or else they zero you," Kyle said before he and the other two Ron's Raiders hopped out.

Turnbull looked over the phone. It had a basic scrambler, but that would not hold up to serious signals crypto cracking. His best move was to talk fast and hang up. Then maybe the algorithms would not even flag the call as suspicious at all.

He dialed the number he had memorized. It rang – twice.

"Go." It was Deeds.

"It's me," Turnbull said. "I'm in 'Frisco. It's Scott, the general. I think he's behind it. Tried to wax me again. I don't have details yet, no motive, but I'm going where I was going to try to find out."

"Got it," was all Deeds said. He knew they had no time to chat.

Turnbull purged the phone number from the memory and opened the door, holding the device out. The owner came over, collected it, and walked away fast without a word. Kyle and the other libertarians got back in.

"Let's roll," Turnbull said.

The Ron's Raiders SUVs headed south on the eight-lane I-280 fast at 2 a.m. It was dark and deserted, with the suburbs on to the east and the watershed wilderness to the west.

"Almost at 92," Kyle said. "On this bridge here, the Doran Bridge, there was a big battle here during the Liberation."

"I remember. I shot a guy off this bridge right over there."

"You what?"

"Don't worry, he was an asshole." Turnbull briefly considered a detour to see if they could find the hole Rios-Parkinson made in the floor of the San Mateo Creek Canyon.

They exited the interstate at State Route 92 and climbed up over the mountains that ran down the spine of the San Francisco Peninsula. Near the summit, they entered a fog bank and did not exit it until they were coming down on the other side.

Half Moon Bay was a quiet coastal town that had, earlier in its history, facilitated many of the vices of its big city neighbor to the north. There had been gambling establishments there suitable for a weekend jaunt from the City, and during Prohibition rum-runners had used its port and the deserted beaches further down the San Mateo coast to land their wares.

The local provos stopped them briefly, figured out their destination, and waved them through. Adelante, and probably a lot of others, paid them to keep the peace and keep their mouths shut.

Their destination was Pillar Point Harbor, not far from the famous Mavericks, site of the giant waves that surfers used to come across the globe to ride until surfing was outlawed by the People's Republic as being part of "a cisgender-reinforcing ableist paradigm" that was also somehow Islamophobic.

At the port, the lights were on around a white Bayliner that Turnbull pegged as about fifty feet long. Several folks were scuttling around and over it, and it looked like someone was filling it from a diesel pump.

"I guess that's my ride," Turnbull said.

"Subcontractors of Adelante. They're probably happy to make a few bucks on the back-haul," Kyle observed.

"The Occupation is kind of making it the Wild West here. The reds don't have the resources to investigate every boat sailing around, or close down every giant rave – especially if the right guys are paid off. I'm not sure – is this a libertarian or anarchist paradise?"

"Oh, you don't want to fall in with an anarchist militia," Kyle warned him. "They never shut up about anarchism."

The SUVs stopped and Turnbull stepped out.

"Thanks, Kyle," Turnbull said, extending his hand. Kyle shook it.

"Thanks for the money," Kyle said. "I hope you kill all those people you're mad at."

"Thanks," Turnbull said. "That means a lot."

Turnbull took his rucksack and walked onto the gangway down to the floating dock. A salty looking dude in jeans and a blue-era UC Berkeley sweatshirt – it said "Decolonializing Education Since 2023" – who was even bigger than Turnbull saw him coming and picked up a rusty Mossberg shotgun and stood in his way.

"Looking for Dennis," Turnbull said, having come to a stop.

"Dennis!" the man bellowed.

"What?"

"Guy here looking for you."

Dennis was a skeevy-looking character wearing a jeans jacket and had a black Walther P38 pistol on his belt. He was maybe 50. Dennis put down a duffel bag he was about to carry up the gangway and walked over to the face-off.

"You No-Name?" he asked.

"That's me," Turnbull answered.

"You got the money?"

"Yeah. Payable on delivery."

Dennis considered this for a moment, and then gestured with his head toward the Bayliner.

"Get on board. Grab a rack. We're off in a half-hour."

Turnbull nodded and went aboard the *Cherry Bomb*.

They had been underway for a while.

"About fifty, sixty hours," Dennis said, wiping the sweat off his forehead with his ragged sleeve. "We're against the wind and the currents – they come from the north/northwest. We'll come in the San Juan de Fuca at night and we'll drop you north of Seattle. You're on your own from there." This was the first thing Dennis had said to Turnbull since Pillar Point. He was not chatty, which was nice.

Dennis was the captain and there were two others in his crew, including the huge guy whose name was Jerome. The third sailor was named Fish and he sat, prison tatts all over his body, drinking a People's Beer they had probably loaded up in Seattle before they came south with their load. Fish, his unshaven face and neck decorated with several incomprehensible tattoos, had a .357 tucked in his pants. He gave Turnbull the stink-eye.

Turnbull stood on the bridge and watched Dennis work, how he steered, what gauges he checked. Dennis never touched the radio, though it was on and there was occasional traffic. Turnbull noted the radar, with occasional blips of various sizes. Dennis seemed to avoid the big ones.

After an hour or so, Dennis turned to him and said, "I'm getting paid to haul you, not to have you hang on my ass watching me."

Turnbull turned and left the bridge. He had seen enough.

During the day, it was cool out on the water – they were past the horizon and could not see land. But at night it got cold. At least it did not rain, which was something. The smell of the sea permeated everything. Three nights, two days of this would be plenty for Turnbull. He was a landlubber.

Food was sandwiches and chips, mostly, with the fixings bought in Half Moon Bay. Each sailor made his own baloney and white bread creation, usually with mayo and/or mustard – no mustard for Turnbull, of course. It was washed down with People's Beer, which tasted like sweat and battery acid. But it was still better than Corona.

His rack was an internal alcove at shoulder height in the main cabin that could be enclosed with a sliding curtain. There was a head nearby. It was comfortable enough. Mostly, Turnbull sat on a cushioned bench along the port side and ran through his plans for Seattle. He would be cutting it close on his rendezvous with Casey at the Space Needle. Several times he watched humpback whales break water off the bow.

Turnbull was in his rack during the first afternoon, curtains drawn and catching some Zs with his .45 in hand when the engine slowed and it woke him. He pulled the curtains back and looked out, weapon ready.

The three crewmen were up by the bridge huddling. They were interested in something ahead of them, and they were keeping their voices low.

Turnbull rolled out of his rack and onto the deck, then walked up quietly. They were quieter – he could not pick up what they were saying. Jerome's Mossberg was leaning against the instrument panel and Dennis was pointing at the radar.

"What's up?" Turnbull said and they practically leaped.

"We're working," Dennis said, defensive.

"On what?" Turnbull asked politely.

"You're just a passenger. Mind your own business."

The radar showed there was a small boat that appeared to be straight ahead. Turnbull scanned the horizon and saw a sail in the distance.

"I think you can probably avoid a collision at this distance," Turnbull said.

"What do you know about sailing?" Dennis said. Fish and Jerome looked at each other, and wandered off – Jerome taking the shotgun. Turnbull returned to his rack, drew the curtain, and took his short-barreled Mossberg 590 Shockwave SPX out of his rucksack. He did a quick chamber check – there was a double-00 shell seated. He placed the weapon perpendicular under his pillow, muzzle pointed outward, safety off.

Dinner was more baloney sandwiches and sullen silence – maybe it was nothing personal, since the crew did not talk to each other much either. Turnbull passed on the ersatz blue-state beer and drank water. The others were happy to pick up his suds slack.

Dennis was still spending a lot of time staring at the radar screen. Turnbull crashed in his bunk, his pistol in hand.

The engine revved and Turnbull awoke just a moment before the 50-foot Bayliner shuddered and jolted. Turnbull braced himself in his rack so that he avoided spilling out on the floor, but there was a huge grinding sound. Somehow, the boat had managed to hit something out in the middle of the ocean.

There was yelling and shouting. Turnbull ripped back the curtain and landed on the deck in his boots, which he had chosen to sleep in. It was dark, but there was enough moonlight to see the situation. Right off the starboard side was another boat, a sailboat, right up against the side of the *Cherry Bomb*.

This was no accident.

Jerome was up on the deck with his shotgun, apparently trying to board the other vessel. Fish had his Colt Python out, not quite sure what to do. Dennis was at the helm, shouting orders no one could hear and waving his Walther.

Jerome evidently saw someone on the other boat, aimed and fired. The blast ripped through the cold night air. Someone screamed. Jerome was delighted. He lowered the shotgun to get a better look at the guy he had just blasted when another man popped his head out of a rear hatch – a man with an HK MP5 submachine gun.

"Mother–!" the shooter began, but the obscenity was drowned out by his long blast of 9mm fire directed at the hulking deckhand who had just blown his buddy away.

Jerome shook and shimmied under the impact of a dozen rounds, the Mossberg flying off into the water, but somehow the ogre remained standing even with his chest, stomach, and legs splattered with weeping-red holes.

The MP5 shooter stopped firing, astonished that anyone could survive that onslaught.

"Uhhhhh," howled Jerome. The MP5 shooter fired again, terrified. More splotches erupted across Jerome's chest, and the big man finally went down.

At this point, Fish took a shot at the MP5 shooter. It went high, and the man pivoted back toward him. Fish determined that discretion was the better part of valor, and in this case, discretion meant diving off the deck and out of sight while his opponent emptied the rest of his mag into the side of the *Cherry Bomb*.

Now another crewman popped up from a front hatch, this time with an AK-47 that looked like it had been lifted from some People's Security Force squad car. It was battered, but the thing worked – the shooter put a burst into the Bayliner's bulkhead even though no one was near there.

As the MP5 shooter slipped a new mag into the well, Turnbull decided he had to dance with the ones who brung him, though he hadn't wanted to come to a dance at all. He lifted the Wilson and got a clear sight picture on the shooter hanging out of the rear hatch. He fired three times.

The hatch cover splattered with blood, which appeared quite black in the moonlight, and the MP5 shooter dropped back below.

The AK shooter now had a target, but Turnbull was moving and the hail of lead slammed into the wood deck where he had been a second before. Turnbull fired on the run, round after round. He only needed one Lehigh Defense XD round to hit, but two did. The first hit vaporized the shooter's spleen, while the second slapped into the left side of the shooter's forehead and sloughed off the upper left quadrant of his face. He spun and flopped to the deck trailing a gusher of gore, his rifle clacking and clanging across the deck before falling overboard.

Turnbull dropped his mag and reloaded, the slide seating the fresh round hard. He scanned the deck through the sights.

"Oh, no, I'm hurt. I'm hurt!" someone yelled. It was probably the guy Jerome hit.

"Dennis!" Turnbull yelled, still behind cover. "Fish!"

"Yeah?" Dennis replied, as if he was wondering why he was being interrupted.

"You see anything from up there?"

"Any what?"

"Any freaking bad guys!" Turnbull shouted. It occurred to him that he probably needed to be more specific.

"I'm okay," Fish yelled, though he was still out of sight. "I think I got one."

"You didn't hit shit!" Turnbull shouted. "Get up here and cover the deck!"

Slowly, reluctantly, Fish's head rose out from below deck, his .357 an afterthought.

"Point your gun at the deck and shoot any of them you see!" Turnbull instructed. Fish complied, scowling.

Turnbull rolled onto the sailboat's deck, covering backward and forward. The sailboat was about 35 feet long and it seemed like a nice little vessel, except for the splotches of blood and the gut-shot guy rolling around up front.

Turnbull went to the hatch where the MP5 shooter had been and flipped it open as he jumped back.

There was no hail of bullets, which was nice.

"Anyone in there, you best come out and you'll live. If not, I'm setting this boat on fire and you'll toast."

Nothing.

"I'm shot!" the wounded man cried from up front. Turnbull looked over and there were no firearms lying around the casualty, so he ignored the man's literal belly-aching.

Carefully, he peeked down into the hull. The MP5 shooter was crumpled at the bottom of the short ladder down to the inner deck. There was darkness beyond.

"Grab a flashlight," Turnbull yelled to Fish, who was now standing up and staring, his weapon hanging at his side. Fish turned and went to get a light.

When Fish returned with a yellow flashlight in his non-gun hand, Turnbull waved him over to the hatch. Fish loped over and squatted down.

"Anyone home?" he asked Turnbull.

"I don't think so, but you need to go in and make sure."

"Me? Why me?"

"Because you're expendable. Now get your ass in there and clear it."

"I ain't going in there."

Turnbull lifted the Wilson and pressed it to Fish's forehead.

"You can get down there alive, or I can drop your carcass down there to draw fire. Choose."

Fish shakily held the flashlight and the .357 while climbing down the ladder, bellowing "I got me a gun and I'll blast you if you don't come out peaceably!"

Above, the black emptiness of the barrel of Turnbull's .45 loomed over him.

Fish got to the bottom, straddling the dead MP5 shooter and swinging the flashlight beam around, his pistol not coordinated with the beam.

No one shot him. At least not yet.

"Don't come up until you clear it all," Turnbull commanded. "Every berth, every room, every closet, the john. Don't stop until you are sure there is no one down there." Turnbull did not add the other possible stop criterion – a fourth crewman blasting Fish at close range in the dark.

Dennis was lashing the sailboat to the *Cherry Bomb* with ropes so it would not float away. He had dropped the sails and cut his own craft's engines. The wounded man moaned again.

"Shut that bitch up!" Dennis yelled, though it was unclear to whom.

Turnbull approached him as he tied on another line.

"The bitch needs to–"

Dennis did not finish his sentence because Turnbull punched him hard across the jaw. He flew back onto the *Cherry Bomb's* deck, his P38 flying out of his belt and away, which probably saved his life.

"What the hell?"

"Yeah, what the hell?" Turnbull shouted. "What the hell were you doing?"

"We were doing fine without you!"

"Fine? You were doing fine? Have you seen your boy Baby Huey? He's a lot of things but fine isn't one."

Dennis, scuttling backward, shot Turnbull a look of pure hatred.

"Are you guys pirates as well as drug mules? Are you Captain Jackass Sparrow? I don't see any parrots, so how the hell are you a pirate?" Turnbull kicked him viciously in the gut, and Dennis groaned.

"There ain't nothing down here!" Fish shouted, popping his head out of the hatch "No people, and no damn cargo. None! You said there'd be cargo!"

"You idiot," Turnbull said to Dennis, who cowered at his feet. "You decided to play Long John Dumbshit on a boat coming *back* from a run. You hijacked an *empty* boat!"

"Son of a bitch," moaned Dennis.

"Take care of your idiot friend, Fish," Turnbull said. Fish came over.

"Gun," Turnbull said.

"Gun?"

"Your gun. Give it to me."

Fish handed it over, butt first, and Turnbull tossed it over the side.

"Hey man!" Fish howled.

Turnbull walked over to the P38 on the deck and chucked it into the deep too.

"You morons have lost your gun privileges."

"I'm shot!" howled the wounded sailor.

Turnbull sighed. He considered having Fish clean up that mess, but decided it needed to be done right. He walked over to the wounded man and shot him in the head. It was that or rolling him into the water, or worse, letting him slowly die of internal gangrene fueled by the contents of his shredded bowels.

Turnbull cleared the empty lower deck of the sailboat himself, making sure to toss the MP5 into the water. He assigned Fish to toss the sailboat crew's bodies over the side and to wipe up the blood so whoever found the abandoned sailboat would not know it was the site of a massacre.

Dennis was untying the sailboat as Turnbull was giving him and Fish their orders.

"You're taking me where you promised with no more screw-ups and maybe, maybe, I will pay you. But if you so much as deviate for a nanosecond, I will cap you and feed you to the fish. Do you dipshits read me?"

Turnbull interpreted their grumbling as an affirmative response. The sailboat came loose and slowly floated away.

"And you need to wrap up Jerome in a tarp, because he's going to get fusty," Turnbull said.

Dennis spit, and kicked his dead friend's corpse over the side.

They would hit Seattle the next evening, not a minute too soon for Turnbull.

The atmosphere was even chillier over the next day. Turnbull ate his crappy baloney sandwich off to the rear of the ship, with his back to a wall. He received considerable stink-eye, but no overt aggression. His .45 was on his hip and both Dennis and Fish understood vividly that their passenger knew how to use it.

At lunch, both men seemed to take to the People's Beer extra hard, knocking back their own allocations as well as Turnbull's and the late Jerome's with rigorous intensity. Both were notably slower and unsteady thereafter. This was fine with Turnbull, as long at the boat got where it was supposed to go. By this time tomorrow, he should be meeting Casey at the Space Needle and getting some answers.

He headed for the latrine.

When Turnbull stepped out of the head, it occurred to him that his shipmates had been pouring their beer over the side when he was not looking and the drunkenness was an elaborate pantomime to lull him into lowering his guard. He gave them some mental credit for pulling it off even as Fish smashed the fire extinguisher into his gut and he fell back toward the toilet seat.

Dennis made the play for the .45, grasping and pulling at it in its holster even as Fish slammed Turnbull again hard with the butt of the red metal canister. Turnbull absorbed the blow, but then pressed forward toward Fish even as Dennis slipped the loaded weapon out of the holster and began fumbling with it.

Turnbull felt the weapon leave him.

Now Turnbull's hands and fingers reached forward to the top of the canister, his right index finger slipping inside the safety ring and pulling it out. Turnbull lifted his head hard, the crown of his skull slamming into Fish's nose from below, generating a torrent of blood. But it was his left hand that was Turnbull's main effort, and his left hand found the handle of the fire extinguisher and squeezed even as Dennis was bringing the handgun to bear.

The CO2 spray filled the cabin but the bulk of it went directly into Dennis's face. He fired anyway, the Lehigh Defense XD round punching through the wall, with the report echoing so loudly in the cabin that it disoriented both aggressors. But Turnbull was used to the noise of close-quarter combat. He pushed Fish aside and went for his bunk, his hands slipping under his pillow.

Fish was on him from behind now, the ex-con having dropped the fire extinguisher and settled on throttling Turnbull from the rear. Turnbull pulled the Mossberg Shockwave that lurked under his pillow toward the tussling pair, having placed it muzzle out, and the barrel slipped over his shoulder until it was flush against Fish's unshaven right cheek.

"Shit!" Fish screamed as his perilous situation became clear. Turnbull pressed his right ear into the mattress to keep from blasting out his eardrum and pulled the trigger.

Fish's face disintegrated in a storm of red goo, bone frags and double-aught buckshot that blasted out in a scarlet cone to his rear. Dennis was about to take another shot with the Wilson CQB – one that might well have hit his running buddy – when the storm of gore and metal came his way.

Dennis wiped his eyes with his left hand and could see well enough to make out Turnbull standing there with the Shockwave pointed at him.

"I told you," Turnbull said. Except for the subsequent 12-gauge blast, that was the last thing Dennis ever heard.

10.

The ringing in Turnbull's ears subsided slowly during the next few hours. He figured out that Dennis had set the autopilot and that the course was generally toward the Strait of Juan de Fuca, the inlet shared by Canada and the remnants of the People's Republic that provided access to both Vancouver and to Seattle within the state of Hillaryia.

While he figured he could maneuver the boat in the open ocean, where there was nothing to run into, going through the Strait, which was bound to be patrolled, was too risky.

He determined to make for the western coast of the Olympic Peninsula and make his way east to Seattle. But that would mean abandoning the ship, and if it looked like an abattoir that might get the People's Security Force interested.

He stripped to his skivvies and began cleaning up the mess as best he could. First, he dragged Fish up and fed him to his namesakes, then did the same to Dennis. Next, he set to wiping up the splatter on the floor, the walls, and even the ceiling of the cabin. Shotguns, he sighed. What a mess.

It looked significantly better after the initial cleaning, though the boat was now bereft of towels. These all went overboard, as did the shell casings. There were bullet holes throughout the ship – 9mm, 7.62x39mm, .45 and buckshot – but that was too bad. He was no carpenter. He would just have to hope that no one noticed them.

Now came the tough part. He had to get to land. A port was out, even one in a small town. Turnbull decided he would have to beach the craft, but he had no idea of the draft. He might find himself beached a quarter mile out.

Turnbull emptied his ruck and used garbage bags to wrap up his clothes and the other contents. Hopefully, that would give himself something dry, or dryish, when he hit land. Then he considered the problem of where he would be landing. He did not want to land out in the boonies miles from human civilization. After all, he had a lunch date at the Space Needle.

He resolved to steer the boat toward land and look for lights. With some luck, he might find some humans. Without luck, he might find himself having to walk miles through a forest and miss his date with Casey.

Turnbull set what he hoped was a course for the Olympic Peninsula. From the radar picture, he figured he was headed the right way, and an hour after sunset lights appeared on the horizon where the radar screen indicated land. He headed toward them, but not directly. Putting on a life jacket and setting his newly water-resistant ruck nearby, he steered the boat toward his objective. The black mass ahead came into view under the moonlight as he approached. He saw a pair of lights move by right to left on the shore – a road.

The boat continued forward, though he throttled back on the speed. There was a shake and a screech – had he scraped a rock? Looking up, the shore appeared much closer than it had just seconds before. He tried to cut the speed, but there was another jolt and more scraping. Now he could hear surf. The boat continued on, jolting again. The shore was close now, very close – he could see the luminescence of the waves.

The scraping was very loud and the boat was slowing considerably. The shore was just over there, but he could not estimate the distance.

The *Cherry Bomb* shuddered and stopped, dead in the water but with the engine whining. He cut it, then stood back and listened. Nothing but surf. He looked over the side into the blackness. He had no idea of the depth, as he had no idea of the boat's draft.

Turnbull dreaded the cold water – you always seemed to train in cold water. But that was preparation for times like this. He took his ruck and hopped over the side and into the water.

Two feet deep. He fell over, and the cold sea water roiled around him.

"Spectacular," he muttered, but it was comparatively spectacular. It could have gone so much worse.

Turnbull made his way to shore and onto the sandy beach. There was a cliff, and on top of it was a forest of pine trees with the road somewhere beyond that.

He changed into dry clothes, though his boots were still wet. The jury-rigged waterproofing had done its job. After placing his Wilson and its holster in the ruck, he made his way up a cut to the trees at the top of the cliff. The road was 50 meters in, and when he got to it, he turned and started walking north to where the lights were.

He got about two hundred meters when a vehicle came from the north toward him. Without any better idea, he stuck his hand out. A light blue pick-up truck, pre-Split, slowed and stopped beside him.

On the door was painted "QUINAULT INDIGENOUS PEOPLES – PRIVILEGE LEVEL 9. DO NOT OPPRESS."

The driver was a handsome man in his forties with his grey-flecked black hair pulled back in a pony-tail.

"You belong here about as much as Elizabeth Warren," he said.

"I'm lost," Turnbull said.

"Bullshit. You're something, but not a poacher, not a robber either I don't think. But you are damn sure in trouble with the law. Well, the white man's law, at least."

"I need a ride. Just to where I can pick up some transpo to Seattle."

The man smiled. "A ride to Seattle is expensive."

"I got money. I can pay you to get me to town."

"You can pay me to get you to Seattle. I'm a Quinault Indian. No PSF is stopping me. Privilege level 9, buddy. The only way I could get any higher is if I thought I was a squaw and had a limp. See, and I can even say 'squaw.'"

"Five thousand."

The man laughed. "Five thousand People's bucks? That ain't worth shit. The whole PR is on the verge of falling apart. Why don't you just offer me some beads and a smallpox blanket?"

"Dollars. Red American dollars."

The man whistled and extended his hand. "I'm Donny Running Bear and I'm your new chauffeur. Get in. We're going to Seattle."

Donny Running Bear – "Don't confuse me with the Sitting Bears – they aren't related" – liked to talk. Normally, this would have made Turnbull consider other options, like telling him to stop talking, or bailing out of the truck, or shooting him, but Running Bear had some useful information.

"Back before the Split, it would have been about a three-hour ride," Running Bear said. "We're stuck together for six at least, and that's only because Privilege Level 9 gets me through the checkpoints."

"I'd like to avoid interaction with authorities," Turnbull said.

"Oh, I bet you would," Running Bear replied. "You going to tell me where you are really from?"

"Nope."

Well, I know it's not here. You going to tell me why you need to go to Seattle?"

"Nope. I just need to be there by noon."

"I think we can make it. With a little luck."

Their path was east straight across the Olympic Peninsula on State Route 12 to State Route 8 at the nearly deserted town of Elma.

"There are bandits," Running Bear said. "Keep an eye out for trees across the road, stuff like that."

"Bandits?"

"Yeah. They want the gas. I get fuel because I am an Indian. Especially after the war started, there's almost none for anyone. They'll try to stop cars and trucks and siphon it out. Leave you dead, throat cut. Wish I could keep my shotgun, but if you have a piece even Privilege Level 9 is not going to help."

They did not encounter any bandits, but they did get waved through a couple PSF checkpoints. Running Bear gave him a hat and told Turnbull to pull it down over his face and slump in the seat.

"I'll tell them you're my buddy and you're drunk. They'll believe it."

They did.

Saved by the stereotype, Turnbull thought.

Eventually they came to Interstate 5 and headed north, past Olympia and then what had been Joint Base Lewis-McChord. Joint Base Milley-Levine, named after the feckless pre-Split chair of the Joint Chiefs and the trans admiral in the old Public Health Service, seemed almost deserted from the road. Beyond the statue of the man in a skirt with a uniform saluting the few passing vehicles, the old fort seemed to be decaying. But a sign at the main gate announced, "JOINT BASE MILLEY-LEVINE INPROCESSES AND TRAINS THE MOST DIVERSE PEOPLE OF SOLDIERING IN THE WORLD!"

The airfield area farther north was worse – the runways were pitted with craters and you could see several destroyed structures from the road.

"The reds hit the base and knocked it out early in the war," Running Bear said. "It's been a year and they haven't fixed it."

"What do you know about the war?"

"I know they say on TV and the radio that we are winning and also that the wreckers, looters, transphobes, racists, sexists, whatevers are making us lose. Hey, you notice how there's no special word for someone who hates Indians? Like Islamophobe, except for indigenous peoples? That's kind of bullshit, right?"

"I never thought of that," Turnbull conceded.

"At least they bend over backwards for us. I mean, we take what they give us but it's pretty funny to have a bunch of butt-white richies from Seattle coming out apologizing for oppressing us and then giving us stuff like gas that no one else gets. We take it, but it's funny."

The truck shuddered – another of the many potholes. This was the longest stretch of freeway without any kind of repair or construction that Turnbull recalled ever driving, except maybe in California.

"We do okay in the reservation, but you better be careful in Seattle. I hear there's almost no food. And you, well, they are going to notice you."

"Why?" Turnbull asked, his curiosity piqued.

Running Bear laughed. "Look in the mirror. Go on."

Turnbull twisted the rearview in his direction. The sun was coming up so he could see all right. He examined his face. Nothing unusual.

Running Bear saw his consternation.

"You aren't thin," he said. "You aren't fat, but you aren't thin either. Last time I was in Seattle, it was all like – what do you call them? – wraiths, at least outside the Controlled Zones where the richies live. We can hunt and fish and do okay, but the city people are hungry. And you look like you aren't, at least not yet."

Seattle was socked-in with clouds, but even if it had been sunny it would have looked even more depressing than the last time he was there on Army temporary duty pre-Split. There were few cars and little activity, even though it was about 8 a.m.

"I hate coming here," Running Bear said. "I especially hate that grunge music."

"That was forty some years ago."

"And they are still milking it. There was a Museum of Grunge for about a week but it got closed."

"Let me guess. Feminists thought it was phallocentric."

"It was racist somehow. I forget. Courtney Love was at the opening, but later she got arrested for hate crimes. I don't know what happened to any of the famous people. We don't pay much attention to this crap out on the reservation. Except Tom Cruise. We really liked him. Sad he went to the red."

"I hear he still looks 37."

"He must have one hell of a medicine man."

The pick-up passed through an overpass where a tent city was set up underneath, sheltered from the near constant rain. Two derelicts fought over what appeared to be a tricycle. A few others huddled around a fire.

A PSF cruiser came up even on their right and looked them over. Running Bear waved at the two officers, who accelerated past. He noted that Turnbull's hand had gone to his ruck.

"Privilege Level 9. You gotta explain hassling a 9. So they leave us be. No need for whatever you got in that backpack of yours."

"Mercer Street exit," Turnbull said. "Coming up." He was looking at a paper map Running Bear had in his center console.

"This is a seedy-looking part of town," Running Bear observed.

"It's all seedy," Turnbull said.

"I expect you can handle it." Running Bear took the exit. Turnbull surveyed the passing terrain. Broken windows, people walking fast, heads down. A brownish haze hung in the air, which Running Bear explained was because people had to burn things for heat. Even the propaganda looked tired.

"ALL PEOPLX ARE WELCOME TO JOIN THE PEOPLE'S REPUBLIC ARMY TO FIGHT THE NAZI INVADERS!" read the black words on a white background, with a long-superseded version of the PR's flag in the upper right corner.

"Nobody is enlisting," Running Bear said, seeing Turnbull take in the sign. "None of our people, for sure. Probably put us in the cavalry."

"I can see how that might rankle."

"Yeah, they take anyone now, anyone who wants to enlist. And while they don't have a draft, they do shanghai folks. Can I say 'shanghai,' or is that a hate crime?"

"I just assume everything is."

"Well, you watch yourself or you might get grabbed and put in uniform and sent south to fight the reds."

"The Needle," Turnbull said. He only just noticed it, and he was a bit surprised that it was still there. Off the top was a high flagpole, and from it flew yet another version of the People's Republic flag. This one added what seemed to be a pink "W" and a mauve symbol that looked like a fusilli pasta.

Maybe it represents differently-abled bicurious Italians, Turnbull considered.

They were getting close to the park around the Needle, and locals were eyeing the pick-up. It was rare to see a non-governmental private vehicle. Running Bear stopped talking, and Turnbull took that as an indication that his driver was getting nervous.

"Pull over. We're close enough." It was almost nine.

Running Bear obliged. A double-masked woman – both were very dirty and obviously were being reused – stomped by scowling at their facial freedom. Turnbull ignored her and dug into the ruck as Running Bear watched. The Wilson came into view.

"Nice piece," he observed. "I knew you were trouble."

"Not to you," Turnbull said. "Not if you keep this all to yourself."

"Hey, I'm no friend of the government."

Turnbull found what he was after and withdrew the five thousand he had promised his chauffeur.

Running Bear took it and slipped it into his jeans jacket without counting it.

"Good to know you, stranger," he said.

"You don't know me. I don't exist. This never happened."

Running Bear nodded and Turnbull got out with his gear. As the pick-up pulled away, he pulled it around one shoulder and, hoping he looked enough like a transient to pass for one, he started walking.

Turnbull kept his distance from the Needle, instead walking the perimeter several hundred meters away, looking where he would set up if he was planning on observing – or busting – a clandestine meeting nearby.

It was not that he did not trust Casey Warner. It was that he did not trust anyone.

He made a sweep, seeing nothing more amiss than usual. Bums were fighting here and there – there seemed to be a lot of junkies. There were no tourists, tourism being a thing of the past between climate change restrictions on travel and the fact there was a war going on.

In the sky, he occasionally heard the whine of a jet engine. They looked to be a pair of Chinese Chengdu J-20C "Mighty Dragon" fighters flying over the city. Above them, he could make out what seemed to be a KJ-2000, a Chi Com People's Liberation Army Air Force AWACS jet with a large rotating radar disc suspended above its fuselage.

He did see some PSF cruisers roll by, blue and white, but the officers did not get out and mingle with the masses.

Initially satisfied that there was no platoon of blue secret police waiting to swoop on him the minute he showed, he moved closer and did another circuit. He noted no out-of-place vehicles – in fact, he noted very few vehicles. He saw no one sketchy in a police kind of way, though there were plenty of sketchy folks. He scanned the edges of the rooftops for watchers, or snipers, and saw nothing. There were no helicopters aloft, and he did not hear or see any drones. It was now almost 11 a.m., and he suspected that if they were going to bushwhack him at noon, they would have set up long ago.

He made his way to Kerry Park, which was on some high ground formerly known as Queen Anne Hill. "Queen" being gendered, it first morphed into "Royal Person Hill," and when the Otherkin complained that "person" excluded them, it became simply "Hill X." Whoever Kerry was must have never owned slaves, fought Indians, or wielded a penis without shame, as the name "Kerry Park" endured.

The high ground of Hill X gave him a good view to the south and the area around the Needle. Beyond it were the high-rises of the city itself, and beyond that Mt. Rainier. The mountain looked exactly the same as it did when he had done TDY at Lewis before the Split.

He found an observation position on a bench about 200 meters from a dozen unnaturally white people out on the grass holding a banner that read, "ACCEPT YOUR RACISM AND STRIVE TO MAKE AMENDS." Turnbull watched them chant for several minutes until there was a screech of tires and a black van along with two PSF cruisers roared up over the sidewalk and toward them. They dropped the banner and scattered, with a squad of officers and some soldiers running after them. They caught three of the fleeing demonstrators, who twisted and struggled as they were dragged into the van. On the side panel it read "PEOPLE'S ARMY."

Now you're working for Uncle Samantha, probably, Turnbull thought to himself.

The recruiters having departed, Turnbull kept observing. Satisfied that it was at least superficially safe – maybe these guys had exceptional tradecraft that kept them from being spotted, but he doubted that – Turnbull resolved to go find some coffee and maybe even some grub. After all, wasn't Seattle once famous for joe?

It was a pretty long walk before he found a place. Common Grounds Coffee House was built inside what had obviously once been a Starbucks. Why it was still open when most of the other storefronts around it were boarded up was not clear, but it was open even if not jammed. Few people had the money to spend on coffee.

Turnbull stepped inside. There were two other customers, (both masked) and seven people working the counter. It was illegal to fire or lay-off workers in the PR without permission of the Board of Economic Justice.

"I am Chris. I will be your baristx," the gender indeterminate being at the counter informed him as Turnbull stepped up. Turnbull had not heard that before, but he went with it. Going with it was always the key to survival in the blue.

"Responsible coffee," he said. Chris sighed, because there was no other kind. While Chris measured out a few spoonfuls of moist used coffee grounds into a sieve, Turnbull turned his attention to the food offerings. There were some muffins, but they seemed small and hard. There was some sort of yellow cake, but an oily puddle had formed on the plate beneath it. There were several orange single-serving bags of something – chips perhaps? – but the Chinese lettering made it impossible to tell.

Pass.

"You got a key to the head," Turnbull asked.

Chris gazed at him puzzled. Turnbull almost said "Men's Room" but caught himself.

"Toilet."

"No key. A guy's in there shooting up. I don't think he'll be too long, unless he passes out. You can go in the alley." Chris handed over the coffee in a flimsy paper cup. There was tiny Chinese writing on it – "Dixie" in Mandarin perhaps.

Turnbull took it and drank a gulp. Even if he took cream or sugar, he knew not to bother asking for either. Maybe inside the Controlled Zones where the rich folks were, but these were delicacies in the blue even before the war.

There was a noise and a groan and the junkie staggered out of the head. Turnbull moved past him quickly and caught the door before it could shut and lock. That was unnecessary – there was no lock, not even a doorknob, only a hole. Turnbull slipped inside.

Trying to stay out of the visual range of someone gazing through where the doorknob assembly should be, Turnbull took out the .45, checked the chamber, and slipped it into the small of his back. He pocketed three more mags. If this was a set-up, he would go down shooting. And take Casey Warner with him.

At noon, Casey Warner came up the walkway directly toward the Space Needle all alone. Turnbull spotted him a couple hundred meters back and followed him in, with the intent of spotting anyone else following his date.

Casey was clean. He stood in front of the Needle, checking the time on his burner cell two or three times in the five minutes Turnbull waited before approaching. Casey saw him fifty meters out and immediately looked away.

Good tradecraft, Turnbull observed. No outward signs of recognition until he was sure Turnbull was clean.

He gave Casey a moment to get comfortable and then walked up to him.

"I'd ask you for a light but no one in this shitty place has any cigarettes," Turnbull said.

Casey smiled. "If anyone asks, we are meeting here because I right-swiped you on Humpr."

"I don't want to know what that is, do I?" Turnbull asked.

"No, but just remember that if the PSF rousts us that you're the bottom."

"I thought I hated you before for bringing me here and now I hate you even more."

"Let's walk," Casey said. "I mean, I'd suggest going up in the Needle but they don't do maintenance in the blue and it's closed because it'll probably collapse the next time there's a strong wind."

"After St. Louis, I have an aversion to high landmarks," Turnbull said. Casey knew he meant the Arch.

"Funny you should say that," Casey replied as they started walking in a giant circle around the monolith.

"These people sent Joe Schiller to shoot my fiancée and try to shoot me," Turnbull growled. "At my house. My house." He used all his effort to keep his rage in check.

"I know. I'm sorry. And it was my fault."

"Yours?" Turnbull said, stopping.

"I set it in motion by being, well, me. I got bored and curious."

"Explain."

"There's a project called INFERNO."

"I know what it is. You were running security for it."

"And it's remarkable. You can use it to spot and uniquely identify every single nuclear warhead on the planet." Even though there was not a soul within fifty feet, Casey still lowered his voice so that Turnbull had to strain to hear him.

"I don't see how some useful tech for tracking nukes led to someone on our team trying to whack me, you, and everyone else we worked with back in the day."

"Everyone who worked with us in St. Louis during the Crisis," Casey said. "We were stopping a bunch of terrorists who wanted to wipe out the national leadership of both red and blue while the Split was being negotiated."

"I remember."

"Using a nuke," Casey explained slowly.

"Yeah, they would vaporize everyone in charge and take power for themselves."

"Using a nuke," Casey repeated.

"You keep saying that, Casey," Turnbull said impatiently.

"Kelly, what happened to that nuke?"

"What?" asked Turnbull, puzzled.

"The nuke. What happened to it after we stopped them?"

"I guess they took it back to the Air Force."

"You guess? Who took it? Specifically."

"Joe Schiller," Turnbull said.

"Yeah, the guy who personally came to your ranch to blow you away a dozen years later."

"Shit," Turnbull said.

"I was just screwing around with INFERNO in the SCIF," Casey said, referring to the Sensitive Compartmented Information Facility that housed it. "Late shift, bored. So, I decided to look around. Now, a nuke doesn't just pop up. You have to find a location, and scan it, and then set the artificial intelligence on it. It takes time, which is why we have not scanned the whole world. You can find subs, but you need to scan where we know the Chinese and Russian boats patrol and then you can find them, but it isn't instantaneous. So, I would pick an area and scan it. Looking here, looking there. Did you know Switzerland has three nukes?"

"Sounds like a Swiss thing."

"Well, I found it, Kelly. I found it. There was this one random warhead where one should definitely not be, and I know I was out of my lane, at least a little, so I turned the AI onto it and it assessed the radiation and whatnot – every bomb is pretty much a unique thing, with a unique signature – and it's clear this bomb I found where it mos def should not be is our bomb since all the others of its type were accounted for. It was the one we thought we marked return to sender."

"Where is it?" Turnbull asked.

"Here."

"Here? In the blue?"

"Here in Hillaryia. Old Washington state. At the Hanford nuke facility. The facility we thought was all closed down when the People's Republic gave up all its nukes."

"But why would Joe Schiller keep it, much less bring it into the blue?"

"I thought about that too. The only thing that fits is that he wanted to keep it hidden. See, INFERNO was originally intended to stop another nuclear terrorist. The scan pattern is set – all of red America, over and over, looking for a nuke that is not where the database says one should be. It never looked at Hanford until I got bored."

"So, your ADHD started all this?"

"Yeah," Casey said. "Pretty much."

"And I think I know what Joe Schiller was thinking."

"What?" Casey asked.

"The bomb was not for Schiller. It's for Schiller's patron, General Karl Martin Scott. That bastard can't guarantee that he'll ever get elected president, but if he reruns St. Louis and vaporizes the competition, he won't just be president. He won't even be Caesar. He'll be freaking Emperor Augustus with carte blanche to wage any war he wants."

"Freaking Scott," Casey said. "He's a walking, talking dildo. But it's hard to believe that he thought of this scheme a decade ago?"

"You ever meet the guy? He probably touches himself in the bathtub thinking about absolute power and how to get it."

"I made a mistake," Casey said. "I told my boss what I found and he told me to say nothing. He was a general. I'm guessing he was tight with Scott. It makes sense though, taking us out. There can't be anyone left outside the clique that knows about the St. Louis bomb. I assume all the high mucketty-mucks who knew were going to be inside the blast radius when it went off, except General Scott, of course."

"Us guys in Task Force Zulu were loose ends," Turnbull said. "And he was burning them off before the big show."

"When I was told to wait at home for orders, my suspicious nature started up. You read enough about internet conspiracy theories and you get a little paranoid. So, I basically broke into a neighbor's house while he was on vacation and hung out there, just in case, you know. And then they hit my place. I watched it go down, and then I went on the run. With a conspiracy that deep, I knew the only place I might have a chance was where they can't reach me."

"The blue," Turnbull said.

"Yeah," Casey said.

"You could have called me and given me a heads up."

"Like I had your number," Casey replied, annoyed. "You are kind of anti-social."

"I guess," Turnbull admitted.

"Well, now we're in the blue," Casey said. "And if you're smart, you'll stay here with me."

Turnbull considered this for a moment.

"Oh, that's not how this is going, Casey," he said. "That's not how this is going at all. I'm getting back in the game, and so are you, my friend. This son of a bitch is going to pay."

"He's a four-star general. He commands an army."

"Yeah, so I give him even odds. Look, he shot my girl. I'm putting him down, him and his cronies. And you're helping."

Casey sighed. "I knew I should not have swiped right."

They stood, looking over at the unchanging, indifferent volcano to the south.

"We have no idea of their timetable. They could be moving right now."

"I think they are. Scott is nailing down the support of a personal army of provisionals who will do whatever he tells them, loyal only to him. Time is not on our side."

They kept staring into the distance, their minds assessing the situation and their potential courses of action.

Casey finally asked the question Turnbull had been putting off answering.

"So, what's your plan, Kelly?"

"Lots of bullets into lots of faces," Turnbull said.

"That's not your plan. That your lifestyle," Casey said. "What do we do next?"

"You go home," Turnbull said. "Hook up with Clay Deeds. Assemble as many solid guys as you can. I have no idea who else might be alive. Just be ready to help me when I call."

"And you, Kelly?"

"I'm going to Hanford to get me a nuke."

Casey snorted.

"That's past the frontlines, in the Gray Zone where no one's in charge. I hear it's nuts in there. Cannibal kind of stuff."

"Great. I hate cannibals. But that's where I'm going."

"Well, have you figured out how you are getting there?"

"Yeah," Turnbull said. "Step one, I'm joining the Army."

BOOK TWO

11.

Karl Martin Scott sized himself up in the mirror of his bedroom in Quarters One, the commander's house at the Presidio. He was shirtless.

Not bad for sixty-one, he thought. He had been in prime physical shape since before he first set foot in West Point as a plebe. He did not even notice the discipline it took anymore. It was simply part of who he was, part of the package, part of the price.

Behind him, on the canopy bed, his companion for the evening stirred. He had forgotten her name, or rather, he had never learned it. There would be a different one the next time he required company. For her part, she was a local thrilled at the opportunity her looks had provided her to double her rations.

He dismissed her gruffly, and she gathered her clothes then left the room without a word. His men – the loyal men who had surrounded him and who had hitched themselves to his rising star since the Split and before – would see that she was discreetly driven home. There would be no walk of shame, no chance of tarnishing the image he had worked to perfect since that first day in uniform so long ago.

The youngest brigadier general in the United States Army, the youngest major general, the youngest lieutenant general. He had always had his sights on the prize, always driven harder than his peers. They would call him "political." He knew it and ignored the epithet. He consciously calculated his image as an up-and-comer, an officer to watch. He was an aide-de-camp as a lieutenant and a protégé to the brightest star in whatever battalion, brigade, division, or corps he found himself assigned to. Others grumbled as the assignments and accolades came his way and not theirs.

Let them grumble, Karl Martin Scott had thought. He had a vision of power without limits. That drove him, that and the adulation.

He was the first of his peers given company command, battalion command, brigade command. And what rankled the competition is that he did his job so well. He was no stodgy martinet. He was ruthlessly ambitious, but took no particular pleasure in cruelty. That did not drive him, and he considered it counterproductive, an unnecessary tangent – which is not to say that he would forgo destroying an enemy without a second thought. But why not win loyalty, earn loyalty by returning it? The jealous hated him, but many more loved him. And that was the only love in his life – he never married because a woman was a variable he did not need or want. There was only The Career.

Scott was no slacker and no coward. He earned his medals and badges. Ranger school, airborne school – those required a personal gut check, and he checked out. Lieutenant Scott graduated from West Point on the threshold of the Long War, and he did his time in Afghanistan and Iraq. He fought and earned his Combat Infantryman's Badge. He bled and earned his Purple Hearts. He really did pull in three wounded troops under Taliban fire from the kill zone in some unnamed valley outside of Kandahar to earn his Distinguished Service Cross. There were other medals as well. There was no fraud – he was the real deal, even if inside him there was only an insatiable lust for greater power and glory.

Scott always understood he was different than his peers. None of them had his drive, or more precisely, the need that fueled his drive. But at Harvard, where he did a fellowship, Scott discovered that he was not unique. He found others with the same will to power. He found them in books.

Scott wrote his thesis on the last generals of the Roman Republic – Sulla, Marius, Caesar, men who would die rather than live mediocre lives, men who understood power and needed it like others need air, food, and love. His paper was excellent, of course, but cold, and he did not include the great lesson he learned from studying their rise to absolute power.

Those men would do whatever was required to prevail, to be the first man in their country. And so would Karl Martin Scott.

After being promoted to O-9, three stars, faster than even the top performers usually saw their first star (his stint as a White House military aide to politicians he quietly despised gave him the career boost he needed), Lieutenant General Karl Martin Scott chose to throw it all away.

He *chose* to. Consciously.

As the youngest lieutenant general in living memory, he was finally inside the club, if not in the Champagne Room where the four-stars dwelled. But it was clear that he had been forced upon the brass. Scott was fine when he was making his bosses look good, but now he threatened their positions. The jealousy that he once felt coming from passed-by peers he now felt from his seniors who had nowhere to go but out to make way for the ambitious *wunderkind*. He was passed over for corps command.

Scott would not be denied. He assessed the situation and it was clear that the inside path was blocked. He resolved to take the outside path and perhaps catapult himself into a new arena far beyond the flag officers and their cloistered world.

He went to the media, the conservative media, and expressed his concerns about the state of the Pentagon and the Department of Defense in general, about the lack of strategic vision and the lack of accountability for lives squandered. Nothing he said was a lie; the fact that he, an insider, was saying it was what changed everything.

The fact that his critique was true was a fringe benefit. If it had been false he would still have said it. The truth was simply a terrain feature, to be used if it was useful and avoided if it was not. It was about the goal.

The Pentagon clique was frothing at the mouth at this betrayal of their flag officer caste, but now this upstart was on a stage beyond their control. They went to the president planning to relieve him; the president told them, "The hell you will! Have you seen Gallup? He's the most popular man in the whole federal government, more than you guys, more than me."

Scott was untouchable, for the moment. Poohbahs of both parties came to him behind the scenes to see if he might want to run for a Senate seat in Virginia that had become vacant. He declined, partly because he had no more connection to Virginia than anywhere else and partly because he had no intention of wasting time as one of one hundred political popinjays.

He was aiming higher.

But history interfered. The United States destabilized, first slowly then very fast. He was approached by more influential men and sounded out about what was to be done. Scott assessed that they were testing his willingness to participate in some sort of coup. He demurred, not because of any dedication to the current political structure but because he was not convinced either that these individuals, powerful as they were, could pull it off, and because at the end of it there was no guarantee that he would be the one on top.

If he was to risk everything – and he was perfectly willing to – he needed a jackpot worthy of the risk.

The Crisis erupted and the military slowly realized that it must take a side. But it was not that easy. The military was fragmented just like the country was. Those at the top chose to throw in with the progressive establishment in Washington, DC, and the benefits of confronting Scott gradually began to outweigh the risk. They tried to take him out. They saw him, correctly, as a threat – a military leader who not merely the troops but the people would follow anywhere.

Scott assessed the two sides and chose the strong horse, the red. He sided with the new United States and took his fourth star. He retired and waited, letting others march the country into the mire of war. And when the Occupation began to drag on, he volunteered to return to the colors to command the Pacific Coast forces – but only after they pleaded with him to take it on. Again, he leap-frogged ahead by going outside the established lanes to attain power.

Now in the Presidio's Quarters One months later, Scott slipped on his camo trousers and began lacing up his boots. His SIG M17 lay on the bed beside him in its holster.

He smiled, because it was all coming together. Nothing could stop him. The blue brass had tried to stop him during the Crisis. They came for him with the intent of trying him as a traitor and making an example of him. But Scott was spirited out of the Beltway by some shadowy operatives, including the operator he now knew was named Kelly Turnbull.

He frowned. Turnbull had somehow avoided being eliminated the week before even though his loyal henchman Joe Schiller had personally taken on the task of ending him. Now Turnbull was on the loose, and he was dangerous, but did he understand what was actually happening?

Did Turnbull know about Scott's most audacious decision, to have Joe Schiller and his men spirit away the stolen nuclear warhead that could have wiped out the blue and red governments all in one fell swoop during the St. Louis summit that brought about the Split?

Why had he done it? Because he saw the opportunity and seized it. Schiller had broken security to tell him of the bomb plot, and suddenly it was all clear to him.

"We are keeping the bomb," he said. Schiller had blinked, not comprehending. Scott went on.

"No one but us and a few senior politicians know there is a stolen bomb," he said. "And none of them will double check to confirm that it went back to the Air Force. When we tell them it did, they will move on. And the Air Force has no idea it was ever recovered."

Schiller's eyes grew wide at the sheer audacity of the plan. He nodded, and it was on. Karl Martin Scott was a one-man nuclear power.

Was it madness? No, it was insurance. Scott had no idea what he might actually do with a nuke, but it provided him with unprecedented options. He had learned from his experience with the generals that, at some point, he might need to step outside the paradigm once again – perhaps very far outside indeed. A nuclear device gave him that capacity, and the morality of it never even occurred to him. There was only reaching the prize.

Scott was right. The knowledge of the bomb was limited to a few senior red leaders and the Task Force Zulu operatives who stopped the disaster, and during the next decade none of them would follow up on what happened to the bomb after it was recovered by Kelly Turnbull and the other Zealots.

And the general was especially proud of how he hid it away. It sat, safe, until that day when he and the other American four stars were briefed about INFERNO and he understood that it was only a matter of time before the lost warhead was found.

It happened at an auspicious time. He had been considering how he might best use the bomb to make his final move.

Scott thrived in the praise and adulation of his supporters. He thrilled to the power. But he also understood, from his experience with the generals, that the way to the top was blocked by others clamoring for the same prize – this time, civilian politicians. Certainly, his profile was rising as commander of the Occupation, but he was just one of several competitors – mostly civilian politicians – clamoring to get inside to the throne. He needed something to blast open the walls.

Literally.

He briefed only his closest confidants on his plan. To a man, they swore to follow him. It had to be done. The lives lost would be a small sacrifice to save the new United States of America from falling apart.

General Scott had volunteered for the thankless task of overseeing the Occupation even as his political agents at home decried the mishandling of the war on his behalf. To his adoring followers, he was again sacrificing himself for the good of the country. But he saw it as an opportunity to ape his heroes in togas, and build an army loyal not to the state but to the general who led them.

Now he pulled on his brown t-shirt then his camo top, and hung his dog tags around his neck. His hair was short, but still black though it was flecked with more silver each time he inspected it.

The plan was solid. He had eliminated almost every variable.

But that one thought still nagged at him.

One unresolved variable.

Kelly Turnbull had cheated death at the hands of both his own covert operatives and his Mutilated militia. Now Turnbull was out there, somewhere. He knew the bomb existed because he had recaptured it from the terrorists. No one who knew of the bomb's existence who was outside the Karl Martin Scott circle of trust could be allowed to live.

He resolved to set that task before his personal Green Beret detachment once they got back from the Gray Zone between California and Hillaryia with his nuke. They would hunt down and eliminate this vexing Lieutenant Colonel Kelly Turnbull.

Scott placed his camo cap with four silver stars across its front upon his head. It was crisp and starched, like his entire uniform. He looked, he told himself, like the warrior-king he had spent decades working to become. Woe to those who stood against him. He talked peace for the benefit of the folks at home who were tired of conflict, but when he was in charge, it would be war. And more war.

War brought glory.

He smiled thinly and about-faced to go downstairs to his SUV and off to the headquarters. Except for this unfortunate business with Kelly Turnbull, all was going according to plan.

Within days, the nuke would be recovered from its hiding place and in his custody. Then, at the right time, it would be used, and his massive provisional army, joined by his supporters in the red and defectors from the active military, would call on him to save the Republic by acclamation.

President Karl Martin Scott.

He smiled. It would have to do. "Dictator for Life" had been Caesar's title, but his enemies had left him to bleed out on the marble floor at the feet of a statue of his rival Pompey the Great after the legendary Roman had adopted it.

So, "Dictator for Life" was out and "President" was in. But then, what's in a name?

"I want to join up," Turnbull informed the rather baffled crew of a People's Army recruitment van that was parked next to a street vendor. They were eating tacos, but Turnbull was savvy enough not to try to guess the kind of *carne* that had been *asada*'d.

"You *want* to join up?" asked a short-haired female – the pronouns on her uniform nametape were (SHE/HER) – as she chewed her taco.

"Sure," Turnbull said. "I hate racism and sexism. Transphobia too. And I hear they feed you."

The female looked to her partner, who seemed to be male but whose nametape pronouns were also (SHE/HER), and they both shrugged simultaneously.

"Okay," she said. "I won't even cuff you since you're a volunteer and everything."

"Thanks," Turnbull said. "I can take my stuff, right?"

"You better," said the gender-ambiguous one. "I think they have some uniforms for recruits but not much else. Except a gun."

"Oh, I like guns," Turnbull said, nodding eagerly.

They regarded their recruit skeptically for a moment, but finished their tacos and stood up.

"Come on," said the clearly female one, waving him over. She reached into her pocket and got out a key then opened the rear door. The cavernous interior was dark, but there were five unhappy people sitting inside, each within the target demographic, fifteen to forty-years-old. They were all cuffed to a steel wire running diagonally from the roof near the front to the floor by the door. And they were angry, outraged, at their predicament. The compartment was a cacophony of protests, complaints, cries, and howls.

"You're murdering me!" screamed one male who was, improbably, 250 pounds minimum.

"I'm privilege Level 6!" shouted another, superficially female, recruit. Evidently that was not high enough.

"Get in," the recruiter told Kelly. He complied, dropping the ruck at his feet.

"So," he said, turning to his new companions as the doors swung shut. "Who's psyched to fight the reds?"

None of them.

It was a long drive south to the half-deserted Joint Base Milley-Levine, where the People's Republic Army in Hillaryia conducted its in-processing and basic training. The involuntary volunteers in the van were largely aimless youths with low to middling privilege levels and lower prospects.

Of course, none of the new soldiers were from the Controlled Zones – the walled areas where the elite lived were immune to such hassles as defending the country they ruled over. Several of the reluctant recruits described themselves as "students," though it was unclear any were actually studying anything. A couple were obviously still high from before being grabbed. When their buzz wore off, it was going to be a serious drag.

They all regarded Turnbull, who insisted he wanted to be there, as a lunatic and avoided making any sudden movements around him. Better, from Turnbull's perspective, they avoided making any conversation with him at all. Unsure of exactly what lay ahead, Turnbull utilized his infantry superpower of falling asleep even though the van was constantly jolted by the myriad ruts and potholes of I-5.

They entered the decaying base with a cursory wave at the main gate and headed to West Post. Pre-Split, that was where the active component had relegated the Guard and Reserve units to stay during their pre-deployment train-ups post 9/11. It was the ghetto then, and it was still a dump decades later.

The truck disgorged its human contents, raw clay to be molded into PR soldiers, on a parade field near some ancient barracks that had probably been dilapidated during the Tet Offensive. Not that anyone present knew what that was. The military component of this military seemed sorely lacking. The officers were almost completely absent and the non-commissioned officers who ran the in-processing were basically recruits themselves. The troops were left wearing the civilian gear they arrived in; there were vague assurances that in a couple days they would be issued uniforms. No one inspected or collected the personal belongings of the relatively few recruits who had been impressed into service while carrying any. Turnbull kept his ruck with or on him, and his mouth shut.

The old model of military training was to break the newbies down and build them back up as soldiers. Here, it was the opposite. The recruits were immediately spirited to a seminar on how the People's Republic Army itself was "a colonializing presence that reinforces sexist, racist, and cisgender paradigms." They were then invited to share their feelings about the microaggressions they have suffered so far. A bored political officer took notes on their complaints, and made a short speech about the combat power of diversity. It was, xe informed the assembled future warriors, the PR's strength.

The recruits, used to enduring this kind of rote cant as civilians, simply stared.

Then came branch assignments. One young Spartan standing next to Turnbull in what passed for a formation identified himself as a poet; he asked if there was a poetry military occupational specialty. Like everyone else swooped up off the streets, they gave him the infantry MOS. He started crying.

Next, it was over to the chow hall, a low and ancient building with a dining area on one end and a kitchen on the other. The recruits informed the servers of their particularized dietary needs in great and never-ending detail. There were vegans, but they were easy. They got boiled spinach. The nonbinary Otherkin cow who insisted moo – that was moos pronoun – could only eat cud baffled them. Moo ended up with a plate of boiled spinach and began screaming that "THIS IS FOOD RAPE!" until moo was hustled out.

Turnbull ate the chicken and boiled spinach they plopped on his plate – a double helping as a reward because he hadn't bitched about anything. It tasted like wet newspaper on a bed of moist sawdust, but it was calories and far from the worst thing Turnbull had ever had to eat in enemy territory. He forced it down and, when he was pretty sure no one was watching, gobbled a Cipro pill. Then he grabbed his ruck and walked outside as if he was looking for the latrine.

He was not. Instead, he hiked south, trying to recall the layout of the old Fort Lewis. He recalled that there were officer billets somewhere ahead, still sub-par but miles above the enlisted troop quarters on West Post. He walked and walked, ducking behind trees whenever a pair of headlights appeared and passed by.

Reaching the bachelor officer quarters building, he found a hide spot in a copse of pine trees across the road and waited. Most of the lights were out. There was music from the open second-floor window of one room. Turnbull ran his finger along the razor-sharp edge of his Gerber knife and bided his time.

A Hummer appeared and slowed, finally stopping in front of the BOQs. Three figures got out, clearly buzzed. They stood under the front porch light as the vehicle pulled away, talking. Turnbull could not make it out, but it seemed like drunk-talk.

One took something from his uniform top and popped a flame. A cigarette? That was someone with rank. The other two took their leave and went inside. The smoker stood alone.

Turnbull approached, his ruck back by the trees. The smoker did not see him until he was near. Turnbull looked over the man's uniform in the light. His nametape read "DUNCAN (HE/HIM) and his rank, centered in his chest, was a single pine tree.

A colonel. And a large one at that. Nice.

"You don't salute?" the unsteady colonel asked upon seeing Turnbull. In fact, no one really saluted in the People's Republic Army. It reinforced classist stereotypes, and besides, people saluted George Washington and he owned slaves, so it was racist.

The field grade officer, fueled by whiskey and bitterness at where his life had taken him, was clearly flashing back to his pre-Split tenure in the old US Army.

"Why would I salute a PR colonel?" Turnbull asked. He was still in his civilian duds.

"Respect. Discipline," Colonel Duncan said.

"I'm batting .500 there," Turnbull said. He stood next to the officer.

"You some sort of special forces guy?" the colonel asked after looking his civilian duds up and down.

"Bingo," said Turnbull.

The colonel snorted.

"Fat lot of good you guys have been."

"What do you mean?"

"I was in California," said the colonel. "You guys didn't do shit."

"I did do shit," Turnbull said, offended. "I blew up the Golden Gate Bridge."

"What?"

Turnbull repeated himself, slowly.

"I blew up the Golden Gate Bridge."

The colonel's jaw dropped and Turnbull struck. The knife flashed and was in the man's temple. Turnbull lowered him to the ground fast and dragged him out of the cone of light quickly. He took care not to let blood splatter on the uniform.

Colonel Duncan (HE/HIM) walked into the tactical assembly area on main post just after dawn and quickly identified the sergeant who was probably in charge. Dozens of vehicles were getting ready to move, with troops filling them in nothing resembling military order. Turnbull knew their destination: a little town on the forward line of troops called Cle Elum.

"Sergeant," Turnbull said, his ruck over his shoulder. "I need a lift in your convoy. I'm heading south too."

The sergeant regarded the colonel with misery. This was just what he needed.

"Colonel, can you ride with the battalion commander?"

"No," Turnbull said. The battalion commander might have known Colonel Duncan. For all he knew, Colonel Duncan *was* the brigade commander.

"I am on the down-low. Put me in with the troops. I'll sit in a truck. I want it low key. My movement south is top secret."

"Okay," said the dubious NCO. He smelled bullshit, like any NCO in any army would, but he also understood that whatever problem this weird colonel might be was not *his* problem.

"Colonel, why don't you ride in Alpha-46?"

Turnbull/Duncan smiled and nodded. Then he got up into the truck.

He slept most of the way. The enlisted soldiers did not speak to him and instead griped non-stop – about the food, the leadership, the rampant atmosphere of cisgender paradigm reinforcement.

It was a long but pleasant drive, in the sense that Duncan/Turnbull could look out the back at the passing forests and mountains. The blues had not gotten around to ruining all of nature yet. The antics of humans seemed to make no difference to it, which he somehow found reassuring.

Outside the town of Cle Elum, with a few miles to go to the forward operating base, the truck got off the interstate and came to a stop in a back-up of trucks on a surface street. Turnbull stood up and looked at the troops. He put his finger to his mouth and said, "Shhhhhh."

The troops watched silently as the colonel went over the tailgate and dropped down onto the road, then disappeared into the woods. The troops went back to griping.

Casey Warner walked through the Vancouver International Airport to his gate, having shown the People's Republic passport that bore a name (Francis Kaufman), a picture (his, with a nose ring), and his gender identity ("Questioning non-binary two-spirit (femme)"). There were lots of soldiers on duty with guns, long guns, a reminder that Canada was enduring its own civil conflict. Justin Trudeau still ruled here – his picture stared down at the passengers from posters that bore slogans like "FIGHTING FOR FIRST PEOPLX RIGHTS" in English, French, Cree, Inuktitut and Ojibwe, thereby taking up most of the space. But outside of the urban areas, he did not rule and barely pretended to. Though he had outlawed firearms for everyone else, red America had allowed and even encouraged arms smuggling into the north. Though the resulting insurrection was extremely polite, it was still an insurrection, and the leftist forces did not dare venture into the bulk of the country except in large numbers lest they disappear into the vastness of the Great White North.

Canada was as split as the old United States, just not formally. The rebel provinces in the center of the country simply excused themselves from Ottawa's control, and the first thing they did was restart the Keystone Pipeline project with the new United States. Trudeau was outraged – "This is an assault on our Mother, the Earth!" he shouted to the cameras – but there was not much he could do about it even with the Chinese forces he allowed to train and stage on British Columbian soil. The foreign forces were focused for the time being on the war to the south.

Casey had crossed the border that morning, as the Sea-Tac Airport was barely functioning. His Air Canada flight to Munich would leave in an hour. Then he would fly from Germany to Havana on a US passport, using still another false name, and then from there into Dallas.

"We show solidarity with the just struggles of the People's Republic of North America," a voice boomed over the loudspeaker in English, and then in French, Cree, Inuktitut and Ojibwe. Casey ignored it, stepping over to the Tim Hortons to get the first real coffee he had swallowed since Dallas.

12.

On a map, the front line of the People's Republic troops wound like a snake around Mt. Rainier and roughly northeast across the state of Hillaryia. To the south by southwest was the Gray Zone, unoccupied by either side, providing a buffer between the two armies.

But on the ground, it was not a solid line of fortifications – garrisons and outposts popped up at uneven intervals, but there were no interconnected set of trenches, no walls, and few other obstacles. It was mostly clumps of PR soldiers, ill-trained, poorly equipped, and constantly complaining, strung out along a hypothetical line. Back behind them, somewhere, there might be some better forces lurking to plug holes if the reds came through – mechanized units, maybe even Chinese ones. The Chi Coms stayed off the front line – that unpleasant frontline work was for the blues.

Turnbull made his way just behind the line of blue troops at a short distance, looking for where to cross through to the south.

Turnbull immediately confirmed that the blue defenses were poor – large parts of the front were covered neither by observation nor direct fires. Maybe there were indirect fires delivered by artillery batteries somewhere to the rear, but Turnbull doubted it. If the reds could generate even a little combat power they would smash right through – but that was a big "if." What was stopping them from crossing Oregon and half of Washington, or whatever it was called now? Several things, including the fact that if the reds took the Gray Zone territory, they would have to occupy it.

There were just not enough red bodies to do that, at least not at present. Both sides had their own good reasons to let the Gray Zone exist. For the time being, both sides were content with a stalemate with their armies far apart and a no-man's land in between.

Turnbull kept moving. Several times he heard the roar of motor bikes. That was the primary way they patrolled behind the lines. It was easy for him to go to ground until the one or two-man patrols roared by on the otherwise deserted road, kicking up a tiny storm of leaves and pine needles.

Turnbull did pass several emplacements that were obviously Chinese, recognizing several Hóng Qí-22 "Red Banner-22" anti-aircraft missile systems, consisting of a radar/control vehicle and three transport/launchers that each held four missiles. They were oriented south; between the ground-based missiles and the AWACS-guide advanced PLA Air Force fighters, the integrated air defenses over the Gray Zone made it a very bad place to be in the air if you were red. The red air defenses to the south returned the favor for the blues or any Chinese fighters that might cross over.

Turnbull kept out of sight walking behind the front, with the eyes of the blue garrison mostly oriented south. There were a few, very few, refugees coming north. Turnbull observed one pack being stopped and robbed by the blue detachment that detected them crossing north. After some hassle and after liberating some of their meager supplies, the blues let them continue their escape. It was unclear if the blue troops were supposed to stop people coming in from the Gray Zone, but perhaps they just did not care.

Turnbull watched the party of maybe seven folks continue on their way after being released. They were ragged, mostly middle aged. No young women, Turnbull noted – he suspected such travelers would not have been so quickly sent on their way, if they had managed to escape from the Gray Zone at all.

There were no weapons visible among them. That was good for his purposes. Turnbull had his pistol on his hip, the shotgun hanging on his back-pack, and his HK416C fully assembled and carried. He tracked them for a mile or two, even though it drew him away from the border.

He needed intel. He needed to know what lay between him and Hanford.

They were slow and loud heading up a lightly traveled two-lane blacktop dusted with leaves and pine needles, and it was easy for Turnbull to get around to their front. He found a good location at a blind curve in the road where there was an embankment on one side and a steep ravine to the other. If they bolted, it would be southward and he could catch them instead of having to chase them all over the pine woods.

He waited by the side of the road, eating a Quest bar for energy. There was a creek down at the bottom of the ravine, and he had filled up his bottle and dropped a couple purification tablets into it. Once a motorbike ridden by a helmeted blue soldier passed by while Turnbull hid behind a tree.

The sun was falling down. He estimated it would take the little band about ten minutes to arrive, but they took nearly a half-hour.

When the travelers turned the corner, he stepped out, his weapon a low ready.

"I'm not going to hurt you," he announced. "I want to talk, nothing more." Their faces showed resignation and exhaustion. None bothered running. Several sat down on the pavement, resigned to whatever fate the big man with the big gun chose to deal out.

Their leader was an older woman, her face creased and her eyes moist. She had a large blemish on her neck that Turnbull thought cried out for the intervention of a dermatologist. But potential melanoma was probably the least of her concerns back where she had just come from.

"We don't got nothing left," she said.

"I'm not here to rob you," Turnbull said. The woman looked skeptical.

"I want some information," Turnbull continued. "I'll pay you for it." He tossed over three of his Quest bars – peanut butter ones. The travelers looked at them like they were gold bars, but no one moved to pick them up off the asphalt.

"What do you want to know?" the woman asked.

"Tell me about the Gray Zone."

She paused. "There's no law there. No power, no running water. There was, some, until the war. Then the blues all pulled out. Most of us had no use for them anyway, but there was something like order. We could get food, most of the time. That ended. Now, it's the strong living off the weak."

"You made it out."

"We're seven. We started with two dozen."

She wiped her eyes and went on.

"The blue was closer – we heard the reds were coming but then they didn't. We could have gone south, but we would have had to walk through Oregon. We were all from Yakima. I was a teacher. We held out there longer than most. But there's no food, no gas, and..."

"And?"

"And the crazies rule there now. They steal, rape, kill. Mostly kill."

"The crazies?"

She nodded. "That's why we won't go east to the reds in Idaho. They think it's their divine mission to scourge the earth of life, and they do."

Turnbull sighed. "I've had experience with those types before."

She kept going on, oblivious to him. "We tried to hide, move at night. Some of us got sick, or hurt. They caught some of us. We had to leave them behind, had to run. We had no weapons."

"These crazies, are they armed like me? You know, with guns?"

"Mostly axes, picks, spears. They have arrows. They prefer to do their dirty work by hand."

"Any other advice for me?" Turnbull asked.

"Yes," the old woman said. "Don't go in there."

"Not in the cards," Turnbull said. He tossed them a couple extra bars, and headed south past them.

It would be a very long walk to Hanford, if he walked.

Turnbull pulled on the OD green 550-paracord he had affixed between two pine trees about 30 feet apart. The taut line was about four feet high off the ground and crossed over the road.

In the dark, it was invisible until you got right up to it, and then it would be too late.

He found a spot off the road and set the HK416C down against a stump before sitting back against the wood. Its suppressor was screwed on, making the weapon a bit longer, but overall it was still relatively short. He ate an energy bar and drank some water. It tasted of bleach.

The roar and the headlights came from the east, which he did not expect. The patrols were usually east-bound, but it didn't matter.

Two headlights – perfect. Three was too many and one, well, there was some risk of damage to the bike, and he preferred two opportunities to secure a ride over just one.

Turnbull estimated that the motorbikes were coming at maybe 25 miles per hour, though the use of miles was Eurocentric and outlawed in the blue. Turnbull wondered how long it would be before someone in the rump People's Republic of the West Coast or the larger remaining portion in New

England learned that the metric system was also developed in Europe. How would they measure then? Cubits and hogsheads?

He focused on his prey. The one biker on the left was a little ahead of his compadre. Turnbull took his rifle into his arms and waited. It did not take long for the first one to hit the paracord at sternum level.

The line snapped, but it did its job. The first rider lost control and slowed before his running buddy figured out there was even a problem.

They collided, sparks cascading into the air, and both wavered and fell, skidding along the asphalt past Turnbull's position.

Turnbull sprinted out of his hiding place to the asphalt, his weapon ready, even before the bikes and their riders came to rest. One motorbike shut off; the other was still revving.

The first rider was on his face and he pushed himself up. The second sat up, until Turnbull put two suppressed 5.56mm rounds into his chest and he fell backward. Then Turnbull pivoted and shot the other rider twice, once in the head. The rider collapsed on his face. Both were still, and when Turnbull cut the ignition on the revving bike, it was absolutely quiet in the woods.

Under the moonlight, he evaluated both bikes and decided that the one that had not been revving was in better shape. It was an OD green-painted Kawasaki KX450 from the early 2020s that probably pre-dated the Split. He got them upright, since leaving them on their sides would increase the risk of fire and that would defeat the purpose of the whole exercise.

Using one of the dead men's canteen cups, he took fuel from the other bike and filled the tank to the brim on his choice of rides.

He searched the bodies. They had AK-47s, which he tossed over the side and off the road. He found four weird PLA meal packs with Chinese characters, two with a smiling carp, one with some dancing noodles, and the last with what he suspected was a happy pangolin. Whether these were helpful illustrations for illiterate soldiers was unclear, but food was food. They went into his ruck.

The unused bike and the bodies of the two riders joined their guns over the side. But he retained one of the helmets, though if he wiped out bad enough in the Gray Zone, helmet or not, he was dead meat.

Turnbull waited for dawn on the side of the road on a hill overlooking a draw that headed south through the border into the Gray Zone. He needed the light to make it down the hiking trail he would use instead of risking going down a heavily-defended road – the bike's headlight would not be enough to make it on the dirt path in the dark, and it would have also given the blue border guards on the high ground on both sides of the trail an easier target if they decided to shoot.

There was no noise from the enemy positions even as the sun began to rise – no standing-to for them like real soldiers. He did hear some noise of people blundering around, probably to take a morning leak. Otherwise, it was a cluster.

He waited.

His plan was simple. Get through the border here and into the Gray Zone. Head out to I-90 and then pick up State Route 243 south and head into Hanford. He had little idea of what he would find there besides the bomb; right now, his focus was on just getting there. A detailed plan for actions on the objective could come later.

It was now light enough to see, and Turnbull mounted the motorbike. He wore his pack, which was a bit unwieldy, and his HK416 was hung around his neck cross-wise.

He cranked the bike and turned it off the asphalt onto the hiking trail. A sign, old and predating the invasion that turned this area into the front line, read "NATURE EXPERIENCE TRAIL FOR DIVERSE PERSONX ONLY – BATTLING WHITE SUPREMACY BY INVITING MARGINALIZED PEOPLX TO DECOLONIZE OUTDOOR RECREATION." Another sign warned about the danger of forest fires using a trans Smokey the Bear cartoon that helpfully explained that their pronouns were they/them. "ONLY DIVERSE COMMUNITIES CAN PREVENT FOREST FIRES," they announced, decked out in a kind of drag ranger outfit that was fabulous despite being heavy on earth tones.

The trail itself was a mess, with branches and rocks littered across it and occasional portions that had slid away. Decolonization did not appear to include basic maintenance. Turnbull grimaced. It would be slower going than he wanted. Speed and surprise were his allies. On the upside, the guards were probably used to motorbike patrols, so that might give him a little edge.

The bike jolted and kicked as he ran over small branches and dodged big rocks. The downward angle was pretty steep, but nothing a casual off-roader could not handle. Turnbull had a Yamaha at the ranch that he used when he had to go far or fast – he preferred walking, but he knew how to handle a bike. The trail ahead was about a mile until the forest opened up into plains past the forward line of troops. The enemy positions he picked out from his observations were up on the high ground to each side of the draw. He hoped there was no one at the bottom straddling the trail, but if there was, he would deal.

The bike was loud, very loud, and the noise echoed in the draw. As Turnbull picked his way along, much slower than he had expected and hoped, he could hear some yelling and shouting from the blue positions. That was annoying. Nothing to do but press on.

Ahead, he could make out a break in the trees, and beyond it the terrain looked relatively flat intermittently broken by bare, brown hills. That was the Gray Zone. He pressed ahead.

"Stop!" he heard someone yell, but it was not clear from which side of the draw. He accelerated, swerving around a log that had fallen onto the path.

"Stop!" he heard once again. Had someone found the bodies of the patrol?

There was a shot, definitely an AK, then another. This one was closer – the bullet cracked over his head. He punched it, picking up speed. There was a little landslide across the path to his front and he went over it, catching air.

More shots – a branch was clipped off by a round and fell just ahead of him. Where were they? He felt a blow to his ruck. It had taken a round but not punched through into his back.

The path just ahead was much better and the grade shallower. He picked up speed, heedless of the shouts and shots behind him. The trees were becoming sparser. Almost there.

To his front he saw shapes even as he maneuvered the bike around the obstacles in his path. Men – armed men in camo, at least two of them.

They seemed confused, and Turnbull figured they were not in radio contact with the others and were not sure of what all the commotion was about. He was coming toward them fast, but they were not brandishing their AKs as much as holding them and looking confused.

"Shoot him!" someone off to his left on the high ground shouted. "Shoot him!"

The pair of blue troops heard the command but hesitated. Shoot who? Turnbull wondered if they were confused by the pronoun.

Then they looked at him, in his civilian duds riding a People's Republic Army recon motorbike, and they figured it out.

They were supposed to shoot he/him.

Turnbull had made his shooting decision earlier, and by the time the guards on the path ahead figured out who they were supposed to engage, he was ready to engage them. He pulled his MK416, which hung across his chest by a strap around his neck, back with his right hand until it pointed out forward, like a knight's lance, except both shorter and deadlier.

There would be no finesse here. Turnbull's thumb clicked the selector switch to AUTO.

The taller of the two to Turnbull's front managed to swing his AK around as Turnbull pulled the trigger. The HK416 kicked as he fired one-handed, but Turnbull lowered it to lie across the handlebars for stability. There was a long "PFFFFTTTT" as the suppressor did its job, but there was no way to see where the rounds hit as he jostled and shook from the bumpy path.

The taller one took aim, barely, and fired. The approaching bike was a small, moving target and he missed. Turnbull squeezed again.

This time, different story. The shooter had managed to gain a sight picture this time and would have pulled his own trigger if two 5.56mm rounds had not slammed first into his shoulder, and then into the center of his chest.

The guard went down even as his running buddy squeezed off a long burst off to Turnbull's left. It tore up a pine tree by the side of the trail ahead, and Turnbull rode through the cloud of bark fragments even as he pivoted his HK416 slightly.

Turnbull was now about 40 meters away.

There were more rounds coming at him, now from each side of the draw raining down from the guards above. Turnbull ignored them and aimed at the guy ahead of him by dead reckoning. He fired a burst at the surviving guard on the trail. No effect.

The guard began shooting, a long burst – he was going to empty his mag. Even over the roar of the motorbike, the noise was tremendous. Turnbull pulled his own trigger as he closed the distance between them.

Spent shells kicked out of the HK416 and off into the brush in a golden arc of brass as the target got bigger ahead of him. But the guard was firing too, his aim improving – rounds cracked above and beside Turnbull, each one nearer than the last.

Like medieval knights in a tourney, both men were fixed on the other, on killing each other.

The blue border guard was spraying a wild stream of 7.62x39mm rounds when he suddenly staggered. One of the bullets from Turnbull's gun had found his forehead. When the blue fell, a pink mist hung in the air and had barely dissipated when Turnbull passed through it as he guided his bike between the two dead men heaped on the forest floor.

The Gray Zone was just ahead, a golden-brown wasteland stretching out to a line of low hills on the far horizon. There was still firing from behind him, but they would have to be very lucky to score a hit now.

They were not lucky – today, lady luck was riding backseat with Kelly Turnbull. He passed the last of the trees and tore off south into the wasteland of the Gray Zone.

Turnbull was wrong about luck. He felt the wetness on his khaki 5.11 pants.

Gas.

It was not a big hole. The 7.62x39mm round had barely nicked the tank, but it was still leaking. That was bad. It was a long walk to Hanford.

He decided to grind out as much distance as he could before the tank dripped dry. He headed east cross-country over the flatlands, pausing occasionally to pass through a barbed wire fence. He saw nothing and almost no one. In the distance, he observed small clumps of travelers moving north and going to ground as they heard his bike.

The Gray Zone must suck something awful if its inhabitants preferred the blue.

He hit I-90 north of where the freeway met the Yakima River and then ran alongside the waterway that lay to the east, saving him the effort of finding a river crossing. The road was deserted, except for all manner of vehicles pulled to the side and simply abandoned. Many were old private vehicles and most looked relatively undamaged, though every one of them was pillaged. They probably ran out of gas. Every gas door was open.

He rode on, making decent time.

The town of Ellensburg, with a pre-Split population of just under 20,000, was ahead. Beyond it were hills, and the Yakima River ran beside it. But the town itself was behind a series of walls, obstacles and barbed wire, lots of barbed wire. Smoke from cooking fires rose from the town, and a haze hung over it.

A sign was planted next to the road: "FREE TOWN OF ELLENBURG – ALL ARE WELCOME TO TRADE NO SCUM NO TROUBLE NO WEAPONS WE WILL HANG YOU."

Charming, Turnbull told himself. He checked his gas gauge. Not much left. He considered his options.

Reluctantly, he turned the motorbike toward Ellensburg.

Turnbull did not go immediately to the main city gate. A good chunk of the city was outside of the wall and it was entirely deserted – street upon street of residential homes, all thoroughly abandoned and thoroughly ransacked. A surprising number of the houses were burned out.

He found a once-nice ranch-style house with the skeleton of a swing set out front and took the motorbike around back. He crept to the front yard and observed for a half-hour, listening and watching. Some coyotes wandered through until a pack of feral dogs drove them out of what had been their homes in better times when the people who lived there fed them, before the pets had had to fend for themselves.

Satisfied that he had not been followed and that he was probably alone, at least alone in terms of humans, he went inside. Every door and drawer in the house had been pulled open. The place had been pillaged, and then pillaged again. There was nothing useful left, nothing except what Turnbull was looking for – a hiding place.

He found a closet in what had been a kid's room – there was an old poster of Justin Timberlake on the wall from his "My Penis Does Not Define Me" comeback tour a few years post-Split. Apparently, his penis did define him – he had been arrested by the blues for a felony "cis-crime," making the kid who owned this room a rebel, at least in the context of the People's Republic. Turnbull left the HK416, his Shockwave shotgun, and the Wilson Combat, plus their accoutrements and ammo, with the ruck in the back of the closet covered by a piece of cardboard.

He slipped the Springfield XD-S 4.0 9mm pistol into his crotch, plus a spare mag. With five in the magazine and one in the pipe, he felt practically naked. He took the Gerber knife too. And a pile of cash plus some Quest bars.

Then he started riding toward town. On the way, he saw a wooden handle in the grass. He stopped. It turned out to be attached to a rusty axe head – at least, he hoped the red stuff was just rust. But he picked it up nonetheless.

There was a family with a horse-drawn wagon ahead of him at the gate to Ellensburg. The guards were men with a collection of spears and clubs, but not far off was a three-story tower and the guy in there seemed to have a rifle. He was probably the fail-safe in case the dudes with the melee weapons were outclassed.

A flag he guessed was that of the old Washington state flew off the top. Turnbull suspected that this place was no longer Hillaryia, if it ever had been.

The wagon, pulled by two horses, held what looked like a dozen metal milk containers. And the family was a large one, five young males – sons? – each of them with a club or spear or, in one guy's case, a compound bow and quiver of arrows.

They laughed and joked with the guards and were obviously locals and regulars. They did not protest handing over their weapons, which the guards took inside. Nor did they protest the cursory pat down by the youngest of the sentinels.

When the wagon was clear, Turnbull approached slowly on foot, pushing the bike, helmet off, eschewing sudden moves. He held the axe by its head, but the guards were wary and three more appeared, acting nonchalant but closely watching the stranger. Turnbull noted that their gear seemed clean and maintained. They might not be pros, but they were not clowns.

The guards motioned him forward, relieved him of the axe, and then the young man patted him down, poorly. The guard missed the compact pistol in his crotch. Turnbull relaxed – he counted on the fact that amateurs rarely effectively searched that neighborhood.

"What's your business?" the guard leader, an older and serious looking gentleman, asked.

"Traveling. I'm not from here. My bike's damaged. I want to get it fixed."

"Traveling?" the guard asked. "Going north?"

"Wherever. I just want to fix my bike. I can trade for it."

"What do you have to trade? You aren't carrying nothing. And where did you get gas?"

"That's my business," Turnbull said, but that seemed to be a poorly received response so he elaborated. "Services, if it matters. I have skills."

The lead guard regarded him coldly.

"You one of them, boy?"

"One of who?" Turnbull asked. The guards were making a circle around him, subtly, nothing fast, but they were definitely preparing in case this conversation went south.

Turnbull figured his move. Plant the axe in the boss, then kill several with the Springfield and hopefully scatter the others and ride off before the rifleman in the tower could take him. It was not a great plan, but it was a plan. And it was the best of a bunch of bad options if the situation escalated.

"Let me see you without your shirt."

"Not that kind of services," Turnbull said.

"Shut your mouth and show us your chest."

Turnbull considered the options, and went with indulging his interlocutor. He pulled off his shirt. If he had to take off more, he would be in trouble.

"You got a lot of scars," the guard marveled. "You're a mess. But you've had plenty of food. What the hell is your story?"

"Long and my own," Turnbull said. "If you're done admiring my physique, can I put my shirt back on?"

The other guards laughed a little. Apparently he had passed some test.

"No tatts. No straight cuts. Okay, you're not one of them."

Turnbull pulled the shirt back over his head.

"Who is 'them'?"

The lead guard laughed bitterly.

"You really are new here. You never met one of the scum while you were riding around?"

"I've met a lot of scum, but not *the* scum."

"You'll know them if you meet them," The guard assured him. "Okay, come in. Mind you, we don't tolerate bullshit in Ellensburg. Keep the peace, don't steal, you'll be fine. Break the law, you won't leave. Got it?"

"Sounds reasonable."

"Give me that axe."

Turnbull handed it over.

"You ought to clean this," the guard said. "It looks like shit."

"I'll get on it when I get it back."

Another guard approached with a piece of paper. It read "AXE."

"Your receipt," he said, handing it to Turnbull, who took it and stuffed it into his shirt pocket.

The lead guard waved him inside, and Turnbull walked into Ellensburg.

13.

Ellensburg had been a picturesque American town that would have done just fine as the backdrop for an Andy Hardy film. The buildings were old-fashioned, with no modernist nonsense until the Split, except for the squat, ugly courthouse. After the Split, the brutalist People's Security Force building replaced the old police station on 5th Avenue and clashed with the garrets and shutters of the rest of the main drag. It was now the home of the town sheriffs, which the city guards called themselves. The People's Security Force had abandoned the town in the middle of the night when the rumor mill claimed that the United States forces were about to reconquer it. But the reds never came, and the blues never came back.

It seemed to Turnbull to be like Dodge City if it was in medieval times and not in the Old West. The sheriffs patrolled with spears, clubs, axes, and such. The blues had devoted a great deal of effort into disarming the rural folk in Washington after the Split – they did not want to have to deal with another Indiana and felt the best way to squash an insurgency was to deprive them of firearms before they started getting uppity. That worked better in towns like Ellensburg than out in the hinterlands, where there was active resistance and the PSF only ventured if absolutely necessary and in large numbers.

Another difference was the wall, or rather, the barrier that surrounded most of downtown and much of the residential area. It was not perfect, but it was something. It was sufficient to funnel traffic through the main gate, where it could be controlled. And it was defensible, good for keeping casual interlopers from wandering in, and for keeping kids and knuckleheads from wandering out.

Just inside the gate, in a parking lot of some long-shuttered box store, there were dozens of wagons and maybe a hundred people gathered, men, women, children, and no one who appeared non-binary. It looked like a wagon train getting organized.

They move in convoys, Turnbull thought. *Makes sense.*

There was a Main Street, of course, and commerce was centered there. The store fronts were all open, but most of the traders were working out of stalls erected along the sidewalk. Without much automobile traffic – there was some, but there were many more horse-drawn carts and wagons – the streets were open for walking and, while not exactly crowded, during the mid-afternoon there were more people than Turnbull expected.

He slowly pushed the Kawasaki down the street – signs forbade riding motorbikes and the like. There was some level of civilization here. There were even public latrines, complete with running water from the Yakima River. A sewer system was an emblem of civilization. Good for Ellensburg. He decided to make use of it. In his stall, he took the pistol and mag out of his pants and put them in his pocket. Then he continued down the street.

The people looked rough, with dirty clothes and more scars than he was used to. Only the strong survived here. Turnbull continued on. He was looking for something.

He saw thick black smoke rising. That was the ticket. He turned the motorbike in that direction. It was off Main itself, around back in what appeared to have been a car dealership. The garage was open and there was a furnace that kids were feeding with wood. The hand-painted sign overhead read "BLACKSMITH METAL WORK."

He found the proprietor and the man regarded the rupture in the gas tank carefully.

"That looks like a bullet hole," he said.

"Holes are holes," Turnbull replied. "Can you fix it? Like, now, this afternoon?"

The blacksmith regarded him warily. "Sure. I don't know how you'll get gas, though. Or how you'll pay for it."

"Gas is my problem. And US dollars are your solution."

The blacksmith laughed. "US dollars? Right."

Turnbull pulled four hundreds from his pocket and the man went white.

"Those real?" the blacksmith asked, doubtful.

"You see a printing press?" Turnbull asked.

The blacksmith considered the proposal. The money had no inherent value, but traders passing through either north to the blue or south or even the crazy ones heading east to get to the red would want it.

"Deal?" asked Turnbull. The blacksmith nodded and they shook hands.

Turnbull headed back to Main.

"Bread!" someone shouted at him from a stall. Another vendor offered him candles.

"Deer fat," the man told him without prompting. Turnbull demurred.

He decided to get something to eat.

The Dakota was a combination restaurant/saloon/hotel that would have fit right in out in Deadwood a century-and-a-half before. It did not seem particularly rowdy, which was good. Turnbull wanted a meal, not trouble.

The menu was simple. He asked his waitress, who wore a skirt and did not offer her pronouns, for venison, potatoes, and beer. The request for meat impressed her, but not as much as the hundred-dollar bill. Her eyes got big when he handed it over, and other eyes alighted upon him.

Turnbull remained quiet, hoping the attention would fade.

Hunters, many of them Indians, brought the field-dressed deer into town and sold it to butchers. Farmers brought in the potatoes, and brewers did what they could to make their draughts. Capitalism had returned to the blue with a vengeance, though it had never fully left this rural area of western Washington state. The People's Republic was nominally in charge after the Split, but besides making sure all the guns they could find were confiscated – the leftist state's gun registry made that easy – the PR had not gotten around to transforming Ellensburg and its environs into a rustic Seattle before everything collapsed. To compensate for the disastrous economy of the new nation, the locals built a rudimentary one based largely on barter soon after the Split. They were therefore better able to fend for themselves when the PR fled the allegedly advancing red army.

But there were complications.

Something was happening out in the street, and people were running to the front door and windows to see. Turnbull took another gulp of the beer – it was something like an IPA and he hated IPAs – then joined the audience gazing out the window.

There was a wagon pulled by a pair of horses coming down the street, with a number of sheriffs. In the back were three bundles, man-shaped bundles wrapped in dark-stained blankets. And there were two wounded men who were, for now, among the living. One was quiet with a scarlet bandage wrapped around his arm. The other was struggling and groaning, and three arrow shafts protruded from his upper legs and abdomen.

"Scum did it," someone muttered.

"They'll kill us all," another said.

"You're safe in town," the proprietor shouted. If they were gaping, they weren't eating or drinking. "You've seen it. Show's over. Sit back down."

The crowd gradually went back to their places. Turnbull finished his venison. It was good. Having paid up front, he left his empty plate and walked out. He did not notice the three men who followed him.

There was a fistfight that poured out of another bar as Turnbull killed time walking through the trading street. A couple of idiots hopped up on too much bad beer and testosterone came flying out the door and into the road, where they slugged each other surrounded by vaguely interested observers until a half-dozen sheriffs came and took them to the ground, then dragged them away. The people went back to their business. They did not seem surprised. Turnbull hoped he would be out of town by nightfall. It might get rowdy, and he did not need trouble. What he needed was his bike.

He walked down one side of Main and up the other. Most of the propaganda signs were long gone, but he did see a fading, painted legend on one brick building that read, "TRANS FARMERS SUPPORT INTERSECTIONALITY." If there were any trans farmers still around, he had not seen any and he bet that they had bigger concerns than intersectionality.

There was a school, and while Turnbull did not go inside, he expected that it would not contain any of the kind of woke nonsense that had fueled the conflict leading to the Split. And it was probably legal here to use the term "woke" – in the PR, if you used that term you risked being arrested for linguistic appropriation.

Turnbull also noted several signs on or around public buildings with what he suspected was the word "HILLARYIA" spray-painted out and the word "WASHINGTON" inserted.

He gave it a couple hours and then returned to the blacksmith's shop. The proprietor proudly pointed out the fix – a patch welded onto the tank. It was unpainted, but the hole was sealed.

"And here's your gas," the blacksmith said. He handed Turnbull a glass beaker with a few ounces of fuel that were drained from the tank before the repair. Turnbull nodded and poured it back inside the gas tank. Nothing dribbled out of the hole.

"Good to go," he said and handed the blacksmith his money.

"Where you headed, boy?" the man asked, shoving the bills into his dirty jeans. "North?"

"East," said Turnbull. It was an OPSEC violation, but it invited helpful information. He got some.

"East? They'll kill you."

"Who?"

"The scum. They're out there, picking people off. You gotta travel in a convoy, and a big one, well-armed at that. They sometimes come around here, but we're too hard a nut to crack with the walls and the sheriffs. Out there, alone, they'll kill you. That's their religion."

"Killing people is their religion?"

"Yeah," the blacksmith said. "They worship killing. They ride around, steal gas, food, whatever. Dress like maniacs. They want to kill everyone. They're crazy."

"I met some people like that a while ago. But they all burned up. Annihilationists, they called themselves."

"Yeah," said the blacksmith, nodding. "Annihilationists."

"I doubt they are the same sect," Turnbull said.

"Who knows? Everything is crazy now, boy," the blacksmith said. "Everything. I was an auto mechanic before the Split. Worked right here at Ellensburg Dodge. And then the Split happened – I didn't even know. I never read or watched politics. But it happened. And then the PR was in charge, and then the reds were coming, and then this."

"Tell me about it."

"It's like," the man said, his eyes on something far away. "Evolution, only backwards. I remember before, before the Split. Everything worked. You remember Amazon? We could order boots or a blender and then it would just come overnight. Cell phones. We had the internet."

"Mixed blessing."

"But stuff worked. And then everything got worse. I mean, we were Americans, right, all of us? Things are supposed to get *better*, not worse. I used to have a Dodge Ram truck. I haven't driven in years. How did this happen? We were Americans. That meant something once."

The man looked at Turnbull like Turnbull might have had an answer for him.

He didn't.

"People are idiots," was all Turnbull could say.

The few ounces of gas were not going to get him far, but he had seen a gas seller along Main during his walk and he rode back there, the motorbike earning a fair number of stares. He accepted the risk – he would be gone once he got filled up and then he would get his stuff and be off to the land of maniacs. That was his big problem.

The gas vendor had about fifty gallons to sell. Turnbull needed one and a half gallons. The vendor's eyes lit up at the US dollars and he stared at Ronald Reagan's face on the twenties.

Turnbull had his gas for two hundred bucks and considered it a deal. He fueled the Kawasaki, shut the cap, and was getting up on the bike when a man put his hand on Turnbull's shoulder, gently, so that Turnbull did not rip it off.

"Sir," he said. "We need to talk."

"Doubtful," Turnbull said. The man, with bad teeth – everyone here seemed dentally challenged – and stringy hair, looked at him earnestly.

"You will want to hear what I have to say."

Turnbull regarded him carefully. The guy seemed vaguely familiar, but everyone here looked like hell.

"It's about the red," the man said. He looked into Turnbull's eyes for a reaction.

A fellow agent, Turnbull wondered.

"Talk," he said.

"Not here," the man said. "Too many eyes. Over there."

"The alley?"

The man nodded.

Turnbull considered the request.

"Okay," he said, though against his better judgment. The man led the way, with Turnbull pushing his bike across the road, around the stalls and back into the alley. It was dark in the dying light of the afternoon. The man stopped and turned.

He was smiling now, leering at Turnbull.

"I'm guessing you don't have anything to tell me," Turnbull sighed. He noticed movement to his rear. The man's two amigos had swung in behind him to block the alley entrance.

The Dakota. That's where he saw them. And where they saw him and his cash.

"Well, you gotta be from the red," the man said. "You got real dollars and look at you, all plump."

"I've been carb loading," Turnbull said, assessing.

"You're funny. Won't help you."

"One, two," he said over his shoulder, then looking at the guy who had lured him into the alley, "Three."

Number Three produced a buck knife. Turnbull assumed the others were similarly packed.

"I thought this was a weapons free zone," Turnbull said. "You dudes are breaking the law."

"I think you need to worry about your own self right now, boy."

"Why is everyone around here always calling me 'boy'?" Turnbull wondered aloud. The two henchmen behind him were shifting their weight but not moving forward. The guy to his front was fifteen feet away.

"The money and the bike and *maybe* you walk away."

Turnbull considered.

"I have a counter-offer. Wanna hear it?"

The man regarded him with a sly grin. Turnbull continued.

"You get out of my face now and I don't kill all three of you."

"Maybe you didn't hear me, boy."

"I know you heard me," Turnbull said. "Boy."

The two to his rear leapt forward and Turnbull spun right, drawing his Gerber in his right hand as he turned.

This had the effect of placing the right rear attacker between Turnbull and his partner, making it – for a second – a one-on-one fight.

The man charging him had a large cooking knife, big but awkward, and he had no moves but an all-out charge. Turnbull grabbed the attacker's knife-hand with his left, pulling it past him, while burying the Gerber up to the hilt in the man's right thigh. Then Turnbull yanked, not out but across, and as the man fell forward he ripped the blade across the flesh. A shower of blood erupted and the man screamed and he toppled over.

The second man had a claw hammer and swung now that the obstacle was on the ground shrieking. The blow was aimed at Turnbull's skull, but Turnbull blocked it with his dagger. The hammer struck the blade and the Gerber went flying. The attacker drew back for another swing but got a boot in the gut that sent him back against the brick wall.

Number Three was charging, buck knife high.

"Shit," Turnbull said. He had wanted to keep this quiet but that was not in the cards unless he wanted a buck knife planted in his cerebellum.

The Springfield XD-S 4.0 was out and Number Three was about four feet away when he saw the barrel aimed at his face. His mouth formed into a circle and he started to make a sound. But Turnbull fired twice, the first hollow point 9mm round pulping his target's right eye and blasting a fearsome wound channel through his brain. The second went into the man's forehead and was entirely superfluous.

Even as Number Three's legs turned to fettucine and he dropped, the one with the hammer rallied – for a second.

Turnbull pivoted and shot him twice in the face. This time, each round found an eyeball.

The last guy was on the ground, trying to stop the bleeding from his severed femoral artery.

"In for a penny, in for a pound," Turnbull said and put two rounds into the wounded man's forehead. If he needed to explain the situation, it would be better not to have a living witness on the other side perjuring himself about how he and his friends were on the way to help out at the orphanage when the illegally-armed gun-wielding stranger attacked them for no reason.

But Turnbull had no intention of explaining anything to anyone. He walked the Kawasaki out of the alley, pausing to exchange the empty mag for a full one and close the locked-open slide, and to retrieve his knife. A small crowd began gathering and murmuring.

"Denton's dead!" someone yelled. "So's Jake Schooner!"

Turnbull pocketed the pistol and turned over the motorbike's engine, then rode off up Main Street.

People were scrambling all over the road and coming out of doors, as if the news of the incident had preceded him. He was headed toward the gate, but a hundred yards away he saw the sheriffs scrambling to shut it tight. How they knew he had no idea – maybe they heard the shots. After all, his own ears were still ringing from firing in the confined space of the alley.

He wheeled the bike around and went in the opposite direction, crossing Main Street once again. It was a flurry of activity, and the people pointing and shouting as he roared by demonstrated that the hubbub was about him.

Was there another gate? He did not know – there had been no gas to do a full 360-degree recon of the Ellensburg barrier before he came inside. And if there was a gate, there was no guarantee it would not be shut too.

This was a problem.

He roared into the residential section of the secure area, heading generally east, until he saw it ahead – the barrier. It was a mash-up of cars and barbed wire blocking the street, between four and six feet high. On the other side the residential street just continued, but no one lived out there anymore.

There were shouts coming from behind him. He surveyed the barrier. He could get through, but not with the bike and not in a hurry.

He drummed his fingers on the handlebars.

Something caught his eye. He tore down the street to the last house by the barrier. The front yard was not entirely flat. It rose in a small hill toward the barrier. But was it enough?

It better be.

He turned back and returned up the street. More voices now, and they were coming.

Damn it, Turnbull said.

He gunned the engine and the Kawasaki flew forward down the street. At the last house, he turned into the driveway and onto the rise in the grass at full speed.

He flew up, and the barrier passed below him. He was coming down in an overgrown lawn. He landed, and the bike shimmied and shook as it landed. But he did not lose control. He slowed, and turned out into the street. Behind him, through the barrier, he could see his pursuers. He turned back around and gunned the engine, roaring away down the empty road.

It took him a while to figure out how to get back to the house where he had stored his gear since he was returning by an entirely different route.

The sun was going down as he arrived, and he left the bike out back as he went inside and gathered his things. The Wilson went back on his hip, the shotgun was attached to the side of the ruck, and the HK416 he carried in his arms. He briefly considered spending the night holed up there, but he needed to get moving. With a full tank, Hanford was probably a couple hours away, and he could do his recon in the early morning light.

He went out the back door, got on the bike, and carefully drove it around front.

A dozen sheriffs, with spears, clubs, and one guy with a bow, were arrayed in an arc on the street out front.

He suppressed his question about how they found him – it didn't matter. They had.

The lead sheriff from the gate was in front of his men.

"Put down that weapon," he said. "Come peacefully."

"No." Turnbull said.

"We hold fair trials, in Ellensburg," the sheriff said. "If you have a good reason for killing those three men, you will walk out of the courthouse a free man. But three men are dead and that has to be answered."

"No," Turnbull said.

"You can get some of us with that rifle," the sheriff said. "But not all of us."

"No," Turnbull said. "I'll kill all of you. And I don't want to. The fact is that I have a job to do, a job more important than my life, and more important than yours, and everyone's in your town, in fact. But I'm not going to ask you to believe that."

He held up the HK416.

"You need to believe this. I've killed a lot of people to get here. I'll kill a lot more before I'm done. I'm not sad about any of them. I will be sad if I have to kill you, because you're all good men, just trying to protect your people, and I respect that. But I have a mission, and if you don't let me pass, I will kill every single one of you."

"What kind of psycho are you?" the sheriff said.

"The kind people like you need, I guess, to do the things no one else will do. Understand that I'll do what I have to do, because a helluva lot more lives will be lost than the twelve of yours if I don't. So I'm asking you, nicely. Don't die for those scumbags in the alley. Get out of my way so I don't have to make your wives widows and your kids orphans, because in ten seconds, if you aren't moving, I'm going to kill you all."

The sheriff and his men did not move. Turnbull resolved to shoot the archer first, since he was the most imminent threat, then the leader, then cut down the others as they scattered with their boss dead. He ran through the play in his head, as he had before a hundred firefights.

"Ten seconds!" Turnbull yelled. The sheriffs started murmuring, but the leader stayed put.

He's brave, damn it, Turnbull thought.

"Five!" Turnbull drew up the rifle and put the optic on the archer. The guy with the bow was maybe nineteen.

"Don't make me kill your men," Turnbull said. "Please."

The sheriff considered. He'd known the archer since he was a baby. Hell, he had dated the kid's mother in high school.

"Okay," he shouted. "You go, and don't come back."

The sheriffs moved off, leaving a corridor for Turnbull to escape. Turnbull took it and roared through them and down the road.

As the sun set and he drove east on I-90, he tried to think about something other than the fact that he was five seconds from killing them all.

14.

Kelly Turnbull continued on I-90 as it turned east just south of Ellensburg. He was largely alone on the road in the dark, but the moon was already casting a pale light over the desert scrub. His impression of Washington state – it seemed Hillaryia had fallen out of favor around there – had been of a moist, rainy forest. But this was desert, with small bushes breaking up the carpet of dry, brown grasses, and low hills popping up in the midst of the flatlands.

There was a good deal of wreckage along the road. North of Ellensburg, most of the derelict vehicles seem to have been simply left behind when their tanks ran dry, but these were largely damaged, many hanging off the soft shoulder or even sitting in the middle of the road. And there was a good deal of debris strewn across the blacktop, making Turnbull slow down since he was riding without his headlights.

He rode on, carefully. Ahead, there was a tractor trailer rig from PEOPLE'S TRUCKING that was lying on its side. The tractor door was open to the sky, the hood open, the engine picked apart, and the windshield was bashed in. No bodies though, but there was some gore.

The trailer was cleaned out, but what Turnbull noticed was the red spray-painted words on the roof facing west: "THE SCUM RULE HERE."

Charming, thought Turnbull.

He tore on, trying to balance the need for speed with the necessity of avoiding shredded steel-belted radials, fenders, fields of shattered glass, and other hazards spread out across the blacktop.

A few miles ahead, the interstate lanes split apart, with the west-bound lanes far off to the north across the terrain. The freeway rose up into some low hills, slicing through the earth between the high ground with rocky scars on each side of the asphalt.

He glanced up. Out here in the dark, the stars were brilliant and spread across the heavens much like they did back home at his ranch. When he saw the shape of a man mounted on a motorcycle silhouetted against those stars off to his right, he reverted to his Army training.

You're supposed to stay on the military crest, dumbass, he thought. You were supposed to stay just below the actual crest so you are not back-lit and observable.

The biker's machine roared to life, and then another did, and there was a car too, what looked like a red Mustang from the early seventies. They were loud, and they were roaring down the hill toward the interstate just ahead of him.

Turnbull gunned his engine, risking the debris hazard to make sure they could not cut him off.

He scanned the way ahead. The cut went on for at least a half-mile. Good choice of an ambush site. No way to get off-road.

The Kawasaki picked up speed even as the two cyclists and the Mustang ripped down on a dirt track nearly parallel to the traffic lanes but intersecting with the blacktop a few hundred meters ahead.

The shapes were hard to make out, but the riders were big dudes and elaborately decorated. One's helmet had horns, and the other was wearing some sort of feathered cape that flapped behind him as he drove. The Mustang ran well, but it looked like hell. It was spray-painted and items Turnbull could not get a clear view of were affixed to it, like gargoyles hanging off a gothic cathedral. And they were going fast, far too fast for the dirt track that led down from their hilltop positions to the road.

Turnbull shot past the intersection just seconds before the motorcycles and the Mustang tore out onto the blacktop behind him. The motorbike was no motorcycle, and it certainly did not have a Cleveland 351 cubic inch V-8 engine like the Mustang.

They would catch him if he stayed on the highway, and they had picked a spot where he could not get off it.

The horned motorcyclist barreled ahead, coming in on Turnbull's left with the Mustang following behind. Turnbull checked back over his shoulder – the sonofabitch had a long axe in his right hand held high aloft, ready to take his head off.

Turnbull struggled to bring the HK416 to bear, but there was no way – the strap hung it up.

There was a screech, barely human, and the rider took a swing. It was close – even at sixty, Turnbull felt the wind as the axe came down past his face.

Another screech, of rage, and Turnbull saw the red eyes of his pursuer, pure hate. Behind the horned guy, the Mustang was closing on him.

The axe was heavy, and the rider yanked it back up into the air, but he was off-balance for just a second and Turnbull saw his opening. He yanked the handlebars hard, and kicked his attacker in the side with his left combat boot. The horned rider, already off-balance with the heavy axe head above him, swerved left.

The Mustang was there, though, its long hood sideswiping the rider. Horned Guy spilled onto the broad hood of the Mustang, the axe flying away and the motorcycle bouncing off the fender and wiping out. The rider hit the windshield with a horn and cracked it, then flew off into the dark.

The Mustang did not slow. Not a bit. It sped up.

Turnbull glanced over. He could not see inside the shattered windshield, but the car was coming fast. He did manage to identify one of the decorations affixed to the vehicle. The one item attached to the front of the hood was a human skull – not a pretty white one, but one with flapping bits of flesh and hair still hanging from it.

The Mustang pulled even with him as Turnbull went for his .45 with his right hand. The passenger window was down; inside was pure blackness. Then a face, a dirty, scowling face that looked like a bigger Charles Manson on PCP wearing a leather harness. He climbed out of the window and prepared to jump.

Turnbull swerved right as the man leapt, his arms grasping, and he may have actually hit the rear tire of the Kawasaki before planting in the blacktop at sixty miles per hour.

The Mustang did not slow or hesitate.

It occurred to Turnbull that there was another rider, but where? He felt a strike on his pack and looked right – there was the shaft of a crossbow bolt planted in the side of his ruck.

The feathered rider was off to his right and a bit behind, holding the handlebars of his bike with his left paw and trying to reload the crossbow with his right.

Turnbull drew his Wilson and twisted back to place the tritium sight on the dark center mass of the feathered rider.

He fired, twice. The motorcycle went unstable and veered away to the right, slamming into an abandoned panel van that sat there on the shoulder without wheels.

Turnbull began to turn his attention back to the Mustang, but he got a glimpse of the road ahead. What was it – an old bumper, a tire? It was a black mass in the middle of the lane and there was no time to avoid it.

The motorbike shook and careened to the shoulder, where it went down as if something had grabbed it and threw it to the ground. Turnbull saw glimpses of stars, blackness, sparks, hills, more stars as he skidded over the dirt.

Then he stopped. He was on his back, the sky reeling above him.

Pain, legs, arm. Not his head, but his head was cloudy.

Blackness over his eyes. Warm. He blinked it clear.

A copper smell.

No ruck, it was gone.

Weapon? Where were his weapons?

His hand was empty, and the HK416 was not around his neck.

He put his empty hand down to the rocky soil of the shoulder and tried to push himself up. No go. Pain in his legs. Dizziness.

Engine noise.

What happened to the Mustang?

A shape above him, silhouetted against the bright stars, with something long with a rectangle at the top.

A sledgehammer.

The man was wearing black, smiling, smiling too widely, eyes ablaze, raising his weapon with two hands.

Turnbull reached for the Wilson in his holster, but it was not there.

Oh, right, it had been in his hand and now it was gone.

He was going to die with his face bashed in by a sledgehammer.

Did not see that coming, he thought to himself.

A pop, loud.

A 7.62mm, he'd know it anywhere.

The guy loomed above him, his sledge raised high, ready to come down on the bridge of Turnbull's nose.

But he didn't. Turnbull could not understand why.

The guy just stood there, staring, then his mouth opened and out flowed a torrent of blackness.

Another pop and the man fell, forward, the sledgehammer falling away but the man collapsing on top of Turnbull and then it was all darkness.

"Lucky you wore a helmet," said a man's voice as Turnbull shook his head, only just becoming aware again.

"I'm infantry," Turnbull said, slowly. "My head's not really a vital organ."

The man laughed – where was the man? Turnbull was aware that he was lying in some sort of bed, and he looked around. He was in a house, a nice one, with yellow walls. It hurt to move his head. Now, where was the man talking to him?

"You were almost the guest of honor at a scum dinner party," the man said. "And the entrée. Not a lot of other protein options out here these days."

Turnbull followed the sound and his eyes found a man in his fifties, trim, rugged, but well-put together. His moustache was trimmed, though a bit longer than currently fashionable, and his hair was neatly cut. He had a large frame chrome revolver in a shoulder holster. He was holding a wooden tray with a bowl and a spoon.

"You want some soup?"

"I want some answers."

"Can you be more specific?"

"My condition?"

The man laughed again.

"Your condition is that you are beat all to hell."

Turnbull sighed.

"Fractures?" Turnbull asked.

"None I can see. I don't have an X-ray, mind you, but I do have some medical knowledge from experience. You need it to survive out here."

Turnbull patted his own forehead awkwardly. There was a bandage over his right eye.

"Ten stitches. I've gotten good at stitches. I don't think you have any internal injuries. Lots of bruises and cuts. A miracle. I think landing on your ruck probably saved your ass."

Turnbull forced himself to sit up. He noted his tattered ruck in the corner, the crossbow bolt still stuck in it. His rifle was there too, and the Wilson, on a table at the other side of the room. Its slide was open.

"Nice gats," said the man. "Makes me wonder who you are. Sorry about the optic on that rifle though. It didn't make it."

"You capped the last bad guy," Turnbull said.

"I was out with my trusty FAL. You're lucky I went hunting by the cut last night. I had a feeling they might be out there looking for prey and I was sure right."

"Thanks," Turnbull said. "For that and all this. Not a lot of folks help out strangers these days."

"You know the good Samaritan story, right? Well, I take the Lord's word seriously. He saved me, so I try to save others."

"I appreciate it. You alone here?"

"Yeah. This is my compound. It's secure, but I'm way off the beaten path and being hidden is my best security. You ever read *Lord of the Rings*?"

"Does that have elves?"

"Yes, and hobbits. I'm like Tom Bombadil, without the songs."

"I don't know what that is."

"I help travelers and fight the monsters. The pagan scum, they would love to find me, make a meal of me."

"What is it with all these cannibals?" Turnbull said. "I hate cannibals."

"You and me both, brother. They showed up a few months ago, not too long after the invasion by the reds. We had always had bandits and bad guys out here in the desert since the blues left and even before. But these folks – they had an *ideology*. I talked to a wounded one once. Before he died, he tried to rip out my eyes even though I was helping him. Said they were going to kill every living thing on Earth, then themselves."

"Annihilationists," Turnbull said.

"That's what he said they called themselves."

"Yeah, I met some others a while ago. I guess this is a more aggro franchise, since I cooked all the others."

"Cooked?"

"Well, I didn't eat them," Turnbull assured his host.

"So, you got a name?"

"You can call me Kelly. And you?"

The man laughed. "You saying you don't know me? Take a look. Take a good look."

Turnbull squinted.

"Not a clue."

"Come on, be honest. Pretty much every man of your age knows me and my work."

"Drawing a blank."

"I was a movie star."

"I know Eastwood, Gibson, Baldwin, Marsden, and Senator Searcy, of course. That's about it."

"I've acted under a lot of names. Johnny Throb? Big Tom Stallion? Ginch Bangwell?"

Turnbull regarded the man quizzically.

"I was a porn star, Kelly. I did it for years. Come on, you look like a guy who has seen *Cheerleader Tickle Party V.* I got an award for that one. Best Performance While Aroused."

"You know, maybe you don't need to share that with strangers."

"Oh no," the man said. "I *have* to. Because if I hadn't fallen I'd have never risen up. I was on the floor of a Motel 6 in Van Nuys, high on meth, it hurting when I peed, thinking about diving off the balcony, and then I saw the Bible. It was in an open drawer, a drawer that I hadn't even opened. I started reading just to keep from killing myself. That was the start. I left LA, sold my Porsche and my condo, and bought this place. It saved my life. *He* saved my life. And I want to help others."

"You were a big help to me," Turnbull said, desperate to change the subject. "What's your real name then?"

"Bill Thomas. Pretty mundane, huh?"

"It's just fine, Bill."

"You know, I once did this special gig for these DC guys called *Conservative Cruise Cuckolds* where I played a pool boy named 'Raul.'"

"Bill, stop –"

"They wrote the script themselves and wanted me to act it out. I think they had a blog called *The Aardvark* or something. It was weird."

"I get the picture." Turnbull said. "And I need to get going. Going from here."

"You need to rest, but I thought you might be on some kind of mission, judging from your gear, just like the other guys."

"Other guys?"

"A group of guys passed by here a few days ago heading east. I spotted them, but when I tried to make contact to warn them they tried to cap me. They did not seem to be in any trouble then, but where they were going sure was. Right toward the Vantage Bridge over the Columbia River. The Annihilationists are all over it."

"These guys...?"

"Definitely military. Camo uniforms, top shelf gear. Even had a dog."

"A dog?"

"Like a German Shepherd or something. A military working dog."

Turnbull considered this development. He was not the only guy after the hot rock. Karl Martin Scott would need to recover it now that the secret was out thanks to INFERNO. And of course the team would have to go in on the ground. Anything that flies in the Gray Zone dies.

Now, there was a problem. He might be too late. And even if he wasn't, there were a bunch of competitors, and they were trained American Special Forces, albeit working for an asshole. They would not be pushovers. And they would not back down.

"Have your soup," Bill said. "Let's talk about you going places in the morning."

Turnbull could walk. It hurt everywhere – he was banged up but good – yet once he got going, and gobbled a handful of Motrin from his ruck, he found that he could function.

Next, he reviewed his gear. The weapons were okay, except for the optic on the HK416. The Wilson was a little scuffed from skidding across the blacktop but it was solid and the function check was a GO. The shotgun and Springfield were fine too.

The motorbike was toast, though, but a vehicle drew too much attention besides. He planned to hoof it.

"You want to move at night and lay up in the day," Bill told him. "Though they go out day and night. Out hunting."

"The best way to Hanford?"

Bill considered.

"It's a two, three-day walk. You want to stay off the roads, so it's cross country."

"What about this Vantage Bridge?"

"You stay the hell away from that," Bill warned. "Stay on the west side of the Columbia River and follow it south until the bend east. Keep following it. That will take you to Hanford, though I have no idea why anyone would want to go there. It's radioactive."

"How do you know?"

"Everyone knows. The whole area had been off-limits for years. The blues were always talking about the red's earthcrime of poisoning the land and such. Elizabeth Warren once came out and accused the United States of waging war on her people with gamma rays."

"Will I see many people on the way? Any settlements?"

"Not really. Putting aside the Annihilationists, there's no water, so no farms."

"What about the Columbia River?"

Bill laughed bitterly.

"The blues declared taking water for irrigation an earthcrime about a decade ago. Then they blew up the Priest Rapids Dam, the Wanapum Dam, and some others too. This place is fertile, only you need water. Without water, everything blew away in the wind. And then there's the electricity. They talked all day about climate change and renewable power, and then they demolished the dams that generated hydroelectric power. You think what power they had left was going to their pals in Seattle, or out here to a bunch of angry country folk?"

"So I am walking through a man-made desert?"

"Pretty much. It was paradise when I came here before the Split."

"The whole country was paradise before the Split," Turnbull said. "People were just too stupid to realize it."

He left at sundown, rifle in hand, ruck on his back. Bill had a well and Turnbull had all the fresh water he could carry. Hopefully it would be enough to get him to the Columbia River. There was not much moisture in between.

Bill's compound was south of the interstate a few miles and located in a secluded and wooded draw. You would have to stumble on it to see it. Bill tried not to use his motor vehicles so that there would be no tracks leading back. He could have driven, since his gas tank on the property held almost a thousand gallons – quite the prize for bandits and Annihilationists had they known. He had managed to bring back the Mustang intact and salvage five more gallons from the wrecked motorcycles.

Bill was burying the various body parts that had been attached to his newest vehicle. After thanking his host, Turnbull started off, the sun setting behind him in the west. He walked out of sight as Bill said a prayer over the remains.

Turnbull walked at a reasonable pace, but frequently dropped to his knee to listen. Listening was underrated. It would be initially quiet when he did, as if the whole word held its breath. But, after a couple minutes, he would be aware of the noises. The wind. The bugs. The cries of animals. Sometimes, he thought he heard the whine of engines from the north, where I-90 ran parallel to the first leg of his route.

He saw no other humans, and very few animals, except perhaps the odd jackrabbit or crow. Above him, the stars were bright and he had plenty of illumination. There were occasional dirt roads, and if they looked unused – and most showed no evidence of recent vehicular transit – then he would follow them a ways, but carefully. If they led into a defile or if the terrain ahead looked like where he would choose to set an ambush, he got off the road and went around the danger area.

The sun was below the horizon ahead. He had made slow progress, but the terrain was not easy and he listened and rested frequently. Slow, he told himself, was fast. Fast was sloppy, and sloppy could get him killed.

Besides, he needed some time to figure out his play when he got to Hanford. He would be facing an Operational Detachment-Alpha plussed up with a working dog and some EOD guys. Explosive ordnance disposal, well, now that made sense.

They were not going to just give him a thermonuclear warhead no matter how nicely he asked them.

He found a good little draw to make camp in. He figured the Columbia River was over some hills a half-mile ahead or so, give or take. There were no tracks in the area; it did not appear anyone came there. And it was sheltered – he could have some shade, but enough concealment that an enemy would have to stumble on him to find him.

He got out his ruck and laid his HK416 beside him. He changed his socks, one at a time, and would sleep in his boots. After a couple Quest bars and a slug of well water, he lay back and listened. He listened for a long time.

Nothing out of the ordinary.

Assured that all was secure – at least, that all was as secure as it could be in the middle of a failed state on the North American continent – he allowed himself to fall into sleep.

15.

A growl.

Low.

Close.

Turnbull opened his eyes.

The dog was at his feet, sitting, staring into his eyes. It looked like a German Shepard to him, but smaller.

A Belgian Malinois.

The handsome animal wore a black harness around his thick chest. There was a black name tape with gold lettering.

"Gibson."

Turnbull reached for the rifle resting to his right. The dog growled again.

Teeth.

Turnbull pulled his hand back and the growling stopped.

Where was the team? He wondered. They should have been rolling him up and zip tying him by now. But there was just the dog.

Watching him.

Turnbull looked the animal over more closely.

He was dirty, bedraggled even. And he had burrs in his fur and some cuts on his body caked with dry blood.

Turnbull craned his neck to look around.

Nobody. The dog was alone.

"You want some water?" he asked the dog, who did not answer. He just stared back.

Carefully, slowly, Turnbull sat up. The dog did not react, did not try to tear out his throat. That was a relief.

Very, very slowly, Turnbull pulled himself out of the sleeping bag. The dog registered no objection. He was very careful not to touch his weapons or make any move toward them with his hand – he was no dog handler and no expert, but he suspected that the intelligent animal knew what a weapon was and was trained to take out anyone who was not authorized to have one.

Was Turnbull authorized? That was the question.

He was an American soldier, and the dog had met him before in garrison. Maybe that gave him a bit of wiggle room that some civilian the animal just encountered out in the field would not get. On the other hand, maybe it would not.

Turnbull resolved not to find out. Hence, he did not reach for his weapons.

"You want some water?" he asked again. He slowly reached for his water bottle. The dog watched intently. Turnbull looked for something to pour it in and, realizing the Gortex of his fartsack might work, pressed a little bowl into it and poured in a half-cup of water.

Gibson looked at the water, then looked at Turnbull. Turnbull splashed his fingers in it.

"Go on."

The dog came forward cautiously, smelled the water, then lapped it up, first slowly then quickly. Turnbull added more when it ran dry, then refilled it again a third time. The dog finished it and licked the damp surface of the waterproof fabric.

"How did you get out here?" Turnbull said aloud. The dog looked at him.

One thing was certain. His master was out of the picture, maybe captured, probably dead. Dog handlers were fanatics for their animals. There was no way he was getting separated from his dog if he had a choice.

And if the handler was dead, the rest of the team probably was too.

He decided to feed the dog with the Chinese military ration that featured the cartoon caricature of the pangolin. Gibson was puzzled by the mass of gray meat and the orange, gelatinous sauces, sniffing it before taking a tentative lick. Hunger has a way of overcoming food fussiness. The canine gulped it all down, along with a packet of pale, moist noodles. Turnbull himself ate another Quest bar, though he was running out of them.

The dog licked the plastic packaging clean.

"You must really be hungry," Turnbull said.

Gibson allowed Turnbull to examine him and gently pick off the burrs. His paws were okay. His cuts were shallow, but they seemed to be made not by random accidents but by cutting edges. Blades.

That meant Annihilationists.

Had the savages somehow gotten the drop on a team of Green Berets? Maybe they had surprised and overwhelmed the operators. Turnbull had no idea how many scum there were out there, driving around looking for victims. Whatever happened, the dog survived. Maybe some of them did too.

The Green Beret survivors would be heading to Hanford.

"Okay Gibson," Turnbull said. The dog alerted. He knew his own name.

"Let's get going."

Turnbull packed up his gear, and the dog wandered off. But it was clear it was not aimless wandering, sniffing around like some suburban Corgi on a walk. He was patrolling, ensuring the area was clear. He came loping back as Turnbull stood up with his ruck.

Gibson sat and looked at Turnbull.

"Okay, the big test," Turnbull said. He slowly reached down to pick up his rifle.

The dog did not tear his throat out. He just waited.

"Come on," Turnbull said, pulling the sling over his head. He started walking out of the draw and turned east.

Gibson followed him down then passed him, sprinting forward about twenty meters before turning to look back.

"Go on," Turnbull said, following. "You got point."

Gibson turned and walked ahead.

They went for a while, seeing nothing, but Gibson then started, his ears up. Turnbull went to a knee, weapon ready. He listened.

Engine noises ahead, over the hills.

He waited. Gibson did not move. The noise faded.

After a time, they pressed on.

"Well," Turnbull said, observing the wreckage that had been an engineering marvel. "It looks like it was a dam, once."

He and Gibson were below the military crest of a hill west of the Columbia River, looking down to the east. There had been a dam there, but it was now just some concrete embankments jutting out from both sides of the river. There were pieces of the blasted barrier immediately downstream of the ruins, and north of it there was a great dry basin on each side of the much narrower river where the former lake had once been.

Probably the Wanapum Dam and the former Wanapum Lake, Turnbull decided. Bill had let him review an old AAA map before he departed.

The terrain dropped from the hills about a quarter mile to the water line. There were dirt roads running parallel to the river north and south, but they did not look like they got much use. Across the river there was a blacktop road running north-south and some deserted farm buildings. There were no farmers here anymore.

They moved on. He saw some coyotes, who eyed him, trying to decide if he was food.

Turnbull and Gibson kept walking.

Noise. Engines. From the east.

He squinted, as the sun was still somewhat to the east. Across the river he could see a pack of vehicles, some cars, some trucks, and some motorcycles, heading south fast on the blacktop. Even from that distance, without binoculars, he could see the chaos.

"Annihilationists," he said aloud. The dog was alert and all business.

The little pack of malignant mutants disappeared.

"Let's go," Turnbull said. They would keep to the high ground as they walked south, alongside, but at a distance from, the river.

They continued on for about 15 minutes, and then the dog alerted again. Turnbull took a knee. His rifle was ready.

"She's crying now," someone said, mockingly. It was hard to hear. It sounded like it was coming over a radio.

"You save some for me!" said a voice perhaps a hundred meters south and out of sight on the other side of a rise. Absolutely no noise discipline.

"Ain't saving nothing!"

"I'm coming down!" insisted the voice ahead of him.

"You best stay put," the voice on the radio said, followed by a chilling giggle. "Boss gonna be pissed if you leave."

"I spotted 'em and I want a piece!" insisted the nearby one. "We're coming."

"Ain't gonna be none left!" chuckled the voice on the radio. He laughed again.

"Asshole!" shouted his antagonist.

Gibson looked to Turnbull, as if asking for the play, but Turnbull was already moving with the HK416 ready.

They went up the rise, Turnbull sweeping the horizon for targets. The dog was low and focused.

At the apex of the rise, Turnbull chose speed and aggression – he came up fast, scanning for targets on the downslope.

There was a primitive camp about twenty feet below them. A campfire cast up a thin tendril of smoke, while a sort of dune buggy creation, with big tires, an open cockpit, and femur bones zip tied to the roll bar, sat as one of the two men occupying the camp loaded it with gear.

The observation post had a wide view of the river frontage below. There was even a pair of battered binoculars on the hood of their ride. You could see everything, from what was probably the Vantage Bridge to the north to a couple miles south where there was what looked like a high, black railroad bridge over the Columbia serving an abandoned east-west train line.

The two occupants looked like a couple of homeless derelicts, right down to the cackling and unfocused, wide-eyed stares. They wore rags and one wore scuba goggles – it was unclear whether that was because the dune buggy had no windshield or because it was a fashion choice.

Next to him were an axe and a Motorola. That probably meant he was the brains of the outfit.

Turnbull drew a bead on the other one, who had just noticed him and paused in tossing a tattered sleeping bag into the vehicle. Turnbull squeezed off three 5.56mm rounds. The suppressor did its job – the noise did not echo off the hilltop. The impacts on the Annihilationist's chest sent up little puffs of dust from his filthy poncho and he staggered backwards and fell to the dirt.

The other was shocked by the onslaught, and Turnbull could see the wheels in his pea-brain turning – axe or radio?

Turnbull pivoted the barrel to him as he trotted down the rise into camp.

"You move and I'll kill you," he said.

The Annihilationist smiled an intermittently toothed grin.

"You think I care?" he cackled.

Gibson sprinted forward and set himself about ten feet to the man's front as Turnbull followed. The dog growled.

Now the man was not grinning. Bullets were one thing. Teeth were something else entirely.

"This is an OP," Turnbull said, the HK416 still locked onto the man's chest. "What are you dirtbags observing?"

The man swallowed, but was silent.

"I'll ask you again before I let Fido eat your spleen," Turnbull explained. "What are you observing from what is obviously an observation post?"

"You and your mutt can't do worse to me than the boss will."

"That sounds like a challenge," Turnbull replied. Gibson growled, low and serious.

"We're looking for runners," the man said. "Spotted some."

Turnbull came forward.

"Watch him," he told the dog, whose eyes never left his prey.

Turnbull walked over to the dune buggy's dented and dusty hood and swooped up the binoculars. He scanned the terrain below.

There it was, off the dirt road on the near side of the river – an Annihilationist jalopy and what looked like an old government issue white pick-up truck that had gone headfirst into a ditch.

Two scum were walking around down there. A man, not an Annihilationist, was on the ground and not moving. And there was a woman, still moving, but naked and bleeding...

"I'm taking your party invitation," Turnbull said and shot the man through the temple.

The dog looked indifferently at the man's corpse as it twitched, then trotted over to Turnbull to get a pat.

The dune buggy came down the hill toward the pair of vehicles, kicking up dust as it came. One Annihilationist dressed like a Tusken Raider from some dumb *Star Wars* show was trying to siphon gas out of the white government Chevrolet Silverado and having trouble getting the hose into his jerry can. The truck said "Hanford Base Operations" in fading black block letters on the door. Nearby was the Annihilationists' ride, a 2020s Mustang that looked fifty years rather than a dozen years old. The hood was spray-painted in red with the words "DIE DIE DIE."

These freaks sure love their pony cars, Turnbull thought.

The other Annihilationist was dressed in an elaborate leather harness worn over cutoffs from a baby blue tracksuit with black combat boots. He had a leather codpiece too, but that was lying in the dirt where he had peeled it off earlier. He had spread out a plastic sheet on the dirt and was taking out a bag filled with knives. He selected a gleaming, black-handled boning knife from the collection, which he had looted from a particularly nice McMansion near Yakima. He looked up at the approaching dune buggy and grinned. He obviously cared more for his blades than his teeth.

"Shut up, bitch," he snapped at the bloodied woman crumpled on the ground a few feet away after she moaned. He turned his attention back to the fully-clothed corpse of a man that lay beside his workspace. Its head had been bashed in by the Raider with a crowbar.

Near the front of the truck were two M16A2 rifles leaning against the pick-up's front fender with a couple of ammo bandoliers lying on the dirt beside them.

The dune buggy slowed and stopped about ten feet away at an angle, presenting the passenger side. There was one man in it, dressed in a stained poncho and wearing scuba goggles with his face wrapped by a stained brown rag.

The butcher put down his knife and stood up, grinning even wider, then walked toward the new arrival.

"Saved her for ya," he cackled. "But you better go quick cuz she's draining good."

He reached the dune buggy.

"Get him," ordered Turnbull from the driver's side.

Gibson was on the man, leaping upwards from the passenger seat. It occurred to Turnbull that there must be a key word, probably in German to minimize the chance of it being uttered by mistake, that launched the dog at a target, but Gibson was absolutely clear on Turnbull's intent.

He went directly for the face.

Turnbull rolled out of the driver's seat, tearing off the scuba goggles and the bandana with his left hand while drawing his Wilson with his right.

The Raider looked up and screeched, an inhuman sound that seemed it could not have come from a man. He left the siphon line spitting fuel on the dirt next to the can and picked up his bloody crowbar, as the rifles were in the other direction.

He charged.

Turnbull took aim and fired. The first round slammed into the center of Raider's chest, then another followed. The raider staggered backwards and howled again – loud enough to be heard over his buddy's frenzied screams and Gibson's growls.

The raider lumbered forward. Turnbull fired, again and again and again, the rounds kicking up little eruptions of dust on his chest and pushing him back each time.

The shrieking Annihilationist kept coming – he was a dozen feet away – so Turnbull tried a new tactic.

He shot the man in the face.

That did the trick. The raider collapsed in a heap, the pinkish puff of vaporized occipital lobe lingering in the air for a moment as the man fell face-forward into the dirt.

Turnbull walked over to where Gibson was working on his prey. It was very loud, and Gibson was very thorough.

"Ouch," Turnbull said aloud, watching for a moment. Gibson had exhausted the possibilities of the soft flesh of the face and moved on, with gusto, to the soft flesh of the crotch.

Should have put on your codpiece, Turnbull thought to himself.

Turnbull lifted his pistol, then saw the woman and decided to save the round. He reloaded a fresh mag and visually confirmed that the Hanford man was dead. Turnbull walked over to the woman, holstering his handgun, as Gibson kept at his target.

There was a ragged wound in her abdomen, and copious amounts of blood. She was alive, barely, but pale.

Turnbull knelt beside her. Gibson's chew toy was still shrieking.

Before he could say a word – he was searching for ones to offer the dying woman – she rallied and took his forearm in her hand.

"The gear," she sputtered, scarlet lining her teeth and gums. "Get it back."

"Quiet," said Turnbull. He looked at that wound, then he took out a field dressing packet that he had slipped into his pocket before assuming his ruse identity. Direct pressure was all he had to offer, and it was not going to be enough.

"Get it to Hanford," she sputtered. "The gear."

She coughed up a great mass of blood and fell backwards on the dirt, her breathing heavy and labored.

Turnbull ripped open the dressing pack and pressed it to her ragged cut, bracing for her scream.

Nothing.

Her eyes were open but lifeless. Turnbull stood up, leaving the dressing on the wound, and walked over to where the dog was still going to town on the survivor.

"Here, Gibson," he said. This was not a formal command either, but the dog understood and backed off. The Annihilationist lay on his side in something like a fetal position, rocking back and forth in agony. Turnbull looked over his wounds.

Well, this guy's days of raping were over. And seeing. And tasting, Turnbull concluded.

Gibson's muzzle was bright red, and he sat next to Turnbull.

"Good boy," Turnbull said, petting him. He wiped the resulting blood off on the polluted poncho, which he took off over his head and dropped on the ground.

A visual check of the guy who was sort of alive confirmed that the mangled rapist had no weapons hidden in his crisscrossed leather gear.

Turnbull walked over to the raider and kicked him solidly in the ribs to confirm that he really was expired. The boot hit something solid, and Turnbull checked it out. The guy was wearing a Kevlar plate under his rags.

He was most certainly dead now.

Their gear, Turnbull remembered. He walked to the pick-up and peered into the cab. The rear window of the Silverado had been smashed in by something, probably that crowbar.

But there was no gear in the cab, no rucks or packs. No TA-50 or tacticool crap. Just glass, blood, and some scrap paper lying on the seat. No shell casings either. The Hanford folks did not even get a shot off. But they clearly were not warriors, and they were clearly outclassed by these savages even with firearms.

He checked out the truck bed. There was a dirty canvas bag lying open with a bunch of worn tools – wrenches, screwdrivers, that sort of thing – having spilled out. There were some parts lying there in the bed that looked like they came from a vehicle – some black hoses of various lengths with undone clamps on each end, a headlight with red and blue wires hanging off it, and a large round circular metal object with teeth along its outer edge.

No gear though. Did she mean the rifles? It couldn't be them. Hanford was a nuclear installation. They had to have plenty of rifles. They would never miss these two.

So, where was the gear?

Turnbull pondered the question for a moment.

Gear, he thought.

"Oh shit," he said aloud, and went to the cab. The big, toothed wheel – was that a gear? Like a machine gear, instead of personal effects gear.

He went back to the cab and leaned in, looking at the papers. He found what he was looking for – a piece of paper with neat handwriting.

Hoses. Headlight. Timing gear. With little check marks by each.

A shopping list.

For some reason, this timing gear was very important to these two, important enough to risk their lives and to lose them.

He would take the Annihilationist's Mustang. It looked like it sported a V-8, and it was a piece of history to boot. It would have been a shame to pass it up. He added the siphoned gas from the other vehicles to the Mustang's tank. That gave him a quarter tank, plenty for where he was headed.

Turnbull threw the scavenged parts into the backseat. He took both M16s plus the ammo and the binoculars too. He put his own gear inside as well.

Turnbull toyed with taking the bodies of the Hanford pair, but he decided not to. He put the man and woman into the cab of their truck and shut the door.

Gibson hopped inside the Mustang when Turnbull opened the door. There was a groan, and Turnbull looked over at the writhing rapist for a moment before getting in, firing up the engine, and driving away.

Gibson would not be the only animal that piece of trash fed today.

16.

It would be a rough drive on the dirt road through the hills that ran south to the west of the Columbia River. Gibson sat in the passenger seat, occasionally poking his head out into the dusty wind. They did not see any more Annihilationists until well after the bend in the river.

The Columbia turned east about ten miles south of the site of the killings, ran a few miles, then fishhooked north and back south again. Inside that fishhook was the enormous, nearly 600 square mile Hanford site. But, at least according to Bill's AAA map, much of it was undeveloped desert. The actual buildings were in discrete clumps, much like how a military base often has a main post surrounded by miles and miles of empty training areas. And this was not surprising. The Army built Hanford in 1943 to house the nuclear reactors necessary to produce the plutonium that would go into the Nagasaki A-bomb. For decades, throughout the Cold War, the Hanford complex had generated the materials needed for America's nuclear arsenal. But when the Soviet Union fell, the focus became closing down the remaining reactors. Of course, with radioactive materials, there is no real closing. Up until the Split, there had been some further research and work, but the focus was on figuring out how to clean up the contamination, with particular attention to protecting the Columbia River and the millions downstream.

That was all Turnbull knew, because that was all Bill knew. Except for the fact that the entire area was poisoned by deadly radiation.

"The signs warn you that if you go in, you'll glow," Bill had told Turnbull. "I'm paraphrasing. They talk about extreme radiation hazards and tell you that it's deadly. I've gone as far as the signs and the barbed wire fence across the desert."

"You never went inside?" Turnbull had asked.

"Kelly," Bill replied, "when a sign tells me something's deadly, I'm giving it the benefit of the doubt and a wide berth."

Now, driving the Mustang he had earned through combat, Turnbull considered the facts.

The signs said the place is a nuclear death trap, but there were obviously people living in there. And in some sort of organized community.

The promise of a grisly death from radiation sickness was a pretty good way to deter intruders, but then that assumed something that was not necessarily true.

That the intruders feared a grisly death.

Turnbull and his dog passed by another blown-up dam and dried-out reservoir down below them. This was where the Columbia River turned toward the east. It was also where the dirt road they were on continued south.

It was hard going. The Mustang was not designed as an off-road vehicle, though someone along the way had tried to make it one by working on the suspension. After a couple hours of slow going, they crossed a two-lane blacktop road running generally southwest to northeast.

Turnbull considered his options and decided to take his chances on the road. He got on it and headed toward Hanford.

There was a four-way intersection in the middle of nowhere. A barbed wire fence ran north to south along the east side, and the road heading east led to what had clearly once been a guard shack a couple hundred meters past the intersection. The gate itself was gone – you could drive through it if you swerved around some derelict cars and various other bits of debris.

And Bill was right about the signage. There were plenty of signs and they were lurid. The different signs were all under a decade old, as they all carried the legend "BY ORDER OF THE PEOPLE'S REPUBLIC OF NORTH AMERICA," and bore some version of the multi-colored PR national flag.

"RADIATION HAZARD – KEEP OUT," was the simplest one. It had a pictogram of a diverse group of people – a male, a female, a male-female hybrid, a fat guy, and a dude in a turban plus one in a wheelchair – all with Xs for eyes. Turnbull assumed that meant they were dying. Another sign warned, "DEADLY RADIATION HAZARD – FATAL TO HUMANS AND OTHERKIN." The sign featured a pictogram of a person with a tail.

The largest sign read, "THIS POISONED AREA CONTAINS FATAL RADIATION AND THE PRNA ACKNOWLEDGES IT EXISTS ON LAND STOLEN FROM INDIGENOUS PEOPLX INCLUDING THE WANAPUM, YAKAMA, NEZ PERCE, AND UMATILLA PEOPLX." Someone had spray painted over it "ALEX ABEY IS A PARTY BUNGHOLE" with no further explanation.

Turnbull drove forward, slowly because there was debris on the pavement. Then he stopped. A man in a torn sundress carrying what looked like a halberd and a shield came out of the ruined guard shack, his sunburned face twisted with a smile that highlighted a set of yellow teeth.

He waved his weapon as he stepped out – apparently he was the guard. His smile changed when he walked toward the driver's window and saw the barrel of the .45.

It was the last thing he saw.

Turnbull rolled out of the vehicle and charged the guard house, clearing it without finding any more Annihilationists. There was a Motorola handset left on, and there was some chatter, most of it incoherent grunts and shouts. But one voice was clear.

"Soon, we will kill them all."

That's not auspicious, Turnbull thought to himself as he got back in his ride. He hit the gas and entered the Hanford Site.

There were a lot more signs on the two-lane road, which went straight east across the flat desert terrain. A long series of them, like a Burma-Shave gag except strung out on a dozen signs in sequence, explained how the site itself was a giant atrocity perpetrated by the "RACIST EARTHCRIMINALS OF THE FORMER UNITED STATES" and then apologizing to "THE EARTH MOTHER SHE-BEAR HELD SACRED BY THE INDIGENOUS PEOPLX" of the area.

Turnbull was unsure that was even a thing, but whether it was a thing or not a thing did not matter. He searched ahead for other vehicles. And he noted that he was at about an eighth of a tank of go juice.

"Well, that's interesting," Turnbull said, scanning the scene ahead with the binos. The car was behind him in a shallow draw, and he was on his stomach was looking at a stockade, a fort in the midst of the desert. The sign back behind him at the turn-off had called it "200 East." There were a bunch of large tanks containing who knew what, but there were a few blocks of buildings, many industrial, protected by an honest-to-goodness wall at least 15 feet high. It was of black sheet metal, with barbed wire lining the top.

And the Annihilationists were driving around it, at least a few of them were, roaring in long, lazy circles. The majority of them were camped out of rifle range on a slight rise a half-mile west of the fort. There were at least two dozen vehicles, a number of them RVs. They had an actual encampment, with cooking fires and tents.

It was a siege. The Annihilationists clearly wanted to take the fort, probably slaughter the inhabitants and help themselves to whatever food, gas, and guns the defenders had hoarded.

"They have no idea what those people have in there," Turnbull told Gibson. Gibson was not interested.

Turnbull moved the binos to scan the walls. There must be a walkway on top because he saw bobbing heads and rifles – M16s, like the ones the unfortunates had and had failed to use. Several vehicles lay wrecked or smoldering outside the wall near the main gate. The attackers kept moving, and if they were not moving they were back outside the effective range of the defenders' firearms. It was pretty obvious to Turnbull that the circling vehicles were there to keep the defenders occupied – and to wear them down.

Turnbull kept observing. The cycle of harassment went on. Occasionally, a defender would pop off some rounds if a motorcycle or car came too close, but that was it.

Now it was mid-afternoon. Turnbull had been watching at a distance for a couple hours and nothing seemed to be happening except there were fewer raiders circling the fort – just a couple cars and some motorcycles. Enough to keep the defenders on edge without wasting too much gas.

I'd attack at sundown, or dawn, Turnbull thought. And he was aware that every minute he stayed where he was risked discovery.

"You know what they won't be expecting," Turnbull told Gibson. "Someone trying to break *in.*"

He stood up.

"Get in the car, dog."

Turnbull drove toward the encampment just a little faster than made sense, to better fit in with the crowd. There was no reaction from the campers. They were going about their business, which included working on vehicles, cooking, and fist-fighting with each other. They did not pay any mind to the Mustang coming their way, or to how it turned toward the fort and hit the gas.

Of the four or five vehicles still circling the fort, only a pair of motorcycles were on the gate side when Turnbull approached.

One rider broke off to meet him coming in. He wore a blood-stained Patagonia down vest with a bandolier of steak knives across his chest. The rider slowed and pulled up beside the Mustang, squinting and baffled.

"Ya ain't Jake!" he shouted, audible even over the engines.

Turnbull smiled as he lifted up one of the salvaged M16s, and said, "Jake's dead."

He fired a three-round burst, then another. Several of the rounds slammed into the rider. His bike wobbled, and it fell, his corpse tumbling through the brush.

Turnbull glanced in his rear-view.

The encampment had noticed that. He just hoped the defenders had too, since it was for their benefit.

Turnbull turned his attention back to his front. The gate was about 400 meters ahead of him, and the other biker was charging him head-on with a spear he was using as a lance.

Turnbull aimed the car directly at the oncoming motorcycle but the rider did not turn or evade – he came straight in.

Turnbull pressed the accelerator.

The spear point hit the windshield directly in front of where Turnbull's face would have been had he not bent to the right. The point impacted, spreading a spider web of cracks across the glass, but it did not catch and deflected upwards. By this time, the front grill and the motorcycle had collided and the rider was flying over the hood. He struck the glass in front of the passenger seat and his head, shoulders, and an arm broke through and wedged in the hole.

The rider's eyes opened, bloodshot and wide, and his arm inside the cabin came to life and grabbed at Turnbull with greasy fingers wielding overgrown, dirty nails. Pulling the M16 around, Turnbull pushed the barrel into the rider's throat and fired a burst. The body went limp and when his mouth opened a torrent of red vomited out on the floor.

Turnbull kept going, even after the crunch of the motorcycle under the tires that caused the Mustang to make a grinding sound as it went. It was a couple hundred meters to the gate and he did not slow down until he was directly in front of the portal. There, he stopped.

No fusillade of gunfire from the wall. That was good.

He opened the door and stepped out with two objects in his hands, the M16 and the timing gear.

"Don't you move!" shouted a young voice from above. "If you move, we shoot!"

Turnbull looked over his shoulder. The encampment was alive now, and cars and bikes were streaming his way.

"I saw your people," Turnbull yelled. "And I got this." He held up the timing gear.

"You just don't move! You wait!"

"No time to wait," Turnbull yelled. The mass of Annihilationists was coming. Inside the car, Gibson growled.

"Who are you?" It was a different voice, older.

"I'm the guy with the timing gear and the answers. Now, you best open that gate and let me in or you aren't getting either."

Silence.

"Shit," Turnbull said, observing a bright pink Chevrolet Camaro with a dead body strapped to the roof coming in from the side – it was one of the circling vehicles.

Turnbull threw the timing gear back into the Mustang and lay the M16 on the roof. He took aim, and began firing three-round bursts. The oncoming windshield erupted in geysers of pulverized safety glass but it kept heading straight in on him. He fired another burst, and another, and the third burst of three rounds was the charm. The Chevy pitched right and slid to a stop against the fort's steel wall. The two occupants inside were not moving.

Looking up, Turnbull saw the rest of the Annihilationists bearing down on him.

"Are you letting me in or what?" he shouted at the faces looking at him from above.

There was silence.

Then the gate split and the hinges protested as several figures pulled the two doors wide open.

Turnbull dived back behind the wheel, shifted to "Drive" and hit the gas. The Mustang accelerated into the compound and slid to a stop. Behind him, the defenders were now pushing the doors closed again. And outside the gate, the horde had arrived.

A crossbow bolt flew through the gap and planted itself in the sheet metal of the Mustang's trunk just as the gate clanged shut and they dropped the crossbar.

So many guns in his face now.

He heard a growl.

"Gibson, chill!" he commanded.

The people were not warriors, though they had guns and were dressed in old American military camo. He could see they were scared, and they were right to be, but scared people make mistakes and he did not intend to get himself or his pet dead because one of these amateurs was jumpy.

He held his hands up. Other hands took his Wilson and his Gerber and roughly moved him along across the compound. There were many buildings, all definitely government issue, and he was headed to the one that appeared to be the headquarters.

"Don't mess with my dog," he said loudly. "Hurting him will get us off on the wrong foot."

"Just move," said one of them, a woman, who was hustling him into the building.

He was sitting in a government issue swivel chair in an office with a linoleum floor. It smelled like industrial disinfectant. Gibson sat on the tile at his side, watching. An older man who had introduced himself as Dr. Mondavi was apparently the head honcho. Of course, he had not had to introduce himself verbally. Like all the rest, he had a nametag pinned on his uniform where the nametape would be. It read "Dr. Peter Mondavi, Physics Supervisor."

The rest of the defenders in the room were middle-aged, mostly, men and women. They all carried M16s, and they carried them like people who had never been trained to carry them. And they all had name tags pinned on. Most were some type of doctor. Apparently, their exact titles were very important to them.

The one whose badge read simply "Leia Purcell" was not. She had short brown hair and an attitude. A SIG 17 pistol was holstered at her side in addition to her rifle. She was Turnbull's guard.

"Who are you?" Dr. Mondavi asked, leaning in. "Why are you here and what do you want? How did you get this?" He held up the timing gear.

"You can call me Kelly," Turnbull said. "A few miles back I came across two of your people. They were bushwhacked after their shopping trip."

"Where are they?"

"They didn't make it. But neither did the assholes who killed them."

Dr. Mondavi sighed, and there were groans. One of the women in the group sobbed. The doctor composed himself and wiped his head. He seemed sweaty.

"We worked together, all of us, for over a decade. We're not fighters."

"Speak for yourself, Doctor," Purcell said.

"Leia spent a lot of time with our security folks, before they ran off."

"Well, you better learn to be fighters because those freaks you got camped outside – they are bad news."

"We learned long ago that we can only help ourselves," the doctor said. "Why did you come in here and risk dying with us?"

"Because you have something, doctor, something you've been keeping for a long time. And I need it."

"What are you talking about?" asked the doctor. He was not good at deception.

"The bomb."

Dr. Mondavi paused, thinking.

"You're here to get it?"

"Yeah."

"We don't know who he is!" Leia said.

"I'm the guy who's here," Turnbull said. "And I don't see anyone else coming."

The doctor continued.

"We were told there would be a whole team. Where's the rest of the team?"

Turnbull reached down and pet Gibson.

"He's the rest of the team. The others didn't make it. Now let me see it."

Dr. Mondavi nodded. "Come with me."

"You can't show him!" Purcell protested.

"It has to go Leia. It has to."

They went to another building, marked "SPECIAL MATERIALS 200E-79." Inside, there were several doors, each of which had a lock. Then it was down a ramp and through another vault door.

"This is it," Dr. Mondavi said.

The bomb was on a cart. It had been worked on. Lights were flashing. It looked like Turnbull vaguely remembered it, except now it seemed to be pristine.

"Will it work?" Turnbull asked.

"That was our order. Repair it and safeguard it. We have, for a decade."

"Who gave you the order?"

"Didn't your people?"

Turnbull decided not to elaborate.

"What about the blues?" asked Turnbull.

"What about them? They left us alone, except when we asked for some signs and to build the wall early on. There have been bandits here since the Split, though obviously nothing like what you see out there now. The radiation thing scared the blues, so they obliged. The reds were paying for the maintenance here at

Hanford for a couple years after the Split, part of the Treaty of St. Louis. The blues did not want anything to do with us. They thought the whole place was contaminated, and there are tanks of radioactive sludge, but it's mostly under control. Mostly. They left us alone. And we did our job – making sure the radioisotopes don't find their way into the river, keeping thieves out of the equipment, and maintaining that." Dr. Mondavi pointed to the hydrogen bomb.

"You didn't think it was weird that they asked you to hide a nuclear weapon?"

"I worked with nuclear weapons my entire career. And after the Split, nothing struck me as weird anymore."

A young man, maybe twenty, came running down the ramp.

"They want to talk," he said. Turnbull recognized the voice – it was the one who was initially shouting commands to him at the gate.

"Let's go," said Dr. Mondavi, carefully closing the vault door that hid the bomb. They left the building and went out into the open compound, heading to the gate.

Turnbull followed the others up the stairs to the catwalk. They had not agreed to return his weapons yet and he felt naked. Dr. Mondavi was by his side, and so was the young man. His nametag just said "GLENN MONDAVI."

At the landing at the top of the wall, the panorama came into view. Out about four hundred meters were the lined-up vehicles of the Annihilationists. It was supposed to impress upon the defenders their situation, and it worked – at least on Turnbull.

We're screwed, Turnbull thought.

In the center of the line was a man in a jockstrap waving a white sheet affixed to a pole.

"Parley, parley!" he was shouting, flapping his flag back and forth. He wore what looked like – what Turnbull realized were – US Army night vision goggles.

"Come forward, slowly," Dr. Mondavi shouted. Like everyone but Turnbull, he held an M16.

Flag Waver turned and walked to a pink convertible Cadillac El Dorado, probably from the seventies. It was heavily tricked-out, with jacked up wheels that allowed it to cruise over the dirt. He assisted a man to climb down from the backseat, and then began helping the man to come forward. The other man limped, favoring his right leg.

"No way," Turnbull said.

The pair came forward until they stood right outside the gate, the sheet fluttering in the wind.

The limping man was horribly burned. The right side of his face looked like a melted candle.

"I offer you a chance for life, for at least a little while longer," the hideous creature shouted.

Turnbull was acutely aware that he was unarmed. He pivoted to Dr. Mondavi.

"Shoot this guy," he said. "Shoot him now."

"He's under a flag of truce," the scientist replied, annoyed.

"He's a psychotic who wants to kill you all. Take him out!"

"He's right," Purcell said. She hefted her rifle.

"Stand fast," said Dr. Mondavi. "We're not savages."

"That's what he's counting on," grumbled Turnbull.

"Listen to me," the melted man shouted. "You can live, at least as long as everyone else lives. But I need what you have."

"If we give you some food and some gas, will you go away?" asked Dr. Mondavi.

The man cackled.

"That's not what I want. You *know* what I want."

"I don't."

"Your guests, they were coming to get it. But they met up with us and they aren't coming anymore. Though they were delicious," the man said merrily. "They told us, after some convincing, what you have in there."

"Shit, they know," Turnbull said.

"What do you mean?" Dr. Mondavi said, lamely trying his hand at deception again.

"I want the bomb," the man said. "The hot rock, the big fire!"

"You would think I taught you not to play with fire," Turnbull said, peering over the wall.

"You!" shouted the man, taken aback.

"What are you doing?" hissed Dr. Mondavi. He coughed.

Turnbull ignored him.

"So, you still going by Tommy Doom? Because I thought that was a stupid name. Same with The Last."

"I'm still The Last," Tommy Doom said. "And I have got a new flock."

"I guess a bunch of soft college nerds weren't cutting it genocide-wise, huh? What did you do this time, open up the loony bins and pick the MVPs?"

"Well, the People's Republic did not believe in mental health in-patient treatment," The Last said, now seeing the humor in the situation. "I just recruited likely candidates where I found them, and we have built a family dedicated to restoring to Gaia what is hers!"

"Kind of like the Manson family, except uglier."

"You be silent!" shrieked Flag Waver. "We will die for him!"

"Okay," Turnbull said. "Your terms are acceptable."

The Last put his hands on his toady's shoulder.

"Be still," he whispered. Then he addressed the defenders again.

"It's selfish to keep what you have to yourselves."

"Now you want us to just hand you a bomb?" asked Turnbull.

"I've learned to appreciate fire," The Last said. His mind reeled at the possibilities it presented. So many cities to choose from.

"You know, next time I'm going to make sure you're dead," Turnbull promised.

"What ever happened to our girl, what was her name? Sunflower?"

Turnbull said nothing but his eyes went icy.

"Ooops," The Last said with faux sorrow. "Did she finally get her wish?"

"Like I said, next time we meet I'm putting you down."

"Well, I know how bloodthirsty you are, but the rest of these fine people might not want this to end in blood. If I get what I want, it doesn't have to. They can go on their way until death finds them on its own. You have until tomorrow noon."

He turned and began limping back to his caravan. The flag waver was beside him.

"Shoot him now," Turnbull said. "Give me the rifle and I'll do it."

"Take him out," Purcell urged.

"No," Dr. Mondavi said. "No, we have to discuss his offer."

"He's going to kill you all," Turnbull said, but Dr. Mondavi was already heading down the ladder.

"Last, you can't mean you will really let them go," Flag Waver said as they walked slowly back to the rest of their people. "They are so well-fed!"

The Last chuckled.

"I will be good to my word. There will be no blood. But there will be fire."

"We can't consider giving in to that psychopath!" Leia Purcell shouted to the assembled defenders. There were forty-three of them left, including the dozen on the walls.

"We have to discuss this," Dr. Mondavi said. "We have to decide together. This cannot be a dictatorship. We are better than that! We have not worked here for a decade to become that."

"I don't want to die like the others for some bomb!" one woman said.

"What choice do we have?" said another.

"I say we fight!" Glenn Mondavi said.

Turnbull stood on the outskirts of the conclave, watching and listening, and stewing as well. The arguments continued. Finally, he spoke.

"You are wasting time," Turnbull shouted. The group fell silent. He continued.

"I have dealt with this guy before, and guys like him. He's relying on your fear. He's relying on you to default to believing everyone else is like you, honest and decent. But if the last couple decades taught me anything it's that they aren't. These freaks are going to kill all of you. And eat you, after they finish with you. You have one possible plan. Give me the bomb. I will draw them away. If you try to hold out, you'll lose eventually."

"We have guns," Purcell said.

"And they don't care if they die. That's their ace in the hole. They will keep coming and you will eventually die. And then they will get the bomb and they will find some city packed with people and set it off."

"How will they know how to use it?" demanded a defender. He was a physicist, according to his nametag.

"Because you will tell them. You will tell them anything they want to know."

"He's right," Dr. Mondavi said. "The trigger mechanism is functioning and since Dr. Denver died, no one knows how to disable it. We can't just smash it – it contains explosives and plutonium. We all know the problem with that. The best case is they get a pound of plutonium, the most toxic substance on earth. Pulverize it, release it in a city, and you have thousands dead within months."

"But it will kill them too," the physicist said.

"They don't care," Turnbull answered. "To them that's a bonus."

There was more mumbling and grumbling.

"We vote," said Dr. Mondavi.

The tally was twenty-three to twenty in favor of Turnbull's plan. Turnbull turned to the doctor.

"I just need a vehicle big enough to haul it."

"We have one," said Dr. Mondavi. "Come meet Bertha."

17.

"Are you kidding me?" Turnbull said, astonished. "What the hell is that thing?"

"That's Bertha," Dr. Mondavi said. He began coughing again, and it took him a moment to recover. "And she's what needed that timing gear. The last one cracked. Not a surprise, after over a decade."

Turnbull beheld the beast.

O'Neil, the mechanic, walked up to Turnbull and Dr. Mondavi, beaming.

"SWSTTACV" – O'Neil pronounced it "SwissTac-V" – "AKA the Special Weapons Secure Tactical Transport and Containment Vehicle," O'Neil said proudly. "One of a kind. Never thought it would ever run again."

"So, it transports bombs?"

"It looks like a very large gasoline tanker. Until you look closely," O'Neil said. The tractor trailer rig bore an orange-dominated paint job that identified it as belonging to "Musk Fuels."

"Inside joke," O'Neil said.

"Elon actually went big into oil in Texas. He owns Chevron now, and pretty much everything else," Turnbull said. "He also has thirty-four kids. One's name is the semi-colon symbol."

O'Neil ignored the tangent and continued.

"It was meant to fit in, to be inconspicuous. Bertha – that's our nickname for her – carries her payload in the fake gas tank. You load the payload in the back. The rear end is actually a door and it swings open. Of course, the container is armored and it is meant to contain a plutonium spill if there's an accident."

"Dual wheels on each axle," Turnbull observed. "I'm guessing they are Kevlar run-flats."

"Yep," O'Neil confirmed. "The tractor itself is based off an Australian Kenworth C540, the kind they use for mining. The engine is a very modified Cummins QSK 19 liter that does 650 horsepower stock and about 825 with our mods. It has a modified cooling system to facilitate plate armor where the radiator would normally be. No emissions bullshit on this baby. It's mated to a very tweaked Allison H6610 six-speed tranny. The cab is extra-large, about twelve feet high, and it carries four folks with room for two to sleep so you can run 24/7. There are gunports, but they don't look like gun ports. The cab is armored. There's an overpressure system to keep out gas. The glass is extra thick. No regular round is going through it. What else? Self-sealing diesel tanks. Oh, and there are mounts for rotary cannons, but we don't have any here, damnit."

"I can drive this," Turnbull said. He had learned to drive big rigs, and practically everything else with wheels, in training.

"The hell you say," replied O'Neil. "I'm driving it. You're security. If you ride with me, you ride bitch."

"I'll need my guns back," Turnbull said to Purcell. She nodded.

"It'll be ready to go in the morning," O'Neil said. "And it'll smash through anything they put in our way." He pointed to what looked like a metal cowcatcher bolted to the front end of the behemoth. He was proud as well as confident, Turnbull less so.

"The enemy always gets a vote," Turnbull said. "Always."

Turnbull did a chamber check and slid his Wilson .45 into his holster, then checked the HK416 and the shotgun. They had been out of his immediate possession and he was not about to trust his life to a weapon he had not confirmed had a round in the chamber.

Purcell watched him with his weapons. She seemed to like his HK416C rifle best. Of course, living here among a bunch of scientists for the last decade, she had never seen one of those before. She had not seen a lot of things before. According to Dr. Mondavi, her parents were both physicists, and both died after the Split. She was effectively raised by the whole community, and she was fiercely protective of it.

Dr. Mondavi was also standing there, watching Turnbull prep.

"You got what you wanted," he said. He had voted to deal with The Last.

"It's our only chance."

"I'm still unclear about you, though," Dr. Mondavi began. "When your team was intercepted, how did you get away?"

"I didn't. Different team."

"Who sent you, then?"

"I'm from the red."

"So were the others, I presume. Reds, blues, we see ourselves as neither. We're just serving a higher calling. How about you? What are you doing here then?"

"I'm making sure the bomb gets into the right hands instead of the wrong ones."

"I thought that's what the dead men were supposed to do," said the doctor. "You're both from the red."

"Yeah," Turnbull said. "But it's complicated."

"Politics?"

"In the sense that politics is just war by other means."

"I think you have your Clausewitz backwards. In any case, I thought you reds made the Split to avoid that sort of politics."

"Me too," Turnbull said. "But people are still people."

"Then how do we know that you are the good guy?" asked the doctor.

"Sometimes I ask myself the same question," Turnbull replied. "But I don't think you have a lot of options but to trust me."

"No, we don't. You came inside when it seemed like a death sentence, so that's an indicator. But then again, we could call back to the red and see who you really are."

"What?"

"We could call back to our point of contact and confirm you are who you say you are. We have a sat phone. How do you think we knew the team was coming in the first place?"

"Cripes," Turnbull said. "Give me the phone. I gotta make a call."

"Jack Daniels," Dr. Mondavi said proudly, holding up a bottle. "Been saving this for over a decade. The whiskey in the blue was not fit to be a solvent." He poured a glass for Turnbull and another for himself. Turnbull accepted it without comment.

"We've been here since the Split, doing our duty, trying to prevent contamination. Protecting the work, and the bomb. We never left, not for long. All we really know about the blue we saw on TV, or learned from them when they built the wall and put up the signs. We've been on our own planet, for all practical purposes."

"You didn't miss much."

"We adults didn't. But the kids, like Leia and Glenn, they did. They grew up here. They have never seen the real world. That's one reason we have to leave."

"Cannibal death cultists is probably another."

"And the fact this place actually is contaminated. Oh, you'll only be passing through, so it's no threat to you. But there are a lot of contaminants here, not just radio isotopes either. We lost one chemist when he accidently opened an unlabeled bottle from 1947 and spilled dimethylmercury on himself. Died of toxic heavy metal poisoning. We have no real medical facilities. We've lost half of us so far. Including me. This cough is cancer. I don't know for sure, but I'm pretty sure of it."

"I'm sorry."

KURT SCHLICHTER | 257

"Me too. And there are so many things that could have caused it, I can't even figure out what's going to kill me."

"Glenn know?"

"Probably. He's not dumb. We schooled our kids ourselves."

"They are probably ahead of everyone else out there in the real world. At least they weren't groomed."

"The problem is that tomorrow we will need fighters, not scientists," Dr. Mondavi said.

"O'Neil and I will get through," Turnbull said.

"O'Neil's not a soldier. I can see you are. You walk and talk like one. But you're hurt."

Turnbull felt the stitches on his forehead. The bandage had come off along the way.

"I'm fine," he asserted. He took out his Cipro bottle, the conversation reminding him to take his antibiotic.

"You'll need more help. I'll be coming along as security," the physicist said. The doctor began to cough.

"Kind of tells me what you think of our chances." Turnbull swallowed a pill and put the bottle away.

"O'Neil loves his vehicles. He's run our motor pool the whole time even after the others ran off. But I deal in probabilities, and one vehicle against all that out there does not seem to have a high probability of success."

"We just need to get to Waitsburg," Turnbull said. "That's where we'll be met up with my people. I've set it up. They'll be coming west from the forward line of troops west of the Idaho border."

"That's about sixty miles on roads we haven't been able to scout with all those lunatics chasing us. Do you like those odds?"

"That's a trick question," said Turnbull. "I don't like anything."

Casey Warner stepped off the Lufthansa jet from Munich into the air-conditioned comfort of the new José Martí International Airport outside Havana. It was filled with businessmen and women eager to ply their trades at the gateway to the new

United States. Many European countries had sanctions on the US, some even predating the invasion of the People's Republic – the success of the conservative United States horrified the ruling elite of the much-shrunk European Union. Cuba was not under sanctions. Liberated from communist tyranny a decade before, it was the natural locus for getting around the trade bans. As a result, it had grown very rich – only socialism could keep a nation full of Cubans poor.

He instinctively turned his face away from a gaggle of American GIs walking by in uniform, in the off chance one recognized him. He did not want anyone with a pistol waiting for him to disembark at DFW.

A hand on his shoulder.

"Casey," the man whispered. It was a familiar voice, familiar enough that Casey did not reflexively grab the arm and toss its owner through the plate glass window of the Victoria's Secret shop next to them. The models on display in the posters and the videos playing on the screens around the shop were, once again, fit and attractive after the pre-Split flirtation with plus-size and trans Angels that had almost bankrupted the brand.

"Mundi," Casey said, seeing his old friend. "You're not dead."

"You seem surprised."

"I kind of am. I thought only Kelly and I made it."

"They came for me," Mundi replied. "But the village where I live let me know there were a couple of *gringo pendejos* looking for me the minute they set foot in town. They are now feeding the gators."

"Tough but fair," Casey said.

"You're not going to Dallas," Mundi said.

"I have to meet Clay," replied Casey.

"Change of plan," Mundi said, handing over a new, red-covered United States passport with Casey's picture in it. "You are now Mister David R. Markowicz from Miami, and we are heading to Boise, Idaho."

"No contact, General," the Air Force major told Karl Martin Scott. The general did an about-face without another word and walked back into his secure briefing area. His three personal security detachment operators followed discreetly.

He wanted to smash the monitor hanging on the wall that mocked him with that accursed Gray Zone. It would have been so easy to simply fly the team in, load the package on a CH-47, and chopper it out of there, but the damn Chinese air defenses made that impossible. So it had to be a ground insertion, with all the attendant risks. And it appeared the gamble failed.

But what the hell could have taken out a whole ODA team?

There were no organized blue forces in there. According to the intel, which was sketchy at best and often derived from interviews with refugees fleeing south, it was pretty much warriors of the wasteland-style savagery with various gangs roaming the deserts. There had to be a hell of a lot of them to take out a force of Green Berets.

He began to consider, seriously consider, that he would not be getting his nuke back, at least not anytime soon. And the time was coming when it would have been the perfect opportunity to use it – the cabinet would be meeting next week. The entire federal government there in the new White House except, of course, the designated survivor. That was to be the Secretary of Energy, and the joke was on them. He was in Scott's pocket. The moment the rest of the federal government was erased from the face of the earth when the truck innocently parked a quarter mile from the new Oval Office detonated with the heat of a million suns, the Sec Energy would assume the office of the President and immediately resign in favor of the war hero who the people demanded take the reins of power in the time of tragedy.

And then the purging would have begun, designed to eliminate the people who might stand in his way. But that beautiful vision was not going to come true. No bomb, no plan.

But he had another plan. The business of the senior officer corps was staff work, and a good staff officer – Scott was a great staff officer – always had an alternative plan.

Plan B was to do it the hard way, the dirty way, the even bloodier way. Sulla had done it. And Marius. And, most famously, Caesar.

They had wheeled their armies about from facing the Republic's enemies and they had marched on Rome.

Karl Martin Scott, of course, had command of a huge number of US forces, and they were generally loyal to him, but could he rely – with absolute certainty – on the premise that their loyalty would extend to seizing control of the new United States government?

Perhaps, but perhaps not. Some troops would certainly flock to his banner, but would most of them? Other generals would move to stop him, that was a certainty.

Except Karl Martin Scott had a second army. And it was an army fanatically loyal to him because that army knew him and owed him, as opposed to those politicians back in Dallas who they did not know and who they owed nothing.

General Scott had an army of provisionals that he could call upon, and who would answer.

Scott summoned his brain trust, the officers of unquestioned loyalty to him, to a planning session. He arranged for Sergeant Major to be away inspecting troops in Rancho Cucamonga. No need for a wild card hanging around, one who would answer "No" to the question he was about to ask.

"Gentlemen," he said to the assembled officers. "You could be shot for listening to what I will say next. Do you understand? Will you stand with me?"

They would. He continued.

"We need a plan. We are mobilizing the provisionals and we are taking them into the red to drive out the incompetent current leadership. We need to purge the corruption. It is time."

His men were eager. He went on.

"The first step is their mobilization. We must lock in the loyalty of the provisional forces. I must talk to them, look them in the eyes. We need to arrange a gathering, a gathering of representatives of all the provisionals, so I can personally call them to arms."

His men nodded eagerly, and waited for more guidance.

"I want them here, a few days from now, with ten representatives from every provisional unit. And we will do it at the Cow Palace."

The staff mumbled, confused. But Scott had done his homework and issued his intent. Now it was up to them to plan and execute his intent.

"Gather my army together, gentlemen, and we will take it into battle."

"When we go through them, they will follow us. At least most of them, I bet," Turnbull told the assembled defenders. "You shut the gates tight. They don't mind dying for a reason, but we'll have the package and with that gone our pal The Last is not going to squander his minions' lives in a frontal assault against a fortified position. You have food and ammo. Wait out whoever he leaves behind."

The gathered scientists nodded. It was clear they were scared, which was good. They should be.

So should I, Turnbull thought to himself.

They had considered sending some vehicles along for security but decided against that. These were not skilled combat drivers. They were the kind of people who named their daughter after the princess character in a movie about space laser fights and effeminate robots. No, it would be just the four of them in the rig – Turnbull, O'Neil driving, Dr. Mondavi, and Leia Purcell. She insisted, and Turnbull liked her reflexive hostility.

"You got the route?" Turnbull asked O'Neil. Like the other defenders, he wore a SIG 17 pistol and had an M16 with several magazines, though his job was to drive, not shoot.

Of course, once they left the gate, who knew what would happen?

"I got it. Southwest on Route 4, then south on Hanford Route 10 until we hit 240, then southeast through Pasco. The town is deserted. Cross the Columbia and east on 124 to Waitsburg. Sounds easy when you say it."

"It won't be," Turnbull said. "We're limited to the road, so they know where we have to go. The first fifteen, twenty miles are all flatlands. They can come at us from every direction. Our advantage is we are a tank – we can smash through anything they put in our way. And even if they have some small arms, regular rounds won't penetrate Bertha. They need to stop us, and we need to be unstoppable. So don't stop, no matter what."

O'Neil nodded.

"Show Leia and the doctor the plan and then give them a quick brief on driving the truck. It's an automatic, so that simplifies things."

"I'm driving, though."

"Not if you're dead. Everyone needs to know how to do everyone else's job."

"I'm pretty sure the bad guys can't penetrate the cab," said O'Neil, concerned. "Except the roof. The armor is thin there, but that doesn't matter."

"Pessimists live longer," Turnbull said. "Show our folks how to drive the truck."

Turnbull did a walk-around of the vehicle. It was enormous, and it would only just pass under standard overpasses with minimal clearance. The orange livery made it visible, but that was probably designed for easy acquisition by air support. He walked around to the rear. The weapon was on board already; O'Neil had overseen the process. The door itself was cleverly hidden. Unless you knew what you were looking for, it looked like any other fuel hauler. There was a ladder bolted to the rear of the tank. Turnbull pulled himself up and climbed to the top of the tank, then stood on the metal lattice walkway that broke for two faux hatches along the length up to the front, where it overhung the cab. MUSK FUELS was painted on the top in orange block letters from front to back on the top side so there was no mistaking the SwissTAC-V from the air.

From his vantage point, he could see over the wall, and the Annihilationists could see him as well as Bertha.

So much for surprise.

The Flag Waver wiped the drool from his mouth before leaning into the back seat of the Cadillac, where The Last was taking another Oxycodone tablet. They were not hard to find. Following the trials of the pharmaceutical executives early after the Split – not just the ones pushing Oxy but any who made a profit selling anything and who were too foolish not to go to the red – the PR amended its constitution, adding Article 339. This established the right to government-provided substances for the growing number of addicts. Oxy and other drugs became not just readily available but free. The Last had instructed that his looting parties should bring any they found to him. His melted face was still agony without his pills.

Just because he loved death did not mean he loved pain – at least not his own.

"We are lined up," the Flag Waver told him. "Just as you wanted."

The Last looked to his right and to his left. The entire clan was in a concave semi-circle straddling the road out of Area 200 East. The Cadillac sat in the middle, on the blacktop while the wings spread out across the desert, at least twenty cars and a pack of motorcycles. His troops were hopped-up on their favorite substances, and eager for the taste of blood.

"They will try to bash their way out," The Last said. He picked up an olive-green plastic fly swatter and swished away at the bugs swirling around him.

"May we use rifles?" the Flag Waver asked.

"This once. Shoot the tires, shoot the drivers. Don't hurt the vehicle. We need it to carry the fire."

The Flag Waver nodded, excited, and ran off calling several of the Annihilationists over to one of the RVs parked off the road. He passed out the clan's weapons – old deer rifles, random pistols, and various shotguns – and the clan's few bullets and shells to the men gathered outside.

"Shoot the tires," he shouted. "Shoot the driver. The rest, blades and clubs once we bring it to a stop!"

Spilling blood was sacred. The Last had told them as much as he gathered the clan to him over the last few months. He was damaged and limping, but it was what he said that won them over. It was the way he released them from all the arbitrary limitations of life under the PR, and before the Split under the old US. Limitations like not following your urge to hurt and kill, limitations on what and who could be eaten when you were hungry, and out here, before joining with The Last, you were always hungry.

Everything, almost, was allowed, even encouraged.

Gaia asked for only two things – death for the human vermin and that their blood be spilled by hand where possible.

Today, a few bullets would make a slaughter with blades and clubs possible.

They went back to their vehicles and waited for their prey to come to them.

"You really going to bring that dog?" Leia Purcell said to Turnbull from the second row of seats. Behind her was enough room for two people to rack out. Except for occasional breaks for diesel – very occasional, since the fuel tanks held hundreds of gallons – or to download used energy drinks, coffee, and dinner, Bertha did not have to stop.

Gibson was lying down in the far back next to Turnbull's ruck sack. The dog wore a pair of safety earmuffs. He was used to them.

"I'm sure," Turnbull said. You never got separated from your gear or your dog. "Put in your ear plugs or when it gets shooty, you'll get deaf."

They all began stuffing their orange plugs into their ear canals.

Dr. Mondavi was in back too, cradling the M16. Glenn had wanted to go instead. The doctor was not having it.

"I'm dying," he told his son. "I'm expendable. Get them to safety."

Turnbull noted that Dr. Mondavi made no attempt to tell his son that they would meet again. Not the best sign. Pessimists were usually right in his experience.

"Pile up some mags near you," Turnbull said. "Don't have to look around for one when you need a reload. But don't waste ammo either. There's no resupply between here and Waitsburg. We are going to war with the army we have."

"Love that band," O'Neil said. He had a tatt of Retracto the Retraction Alpaca on his right calf.

"Take this," Turnbull said to Leia, handing her the little Springfield automatic that was in his pocket. Next, Turnbull checked the chamber of his HK416C again. He had half-dozen spare mags. His Wilson was on his hip, and the Shockwave cut-down 12-gauge was in the footwell beside him.

Worst case, if all else failed, he could ensure they didn't take him alive using the last round in one of them. But not before he spent every other round taking out Annihilationists.

18.

"Go!" Turnbull said. O'Neil hit the accelerator, and Bertha lurched forward.

The defenders had pulled the gate open to reveal the entire Annihilationist clan spread across the road ahead. Now the huge tractor pulled through the portal, gaining speed surprisingly quickly heading out onto the blacktop. The pink Caddy and a dilapidated Winnebago that The Last used as his house/harem den were parked in the road ahead perhaps 500 meters away.

"Remember," Dr. Mondavi said. "Physics."

"What's that, Doc?" O'Neil asked, confused. Turnbull glanced at the side mirror by the passenger seat he occupied and saw they were swinging the gate shut behind them, as instructed.

"Physics," the doctor repeated. "You have mass and velocity. Use it."

"He means smash through them," Turnbull added.

"Why didn't you just say so, Doc?"

The truck was still gaining speed, with more pick-up than Turnbull had expected. He slipped the barrel of the HK416 through the gun port in his door. The suppressor was in his ruck, and the stock was minimized.

Bertha's Cummins engine roared as O'Neil pressed the pedal to the metal, but even over the noise and through the cab and the ear plugs, Turnbull could hear the pops of rifle fire.

"They're shooting at us," Purcell said.

Turnbull did not reply. The glass of the windshield to his lower right cracked into a spiderweb of white lines. The bullet did not penetrate.

Another shot sparked off the side of the tractor, leaving a gouge, but it did not penetrate the armor.

"Aim at that schmuck," Turnbull said, pointing to the Caddy.

"You got it," O'Neil said. The truck was still picking up speed.

Nothing.

No effect.

The Last had heard a dozen shots and the tractor trailer rig was not even slowing. Instead, it seemed to be accelerating.

He considered his situation. This was perhaps the biggest tractor-trailer rig he had ever seen.

It was special. Specially designed to carry the fire.

Those puny rifle bullets would not stop it.

"Get out of the way!" he shouted. His shaved-headed chauffeur was chained to the driver's seat by his leather harness. He liked it, and The Last liked that he could not wander away, though it left something to be desired hygiene-wise if The Last failed to let the driver out for a regular bladder break. Since the man had no tongue, he could not ask to go.

The Last slapped the driver with the fly swatter for emphasis and the Caddy lurched forward, then to the right, and then off the road.

The Last's Cadillac tore across the shoulder and into the dirt with moments to spare, but O'Neil did the next best thing and aimed at the side of the Winnebago. Bertha hit it off-center on the passenger side with the edge of the cowcatcher, lifting it off the road and smashing it with the armored tractor. The right side of the RV disintegrated, literally. The house itself was all plastic and particle board, and the impact blasted it to splinters. The Annihilationists inside were shredded by the debris and the carcass of the wrecked recreational vehicle flew back off the road and onto its side, right on top of an unlucky motorcyclist who had the tails of a dozen stray dogs flying from his fantail as trophies.

Turnbull, Mondavi and Purcell all opened up with their weapons, spraying the row of vehicles. If they hit anyone as they passed, they did not see it. Ahead of them was the open road.

"Not bad," O'Neil said.

"We're a long way from Waitsburg," Turnbull said, marveling that his side mirror had somehow survived intact.

The Last looked on in horror at the RV, which was nearly unrecognizable. His harem had been in there. He had no harem anymore.

Several of his men were still firing on the tanker while it grew smaller as it headed east.

One of them, who wore a Slipknot t-shirt over corduroy slacks and a string of ears around his neck, approached carrying a Remington bolt action.

"The tires," Slipknot said. "I shot the tires but they wouldn't pop!"

"You missed, you missed!" screeched Flag Waver from the Caddy's passenger seat.

"Shut up, I don't miss. I know how to shoot. I was a Marine before the Split!" This was true, to the extent he was a Marine for six weeks of basic training before being kicked out after his platoon mates reported that he had a dead raccoon in his wall locker and that he was romantically involved with it.

"Give them everything," The Last told Flag Waver.

"Everything?" Flag Waver said.

"Everything!" shouted The Last. Flag Waver nodded and ran to the arms RV. The rest of the clan was driving over to it as he handed out the dozen or so pistols and rifles they had scavenged. Then there was one final item.

KURT SCHLICHTER | 269

"Not that," The Last yelled as Flag Waver was handing a large item to a man dressed as a malicious circus clown with a machete in his belt. The Last pointed to Raccoon Boy.

"You take the Barrett."

Raccoon Boy nodded eagerly.

"There are only five rounds," The Last instructed him. "So don't waste them. Shoot at the meat."

"The intersection?" O'Neil asked. "How far?"

"Soon," Turnbull said. He looked at the dashboard. It was high-tech. Graphics monitored each system. There was a wide monitor in the middle. He hit the CAMERAS button and the view to the front, sides, and rear of the truck came on.

In the rear view, he could see vehicles coming.

Lots of vehicles.

"Can you go any faster?" Turnbull asked.

"A little," O'Neil told him.

"Good, because they're catching up."

The mass of the Annihilationists were clustered around the road. The RVs – there were still several left – were using it, but lagging behind. The other vehicles were at least somewhat off-road capable and going far too fast. The Last saw one of his motorcyclists hit something with his front tire – a rock, a hole, it didn't matter. The bike kicked up and the rider flew forward, landing on his helmetless head and flopping along until his corpse came to a stop at an impossible angle. The others simply swerved around the wrecked bike and rider and continued the pursuit.

The first one to catch up was a female, apparently, biker with a red-dyed crew-cut and a snub-nosed .38 who came up on the driver's side and began firing at the windows. A couple rounds hit, nicking the thick glass. Dr. Mondavi fired out the port with the M16, missing. O'Neil threw the wheel left and the rig slammed into her, knocking her over. She wiped out along the blacktop and a blue Ford F-150 with cattle horns on the front ran over her.

"A few down, a lot to go," Turnbull said.

"I can't get a shot!" Purcell exclaimed.

"Don't worry, you will," Turnbull advised, looking out his own window for targets.

There was a slight jolt, and Turnbull saw the issue on the monitor's side camera – a station wagon with the roof sawed off had bumped into the trailer's passenger-side rear wheels. Now its occupants were hacking at the tires with hatchets.

"Where's that intersection?" O'Neil asked.

Turnbull hit the window button, and his passenger door window dropped.

"What are you doing?" Purcell asked as the wind buffeted her.

"Housecleaning."

Turnbull leaned out the window with his HK416, but planting it under his left arm as he twisted back. He fired a burst at the station wagon. The rounds stitched the white sheet metal of the hood.

The station wagon swung away from the trailer, kicking up a cloud of dirt from the soft shoulder. Turnbull took aim again and fired. One of the Annihilationists dropped.

More cars and motorcycles were coming. Too many.

They did not notice Raccoon Boy, who was in a Chevy Blazer, its suspension raised and a roll bar over the top. The Barrett .50 M107A1 was balanced on it as it accelerated up the driver's side toward the cab.

The Last struck his driver again and again with the fly swatter. The bulk of his force was far ahead and he was not catching them.

"Get up there!" he commanded.

The driver wordlessly hit the gas.

The station wagon gained speed up the side of the tractor, half in the soft shoulder. There were three targets still alive in it, waving their hatchets and spears. Turnbull fired a burst and hit the guy with the spear in the gut. He fell and was rolling around in the back-back.

Empty.

Turnbull dropped the mag and grabbed a new one. The station wagon caught up even with him and there was a clunk. Turnbull looked over as he slapped in the fresh magazine. The freak had planted his axe in the sheet metal of his door – the armor was inside the door, so the axe piercing the sheet metal gave him a grip. The ax man pulled himself up out of the station wagon, and hung off the side of the cab grasping for the open window frame.

Turnbull seized his door latch and pushed the door open. It took some effort because of the wind, but it had the desired effect.

The hanger-on lost his grip and fell directly on top of the station wagon driver, who lost control and turned the wheel left. The front end of the wagon went under the tractor and the rear wheels of the rig ground against it.

The tractor jolted savagely, but O'Neil maintained control, barely, while the remnants of the station wagon rolled away off the road.

More down, but so many more to go.

"Are we almost there?" O'Neil asked just before the glass blew in on his door's window and out the front windshield, taking much of the side of his head with it. Red splattered the interior.

Turnbull dove for the wheel and took it, putting his foot down on the accelerator.

"Leia, up here!" he shouted.

The tractor swerved across the road then back again as Turnbull struggled to take control.

Had to be a .50 cal, he told himself. *Where?*

The side camera view on the monitor had the answer – some sort of modified SUV with a guy behind a Barrett using the roll bar as a brace.

O'Neil was gone, as was much of the side window and the part of the windshield that had blown out at an angle from below and behind.

"I can't get a shot!" Dr. Mondavi yelled, his rifle in the gun port.

The Barrett shooter was taking aim again, his vehicle moving up to get in position. It was all Turnbull could do to keep the truck under control – he wasn't going to be able to bring his own rifle around.

"Sorry, man," Turnbull said. He clicked loose O'Neil's safety belt and reached across his body to open the driver's door. Turnbull pushed, using his legs for leverage, and O'Neil's body tumbled out and down onto the hood of the SUV, where it bounced into the windshield.

The SUV peeled off left, where it was T-boned by an old Dodge Charger. They both vanished in a cloud of dust and debris.

Purcell had climbed up into the front passenger seat.

"You pushed him out," she sputtered.

"And he took two vehicles out. Now cover right!"

She turned and pushed the barrel of her rifle out the open window. There were a couple bikers, one with a spear and one with a samurai katana, in her field of fire. She squeezed the trigger, her selector switch set to three-round burst. The guy with the spear crashed. The other rider swept in and under her, out of sight.

Turnbull took full control now, scanning the video monitor. Annihilationists to both sides and the rear. Lots of them.

"Turn!" Purcell shouted and pointed.

The right turn to Hanford Route 10 due south.

"I have to slow down," Turnbull yelled. "They'll mob us."

"Let them come!" Purcell answered, slamming in a fresh mag.

Behind Turnbull, Dr. Mondavi was firing out his door's gun port.

"I got one!" he shouted proudly.

"Don't get cocky," Turnbull shouted as he took his foot off the gas. The tractor slowed immediately and suddenly there were Annihilationist vehicles all around them as he made the turn.

Purcell shrieked. The rider with the katana was filling her window, hanging on with one gloved paw and bringing up the Japanese blade with the other. He had leapt onto the rig and simply let his bike go – it had taken out another rider.

Purcell elbowed the samurai in the face, loosening a tooth, but he merely shrieked in fury. She could not bring her rifle to bear. Now the katana was in the cab.

Dr. Mondavi reached forward and fired again and again with his SIG pistol – if not for her ear plugs, it would have blasted out her eardrums, and as it was the ringing was intense.

A couple of the rounds found their target in the samurai's face. The rider dropped off the side and his katana dropped into the cab.

"Nice job, Doc," Turnbull said. He was building speed but the mass of the enemy had caught up with him. He could not count them.

The Last stopped by the wreckage of the station wagon and the Charger. The upper half of Raccoon Boy's torso lay on the pavement. His eyes were blinking, perhaps – hopefully – from the remnants of his nervous system still firing. But The Last was not interested in the dead/dying man.

"There it is," he said, pointing it out for Flag Waver. "Get it."

His toady hopped out of the pink Cadillac and ran over and retrieved the battered Barrett.

"Will it work?" The Last asked.

The Flag Waver examined the weapon, worked the action, ejecting a round, and then checked the magazine. Three rounds, for a total of four.

He slid the ejected round back into the mag, inserted it in the well, and charged the Barrett.

"Oh yes, it'll still work," he said proudly, getting back into the Caddy with the heavy rifle, and adding, "I'll die for you!"

"Let's go," The Last told his driver, slapping him with the fly swatter for emphasis.

"Trouble, Kelly," Dr. Mondavi said, pointing at the dashboard monitor. Turnbull did not look immediately. A motorcycle rider had crossed in front of the tractor and exposed himself. Turnbull swerved left and caught the bike's rear wheel with the cowcatcher. The rider flew head over heels by the driver's window. He was splattering along the road behind them when Turnbull turned his eyes to the monitor.

"What are they doing?" Purcell asked, looking too. It was there in the rear camera.

"Trying to climb on board," Turnbull said. A couple of the baddies had already gotten onto the rear-end of the tank by grabbing the ladder from the hood of their tweaked-out Toyota Camry. A third was making the try.

Turnbull locked the brakes. There was a screech and the smell of rubber rolled over them like a wave.

The guy on the hood of the Camry behind them slammed into the rear of the tank, leaving a red smear before he dropped off to the asphalt. The Camry's front-end crumpled and the airbags deployed. The driver lost control as they blew up and he sideswiped another sedan. Both unlucky vehicles rolled over, tearing themselves apart across the brush.

Turnbull hit the gas again and the tractor trailer rig began to accelerate back up to max speed. But there were still at least a dozen Annihilationist vehicles swirling around them.

19.

Five minutes to the highway, Turnbull thought. Getting on Route 240 east would require they slow for the 90 degree turn left at the four-way intersection.

Bertha was still going strong, but with the loss of O'Neil they were now down one of their team. The enemy had correctly identified the SwissTAC-V's vulnerability – the human beings inside the truck.

"Hand me my shotgun," Turnbull shouted. Purcell complied. He placed the black Shockwave on his lap. Behind him, Dr. Mondavi was firing out the gun port with his rifle.

"Got another one!" he yelled.

"Keep it up," Turnbull said.

There was a thud on the roof. Feet, landing on top.

The head of a rusty steel pick came through the ceiling in the rear of the cab. Gibson growled.

"I thought this thing was armored!" Purcell exclaimed.

"I doubt they ever expected lunatics to jump on board and attack from above," Turnbull said. The weakness in the SwissTAC-V design was the assumption that the threat would be sane.

"What do we do?" asked Dr. Mondavi.

"Shoot him!" yelled Turnbull.

Behind him, Dr. Mondavi began firing bursts into the ceiling. There was another thud and Turnbull caught a glimpse of a body rolling off the roof in the cracked side mirror.

The rusty pick remained firmly anchored in the roof.

Shots from his left. Someone with an old Luger hanging out the passenger side window of a souped-up 2000s model Pontiac Bonneville was blasting away at him with the ancient German handgun. A couple rounds came inside the cab through the hole in the side window blasted by the Barrett and ricocheted off the inside of the windscreen. One planted itself in the headrest of Turnbull's driver's seat.

On the monitor, he saw the Luger gunman trying to reload.

"Everyone okay?" he yelled.

"I'm fine!" Purcell acknowledged before firing out her window with her M16 at a target Turnbull could not see.

"Doc?" he yelled.

Nothing.

"Doc?"

"I think," Dr. Mondavi began. "I think I caught one." He coughed wetly.

"Put pressure on it!" Turnbull yelled. "Use the field dressings!"

Turnbull picked up his cut-down Shockwave and opened the driver's door. Leaning out and twisting backward to his left, he saw the Luger gunner slap in a fresh mag.

Not quick enough.

Turnbull took aim at the man's face and fired the 12-gauge with his left hand. The kick was tremendous. The buckshot slammed into the shooter, turning his head into pulpy goo. His body slumped down over the passenger's door, painting the side of the door with scarlet, but Turnbull was not finished. He took his right hand off the wheel for a moment to pump out the empty shell and rack the weapon again, lowering it this time at the driver.

The driver thought to hit the brakes and get out of the line of fire, but the neural impulse to do that was intercepted by a load of heavy lead shotgun pellets, along with a cloud of safety glass from his vaporized windshield, tearing through his face.

The Pontiac swerved rightward into the wheels of the truck then bounced off back to the left too sharply, barrel-rolling four times. A dune buggy following the sedan too closely smashed into it at speed and two Annihilationists were ejected into the desert at fifty miles an hour. Their friends did not bother to check on their condition. It was terminal.

Turnbull pulled the door shut again. A small caliber round fired from one of the pursuers clinked off its armor.

"Look!" Purcell said, pointing to the monitor.

There were men climbing up the side of the tank too, using ropes tied to grappling hooks that had caught on the lattice walkway that ran the length of the top of the tanker.

"I'm beginning to doubt some of Bertha's designer's choices," Turnbull said.

"What do we do?" Purcell asked.

Turnbull didn't answer instantly. A pick-up truck was on his front left and he swerved into it, the cowcatcher slamming its rear axle and shredding its rear tire. The truck did not wipe out, though one of the idiots in the rear cargo area fell out on impact, but the truck was out of the fight.

"Take the wheel," Turnbull directed.

"Me?"

"No, the dog!" Turnbull snapped. "Yes, you!"

"I can't drive this thing!"

"It's a straight shot until we hit 240, then you go left. Otherwise, push the gas pedal as far as it will go and keep it pushed."

"What are you going to do?"

"I'm clearing those assholes off our tanker!"

The Annihilationists' supporting RVs were now far behind him, and the Caddy's driver, incentivized by constant blows from the fly swatter, was slowly catching up to the tanker. The Last looked at the wreckage the moving battle had left strewn across the desert – much more than he had expected, but the lost lives were a small sacrifice considering the reward.

Oh, what he would do with the fire.

There were a number of bikes and a few cars still in the chase and, to his delight, there were several figures on top of the tanker.

"Get them!" he urged. "Go get them!"

Purcell slid over Turnbull's lap and dropped into the driver's seat as he slid out. Turnbull looked back at Dr. Mondavi. There was a red splotch on his uniform, and his eyes were closed. Gibson gave him a look, almost like he wanted in on the action.

"No doggy, you stay here."

He thrust his hand into his pocket, which he had filled with shells, and proceeded to slide them into the Shockwave. There was a thud, this time above him and, in a flash, the head and torso of one of the Annihilationists was inside the open passenger window grabbing at him with one hand and stabbing at him with a kitchen knife in the other.

The blade sliced his right forearm – he felt the fire of the cut go up to his shoulder and his shotgun clattered on the floor.

They were grappling now, the man pushing into the window and Turnbull trying to hold him and his knife back and off.

"Gibson!"

The dog leapt forward, going for the face. The attacker immediately forgot about Turnbull and began slashing at the snarling animal.

"Don't screw with my dog!" Turnbull yelled. His left hand grasped the katana from off the floor and he drove it upwards. The blade punched through the attacker's sternum, emerging to the right of the spine with the tip of the blade burying itself in the padding of the ceiling.

Gibson pulled back, his snout dripping red, and the man's remaining eye blinked while the ruins of his lips moved.

"Mommy," he said.

Turnbull ripped the sword out and kicked upwards. The man flew back out the window.

"Thanks, dog," Turnbull said. Gibson panted.

Turnbull retrieved his shotgun.

The Caddy accelerated. There were now several shapes on top, or hanging by grappling ropes off the side, of the tanker.

"The tires," The Last said to the nodding Flag Waver. "Aim for the tires!"

"I'll die for you!" Flag Waver promised as he lifted up the Barrett, leaned it on the windshield frame, and welded his eye to the optic.

Turnbull wriggled out of the passenger door window, bringing up the shotgun just as a man with a Viking horn helmet leapt from the tanker and down onto the roof of the cab. He had what looked like a medieval battle axe and wore a white hockey mask.

The man, like an ancient berserker, roared.

"No sequels for you, Jason!" Turnbull shouted.

Turnbull took aim with the Shockwave center mass and fired just as the berserker lifted the blade. The impact blasted a single fist-sized hole in his chest, lifting him back off his feet and off the roof and into the air. He disappeared over the side.

Turnbull had loaded a slug, a Winchester PDX1 12-Gauge Defender Segmented Rifled Slug to be exact. That explained the giant hole.

"What did you say up there?" shouted Purcell from inside. "Couldn't hear you!"

"Forget it," Turnbull said. "The moment passed."

There was movement at the edge of the tank. Turnbull racked the slide, still hanging half out of the window, and fired at a shape on top of the tank. The pellets slammed into the lip of the tank, showering sparks. The target withdrew.

Turnbull racked another round and scrambled up and out, getting purchase on the passenger windowsill with his legs. He pushed up and crawled onto the roof, the air ripping past his ears. How these maniacs stood erect in this hurricane was beyond him – it had to be because they were maniacs.

Turnbull used his left hand to stretch out and reach for the pick that remained embedded in the roof. He got it. It let him pull himself into the center of the cab's roof. He raised the 12-gauge and scanned the tanker lip again. Nothing – but he knew they were up there.

If he was going to clear them off, he would have to stand up.

He looked over his shoulder to the front of the rig. The road was straight for a while, but there was a turn way ahead, a few minutes at least. He needed to have something to hold onto when that happened.

And there was a souped-up VW Bug turned into a macabre dune buggy – it looked like it was upholstered in what he suspected, but hoped was not, human skin – that was coming up the left side of the rig. The passenger had a weapon, a double-barreled sawed-off shotgun. Some of those pellets would get into the cab through the .50 cal holes in the windshield and driver's window.

But Turnbull had no shot while stretched out across the roof.

Turnbull slipped the Shockwave under his left arm and used both hands to pull himself up to his knees, the wind buffeting him.

Movement at the top of the tanker above.

And the shotgunner was taking aim below.

He pushed himself erect with his legs, holding himself up in the wind, and pulled the Wilson automatic, passing it to his left hand and taking the scattergun in his right.

The Annihilationist on the tanker stood up and pulled back his arm to throw a spear – where he got a forged metal spearhead Turnbull could not guess. Turnbull aimed the Shockwave as best he could under the assault of the wind and fired. The spear shaft and the thrower's forearm disintegrated in a cloud of blood, bone, and splinters.

Turnbull wheeled left, firing downward with the .45 again and again, the ejected brass zipping back and dinging off the metal of the tanker's front end. The shotgunner jolted and writhed. He lost control of the double-barrel and it twisted to the side, firing at point blank range into the side of the driver's head. The dune buggy bounced off the front tires of the tractor and spun out into the desert.

Now upright, Turnbull had a good view of the three Annihilationists holding onto the walkway that ran along the top of the tanker from front to back. The fourth attacker, now short one arm, was staggering about spurting scarlet from his stump.

The one just behind him had what looked like a British STEN – an all-metal 9mm submachine gun that was simple to make, so simple that metal shops in the blue often made them on the side and sold them for a huge profit. It wasn't pretty, and it wasn't accurate beyond a pretty short effective range, but close in it was deadly.

The STEN gunner fired a long burst that emptied the horizontal mag. Turnbull dropped, wrapping an arm around the pick sticking up from the roof. The rounds flew over his head, except for the dozen or so that slammed into his one-armed buddy. The unfortunate man staggered under the impacts and fell off the side of the tanker.

Kneeling, Turnbull racked the Shockwave then rose again. The STEN gunner was slapping a fresh 30-round mag into the side of the weapon. Turnbull aimed his handgun as best he could, buffeted by sixty mile-per-hour wind, and emptied his Wilson. At least one round hit, judging by the red splatter and how the STEN gunner twisted and fell off the top of the trailer.

The Wilson was empty, the slide locked forward. The other two Annihilationists looked at each other, and then charged at him, at least as much as they could charge when fighting the wind with each step.

Turnbull shoved the Wilson into his holster and racked the Shockwave again.

The pair was still coming fast even against the wind. The first had a Louisville Slugger with a dozen long nails driven through it. The other had a meat cleaver.

Turnbull chose to shoot the meat cleaver guy. It was another 12-gauge slug. The guy's groin vanished and he staggered off the side as the batter, screaming like a banshee, leapt from the tanker's lip bringing the bat down hard directly at Turnbull's skull.

It impacted on the Shockwave, which Turnbull used as a shield to block the blow. The psycho hit hard; the blow sent a wave through Turnbull's arms and the knife cut from earlier erupted in pain.

Turnbull began to think he might have chosen to shoot the wrong guy.

He lost his grip on the shotgun and dropped it. The Shockwave skittered off the cab's roof and disappeared as the batter prepared for a second swing.

Turnbull threw himself forward at his opponent, aiming to get in close to negate the swing. He hit the batter low on his left leg, with the goal of taking him down.

It worked – the bat blow landed on the roof, with several nails punching through the ceiling of the cab – and Turnbull pushed. Off-balance – they were both struggling to remain balanced in the windstorm – the batter fell forward just as Turnbull had hoped.

The rusty upward spike of the pick implanted in the roof drove into the batter's right shoulder, the point cracking the clavicle at the end of the wound channel.

Turnbull pulled back across the rooftop and the man screamed in rage, then pushed himself up off the rusty spike that had impaled him.

Hope he had his tetanus vaccine, Turnbull thought.

Turnbull reached back for his Wilson and drew it out, hitting the eject button and dropping the empty mag.

The batter rose up, blood gushing from the hole, his face a rictus of rage, and he seized the handle of the pick. Turnbull's left hand dug into his pocket, searching among a sea of shotgun shells for the thin rectangle of a full mag of the lethal .45 Lehigh Defense XD rounds.

The batter tore rather than pulled the pick out of the roof, leaving a gaping hole in the ceiling of the cab. His red eyes were fixed on Turnbull, and a string of spittle draped from his scowling mouth.

Turnbull found a mag and got it out of his pocket as the batter raised the pick over his head.

Turnbull was driving it toward the well of his pistol as the pick began to fall.

There was gunfire, shot after shot. The batter stopped his swing, twitching and jerking as round after round blew upwards through the roof and into his body.

The mag mated with the well and Turnbull slid it in until it locked, then he sent the Wilson's slide forward. It locked with a satisfyingly firm click.

The batter stood there, wind blowing his rags off his body like streamers, several weeping red holes in his body, including one that erased the left half of his nose like Nicholson in *Chinatown*, only worse. The batter looked at Turnbull, who took aim between his eyes and blew his brains all over the front face of the tanker.

Turnbull confirmed there was no one else up top and worked his way back down to the passenger side window. Looking back along the side, he saw only a couple vehicles close by the rig. But there was one Annihilationist, the evil circus clown, hanging off the side of the tank from a rope attached above to the walkway.

Turnbull pointed the Wilson and their eyes met.

Turnbull shrugged.

The clown considered his bad options, and then let go and leapt backward. The last Turnbull saw him, the free-falling harlequin was rolling through the brush.

"Bye, Bozo," Turnbull muttered.

Turnbull slid back inside of Bertha's cab.

"What happened?" Purcell said.

"They struck out."

"You're cut."

"Sure am." Turnbull turned to the back of the cab.

Dr. Mondavi smiled weakly. He was slumped in the rear seat, the red splotch larger now. The SIG 17, its slide locked open, lay on his stomach. Gibson was next to him.

"Thanks," Turnbull said. "See, you are a warrior."

The physicist nodded.

"Let Glenn know."

"You tell him yourself," Turnbull said. Then he turned back to the fight at hand, scanning the monitor for the camera views.

"A bunch of them peeled off and just left," Purcell said. There were only four or five vehicles still in sight, but they were following at a distance. The pink Caddy, on the road behind them, was one of them and now in the lead.

There was a flash on the screen. A split-second later the tractor shook and continued shaking slightly – the ride was different, rougher.

The dashboard indicator lights for two of the rear right tires on the tanker trailer turned from green to red.

"Fifty cal," Turnbull said.

"I thought these tires are bulletproof," Purcell exclaimed.

"They are," Turnbull said. "They're just not cannon-proof."

"We have three bullets left," Flag Waver said. He was giddy with his initial success. The round he had just fired had shredded two of the outside tires on the tanker trailer.

But The Last was more concerned with his depleted army at the moment. His best fighters were his most aggressive, and they were the ones lying dead along the highway. There were others, but now they were holding back.

They were waiting, waiting to see what their leader would do to ensure victory.

And The Last knew that if he failed to show them he was worthy to lead them, he would feed them.

"The intersection is right ahead!" Purcell yelled.

The four-way intersection with the old Washington Route 240 was coming fast. Some old PR signs were still up as they approached. One biker broke off from the group then came too close, and Turnbull shot him with the HK416. The rider smashed into a sign that read, "YOU ARE REQUIRED TO ACCEPT DIVERSITY – FIGHT FARMER/SCIENCE/RURAL PRIVILEGE" and featured what looked like a stern human resource manager in overalls wagging her finger at the reader.

No one else was approaching them now – except for the Caddy, which was accelerating, they were hanging back. The terrain was not quite as flat here as before either – small rises lined the highway and the pursuing vehicles were forced to keep on Route 10 instead of easily ranging out to the flank in the desert brush alongside the highway.

"Shoot the tires!" The Last shouted and the Caddy slowed to a stop. He hit Flag Waver on the shoulders with his swatter.

Flag Waver was trying to get a good shot from the moving convertible, using the top of the Caddy's windscreen to brace the Barrett rifle. This was not what it was designed for. The prior shot had cracked it.

"I'm trying!" he whimpered, his face pressed to the optic. "I'll die for you!"

Purcell began slowing to make the left.

"Turn around," Turnbull directed.

"Make the turn?" she asked, confused.

"Make a one-eighty," Turnbull corrected.

"That's going back!"

"Yeah," Turnbull said. "This ends here."

Purcell slowed the massive rig. The brakes squealed. At the four-way intersection, she began to turn the massive big rig around.

As Turnbull expected, the remaining pursuers had slowed and stopped back on Route 10, including the Cadillac.

"What are they doing?" Flag Waver asked, taking his eye off the optic. "I think they're turning around."

The Last looked around him. There were slight rises on both sides, but they were high enough to keep the convertible trapped on the road.

"Shoot the driver!" The Last ordered, flailing away with his fly swatter as the tanker completed its 180-degree turn. "Shoot the driver!"

Bertha the tractor-trailer rig halted and idled facing back up Route 10. The pursuers waited directly ahead.

"Switch seats," Turnbull said. Purcell moved over to her right and Turnbull slid in behind the wheel.

"Everyone, get down on the floor!" Turnbull ordered. He looked over his shoulder into the back and pointed. "You too. Gibson, down here!"

With difficulty, Dr. Mondavi rolled off the seat onto the dusty floor. He groaned.

The dog went where Turnbull pointed.

"Finally, a dog who listens to me," Turnbull muttered.

Mondavi, painfully, reached over to adjust the earmuffs on the dog; it had come askew as the dog chewed on the intruder.

"How will you drive when we're on the floor?" Purcell demanded.

"I'll look at the forward camera screen and push the gas!" Turnbull said.

She scrunched down, as did Turnbull, and he pressed the gas.

"The driver!" screamed The Last. "Kill the driver!"

"I can shoot the engine!" Flag Waver said. "Let me shoot through the engine block!"

"We need the truck, you idiot!" The Last shouted, slapping the side of Flag Waver's head with the fly swatter.

Flag Waver took aim. The Cadillac was coming up the middle of the two-lane blacktop, gaining speed. He moved the crosshairs over the windshield. The optic had proven still accurate even after surviving the crash.

The crosshairs alighted upon the driver's window. The windscreen was opaque and he could not see inside the cab, so Flag Waver centered the shot and aimed low on the driver's side window.

The Hornady 750 grain .50 caliber round hit the glass directly above Turnbull's head at 2820 feet per second. It punched straight through, ripping up the driver's vinyl seat cover with glass spall before punching through the seat back and then the rear of the cab, finally coming to rest in the heavier armor of the tanker behind them. It was incredibly loud.

"Shit!" Purcell shrieked as glass cascaded down on them.

Turnbull lost control of the rig for a moment, but regained it. He never let up on the gas.

"Again!" The Last commanded.

Flag Waver squinted into the optic, and then fired.

The half-inch wide round blasted through the unbroken middle of the window, blowing out a ragged chunk. Glass sprayed all over the back of the cab again; being hunkered down on the floor protected the doc and the dog.

Turnbull looked at the forward camera. The monitor was covered with a fine dust of pulverized glass.

The shooter was in the Caddy, and the Caddy wasn't moving.
The Caddy's windshield was gone.
The shooter was taking aim.
They were only a few hundred yards out.

"This has to stop them!" The Last shrieked. He franticly flogged Flag Waver with the fly swatter.

Tearfully, Flag Waver leaned into the optic, balancing the M107 on the frame of the Cadillac's shattered windscreen. The crosshairs danced over the tanker's pock-marked driver's window. He was hitting where he was shooting, but it was not stopping the tanker.

"I'll die for you!" Flag Waver cried as he squeezed the trigger to fire the final .50 cal round.

The round entered low on the driver's window again, blasting out another remaining chunk of the thick glass. It also punched out a four-inch section of the the top of the steering wheel as the slug roared through the cab, out the back, and into the front of the more thickly armored tank trailer just like the others. Turnbull shook out the tingling in his left hand – the impact of the bullet into the top of the steering wheel had felt like an electric shock where Turnbull held the wheel at the bottom.

In the Caddy, they were silent as the big rig kept coming after the final shot.

"I'm sorry," blubbered Flag Waver. "I'll die for you!"
The Last ignored his minion.

"Turn us around!" he shouted at his chauffeur, who watched expressionless. "Turn us around and drive!" He punctuated his commands with blows from his fly swatter.

The truck was accelerating.
The Last's driver shifted into "D" and began a three-point turn.

Turnbull saw in the dashboard monitor that the shooter had abandoned his Barrett and that the Cadillac was trying to turn around. Beyond the convertible, the other pursuers were turning around too.

He got back up into the driver's seat. The air was blowing through the holes in the windshield like a wind tunnel. He grabbed the remaining parts of the steering wheel and his foot pressed the gas to the floor.

"Hurry!" The Last yelled, whipping the fly swatter across the top of his driver's clean-shaven head. The driver was completing the last of his three-point turn moves, and hit the gas. He hit it too hard. The Caddy went up on the embankment off the west side shoulder and stopped.

He hit the accelerator again. Nothing but the free revving of the V-8 engine. The convertible was now caught on the side of the road, a heap of dirt beneath the undercarriage lifting the rear tires off the ground, spinning helplessly.

The Last looked about in panic. The tanker was coming at them from the south, and fast.

The driver sat nearly catatonic, no matter how many blows landed from the fly swatter.

"I'll die for you!" Flag Waver cried, opening the glove box and taking out a chrome .38 revolver.

He opened the door and bailed out onto the soft shoulder then ran into the road and then south, lifting the pistol and firing at the oncoming truck.

The Last paid his minion's last-ditch defense no mind. He climbed out of the back seat and landed in the dirt, then began limping off into the desert.

Turnbull looked north at the Caddy, which appeared stuck just off the side of the road. One of the occupants had gotten out of the convertible, and now he was running down the centerline of the highway, apparently firing a pistol. One of the rounds even hit the window in front of Purcell.

Turnbull floored it, the truck hitting sixty, the man firing as he came.

It could not be The Last. He wasn't limping and while ugly, he was still too good looking to be the cult leader formerly known as Tommy Doom.

It was the guy who had had the flag.

"Are you going to hit him?" Purcell asked.

"Yeah."

"I'll die for you!" Flag Waver shouted as the truck approached. He pulled the trigger a seventh time and there was no gunshot, no kick, only an impotent click on an empty cylinder.

The huge big rig loomed in front of him, growing larger every second, and he stopped in the road, staring.

"I'll die–" was all he managed to get out before he was vaporized.

A wave of gore splattered across the windshield and some of the atomized particles of the Flag Waver even blew inside the cab through the many holes. Purcell thought she saw, but hoped she hadn't, an arm holding a snub-nosed revolver flying past her passenger window.

Turnbull hit the brakes, hard. The truck slowed as the wheels screeched. They passed the marooned Caddy, then rolled to a full stop slightly past it.

"Take your rifle and cover front," Turnbull ordered. Purcell grabbed her M16A2 and some mags, but the other Annihilationist vehicles in the distance had finished turning around and they were scattering.

Turnbull put the tranny in "P" then opened his driver's door and jumped to the blacktop, bringing along the katana in his left hand.

"Gibson!" he shouted and the dog came forward between the front seats and leapt out the open door all the way to the ground.

Turnbull started walking toward the Caddy. There was a guy in leather gear sitting in the driver's seat – definitely not The Last.

Turnbull drew his Wilson. Gibson stopped to sniff a dead rabbit and then took a long pee.

The driver snarled at him and howled incoherently.

"Stop talking," Turnbull said and shot him through the forehead, ruining the backseat upholstery.

Gibson looked on amused.

"Find the asshole," Turnbull said. He headed up the embankment. The Belgian Malinois sprinted ahead.

The Last hobbled as fast as he could. He shrieked when the dog caught him by the arm and dragged him to the ground.

Turnbull took his time getting to them. When he did, he gave Gibson a minute to gnaw, then finally called the disappointed dog off.

The Last rocked back and forth in the dirt, moaning, clutching his shredded arm.

"I splattered your buddy all over the road," Turnbull said, holstering his Wilson and leaning on the katana, its point in the earth. "Oh, and I capped your gimp."

"They sought death!"

"Yeah, but you're missing my point."

"Your point?" The Last groaned.

"Yeah," Turnbull said. "The point is that this time you really have lived up to your name. You're the last."

The Last looked up at him and opened his mouth, but Turnbull swung before the ex-cult leader could ruin the moment by talking.

"I need practice," Turnbull said, as Gibson looked on at the convulsing, dying man. "I didn't get his whole head off."

He tossed the bloody katana away, and started back to the truck with Gibson trotting beside him.

"You know, this time, better safe than sorry," Turnbull said, drawing his Wilson as he turned around and blew off the top of The Last's skull.

20.

"Let the medics look at that arm," Clay Deeds suggested to Kelly Turnbull as he stood on the road leaning against the side of Bertha's scarred and battered cab. About twenty operators milled about the tanker, securing it. "And those stitches on your forehead too."

"Check out the guy in back first," Turnbull said. "Though he's probably dead."

"I'm not dead," Dr. Mondavi's disembodied voice said from up inside the cab. "I'm feeling better."

Leia Purcell was down on the road with them, her M16 in hand.

"*Monty Python and the Holy Grail* was one of the only Blu-rays we had in Hanford," she explained.

Turnbull grunted.

"Kelly's a big comedy fan," Casey Warner said smugly. He was rigged out too, with a Haenel Defence M556 rifle and an HK P30 pistol on his hip. He was in one of his German arms moods.

Turnbull ignored the jibe. He was just happy to be in Waitsburg among friends. The drive from the intersection where The Last had stopped lasting permanently had taken four hours. Deeds's team had met them on the outskirts of town and then escorted them into downtown Waitsburg, where they had occupied a perimeter that included several abandoned commercial buildings.

Now two camo-clad medics from Deeds's new team had started, but then quickly halted, their climb up into the cab to tend to the wounded doctor.

"Hey Kelly, call off your dog," said Mundi Vega. He had an FN SCAR rifle strapped to his gear as he stood next to Deeds and Turnbull. Gibson was up on the driver's seat growling at the EMTs below.

"Get down here, dog," Turnbull said. "They're friends." The animal leapt down and sat at his side, wary of the strangers.

"You and your dogs," said Casey.

"I like dogs," Turnbull said, looking back at Casey. "They don't talk."

"What the hell happened out there, Kelly?" Mundi asked, marveling at the damage to the vehicle and the myriad blood splatters.

"Bunch of death cultists tried to hijack the hot rock," Turnbull answered. "Went badly for them."

"Oh," Mundi said. He was not surprised.

"Who is this?" Deeds asked politely, gesturing to the woman. He wore a white button-down shirt, blue blazer, and khaki slacks, and stood out among the two dozen tactically-clad operators he had brought along.

"Leia Purcell, from Hanford. That's Dr. Mondavi up there not being dead. He's a physicist, the guy in charge."

"So you folks stayed at your post for over a decade after the Split," Deeds marveled, shaking her hand. "You did a great service securing that site, and keeping the bomb safe. You did bring the bomb, right?"

"It's in the tanker," Turnbull said.

"You sure?" asked Casey. "I mean, maybe they used you as a diversion."

"It's in the tanker," Purcell said, annoyed.

"Well, you guys being movie buffs and all, I just wanted to be sure," Casey explained.

Deeds nodded to several armed gentlemen standing to the side, and they moved to the back of the tanker.

"You're going to give it back, right?" Turnbull said.

"Yes, Kelly," Deeds said. "I like to be more subtle than a hydrogen bomb."

"Lorna's fine," Deeds said. "She's recovering nicely."

"I'm still going to kill all these bastards," Turnbull promised.

"I have her stashed in a hospital under a fake name," Deeds continued. "But she understands you can't reach out in case they are watching."

"Am I getting a wedding invitation?" Casey asked.

"No," Turnbull said.

Casey found this amusing. He, Turnbull, and Mundi were the only guys with a long history with Deeds and they were comfortable together.

"You trust these new guys?" Turnbull asked. Deeds had brought a couple dozen new operators along, all strangers.

The old comrades were all sitting on salvaged chairs in the makeshift task force headquarters in an old brick building the team had occupied. It was located on what had been Main Street before being renamed for Angela Davis by the People's Republic government as part of its effort to "decolonialize Walla Walla County."

The town was deserted now, and the once lush rolling hills that surrounded the little town were barren. A region that had a growing season of 200-plus days per year now grew nothing but weeds, and the only remaining livestock were fat rats and feral dogs that descended from house pets left behind when their owners were deported or worse for their "refusal to accept new modes of social justice in agriculture." In other words, PR bureaucrats told them to give up their family farms to transplanted bums from the city and they refused. There was shooting. The blues won this round through the simple expedient of sweeping every living soul up into "re-education and rehabilitation camps." The newcomers found farming hard, and almost all left before the first pitiful post-redistribution harvest. The rest of the newcomers either died at the hands of the roving bands of marauders or, usually, joined them.

"I trust you and Mundi and Casey, Kelly," Deeds said. "I don't know many of the others that well. But I could only be so picky in re-building my team after Scott tried to wipe us out."

"The new Zealots, a new Task Force Zulu," Casey said. "But we'll always be the OGs, the original gangsters." He threw a sign and pounded his chest.

Turnbull shook his head.

Mundi got up and filled four white Styrofoam cups with the coffee he had just brewed, then brought them over to the group. Casey took one.

"You got any sugar?" Casey asked.

"Of course I have sugar," Mundi said, offended. "And cream. You know I'm Cuban, right?"

"Kelly," Deeds said, taking another cup and leaving it black. "Once you gave me the heads up and we started looking at Scott, all the pieces fit. I've got evidence – comms, witnesses, the H-bomb. I don't have the most important thing."

"The general himself," Turnbull said.

"He's out there, in occupied California still commanding troops, operating without any decent restraint, totally beyond the pale."

"Look, you sound like you're planning a prosecution," Turnbull said. "He tried to cap me. He shot out my fiancée's kidney. I'm going to shoot the son of a bitch."

"Terminate," Casey said, lowering the cup of joe. "With extreme prejudice."

"I get that you're angry," Deeds said to Turnbull.

"You think?"

"Kelly, there is a lot more going on here than your justifiable rage. We are talking about the stability of the new United States of America. This problem is way beyond your personal payback."

"I think Karl Martin Scott twitching on the ground after I put a cap into his brain pan is the solution."

"You can't just kill all the bad guys."

"Why not?"

Deeds sighed.

"We need him alive, to face trial. We have to discredit him."

"The problem," Turnbull said. "Is that the bastard is right about a lot of things."

"He'd be wrong about all those things if he thought it would help him," Deeds said. "A ruthless narcissist. You should see his psych profile. This guy makes you look stable."

"I want him dead," Turnbull said. "That's non-negotiable."

"Then let him hang. But he has to go back to Dallas for trial."

Turnbull pouted. Casey piped up.

"Clay, he's the commanding four star of an army. We can't just walk into his HQ and announce that he's under arrest. That won't go the way we hope."

"It's more than that," Deeds said. "The fuse is burning. My sources tell me that in three days he is having an assembly of representatives from all the provisional units in California."

"There must be a thousand different provo units across the state," Mundi said.

"More," Casey said. During the initial invasion, he had helped organize some of the ad hoc units.

"They answer to him, and most are loyal only to him," Deeds said. "The bomb was his Plan A. His Plan B has to be creating a private army out of the provisionals."

"And with the mobilized regular US forces on the borders facing the blues and the Chi Coms, there's no one to stop them if he leads his private army east to Dallas," Turnbull said.

"He's gathering his forces to lead them to the Rubicon," Deeds said. "And when he crosses it the die is cast."

"I should shoot him," Turnbull said. "You should let me shoot him."

"I need you to bring him out, back home, to Texas and justice."

"My .45 is justice."

"Nevertheless, can you try not to kill him?" Deeds asked. Turnbull noted the assumption that he would be going in to do the job.

But of course he would.

"Yeah, you can trust me to try not to," Turnbull said. "That's the best I can do. But if I can't figure out a way to capture him, I'm going to cap him. Understand?"

"If you kill him, it creates a host of new problems."

"But on the upside he's dead."

"There is that," Deeds conceded. "Take Casey."

"Great," Casey said.

"And the dog," added Turnbull. "I'm not leaving my dog."

Lewiston-Nez Perce County Regional Airport was no longer a sleepy landing field with a couple of scheduled flights a day bringing in tourists or locals flying home from hubs like Denver and Salt Lake City. Instead, Lewiston, Idaho, and its airport, with its 6,500-foot runway, were packed with US military forces. The front line of troops was a few miles to the west, and beyond that, the Gray Zone. Bertha and Turnbull, escorted by a convoy of Deeds's operators, had enjoyed an uneventful drive east from the rendezvous in Waitsburg.

Now, Turnbull and Deeds stood on the tarmac at the airfield. They had to speak loudly, louder than they would like. Fighters and cargo craft rumbled down the busy runway, but no one paid much attention to one more Hercules getting ready for take-off.

"So, beyond the infiltration, do you have a plan?" Deeds asked.

Turnbull's gear was already inside the C-130J aircraft. Gibson, used to flying, sat by him on the cement waiting. The air crew up in the belly of the big beast were all Deeds's men, wearing Air Force flight suits, and the plane itself was seconded from a reserve unit in Montana for this mission.

"You know, I haven't done one of these jumps in years," Casey said as he passed them by, heading up the ramp.

"All you have to do is fall," Turnbull said, then he turned his attention back to Clay Deeds.

"I'm going to improvise," he said. "I've got some potential assets on the ground and one big advantage – he doesn't know I'm coming."

"My intel is that the gathering is going to be at a place called the Cow Palace."

"Like, mooing cows?"

"I didn't name it, Kelly. But my sources say that's the auditorium where this big meeting is taking place."

"Since we took his bomb away, this meeting is his Plan B," Turnbull said. "Do you have a Plan B if we don't get him?"

Deeds shrugged. "I go to the cabinet and show them the bomb and my other evidence and maybe they do something, or maybe they put their heads in the sand until he comes marching into Dallas at the head of an army of provisionals answering only to him and we have yet another civil war to deal with. Having him in handcuffs already makes doing the right thing a lot easier."

"I was hoping that when the Split happened we might get a better class of politicians," Turnbull said.

"Oh Kelly, you're so naïve," Deeds replied, smiling with a hint – more than a hint – of condescension. "The old Republicans formed the base of the red government, and you're probably too young to remember how spineless a lot of them were. All they cared about was cocktail parties, cruises, and losing like gentlemen. We were never going to have perfect politicians. Human nature never changes."

"All society is really just a replay of high school," Turnbull said. He had read that somewhere.

"Except the stakes are a bit higher than not getting a date to the prom," observed Deeds.

The four Rolls-Royce AE 2100D3 turboprops hanging from the aircraft's massive wings sputtered and started. In the air, they would generate 4,700 horsepower. A crewman came to the top of the ramp and gestured for Turnbull to come up.

"A couple things," Turnbull said to Deeds, handing over a piece of paper. "I need you to find my nephew. He got taken from his parents. They're probably gone. He's probably adopted out. His info, what I know of it, is on there."

Deeds took the paper. If anyone had the assets to do it, Deeds did.

"Second," Turnbull said. "Get word to Lorna. Tell her..." He paused.

"I'll handle it," Deeds said.

"Don't tell her about the new dog."

"Good luck, Kelly," Deeds said.

"You know that statistically we have about zero chance of success, right?" Turnbull asked.

"I'll give you one in a hundred." It was unclear to Turnbull if Deeds was joking.

"I'll take it," Turnbull said, doing an about face and walking up the aluminum ramp into the belly of the plane, dog at his side.

The crew chief nudged him awake. The vibrations from the engine had made it remarkably easy for him to fall asleep by the time they flew south over the Nevada border.

"It's time," the crewman said, stepping down the fuselage to shake Casey, who slept upright on the fabric bench seats. The hum of the engines had not kept them awake – they were old hands at getting Zs on the flight into the objective.

Gibson, who had been sleeping on the floor, looked up as Turnbull rose to prepare.

"No, dog," he said. "You are going to stay here with these zoomies and wait for me at SFO, okay."

The dog angled his head, then put it back down. Turnbull started drawing his gear from a flight bag, as did Casey. They pulled out their helmets, goggles, and their off-the-shelf civilian parachutes, gearing up for the jump.

The plane could not land with its passengers on-board at San Francisco International Airport. The blues had re-named SFO for

Nancy Pelosi, who had become even more popular in the PR when she began an affair with Amy Klobuchar just before the Split and after her husband's third DUI, the final time in the company of an exotic dancer named Juggsy McColl. This affair made the former Speaker an LGBTQ+!dD6@?9 icon, and therefore made naming the airport after her a no brainer. However, it was somewhat unfair that she got the hosannas, since Juggsy herself had been assigned male at birth.

The relationship with Klobuchar turned sour after a blazing row at one of Pelosi's several vineyards, where the former senator threw a bottle of a pinot noir at her lover. It had a lot of barnyard on the nose, and it hit Pelosi on the nose. Later, Klobuchar would be linked to Mitt Romney, who moved into the blue after the Split because "red America is not who we are." He apparently appreciated her abuse.

With the airport's name restored after the invasion – General Scott had publicly rejected the paramilitaries' attempt to name it after him in what some critics contended was a stunt designed to demonstrate his virtue – SFO was a bustling military air hub base serving the occupation. Deeds had word that they had tightened up security considerably in the last couple days, and that everyone coming in was being closely screened. Turnbull managing to sneak in without the Occupation knowing it might have been the impetus. In any case, there was only one option for getting back into 'Frisco fast.

They would have to jump.

The pilot would have to wander off course a bit, but that was necessary. The plane was veering out of the normal air corridors and would fly over the massive, open San Bruno Mountain that stretched west from the Bay across the narrow San Francisco Peninsula. The mountain formed the southern geographic boundary of the City. The jumpers would have to try to land somewhere relatively flat.

While the pilot was arguing with air traffic control about his course and position, the crewman at the front of the cabin flipped a switch marked "REAR RAMP – AIRBORNE OPS." They were at 5,350 feet and the aircraft interior was blacked out.

The rear ramp dropped. It was night and the City below was still only intermittently lit, such being the depredations of the People's Republic and the pre-Split California government against the state's power grid.

Turnbull and Casey, clad in dark civilian clothing, did the airborne shuffle to the edge of the ramp as Gibson observed from back inside the plane.

"Geronimo!" Casey shouted, though between the engines and the rushing air no one heard him.

Turnbull pulled on his goggles and stepped off into darkness.

Every jump reminded him that he was at least a little bit insane. Sane people do not leap into the blackness and abandon a perfectly good airplane.

Luckily, it was not foggy. That could have been a real buzzkill. Instead, he enjoyed the view for a few seconds as he dropped, battering his way downward through the air toward terminal velocity. It was all by gut – this was no static line jump where the ripcord is attached to a metal line running down the length of the aircraft and all you have to do is let gravity do its thing.

He disabled his AOD, the automatic opening device, so he could choose when to pull the ripcord. Too soon and that amped up the risk of him being spotted, something that could end badly since the paramilitaries still had a BOLO on him. Too late, and splat.

When it felt right, he pulled the ripcord and watched the canopy deploy above him. It was a perfect dark rectangle, no kinks, tears, or tangles. They were running with civilian chutes that packed themselves, Performance Design Sabre 3s. At 170 square feet, the canopies were significantly smaller than a military issue MC-4 freefall rig. The lower profile, plus the lower opening at about 750 feet, made them that much less detectible.

The yank of the parachute catching the air and controlling his descent was welcome, considering the alternative.

There was enough illumination for him to see where there were trees and where there was brush and where there was grass. He glided toward the latter, landing in a fairly flat area and, to his satisfaction, not suffering any injury. He collapsed the canopy and stripped off his gear. His day pack came down strapped to the front of his legs and was filled with some ammo, some clothes, a couple burner phones, and another $25,000 in cash – Deeds had to pull a lot of strings to make that happen in Lewiston, but Turnbull insisted. He needed to buy help and it would cost him.

He was up the north face of San Bruno Mountain, but it was not particularly steep. There was a road below him, twisting down the hill, Guadalupe Canyon Road. On his internet recon, he had recognized it as where Steve McQueen and his Mustang had ended his chase with the hit men in *Bullitt*. Of course, McQueen did not have death-obsessed lunatics leaping onto his vehicle.

Wuss, thought Turnbull and he gathered the parachute, rolled it up, and hid it under a large sagebrush bush.

He had only the Wilson .45, though he had picked up a suppressor for it from Deeds's team's armorer. He also had the little Springfield; Leia had handed it back to him in Waitsburg. He left the HK416 back in Idaho. This mission would take a bit more finesse than an automatic carbine provided, but if finesse did not work out he could find himself a new rifle pretty quick.

After sitting and listening for a few minutes – he heard nothing but the occasional hoot and the wind – he started heading north down the hill toward the road. He did not bother looking for Casey. They would meet at the rendezvous, the intersection of Guadalupe Canyon Road and the blocked access road up to the radio towers at the summit of the mountain.

Turnbull hit Guadalupe Canyon Road and found it did not have much of a shoulder to walk on, so he was forced to use the pavement. There were no cars coming by – it was only about nine-thirty, but except for the surreptitious furries and other weirdos of the Fisherman's Wharf rave, the town rolled-up early under the Occupation and its curfew.

And from his vantage point, he could see down below, where the undeveloped mountain ended and the City began, a large, looming building surrounded by some outbuildings and acres of parking lot.

It had to be the Cow Palace.

"I was worried about you," Casey said when he got to the intersection about thirty minutes after Turnbull. There was a locked gate across the access road and a little parking area, though no cars. Turnbull had observed the area from a distance just in case someone was there – a guard, a hobo, a couple kids trying to score.

When he decided it was clean he came in, carefully, and swept the area. There was a stand of eucalyptus trees a bit back off the intersection lining the access road, and he took a position in it. Casey came up, stealthily. Turnbull got his attention and they met up on the pavement.

"You okay?" Casey asked.

"My chute worked fine," Turnbull replied.

"No, I mean *you*," Casey said. "It's been nearly forty-eight hours since you killed someone. I was worried you might start having withdrawals."

"Maybe I'll get my fix the day after tomorrow," he said. Turnbull pointed down at the auditorium.

"That's the Cow Palace," he said. "That's where we know he will be."

"Except he will be surrounded by fifteen thousand provisionals and probably his own Army security guys."

"Yeah," Turnbull said, the beginnings of a plan forming in his head. "He's going to feel safe. And that's what's going to screw him."

"What do you have in mind?" Casey asked as they started walking across the parking lot toward the Parkway that would take them off the mountain.

"There is a guy I need to reach out to. Risky, but...," Turnbull paused.

Headlights, coming up the road.

There was no need to talk. Turnbull and Casey both dove into the brush alongside the parking lot.

The vehicle came up the road and Turnbull was hoping it would keep on going to the west, but it did not. It slowed and made the left, a little too fast, into the dusty parking lot at the intersection with the radio tower access road.

His Wilson was out, as was Casey's HK – and Casey was screwing on his suppressor. Turnbull did the same – quietly, carefully, while watching.

The old Ford Econoline van looked like the ride of a guy who would offer passing schoolkids candy or a free puppy. It had two flags flying off the back, one the US flag and another a black flag with an anarchy symbol. On the side in red spray paint, though it looked black in the moonlight, it read "Jello Biafran Militia." It also bore a half-assed Λ symbol.

The van skidded to a stop and the doors opened. There was laughing. The passengers, looking like they were channeling the hardcore kids of a half-century before, got out armed with beer cans and AK-47s. Turnbull counted four total. One had a mohawk; they all wore leather and were giddy.

"Punk provisionals?" Casey whispered.

"Keep it down," Turnbull chided him. They might be stuck waiting for a while until these goons finished getting their Coors on.

The one with the mohawk finished his brew and threw it into the brush a few feet from where Turnbull and Casey were watching. Then he reached inside the cargo area. There was a scream.

A young woman.

"Shit," whispered Turnbull.

The punk pulled her out. She was in her mid-teens, crying and scared, hands bound in front of her with black duct tape.

"Blue bitch," mohawk said when she resisted. He smashed her across the face and she fell to the dirt.

"So much about not killing anyone," Casey said. He pulled back the hammer on his pistol. Turnbull's was already back.

"We did red bitches when the blue was in charge and we do blue when the red's in charge," another of the four Jello Biafrans told her as the girl cried on the ground. "We like it when they cry."

"Go from the left," Turnbull instructed Casey. "I'll go from the right. Leave one. I have questions."

"On three," Casey said. The punk who had been mocking the girl pulled back one of his Doc Martens to kick her.

"Three," said Turnbull.

He stood and the kicker glanced at him a second before two of Turnbull's .45 slugs smashed through his forehead. Turnbull pivoted to the one on his right, who was trying to get the slung AK off his shoulder. Turnbull lined up the sight center mass and fired two suppressed shots into the guy's chest. He went back against the passenger door and slowly slid down it to the dirt. Turnbull declined to complete the Mozambique drill with a round to his brain both to save ammo and to avoid smashing out the windows of the van if the round happened to go through the punk's skull instead of bouncing around inside it.

Casey engaged the two to the left, the first being a rather large punk wearing a Misfits t-shirt under his jacket. Casey popped a couple rounds of Corbon 9mm +P 125 grain JHP hollow points into the grinning skull logo. The target staggered back and Casey moved to engage Mohawk, putting two in his lower gut then pivoting back to finish Misfits Fan with a shot to his face.

Turnbull confirmed his two were dead, and Casey made sure Misfit Fan was with an additional round in the temple. Mohawk was groaning, and Casey knelt and took the punk's rifle, a knife, and a pair of brass knuckles, while Turnbull stepped to the girl.

"You're okay," he said to her, "They're all dead."

She looked around, horrified. Then she looked back at Turnbull.

"I'm cutting off this tape," he said, pulling out the Gerber. "Don't run or freak out, okay?" She nodded.

Turnbull sliced her free of her fetters. She stood, then sat back in the open van doorway.

"I was walking home and they took me," she said.

"They won't be taking anyone else," Casey said. "Except whoever Satan loans them out to."

Casey turned to Mohawk.

"Who are you?"

Mohawk groaned.

"You shot me, man," he said, wincing.

"Yep. Looks like it hurts. Who are you?"

"We're provisionals," Mohawk said. "You can't shoot us."

"That's demonstrably false," Turnbull said, joining the discussion. "He asked you a question."

"We're the Jello Biafrans, man. We're a militia," he said.

"Like, the Dead Kennedys's Jello Biafra?" asked Casey. Turnbull wondered what the hell he was talking about.

Mohawk nodded.

"Like a tribute militia?" Casey asked. Mohawk just groaned.

"You mentioned you did this under the blues," Turnbull said. "Were you working for the blues too?"

"Who cares who's in charge," Mohawk said. "We don't even believe in government."

"So you just sign on with anyone who lets you rape teenagers?" Turnbull said. Mohawk, sensing there was no good answer, just gritted his teeth.

"I need a doctor," he said. "You shot me!"

"Uh huh," Turnbull said. "Say, which one of you was the driver."

Mohawk sat up painfully on the ground, and used a bloody hand to point out the first guy Turnbull took down.

"Thanks," Turnbull said, and then he fired a suppressed round into the punk's temple.

The girl cried out in shock and Mohawk's torso fell over into the dirt.

"Let's go," Turnbull said, walking over to the driver to retrieve the van's keys.

"Where to?" Casey asked.

"Ask her," Turnbull said. "We're taking her home."

21.

The girl's name was Cassidy, and she lived in Pacific Heights. Turnbull was no expert on San Francisco, but he knew that was where the rich people lived before and after the Split. In fact, it was within the Controlled Zone of San Francisco during the People's Republic period; the security wall to keep out the riff-raff still remained around it and some of the adjacent Western Addition neighborhoods, with only the parts blocking the road bulldozed by the Occupation so far. It was no longer a safe haven, protected from the rest of the City.

The van, being a provisional vehicle, was able to cruise the streets without harassment. Both Turnbull and Casey, who drove, borrowed leather jackets from the dead punks to fit in better. Cassidy knew the way once they got far enough north. Pacific Heights was near the tip of the Peninsula, on an east-west ridge providing views of the Bay and even of the Occupation HQ in the Presidio to the west. This was prime real estate for an old ruling class that no longer ruled, at least for those members who had not fled to Seattle when the red forces came up the Peninsula in force.

The streets were empty, except for occasional provisional or Army vehicles, and a few commercial vehicles with special exemptions from the curfew. It was still jarring for Turnbull that there were no bums, none.

He was used to the lack of hobos in the red – you were just not allowed to be a bum, period – but they were such an integral part of San Francisco that it was odd that they were not there. The effect was like the emptiness of the prairie after the buffalo herds had been exterminated. Turnbull wondered just how good the analogy was.

Cassidy, now back in familiar territory, was able to guide them through the streets lined with Victorian homes. Many were clearly unoccupied. The ones that were still inhabited seemed to be in good condition, at least compared to the housing stock outside of the old Controlled Zone. There were few cars, though, despite the fact that the people living here could usually qualify for one under the People's Republic. Thanks to the Occupation, there was no gas for the gas-powered ones, and no cheap electricity for the electric vehicles the PR had been trying to promote.

They got some scowls from the provisionals lurking around the area. Apparently the Jello Biafrans were not the cool kids among the militias.

"Our house," Cassidy said, pointing to a blue Victorian with bay windows. It had a nice northwestern view.

Casey pulled to the side of the road and parked.

"We'll take you up," Turnbull said. It was important her parents understood the necessity of them all shutting the hell up, especially with the Occupation looking for him.

The parents were a couple in their mid-forties, the wife with a goblet of white wine and the husband with round glasses and little upper-body mass. The inside of the house belied the exterior – it was not luxurious, but was functional. He suspected they once had nice stuff, but had sold it off and downscaled.

On the dining room table were a couple open Occupation civilian ration packs and several Tupperware bowls with a white crust. Gruel. When ration packs were unavailable for the locals, the Occupation sent community gruel trucks into the neighborhoods so local blue families could download something to eat. It was calories enough to keep you alive, and it was fortified with vitamin C to prevent scurvy. On holidays, the soldiers would sometimes bring a little cinnamon their families had sent them from home to sprinkle on top.

The family hugged Cassidy and then looked over Turnbull and Casey, uncertain.

"We need to talk," Turnbull said, stepping forward into the hallway.

The wife stood in the way, her eyes on his .45.

"We don't allow guns," she said. "We don't believe in them."

"And I don't believe in letting people rape teenagers," Turnbull said, pushing past her. "So I shoot them."

Casey followed him in and shut the door behind him.

"There are four dead provisionals on San Bruno Mountain and your daughter is okay," Turnbull said. "You're welcome."

"They were going to hurt me, mom," Cassidy said.

Turnbull continued. "I don't know how or if anyone will link Cassidy to them. I don't know if the Occupation is going to care about a quartet of dead creeps enough to even investigate. You may never hear of it again, in which case it will be just a bad memory. But if you do, or they ask about me, you do not know anything. Nothing."

"You killed them," the mother said slowly. "How could you do that?"

"By putting bullets into their skulls," Turnbull snapped. "It works every time. Now focus."

But she did not focus. She could not. Turnbull saw, on the wall behind her, a framed sign that read "Hate has No Home Here."

And she saw where he was looking.

"You're one of the reds, aren't you?"

"Yeah."

"Under your Occupation, they could arrest me for having that sign!"

"The People's Republic arrested people all the time for saying things and you didn't have a problem with that."

"But they were bad people. Disinformation and hate are not free speech. Only a racist constitution would allow that."

"Welcome to the rules you made," Turnbull said. He was done. He pivoted to the door. But the mother was not finished.

"You reds, you brought the hate here! You couldn't stand that the People's Republic rejected your hate! There were no militias before you came. There was no racism, or sexism, or transphobia," she said, getting louder. The husband just stood there.

"Life must have been pretty good for you in the Controlled Zone," Turnbull said. "Outside, not so much."

"You're murderers."

"Your daughter's alive because of us."

"I wish they had killed you!" the mother said, turning and running into the back room. Cassidy ran back to console her.

"We have nothing," the man said when Turnbull's eyes fell on him. "She used to be the head of the diversity department at People's Bank, and now she has to scrub toilets to get our basic subsistence allowance from the Occupation. How is that right?"

"Seems super-right to me," Turnbull said. "And what were you?"

"I consulted on synergy and equity for a non-profit NGO."

"You mopping out shitters now too?"

"Yeah." He seemed offended.

"Good," Turnbull said. "Remember what I said about shutting the hell up. Maybe keep the missus away from the bathtub Chardonnay for a while so she doesn't run her mouth and call down a shit storm on you, from the Occupation or from me."

"You can't talk to us like that. We're not..."

"What aren't you?"

"I had a privilege level of 9 and a Mercedes-Benz!" he said, sputtering.

"Enjoy your mopping."

"These blues are insane," Casey said, driving the Jello Biafran's van toward the Grattan Elementary School, the base for the Ron's Rangers.

"It's like a mass psychosis took over the country when we weren't looking," Turnbull said.

"Larry O'Connor always says on his show that Andrew Breitbart broke the left by exposing who the left really is."

"Do you listen to the radio all day?"

"It's actually a very popular podcast," said Casey. "Regardless, I don't think General Scott is the cure."

"I don't know if there is one," Turnbull said. "We free these people and half of them want to go on a rape and killing spree and the other half are pissed off at us for screwing over their sweet gig in the PR."

"This place is broken," Casey said.

"And I don't know if it can be fixed," Turnbull said before moving on. "Now, remember that the people we're going to stay with are libertarians, so you need to be careful about what you say."

"Hair trigger types? Easy to anger?"

"No, it's just that once they get started talking about libertarianism they won't shut up."

"Oh, like political Cross-Fitters?"

"Or militant atheists."

Turnbull guided Casey through the streets to the schoolhouse base. It was there, up ahead, and Casey slowed the van. There was a roadblock outside the school. Ron's Rangers, Turnbull determined. That was good.

One of the provos, a female with an M4, came to the driver's side window, smiling.

"You know, I met Jello Biafra once," she said, leaning in. "He was signing old underwear for $20 in my college quad right before the Split. I remember when the blues arrested Jello because 'Holiday in Cambodia' was insensitive to Third World peoples and it also slandered socialism."

"Yeah, I don't know who that is," Turnbull said. "I need to talk to Kyle. Tell him it's his pal from the other day."

"They are still looking for you," Kyle said once he and Casey were alone in a room at the old school. "Every day we get instructions to look for you. Maybe that Frankenstein cut on your head might confuse them. Anyway, why did you come back?"

"Because my buddy and I need to go to the party," Turnbull said. "As your guests."

"I don't understand."

"The Cow Palace thing."

"You mean the Kale Palace?" asked Kyle. "I guess it's the Cow Palace again. They changed the name after the Split."

"I'm guessing offensive to vegans."

"Probably. Maybe offensive to otherkins who are cows," said Kyle. "Anyway, all the provisional groups got told to show up. No one knows why, though. We are all supposed to bring ten folks each. Should be thousands of people there. They are coming in from all over the state. We were going to put one of the groups up here, another libertarian militia, but we got into a fight with them over Ayn Rand's view of altruism and they stomped off."

"I need two of your slots," Turnbull said. "For me and my pal."

Kyle shook his head. "We auctioned the ten slots off to whoever wanted to go. You will have to buy them."

"I thought you were in charge," Casey said, annoyed.

"Don't," warned Turnbull.

"Well, I'm currently wielding limited executive authority," Kyle began. "I can make certain smaller decisions, but for major issues and policies I can bring the matter to our executive committee, or in some cases the entire militia for consideration, debate, and approval."

"I should have listened to you," Casey said as Kyle went on.

"How much to buy the damn tickets?" Turnbull asked.

Command Sergeant Major Lightfoot did not like this one bit. The command post itself was humming with activity, but there were fewer personnel working there than before.

Noticeably fewer.

"We should go behind closed doors," he told the general.

Karl Martin Scott smiled. His three security men milled about a few yards away, out of the way but watching closely. The sergeant major had a nickname for the silent trio – Moe, Larry, and Curly.

"We're fine here, Sergeant Major," said the general.

"Okay, sir, you've signed transfer orders for at least twenty personnel, officers, NCOs, even some enlisted, in the last couple days and I never saw any of the paperwork."

"Sergeant Major, those troops had been working long and hard and deserved a chance to return to their families," the general said soothingly. That was true, the senior non-commissioned officer in the Occupation knew. All his people were busting their humps on this thankless mission. But that was the thing – he was the CSM, and they were his people.

"I was not consulted, sir. Officers, fine. That's your world. But NCOs and junior enlisted, those are mine. And now we are not going to have backfills any time soon."

General Scott paused and made a show of considering what CSM Lightfoot had said. It was Sergeant Major's turn to be indisputably correct, and they both knew it.

"You're right," the general conceded after a moment designed to demonstrate that he was listening and thinking about what he had been told. "This was NCO business and I stepped into it. The newest LT would not have made that mistake and I did. It will not happen again, Sergeant Major."

CSM Lightfoot was not taken aback at the concession, because in his months with the general he knew that the commander would not fight on bad ground. Bypassing the CSM broke protocol – that was beyond debate, and Scott was not trying to debate it.

But why had the general done it? Did he do it because he knew that if he brought the transfers out to his sergeant major, his sergeant major would have objected?

"Sergeant Major," General Scott continued. "I need to get with my staff on the Cow Palace plan. We should talk later about streamlining our processes to avoid future problems."

"That's another issue, sir," Lightfoot said. "I don't like this Cow Palace event one bit. You're having 15,000 provisionals who range from semi-trained to basically street gangs all together under one roof alone with a four-star general – and you're not letting me provide any security inside the building beyond your PSD. Plus, and did I get this right, you're letting them bring in their weapons?"

"I can't think of anywhere I'd be safer than in a room where anyone pulls a gun and 14,999 other people draw on him."

"And no soldiers inside except your PSD?"

"Correct," Scott replied. "I think it's important to keep the provisionals and our active forces in their respective lanes."

"I've had concerns about the provisionals for a while, General. They are not real soldiers."

"Many have been fighting ever since the Split."

"I get that. But some are dangerously undisciplined. They kill civilians."

"The People's Republic's subjects cannot expect that the people it oppressed will forget what they suffered. I don't condone it, but I don't see how we can expect bygones to be bygones."

"Too many of the provos are loose cannons."

"And that is why I am making raising their professionalism a personal priority. You take care of my regular forces. I'll handle the militias. And as for tomorrow night, your personnel can secure the outside of the arena. You can handle my convoy in and out."

"Sir, you should let me do my job."

"Sergeant Major, you have my total confidence. Now, I understand you're rolling out this morning to check on soldiers in the East Bay."

Lightfoot nodded. "I'm going to visit a number of units in Oakland and around there."

"Good. I'm very concerned about morale among our people after being deployed so long. They want to go home. When you have a mostly reserve force, that's a huge problem. Brief me on what you find."

"Roger," the sergeant major replied. He walked away, still unsatisfied and, moreover, unsettled.

General Scott waved over one of his Army majors. He had a dozen of them assigned to his staff – the field grade lieutenants were fungible – and almost all of the ones remaining were considered loyal. The twenty souls he had sent packing back to the red were not – they were likely to object or even obstruct when the mission of the Occupation headquarters changed after tomorrow's speech. The remaining personnel of doubtful loyalty were on a list. They would be detained when it all went down. At the top of the list was Command Sergeant Major Lightfoot.

"Major," the general said. "I want Sergeant Major taken into custody the moment we return from the Cow Palace tomorrow night. I want solid folks to greet him. He's a good man and a good soldier – I don't want him hurt, but I want him on ice. Make sure that's in the plan."

"Yes, sir," the major said. He scampered away, as staff officers do.

The general stood, observing his staff at work in the command post. On the monitors, the Gray Zone continued to mock him. If his Green Berets had gotten the bomb, that would have simplified things. But now the scientists at Hanford were not even answering the phone.

And there was more troubling news.

At the nine-a.m. staff call, his provost marshal had briefed him on a troubling development. There were four dead provisionals from a bizarre unit composed of, according to the briefing, ex-punk rockers who had also been some sort of militia/street enforcers under the blues. The MPs found them in a parking lot up on San Bruno Mountain, killed the night before.

Professionally. Tight shot groupings and a lot of head shots. Their vehicle was gone – there was now a BOLO for it. But they never even got their weapons out – not a shot from any of them.

Kelly Turnbull? It sure smelled like an operator, though the marshal had briefed that there were both .45 and 9mm shell casings. Turnbull had carried a very nice M1911. But if he was smart – and Turnbull had demonstrated that he was smart by cheating death from Scott's minions twice – he would be long gone, out of town, vanished. Either he now had a friend, making him doubly dangerous, or there was a new team here.

Why?

Could someone from the red know what was going to happen?

Was there a spy in his headquarters?

He drummed his fingers on one of the worktables but his face did not betray his concerns. He appeared to all serene, even as his mind played the possible scenarios over and over again.

Damn, I wish they had killed Kelly Turnbull, Scott thought.

But he consoled himself with the knowledge that it would happen all in good time.

With the burner phone pressed to his ear, Turnbull could hear the line was ringing. Deeds had located the number somehow while they were in Lewistown. It was good to work for a guy with deep resources, though actually being one of those resources could be a pain in the ass.

The phone clicked and the other end of the call picked up.

"Sergeant Major Lightfoot."

"Sergeant Major, don't react. Do you know who this is?"

There was a pause.

"I think so."

"Can you talk?"

"Wait one." Turnbull could hear the CSM tell his driver to pull over, and then a door opened. It sounded like he was walking.

"Okay," Lightfoot finally said.

"Is this line safe?" Turnbull asked.

"It's open." Sergeant Major was telling him that the line was not secure. Someone could be listening – and the Occupation did a lot of listening, just as the People's Republic had.

"Can we do a sit-down?"

"They're looking for you."

"I'm not sure what for, but do you believe whatever they are saying I did?"

"Maybe."

"Ten minutes. Where?"

Lightfoot looked around. He was on Ninth Street, heading toward the Interstate-80 on-ramp so he could head over the Bay Bridge to visit some maintenance units and naval forces in Oakland out by the water. Visiting units was a key task for a command sergeant major. He could see if the units were functioning, detect problems, and measure morale.

There was a coffee shop back up Ninth, one of the few that had reopened. It probably would not have much in the way of coffee.

"Yeah, I got a place," he told Turnbull.

Turnbull trusted Lightfoot, mostly. But men changed over time, and the same straight arrow from Baghdad might not be so straight almost twenty years later. He spotted the three-vehicle convoy of SUVs cooling its jets a couple hundred meters down the road. The soldiers were smoking and joking, very relaxed, killing time while the sergeant major went off and did sergeant major stuff.

Turnbull walked the perimeter, scanning the rooftops and windows. No observers, and no snipers – though he would not see the really good ones. The coffee shop itself was small and there was a big window in front. Sergeant Major Lightfoot was sitting inside alone, with a cup. There were only a few customers, probably because so few people could afford coffee.

Satisfied that the NCO had not organized a setup in the few minutes since his call, Turnbull walked in. He was dressed as a civilian contractor and wore his .45 on his hip. He had a San Francisco Lightbringers ball cap pulled low over his face, which he wore ironically. The team, which was not yet playing but was supposed to restart in the spring, was now once again called the Giants. Under the People's Republic, that offensive name had been changed after an outcry by a coalition of midgets, dwarfs, and bitter short people.

Turnbull slid into the seat.

"You want a cup?"

"Is it bad?"

"It's bad."

"Then yes."

Lightfoot motioned for another cup. The woman at the counter sighed and began preparing it.

"You really kill all those Mutilated?" Lightfoot asked.

"Yes," Turnbull said. "But I had my reasons."

"And what were they?"

"Your boss told them to take me out, shoot me, and dump me in a hole."

Lightfoot stared, shocked.

"Kelly, he's a GO and a ring knocker, and that's crazy. You need to come in with me. We can work this out."

"No, Sergeant Major. I got a mission. I have to stop your boss."

"From what?"

"From starting another civil war before we finish the one we're in now."

"I don't understand," confessed the CSM.

"General Karl Martin Scott is planning a coup. Actually, it's more than a coup. Those provisionals he's gathering up at the Cow Palace tomorrow night? He's going to turn them into an army and march them on Dallas while the real Army is on the borders too busy with the blues and the Chi Coms to do anything about it."

"That's nuts, Kelly. He's a war hero. He might be president someday."

"I think he's looking for more certainty than 'might.' Ask yourself, do you see anything strange happening? Because I can't imagine he wouldn't try to keep you in the dark. You don't truck with any foolishness."

"I've seen some things," the CSM conceded.

"Oh, and he sent his guys to my house to kill me and ended up shooting my fiancée in the kidney. So it's personal."

"I don't believe it."

"What, that I'm getting married?"

"That either."

"Look, this is classified above classified, but I'm here to either bring his ass back to Dallas to face trial or to put him in his grave. One of those two things is happening."

"He's my commander, Kelly."

"You owe your loyalty to the country first."

"I know who I owe my loyalty to. This is a lot to process."

Turnbull nodded. It was.

"You go back, do your job, but look around. See what you can find. Tomorrow night's shindig is key. The only reason to get all the provos here from around the state in front of him is for him to issue them their marching orders. And he won't be ordering them north. He'll be ordering them east."

"Shit, Kelly." The CSM shook his head. The girl came over and placed the cup on the table in front of Turnbull. Her name tag said "Christy (her/she)." Force of habit.

"I'm getting inside the Cow Palace, if that's still its name."

"It is."

"I'll get in. But I need to get him out."

"I won't have any Army bodies inside. No soldiers, except his PSD."

"Three operators?"

"Yeah, and they are hard. We call them Moe, Larry, and Curly. The general is letting everyone bring their guns in. Says he's safer if everyone is armed."

Turnbull smiled, appreciating Scott's strategy.

"He's right, though. If I pull my piece, I get a thousand barrels pointed right at my head. I don't dare shoot him. No, we need to do it another way."

"I will have security in and out. My guys will convoy him there and home."

"Will they play for our team, Sergeant Major?" Turnbull took a sip of the coffee. It was bad.

"You are assuming I am playing on your team. I'm not yet convinced."

"You know what you are looking for and you'll see it. When we take him, I have a C-130 waiting at SFO to take us back to Texas."

"Great," said the sergeant major. "You just have to get him in the vehicle and south to the airbase without his three killers or his fifteen thousand provisionals capping you."

"Well, at least if I fail no one eats me."

"What's that mean, Kelly?"

"Long story."

Turnbull gulped down the rest of the lousy brew and got up.

22.

Turnbull, Casey, and Kyle drove slowly through the expanse of the overgrown parking lot in a Ron's Rangers vehicle. Kyle was at the wheel. They were doing a site recon the day before the big event.

The Cow Palace was a huge, beige bulk planted in the midst of acres of faded parking spaces. Weeds and grass grew up through crevices and cracks of the asphalt to such an extent that some parts looked more like a field than a car lot.

The words "COW PALACE" had once graced the arched front of the building, painted in a dull rust-red. "COW" had been scraped off and "KALE" added. The paint had not been up to snuff and had weathered off fairly soon. Neither the PR nor the Occupation had gotten around to replacing it, leaving an unreadable smear then "PALACE."

It was built during the Depression a century before, and had an art deco/brutalist mash-up vibe. Flat-roofed wings extended from each side of it, and a low pavilion extended out to serve as the entrance. The complex had been designed for use in agricultural shows and the price tag had been mocked, with a local gadfly describing it as "a palace for cows." The name stuck. But it was soon hosting more than rodeos and livestock expositions. It had been the home court to sports teams and the site of championship games, as well as being a concert venue. Before the Split, legendary performers like the Beatles, The Who, the Rolling Stones, U2, and D-Yazzy had headlined there. And after the Split, it had hosted mandatory concerts by government-licensed acts such as the reunited 4 Non-Blondes and Dee Snider's new group Twisted Sibling, which was touring in support of its yacht-rock single "Obey and Be Happy." It was the stage where Lizzo had suffered cardiac arrest during a mildly-strenuous duet with trans rapper Morgan Thee Mare, and the last show before the red invasion had been a stop on Hunter Biden's "There's a Meth to My Madness" spoken word concert tour.

The trio of Turnbull, Casey, and Kyle walked nonchalantly into the pavilion. There was a lot of work going on. A solemn plaque in the entrance pavilion was being crowbarred off the wall in preparation for General Scott's conclave. It apologized for the Cow Palace having served as the site of the Republican hate rallies that renominated Eisenhower in 1956 and selected Goldwater in 1964. Another, already torn off and lying on the floor, formally acknowledged that the Cow Palace "WAS BUILT ON LANDS STOLEN FROM THE OHLONE/COSTANOAN PEOPLX BY INVADERS OF PALLOR."

A line of fairly uniform and well-armed provisionals blocked them off from walking back into the auditorium itself. This militia looked organized and professional, which is likely why it got the security mission.

"Serra Boys," Kyle said.

"You seem to know everyone in the militia biz," Turnbull observed.

"Always a good idea to be everyone's pal, if you can be," Kyle said.

"Who's on their unit patch?" Casey said, squinting at the face on the provisionals' shoulder. "It looks like Greg Gutfeld." His Fox show, *Gutfeld's Evening Soiree*, was the dominant late-night show in the red, with his main competitor being raconteur Tony Katz on Elon Musk's Doge TV network.

"It *is* Greg Gutfeld," Kyle replied. "The Serra Boys started as an anti-blue resistance group made up of Serra High School alumni in San Mateo, down south on the Peninsula. Gutfeld is their proudest alumnus, and then Tom Brady and Lynn Swann. I went to school down the street at Aragon. Its biggest-name alum was Neil Schon of Journey."

"Journey?" asked Casey. "I think my dad liked them. Or his dad."

Turnbull was peering past the security into the auditorium. It was humming with activity. Inside, the stage was being erected in the rear with hanging red curtains dividing off the backstage area. The sound systems and lights were being erected, and a pair of giant video monitors on each side as well. Out of sight, the plumbers were desperately working to get the long-neglected sewerage system working before 15,000 provos came through the doors.

Outside, in the parking lot, the provisionals were already arriving, thousands so far. Some stayed in their vehicles, having driven in from the far reaches of California. Many erected tents. Others, the smarter and more prosperous militias, had RVs. Many were cooking outdoors, and a smoky haze hung over the scene. They all carried weapons.

Kyle drove them around to the rear of the complex. There were doors, but it was the ramp leading down beneath the building that got their attention. Obviously, it was an entrance for talent and deliveries.

"That's how they'll bring him in," Turnbull said. It would not do to have the commanding general come in the front door and be mobbed like a teeny-bopper heartthrob by his adoring provisional fans.

But access down below was blocked off. There were US Army military police guarding the ramps. They looked bored, but no sense in testing them.

"Let's go," Turnbull said.

Command Sergeant Major Lightfoot was leading a posse of senior non-commissioned officers through the headquarters of the 576th Support Brigade (Theater Support), stopping to talk to soldiers and generally making it look like it was just another command visit. The units' non-commissioned officers – the O-6 colonel commander had greeted CSM Lightfoot then took her leave, since this was NCO business – were on edge, as was usual. The CSM ignored that, and he paid only cursory attention to the routine issues he was normally concerned with – systemic pay problems, morale issues, and the like.

He saw the S4 Planning Cell office door and put his hand on the knob.

"Give me some space, gentlemen," he said to the gaggle of senior sergeants following him. He went inside, leaving them behind, terrified at what the soldiers of the S4 might tell their visitor about how dicked up the unit really was if they were not there to glare.

The office had about a dozen enlisted troops of various ranks working at computers, and they were surprised to see the CSM walk in. They knew the unit was expecting his visit, but they had been told the 4-shop was not on the agenda and to stay inside their cave doing their jobs until the distinguished visitor could be sent on his way. It was such a surprise that it took the ranking soldier, an E-5 buck sergeant, a moment to remember to put the room "at ease."

"Carry on," CSM Lightfoot said pleasantly. "I'm just here to look around, see how things are working."

The sergeant in charge stood by nervously, not sure what to do, wondering where the hell his unit's senior NCOs were and asking the Lord what he had done to deserve this nightmare.

"Sergeant, I'm just going to walk around and talk to the troops. You just get back to work."

"Yes, Sergeant Major," the sergeant said, happy to be sent away.

Sergeant Major Lightfoot scanned the room. A sign on a computer read "CLASS III OPS" and there was a young specialist in thick glasses looking at the screen.

Time to engage the E-4 Mafia, Lightfoot thought to himself.

He walked over, and pulled up a chair. The specialist was distinctly uncomfortable.

"Class III," the sergeant major said. "Fuel and petroleum products."

"Roger, Sergeant Major. I process requisitions and track positioning for the bulk fuel for the theater."

"Things slow now that combat operations are on hold?"

"Oh no, Sergeant Major, we're jumping through our asses. I mean...sorry. Butts."

"Show me."

The specialist typed on his keyboard and Lightfoot saw it right away. The support units were busy, all right. They were stockpiling gas at refueling points all along the I-10 and I-40 corridors. Those were the main support routes between Texas and California. It looked like the command was getting ready to fuel a multi-corps sized movement east. That was huge. But he has not seen a plan for anything like that, and there was no reason to plan, much less conduct, that kind of operation.

No *good* reason.

"Thanks, specialist. Nice job." He reached in his pocket and handed the young man a coin that had a sword impaling California on one side and, on the reverse, the words "COMMAND SERGEANT MAJOR - UNITED STATES PACIFIC COAST OCCUPATION FORCES COMMAND."

The specialist mumbled his thanks and Lightfoot got up and left. He had what he needed.

If you want the ground truth, you go to the E-4 Mafia.

"He's in," Turnbull said, hanging up his burner phone. Sergeant Major Lightfoot was now convinced about his commander's intentions.

"So what's the plan?" asked Casey. They were cleaning their weapons in their room at the libertarian militia's schoolhouse base.

"Sergeant Major will be waiting outside of the Cow Palace with the convoy by the back exit at the bottom of one of those ramps we saw with a convoy of SUVs to bring the general back to the Presidio once the show is over. Except we're going to frog march him out ourselves, and then the convoy is going to the airport."

"Okay," Casey said. "Sounds great. Except how do we get custody of the guy to frog march him out?"

"That's the issue."

"There are fifteen thousand provos who mostly won't like it."

"Yeah."

"His personal security team won't like it."

"The PSD will object. True."

"And General Scott too. He's not a sissy. He'll be strapped."

"I expect so."

Casey shook his head.

"I see some rather significant gaps in your planning, Kelly."

"You think?"

"Is this one of those playing it by ear things?"

"It is."

Casey sighed.

"I really hate playing things by ear."

They had a day until the Cow Palace convention, and Turnbull made the best of it. He ensured his weapons were clean and ready. He had full seven mags for the .45 and one partial. He still had three for the Springfield compact that was his backup piece.

He touched base several times with Sergeant Major to make sure that he and his convoy would be waiting at the Cow Palace's backstage ramp.

Lastly, Turnbull completed his deal with Kyle.

"Twenty thousand dollars," he said, handing over a stack of US currency. He held back $5,000 for emergencies.

Kyle smiled. Turnbull continued.

"That pays for room, board, security, dumping that shitbox van we stole, transpo to the Cow Palace, and our slots on your crew going in. Plus your unique insights and problem-solving abilities inside."

Kyle nodded. It was a lot of US currency – everyone usually had to use the nearly worthless Occupation scrip.

"Are you going to fill me in on what you intend to do once I get you in there?" Kyle asked.

"No," Turnbull said. "But when things start, get your Objectivist ass out of there."

"I wouldn't call myself an Objectivist," Kyle began, but Turnbull was already holding up his palm and directing his libertarian host to talk to the hand.

Turnbull and Casey slept well, at least as well as they could with the libertarians outside their window arguing until nearly 2 a.m. over how to legalize pot in the red. One side was in favor, and the other side was very, very much in favor.

They got up and got the breakfast from the cooks they had purchased. The provisionals had access to better rations than the local blue civilians, and Kyle's militia supplemented the government food with items they bought on their own. That was a huge selling point for the militias – the fact that you did not have to gobble inedible goo out of the plastic bags that filled the ration packs made service worthwhile even if you weren't paid directly. And you never had to eat gruel.

Turnbull made another call later in the morning to a number he had memorized. The guy on the other end knew it was Turnbull – he had a burner too, and no one else was going to call him.

"Tonight, probably eleven. We may be coming in hot," Turnbull said.

"I need to file a flight plan, get permission to fly. I'm putting down an eleven-p.m. departure. You need to be here then."

"I'll try."

"Better try hard. I can't just take off. I need the tower to give clearance. And don't tell me to just blow out of there. We won't get past Modesto before a couple F-35s catch up and tell us to fly back to SFO or eat a Sidewinder missile."

Turnbull grunted and hung up.

Go time.

Kyle approached Turnbull as he waited with Casey out by the Ron's Rangers' motor pool. It was almost six, and they had a decent dinner of cheeseburgers and chips. Turnbull had been offered, but unequivocally rejected, the offer of mustard.

"Here," Kyle said. He handed over a bundle of thick zip ties.

Turnbull took them and jammed them into his pockets. His pockets were already full of pistol magazines and cash.

"Thanks," he said.

"Not sure what you want them for," Kyle said. "Hope it's kinky sex, because you seem uptight. Consider them included in the price."

"Your guys on the way?" Turnbull asked.

"Yeah, the show starts at eight. We've got plenty of time. No assigned seating. Festival seating, in fact. Or standing, I guess."

"Do we have tickets or something?"

"No, I'm leader this week so I'll check in at the door then we go inside. We get a memo every day from Occupation HQ – it comes as a text – and they told us what to do. Show up. Check in. Stand there and listen. We are supposed to bring our weapons too."

"Mutually assured destruction," Casey said, joining them. He had been off chatting up a cute – technically, a deployment cute – Objectivist but he got bored when she started telling him about how Ayn Rand was a true feminist.

"Yeah, you don't dare get froggy. It's actually kind of smart," Turnbull said. But it complicated things too, especially if he had to go to his alternate plan, which was to blow the general's head off with his .45.

"You must have some idea of what this is about if you want to go so bad," Kyle said. "Rumor is he's going to try to get us to join him in some military campaign somewhere."

Turnbull grunted non-committally. Rumors – always true and wrong at the same time.

"Whatever," Kyle said. "We'll find out soon enough."

The Ron's Rangers contingent passed through the regular Army military police cordon and entered the grounds. The Cow Palace parking lot was packed with every manner of vehicle, from civilian sedans to pick-ups to trucks and RVs. There were even a few military vehicles, many of them formerly blue, that had been turned over to the paramilitaries after the collapse of the California government. Some had flags flying. Most of them bore lettering, which varied from standardized block lettering to homemade spray-painted graffiti. They all looked different, except for the one common feature – each bore a Λ symbol on the side.

"It looks like a gypsy camp," Casey observed, staring out the window of the van he shared with the other representatives of Ron's Rangers.

"You mean 'Roma,'" corrected one of the libertarians, who then apologized after everyone looked at him like he was an idiot.

"Force of habit," he explained, dejected.

Turnbull frowned. Now Cher's "Gypsies, Tramps and Thieves" was playing in his head. His father and his damn car radio…

The van slowly made its way through the crowds in the parking lot, many of whom wandered across the lanes without acknowledging the traffic. The different bands of provisionals varied enormously. Some were squared away, with matching uniforms and what looked like a chain of command. One group even marched in formation toward the entrance pavilion. Others appeared to have had their gear thrown at them. Neither clothes nor kit matched, and their weapons looked rusty.

They were all converging on the entrance to the Cow Palace in the thousands.

The Ron's Rangers' van parked and Kyle reminded them to leave their phones. The others complied.

Turnbull and Casey put theirs on silent mode.

The group disembarked. All of the others carried long weapons. Turnbull and Casey only had their pistols. The other attendees flowing past them were all armed, with some just packing handguns, others with long weapons. One group included a guy with an old M60 machine gun and a couple belts of 7.62mm ammo draped around his neck. He looked like Adam Baldwin in *Full Metal Jacket*, if Adam Baldwin were 250 pounds, tatted up, and was wearing a t-shirt that read "Shoot First, Shoot Again, And Ask Questions Later If There's Anything Left."

They began walking toward the entrance pavilion, keeping together. Turnbull had on his Lightbringers baseball cap and Casey wore one that said "Better Dead Than Blue." They both pulled them down over their faces and had not shaved in a couple days, the better to avoid recognition. Luckily, so far, no one seemed to be paying attention to them.

There were a lot of provisionals, from a lot of different groups, and the ones represented there were only a fraction of those operating with official recognition in California and Nevada.

At the entrance, they stood in a short line, one that moved fast. Several signs warned "NO PHONES NO VIDEOTAPING OR RECORDING." They were not searching people, though.

There was a platoon of Serra Boys with M4s and some paramilitaries from a couple other organizations keeping watch and checking in attendees with iPads. They wore brassards on their right arm reading "SECURITY" and each one had an access pass around his neck. The passes did not have photos, Turnbull noted.

The provisional units on security duty seemed to be on the squared away end of the provo spectrum, as their fighters looked relatively uniform and they even wore rank on their shirts. They also coordinated with Motorolas. Some of the groups they were checking looked like motley crews of amateurs one step up from communicating with tin cans and string.

"I'm not impressed by their quality," Casey whispered as they passed through the check-in process.

"But their quantity has a quality all its own," Turnbull replied.

They entered the main auditorium. The sound hit them first, the sound of thousands of excited men and women. The space was cavernous, with a dais ahead at the rear end backed by a curtain. Two huge stadium video monitors flanked the stage and amps lined the sides. Provisionals filled the floor while some went to the sides of the arena and climbed the stairs up into the rows of seats. The stadium could fit better than sixteen thousand people for a ball game, and it looked like there might even be more than that here tonight to see General Karl Martin Scott.

Kyle led the libertarian contingent up above the floor to the seats, and they staked out a space with an outstanding view not only of the stage but of the groups standing below. Many of the delegations brought flags in on short poles to announce their presence.

"Fresno Labor Resistance, Paso Robles Cabernet Mafia," Kyle said, pointing out the various units. "That's the East Bay Liberation Army. And there's the South Bay Liberation Army. They really hate each other, so probably best not to get between them in case it gets hot."

"The guys with the bats?" asked Turnbull.

"Furies. From Hollywood. Used to ambush People's Security Forces patrols and beat them to death."

"Most of these people look relatively normal, I mean for paramilitary fighters," Turnbull said. "But there are an awful lot of weirdos."

"A lot of these guys fought for years before the invasion," Kyle said. "A lot of them lost family. Some managed to even liberate their areas. The blues wouldn't go up into the Sierra foothills in anything less than company strength because of guys like the

Redwood Resistance and the El Dorado Battalion. Not all of them are, well, psychos."

"Speaking of which," Turnbull said, pointing down to the floor. Among the groups and the banners was one band waving a black flag with a scarlet scalpel.

"The Mutilated," Turnbull said.

"That's a charming name," Casey observed.

"They were victims of blue gender surgery," Turnbull said. "And they are very angry."

"I can see that," Casey said. "I would be too."

"They are very dangerous," Kyle said.

"I would be dangerous too," Casey said.

"Some of them saw me," Turnbull said. "Some that lived."

"That's not good," Casey said.

"No, but they are rather distinctive, which means hopefully we notice them first."

"Attention!" boomed the speakers.

"Is it time for the opening act?" Casey wondered aloud. "Please be Limp Bizkit." Kyle was disappointed he could not be live tweeting the proceedings. He missed being active on the bird site.

The loudspeakers continued.

"The Commanding General of the United States Pacific Coast Occupation Forces Command, General Karl Martin Scott, will address you in five minutes. Take your places."

"Time for us to go," Turnbull told Kyle.

"Nice knowing you," Kyle said. "Not that I think you're going to die or anything."

"We probably are going to die, if you want the truth," Casey said.

Turnbull shook his hand.

"Kyle, you might want to leave. You aren't going to like his speech anyway."

"I'm curious," Kyle said. "And we may be libertarian nerds, but we're pretty tough. We lived through the blue when they were hunting us. I want to see where this goes."

"Suit yourself," Turnbull said. "See you around."

Turnbull and Casey began making their way to the floor. They had no precise idea of where they were going, but they figured the closer to the front the better. Perhaps an opportunity would present itself to grab the general.

If not, Turnbull hoped he could get off one clean shot before these provos blew him to pieces.

The house lights went down. The video screens went black for a moment, then the words "NO VIDEOTAPING" flashed across the screens before being replaced by fluttering American flags.

Turnbull and Casey paused. There was silence, then the familiar notes.

The National Anthem.

The entire auditorium stood to attention, with most paramilitaries placing their hands on their hearts and others – like Turnbull and Casey – rendering the hand salute as they were authorized to do as United States military veterans.

Many of the provisionals were singing along. And a surprising number had tears running down their faces.

Most of these men and women were not savages or sociopaths, Turnbull remembered. They were patriots who had fought tyranny for their freedom, some for years and against great odds at a huge personal cost.

And it infuriated Turnbull even more that Karl Martin Scott was exploiting that for his own grubby ends.

The music faded, and they got moving again. A moment later, they reached the auditorium floor.

A spotlight illuminated the stage.

From the side, a figure walked out. The official cameras picked it up and the image flashed on the screen, a four-star general in camo, with a slew of hooah badges on his chest and wearing a SIG Sauer M17 pistol, striding to the edge of the dais.

"Attention!" the loudspeaker boomed.

The room popped to attention, some faster than others, but all silent and facing the stage.

"Presenting the Commanding General of the United States Pacific Coast Occupation Forces Command, General Karl Martin Scott."

"At ease!" the general shouted. The command boomed out of the loudspeakers. He was obviously wearing a radio mic.

The audience was staring at the stage, and Turnbull thought it looked very odd but could not figure out why. Then it hit him.

No one had his phone out filming it.

"Block me," Turnbull whispered. Casey stood next to him and Turnbull pulled his burner and pressed some buttons, then shoved it back in his shirt pocket.

General Scott stepped to the very edge of the stage.

"Around the side of the stage," Turnbull whispered to Casey. "Let's find out where he came out of, and where he'll be going."

"Show some respect to the commander!" someone behind them snapped. Turnbull ignored him, and he and Casey began to move across the floor as the general started to speak.

23.

"You fought for America!" General Karl Martin Scott began, standing at the edge of the stage before the assembled provisional fighters. "You bled for America! And many of your comrades in arms died for America!"

There was a pause as that last bit hung in the air.

An applause line? Turnbull wondered.

But the line had its desired effect. After a moment, but before the pause got awkward, there were initially shouts of "Yes!" and "Hell yeah!" Then there were more and more shouts and cries until the auditorium was filled with a roar louder than anything it had seen since Pete Townshend's guitar riff and Roger Daltrey's scream during "Won't Get Fooled Again," or the shriek of Hunter Biden at the climax of his epic spoken-word piece, "No More Showers with Ashley, Daddy."

General Scott soaked it in as the audience members howled. Someone had recognized their pain and their sacrifice, and they were in his hands.

Turnbull and Casey moved as fast as they could, working their way through the crowd that was fixated on the man in the spotlight. Some were weeping. Turnbull passed a man with no left hand; an American flag was in his right hand.

Scott listened to the response, measured it, calculated, and when he detected a slight dip, he spoke again.

"And now all you ask for is respect, and for the chance to be heard. Do you feel they have heard you in Dallas? Do you feel your contributions, your sacrifices have been acknowledged? Do you believe that you count?"

The crowd roared again with versions of "No!" and "Hell no!" and "No! preceded by various profanities.

"But you count to me!" Scott told them as they quieted. "And now you need to count! Count your numbers! Count the overwhelming numbers of you paramilitary patriots! Count!"

Turnbull weeded his way through the fist-shaking mass of humanity until he came to a barrier, a line of yellow evidence tape across the left side of the stage running to the wall the seats above rested upon. It struck him as odd – it was just a line of plastic tape but the provisionals were honoring it. Beyond it were several security paramilitaries, their own attention on the stage though they were back far enough that they were watching the general speak from behind. Past them was another curtain, and people wearing passes kept going in and out a split in it that was adjacent to the stairs coming down from the stage.

There was Scott's route to and from the dais.

Casey was beside him.

"I see Larry," Turnbull said, nodding at one of Scott's personal security detachment operators standing at the bottom of the stairs with his M4, watching.

"No Curly and Moe?" asked Casey. "You think they're behind the curtain backstage?"

"No idea, but they are close by."

"If you can count, you will see that there are hundreds of thousands of you, perhaps a million of you, loyal paramilitaries and your families. And it is time that you demand what you are owed!"

The crowd cheered. It was not clear that they fully understood the implications of their leader's words, but it sounded good.

Someone cared about them.

"A million paramilitaries, and a million more active soldiers who are loyal to those who fought at their side, that is something that the bureaucrats and the politicians who have forgotten and betrayed you must take into account!"

The crowd was cheering again – he could barely get a whole thought out before the crowd would roar anew.

Turnbull was only half-listening. He was watching the curtain and the guards. A couple of security men passed under the tape carrying, roughly, an obviously drunk gentleman in handcuffs. The trio was waved by and passed through the split in the curtain into the backstage area. Presumably there were holding cells back there.

One of the Serra Boys security men whispered to another, who nodded. The man made his way forward, lifting up the tape and passing under it into the crowd. He began making his way toward the stairs up from the floor into the seats.

"Stay here," Turnbull said to Casey. He followed the man across the floor to the stairway up to the seats.

"What you must do," Scott continued. "What you must do to get the respect and recognition you deserve, is hard. I will not mislead you as others have misled you. The road you face is perilous. But the alternative is no alternative at all!"

The Serra Boy made it to the landing at the top of the stairs and turned right, following the walkway toward the rear of the hall. Turnbull reached the top of the steps a moment after and saw him heading toward the sign that read, "RESTROOMS."

"The politicians and the bureaucrats have failed to win the war," Scott exclaimed, his tone angry, his eyes scanning the crowd. "They have failed to exact justice upon the blues who imprisoned and tortured and murdered your families. They sit in luxury in Dallas while you pick up the pieces of what they have wrecked. They eat steaks and drink wine while you get scraps and think yourselves lucky because at least it's not gruel!"

The crowd murmured, and the murmur rose to a cacophony of shouts and yells.

I have them, Scott thought, quelling a smile.

The Serra Boy disappeared into the men's room. There was a new sign on the door identifying it as such, and one reading "WOMEN" on the door across the hall. On both doors, the words "ALL GENDER RESTROOM" could be read under the spray-paint attempting to blot them out.

His name was Dale. He was a man, and within the auditorium no group was more focused on gender than his. He stood next to Cindy, who held the pole flying the Mutilated banner. She tried to eliminate the hair on her face caused by the hormones that still tormented her even a couple years after discontinuing them.

Dale leaned toward her ear.

"I have to go," he said, miserable. And he did, even as General Scott was enthralling him with his speech. It was another horror in an endless series of horrors stemming from his mutilation. When he had to go, he had to, as the muscles of his groin had been ruined in the surgery that promised to make him into the woman he once had been convinced, by monsters, that he truly was.

"Okay," Cindy replied. "I'll come too." She handed the flagpole to another of the Mutilated, someone caught between male and female with both an Adam's apple and ample breasts, and the pair headed up the stairs, AK-47s slung over their backs.

The hallway where the bathrooms were was empty. Unless you absolutely had to go – or had other business – you were listening to the general run down his litany of oppressions and insults by the current US government. Turnbull screwed the suppressor onto his .45 and carefully opened the door.

There was a long line of stalls with doors lining one wall. Each stall had a door running floor to ceiling. Apparently, privacy was an important consideration. On the other side were the sinks and a row of pipes jutting from the walls at waist level. The blues had removed all of the urinals there and in most other venues, as the fixtures apparently made some people feel unsafe. The blue government had even gone further, launching a campaign to urge "Peoplx Who Sometimes Urinate While Standing" – the acronym was PWSUWS, pronounced "Pwiss-oows" – to do so only while seated as a show of solidarity with the differently-abled and differently-plumbed.

Equity meant everyone must sit to pee.

All the doors were ajar, except the one at the end. From the noise, the Serra Boy was fighting the power and standing tall as he drained his bladder.

Turnbull walked down the row of stalls and waited. The guy going was innocent – he had done nothing wrong and did not deserve what was going to happen, but life is a bitch and then you die.

But the Serra Boy did not die that day. He opened the door and was stunned to see Turnbull there, and more stunned when Turnbull brought the butt of the heavy pistol down on the bridge of his nose.

He staggered back and Turnbull hit him again in the head. The guy went down, probably with a concussion, but he would survive. He sat sprawled on the toilet, eyes half-open and tongue lolling out with blood cascading down over it. Above him was a pictogram of a woman – she had a skirt on – urinating standing up. The cartoon was under a red circle with a slash.

Turnbull proceeded to liberate the "SECURITY" brassard and the pass hanging around the Serra Boy's neck.

Casey stood back, far enough not to be noticed, watching as the general went on.

"It is a time of decision," Scott bellowed. "It is time for you to decide whether you will live in honor, or as mere peasants!"

Larry from the personal security detail alerted to something by the split in the curtain. Casey watched him step over and the head and torso of another PSD operator – Casey designated him "Moe" – slid through and waved five fingers to Larry, who nodded. Moe disappeared backstage again.

Did that mean five minutes until the end of the speech?

Where the hell is Kelly? Casey wondered.

Turnbull stood up and backed out of the stall, kicking the Serra Boy's shiny combat boots back as he pulled closed the stall door.

Movement down the row of stalls.

There was someone standing there, wide-mouthed.

Turnbull thought he – *He is a he, right?* – looked familiar, not specifically but in general. It took a second to place him.

"You!" Dale said, practically gasping. Before him, shockingly, was the man who Dugan took away and who killed his leader. The stitches on his head were new, but it was him. It was the guy everyone was looking for.

Dale started to unsling his AK-47.

The Mutilated, Turnbull realized.

Turnbull was faster.

The Wilson was up and firing. The first suppressed round slammed into Dale's chest to the right of his sternum at breast level, the second to the left side. Dale staggered back. Turnbull shot him in the forehead and he fell. The clatter of his rifle was engulfed by another massive cheer from the crowd.

Dale lay dead on the floor.

Turnbull considered his options then holstered the weapon, the silencer passing through the opening at the bottom of the rig.

No time to dump him in a stall.

Move, Turnbull told himself.

He went out the door. A stocky woman, clearly another of the Mutilated, was waiting there. Turnbull averted his gaze and moved past her. She paid him no particular mind, except she saw the big line of stitches on his forehead.

She just wondered if Dale, because of his condition, was going to need her help like he sometimes did. It was mortifying, but preferable to the potential mess. How she hated the butchers who did this to him, and to her.

The crowd roared behind her out there beyond the dark hallway. She was missing history. She tapped her boot, muttering "Come on, Dale. Hurry."

"You have the power to redeem yourselves!" General Scott preached to the assembly as Turnbull came down the steps. The crowd was feeling it. It felt like an angry sea, powerful and utterly out of control. But Scott sought to control it.

"And I offer myself to lead you!"

The Cow Palace seemed to shake to its foundation. Turnbull reached the floor and headed toward Casey and the taped-off exit.

"Dale," Cindy said, pushing open the door. She hated, hated, the idea of entering a men's room. During her dark years as Sergio, she had used them, not because she wanted to – she felt wrong doing so, which only made her angrier – but because she felt she needed to make the statement.

I am a man.

But she was not a man, she never was and never could be, and now that she had accepted it, she was at least happier, though after what they did to her she knew she would never actually be happy except during those fleeting moments when she helped make one of those butchers pay.

Maybe she was too impatient, but he needed to hurry. They were missing it.

Cindy peered inside the men's room. Silent.

"Dale?"

Nothing.

It must be bad this time. She felt for him and the humiliation of soiling himself because his perfectly healthy man's body had been carved into a grim satire of a woman's.

She pushed into the latrine and took a single step, then stopped.

Dale was there on the floor, clearly dead.

And ahead, out of the last of the line of stalls, a paramilitary with a bloody face was crawling out.

"He took my security pass!" the man shouted.

Turnbull wended his way through the crowd toward Casey. But then he moved toward the wall for a moment. With the crowd's attention on the stage, he tossed away the Lightbringers ball cap, slipped the "SECURITY" brassard onto his bicep, and hung the pass around his neck.

Up on the stage, General Scott was finishing, and finishing big.

"Together, we will march to Dallas! We will clear away the liars and the thieves. We will clear the moneychangers from the temple!"

That last line got a big response from a group Turnbull was pushing past at the moment, the Knights Templar, an aggressively old-school Baptist militia that started in the Central Valley around Bakersfield and had spread across the state. It got some polite, but a bit embarrassed, applause from the Circle of Faith, a Methodist-oriented provisional unit from the suburbs of Walnut Creek.

"Sissies," hissed one Knight Templar.

Turnbull saw Casey ahead and went straight for him as Scott continued with his finale.

"I see a new day. I see a new America. I see you and yours in your rightful place at the helm, guiding and leading a renewed United States of America!"

Turnbull got to Casey.

"He's like Patton, if Patton was a dick," Casey said, staring at the general.

"Patton kind of was a dick. That's what made him awesome. But this guy is no Patton."

"This looks like it's the climax," Casey said. "You got a pass for me?"

"Nope," Turnbull said, pulling out a long zip tie. "I got you one of these."

Above them, Scott was at the end of the stage, arms wide, drinking in the energy.

"Can you see it?" he cried.

The crowd answered as one: "Yes!"

"Can you see it?" he repeated, more urgently.

The crowd shouted back in the affirmative, even louder.

"Can you see it?" Scott shouted, enunciating each individual word.

The crowd answered with a tsunami of affirmation.

"I can dig it," Casey said as Turnbull affixed the zip tie loosely to his friend's hands behind his back.

"Come on," Turnbull said, pushing and guiding his faux-prisoner with his left hand on Casey's right shoulder.

The crowd was ecstatic, like a heavily-armed revival meeting.

"Together, we will retake America for the people!" General Scott shouted. "We march to victory!"

The place went nuts.

Turnbull and Casey reached the yellow tape, and Turnbull lifted it up then pushed Casey ahead underneath it. The half-dozen security men paid them little heed – Turnbull had a brassard and a pass and was just another member of some random provisional unit. The guards were focused on the stage right above them, as General Scott paced across it, right arm lifted high, drawing in the cheers and applause.

This is my moment, Scott thought to himself. There were no limits. He could not be stopped.

Turnbull aimed Casey to the slit in the curtain. Whatever went down would go down beyond it, backstage. Larry from the security detail paid them no heed. He was watching as his general strode off the stage and toward the stairway down off the dais to the floor.

The noise was incredible. The general reached the stairway, waved at his adoring fans, and began descending to where Larry waited at the bottom.

"Stop him!"

The shout broke through the cacophony even as the cheering was shaking the Cow Palace's very rafters.

"He's a murderer!"

The Serra Boy guards were baffled, their attention drawn to the people by the tape running across the floor.

Scott, still fixated on the crowd, came down the stairs.

Turnbull pivoted, still holding Casey.

The Mutilated were gathered at the tape line, the woman he passed coming out of the latrine standing in front.

They were lifting up their weapons.

Now, so were the Serra Boys as they moved forward to engage the threat.

Turnbull dropped his left hand to the loose zip tie and ripped it off Casey's wrist.

The Mutilated woman fired her weapon in Turnbull's direction even as the Serra Boys fired. Her shots went high as the Serra Boy's M4 rounds shredded Chris's chest. Now her friends were engaging the Serra Boys, who were engaging them back. Other provisionals were entering the fray as rounds tore into the crowd – some shot the Mutilated, some shot the Serra Boys.

Turnbull pivoted back to General Scott and Larry as the pair stood stunned by the firefight breaking out in front of them. Turnbull drew his Wilson.

The movement caught Karl Martin Scott's eye, and then his eyes met Turnbull's.

"You!" General Scott shouted. It was impossible! And yet there he was.

Larry was covering the Mutilated but Scott's momentary interaction with Turnbull caused him to change his primary threat assessment.

Turnbull was faster. He put two into the PSD man's chest; whether the slugs were stopped by a ceramic plate was immaterial because Turnbull completed the Mozambique drill with a round to the man's face. The advanced copper round entered just above the target's upper lip and blew out the man's C1 vertebra. Larry's body was dead before he crumpled to the floor even if his brain was still working for a few desperate moments thereafter.

The general did not wait for Turnbull to cap him too. He did not go for his own piece. Instead, he sprinted the couple meters to the split in the curtain that led backstage.

Turnbull leapt forward even as the arena behind him dissolved into utter chaos.

Scott was almost through the split in the curtain when Turnbull reached him and tackled him, carrying the general through it. They sprawled on the cement floor in the brightly lit, cavernous backstage area beyond. The people back there had largely run away or taken cover – except for a couple of provos rolling around on the floor, obviously having been hit by the barrage of rounds passing through the heavy red curtain from the firefight outside in the auditorium proper. The sound of shooting had utterly banished the sound of cheering.

Turnbull lost his grip on his Wilson when they hit the ground and it clattered away across the cement. Scott was stronger than he expected, turning and squirming as Turnbull sought to get control of him. They wrestled for a moment before Turnbull saw his opportunity and punched Scott hard across the jaw. Blood and spit splashed across the floor.

Movement front.

Moe was running toward them, his M4 coming to bear as Turnbull realized that he was sitting upright over the prone Scott, and presenting quite a target. He grabbed Scott and pulled him close as he rolled over.

Moe stopped and took aim, but the two men were entangled. Moe only needed a clear shot, just for a second. He squinted into his optic.

Then he staggered once, and then a bloom of red erupted from his neck. On the next round, Turnbull actually heard the "pffft" of Casey's suppressed HK P30 as the final 9mm round slammed into Moe's temple. The operator fell, his rifle dropping to the cement as well.

Turnbull pushed away from Scott then punched him again in the mouth. The general fell backwards, his head conking on the cement floor.

"That's for Lorna, asshole," Turnbull said. He reached down and drew out the general's SIG M17, then forced the barrel into his prisoner's scarlet mouth.

"We need to roll, Kelly!" Casey said. He was acutely aware that Curly was still out there, somewhere, and he trotted over and picked up Moe's M4 plus two spare mags after holstering his own German pistol. After all, the proper role of a handgun is to use it to fight your way to a long weapon.

Turnbull leaned in close.

"Listen, shithead," he began. "You're coming with us. When I say jump, you jump. If you do anything cute, I'll kill you. Nod if you understand."

Scott, the gun in his piehole, offered the most passive aggressive nod Turnbull had ever experienced.

"Roll over."

Scott did.

"Come on, Kelly!" said Casey, scanning for targets with the rifle down the backstage hall. Through the curtain, in the auditorium, the shooting would slow, then start up again.

Turnbull locked a black zip tie tight around Scott's wrists behind his back and pulled him to his feet. Pausing to retrieve his Wilson Combat – and to reload it with a fresh mag – he took hold of his prisoner.

"Let's go."

They started running down the hallway, Casey and Turnbull covering ahead and behind with their respective weapons.

They seemed to go on running forever down the long, curving hallway, and the few people they encountered gave them a wide berth. Whatever chaos was still happening in the auditorium could be heard backstage. They were glad to be out of the midst of it.

"Where the hell are we?" Casey asked. "I think we've passed this same forklift three times. I feel like we're Spinal Tap."

"You!" Turnbull said to a man in civilian work clothes cowering behind a pallet of chemical drums. "Come out!"

The man did, scared, hands up.

"We're trying to find the exit ramp. You know, where the talent comes in and goes out."

The man pointed to a hallway that turned off up ahead.

Movement left.

Turnbull leapt and rolled.

A line of holes appeared in one of the drums as golden streams of detergent arced out of the bullet holes stitched across its face. The civilian took off running the other way.

Turnbull backed up, flat against the wall, .45 ready.

"Curly," Casey said, covering back the way they came. No target – Curly was somewhere back behind the curve with a suppressed rifle.

"Kill them all!" Scott shouted. Turnbull punched him in the gut and he gasped.

"If we try to make a break for it he'll get a shot at us," Turnbull said to Casey.

"We can use Discount Patton as a human shield," Casey suggested.

"No," Turnbull said, holstering the Wilson. "Give me the M4 and you take Mr. Seven Days in May here to the ramp."

"Nice reference," Casey said. He handed over the rifle and the two spare mags, which Turnbull stuffed in his bulging pockets.

"Just make noise when you go."

"Roger," Casey replied. "Come on, general, let's move." He grabbed the general and pulled him along both ungently and loudly.

Turnbull dropped to the floor, and aimed back down the hall.

Movement, a flash of khaki.

He fired three times, single shots. The flash pulled back out of sight.

Turnbull waited. Nothing down there all the way to where the hall curved out of sight.

"Hey warrior," Curly yelled from down the hall. "Come out and play!"

There was a flash of movement and then a long burst of fire. Curly was holding his weapon out and firing blindly. Most of the rounds flew past Turnbull down the hall. A couple of bullets hit the wall above him and showered him with a sprinkling of concrete and paint chips.

Turnbull knew that time was on his side. Curly had to break the stalemate or his principal would be gone.

"Come on!" the bodyguard yelled. "Waste me!"

Turnbull waited, aiming.

There was a clattering noise and Turnbull saw it, a lime green canister bouncing up the hallway toward him, a thin red stream of smoke pouring out of one end.

It rolled to a stop and the smoke grenade erupted in a massive cloud of thick red fog that filled the hallway. The fog bank began rolling toward him.

There was Curly's stalemate buster.

Turnbull assessed the situation. In a moment, Curly would be charging now, hoping to get close enough to Turnbull to do him in. And he would be spraying fire at Turnbull's last known position to suppress him.

It might just work.

There was only one thing to do.

The same damn thing.

Turnbull rolled, literally, to the side, as rounds began flying out of the smoke toward where he had just been. It was loud. The guy pulled off his suppressor. Curly wanted it noisy.

Turnbull kept rolling, keeping low, minimizing the chance of Curly getting lucky, until he hit the other wall on the far side of the hallway.

Footsteps coming.

Turnbull got up and charged. Curly's fusillade slacked off for a moment, then started up again. A mag change. Now Curly was full up again.

Turnbull could hear his enemy's footfalls – but Curly's ringing ears probably could not hear his.

The smoke enveloped him, but Turnbull pushed on. The footfalls and the firing got louder – now Curly was to Turnbull's left. Close.

Turnbull flicked the selector switch to full auto – these M4 variants did not have a three-round burst setting.

He fired at what he could best figure was Curly's position in the smoke and kept firing until he ran dry. Curly's fire ceased and there was a noise like a grunt and a thud. Turnbull dropped the empty mag and reloaded by feel – the smoke was impenetrable.

He fired again by dead reckoning at where he thought Curly might be. The gun went dry once more. He reloaded it with his last mag.

Silence. Just the ringing in his ears.

Turnbull moved back up the hall, but his foot hit something. He probed with the barrel of the rifle. It was human-sized and not moving. He fired into it three times just to be sure – he didn't need a round in his back as he made for the ramp.

And then he made for the ramp.

24.

Sergeant Major Lightfoot and his three-SUV convoy were waiting for Turnbull where he had promised, at the bottom of the ramp. Scott was in the back of the middle vehicle with Casey. He had ordered Lightfoot to shoot the operative. Lightfoot told him he was in no position to be giving orders.

"Let's ride," Turnbull said. He jumped in the front vehicle with Sergeant Major and they roared out of the ramp and toward the back exit of the Cow Palace parking lot that had been blocked off for the general's use.

Turnbull could not get a good look at what was happening out in front of the building, but it seemed like a riot. There were occasional gunshots and clearly some fires. The one man who had kept the provisionals from turning on each other was on ice in the backseat of the Chevy Blazer behind his.

They headed toward SFO. They would make their eleven o'clock departure.

"What will you do, Sergeant Major?" Turnbull said.

"Take charge," CSM Lightfoot replied. "I just got word that my guys walked into the command post and disarmed all of Scott's boys without a shot. Turns out they had a list and I was on it. But I had a list too."

Turnbull noted that the sergeant major was no longer referring to his commander by his rank. The shit had truly gotten real.

With the Bayshore Freeway practically empty, it did not take long to get to SFO. They pulled up to the military terminal, and all of them got out. Sergeant Major sought out the head NCO at the site and told him how it was going to go down, and that is exactly how it went.

Casey took charge of the prisoner. Turnbull got reunited with Gibson. As the turboprops cranked, he put his hand out to the CSM.

"I know NCOs get pissy when you thank them," Turnbull said. "But thanks."

Lightfoot shook Turnbull's hand. "You're okay," he said. "For an officer."

"I'd like to think Scott's not representative," Turnbull said. "But I've never liked generals."

The sergeant major smiled. "Me neither."

Turnbull watched General Karl Martin Scott from across the aisle in the cargo bay of the C-130J Hercules transport. The engines roared outside; if anyone wanted to speak, he would have to speak up. So far, no one had.

The general stared back from his canvas bench seat, his face a blank mask, hands zip tied to his rear and a seat belt securing him from the bumps and jostles that went with military aircraft travel. Turnbull was belted in too, and he had his black Wilson pistol on his lap, not being one to take chances. Gibson sat up beside him on the cold metal floor, alert and focused.

Casey Warner was asleep further toward the cockpit, his HK P30 pistol on his chest. His snores were drowned out by the throb of the engines.

Up front, the loadmaster's aircraft phone light flashed red and he picked it up and listened, then hung up.

"Thirty minutes to Dallas," he shouted at the passengers, and then went back to his iPhone game.

"So, you're bringing me in," the general said, dark eyes fixed on his nemesis. "Like a marshal bringing in a dangerous desperado."

"Stop talking," Turnbull said.

Scott gave a small snort of amusement.

"You usually don't take prisoners," he continued. "It's one of the qualities I respect about men like you, normally."

"Shut up, General," Turnbull said.

"And what will you do if I don't?" Scott asked, sounding genuinely curious. "I mean, what your government will do to me is probably similar, if not worse."

"Maybe I'll let the dog at you." Gibson licked his lips on cue.

"Oh, Kelly Turnbull, the bluntest of blunt instruments. You're a tactical man, solving the problem right in front of you. But right now, perhaps you should be strategic for once in your life."

"You think you're going to talk yourself out of this?" Turnbull asked. Now it was his turn to be genuinely curious. "You shot my fiancée, you killed my friends, you tried to nuke the entire government and become a military dictator. That's not even counting you trying to off me I lost count of how many times. I'm not clear on how you see this ending well for you."

"Oh, I'm reconciled to the fact that it won't," Scott said amiably. "The bottom line is that I die. I'm not afraid of that."

"Which is why you're talking to me now," Turnbull said.

"There's dying and then there's dying," Scott replied. "The long-term consequences, though, will not be my problem. They'll be yours, you and every citizen's."

"I think a noose is a solution, General, not a problem."

"No, it's a problem. You and your masters don't need a villain. You need a hero."

"I'm guessing that'd be you."

"Let's walk this thing through, Turnbull. I go back and go on trial. But a lot of my supporters don't see justice. They see their hero being railroaded."

"I just want to make sure I'm clear," Turnbull said. "Because I'm not a genius general officer who ended up in zip ties heading toward a trial and a date with the hangman. You're the hero of this little saga, right?"

"Heroism is in the eye of the beholder."

"So's treason."

"Exactly," Scott said. "Exactly right, Colonel. Your government can try me and hang me and what will that do? Will it bring the new America together just as you are trying to bring the old America back together? Or will what you think is justice make it all much, much worse?"

"I'm not letting you go, General."

"I know that. I'm not suggesting that. I'm suggesting an alternative." The general glanced at the rear door of the aircraft.

Turnbull's eyes followed his and he grasped his prisoner's purpose.

"An alternative? A pretty bleak alternative."

"Wait a sec, Kelly," Casey, now awake, piped in. "Maybe this asswipe has a point."

"I certainly do," General Scott said. "In the end, it's all the same to me. But what about the country?"

"Nice to see you caring about the country again, General."

"Everything I've done was for my country, Colonel," Scott snapped. "I'm offering you and your masters who control you the ability to play this however you want. They can tell whatever story they like. But if I stand in the dock, I get an opportunity to speak not merely about subjects like the St. Louis incident and INFERNO. And you know that what I will say in my defense will tear what's left of this country apart."

"He'd burn it all down in a heartbeat, Kelly," Casey said. "He'll use it as a chance to rally his supporters. And he'd get the inferno he wanted all along."

"Or, General Karl Martin Scott," the prisoner said. "He gave his life in the service of his country. Not a bad epitaph."

"Except for it being utter bullshit," Turnbull said.

"Most of history is a lie," Scott said. "Lies written about the liars who died by the liars who survived."

"And you get to go down in history as a hero?" Turnbull said.

"I would be giving my life for my country, in a way," Scott replied.

"And what about justice?" Turnbull said.

"Justice?" snorted the general. "You sound like a teenager complaining that life's not fair. There's no justice. There's only winning and losing."

"And this way you win?"

"Sulla, Marius, Caesar, Augustus. Do you know what they all have in common?"

"Togas? Orgies? Vomitoriums?" asked Turnbull.

Scott ignored the reply. "Two thousand and some years later, we still remember their names."

"It's like the end of *LA Confidential*," Casey said.

"He's no Russell Crowe. Or that other guy with the glasses."

"But it seems like a smart trade," Casey said. "I mean, I don't like it, but he's got a point about what happens if we take him back and he goes on trial."

"Don't we have trials in America?" asked Turnbull. "I was awake for at least part of my civics classes. We have rules."

"Since when did you ever play by the rules, Colonel?" taunted Scott. "You've killed more men than you can count."

"I'm infantry, so I can't count very high."

"Are you going to start playing by the rules now and risk ripping your country further apart just to see some judge pass sentence on me?"

Turnbull was silent for a moment.

"Hey," Turnbull shouted to the loadmaster. "Get in the cockpit and stay there."

The Air Force sergeant, who had not been paying attention, now got up and went into the cabin, shutting the door behind him.

Scott was smiling as Turnbull stood and walked forward to the control panel. He flipped the switch marked "REAR RAMP – AIRBORNE OPS."

At the back of the plane, the rear door began opening, the ramp dropping from diagonal to flat as the Texas landscape below came into view with the sun just beginning to rise.

Scott was beaming now. Turnbull undid his seatbelt. Gibson growled.

"It's okay, dog," Turnbull said. "The general's planning on leaving us in a moment. Airborne, all the way. All the way down."

Scott stood up, pleased. He had won.

"You should cut me loose. It will complicate whatever story your masters tell if General Karl Martin Scott is found in zip ties."

He turned his back to Turnbull, and thrust his hands out.

Turnbull looked down at the bound hands, then turned him around and looked into Scott's face.

"You're not a hero. You're a convict." Turnbull smiled broadly and walked over to push the "REAR RAMP – AIRBORNE OPS" button again.

The smirk across Scott's face vanished, and he went pale. The general turned and sprinted awkwardly back down the aisle toward the closing ramp. He got about eight feet from the closing ramp when Gibson was on him, his jaws fixed around the general's ankles. The officer fell, face-first, to the metal floor.

The ramp closed.

Turnbull knelt beside the prone general as the prisoner stared forlornly at the blocked exit.

"I don't have masters," Turnbull said. "You'e going in because I chose to take you in like the scumbag criminal you are. Remember that when they put the rope around your neck, you piece of shit traitor."

Turnbull manned the Weber grill, flipping the fresh boar chops from the tusked monster he had put down the previous evening with his Henry .44.

"I could have brought prime steaks," Clay Deeds said. He sat in a wicker chair on the porch nearby, nursing a Shiner Bock. Lorna sat next to him. She was doing fine on one kidney, and her recuperation got her out of any sort of prep duty for their rare dinner guests. She fully intended to milk the injury for all it was worth.

"Lorna, darling, could I borrow your beau?" Deeds asked.

She understood and stood up. "You can keep him if you want."

"Thank you," Deeds said. Lorna went into the house. The dogs, Gibson now part of the pack, stayed outside on the porch in the fading Texas sunlight.

"Do we need to do secret squirrel stuff tonight?" Turnbull asked. "I'd like just one night without all hell breaking loose."

"I can't promise that," Deeds said. A hundred yards away, parked off the road, were the three vehicles of his convoy. His security detachment smoked and joked as they waited for their principal.

"I found out what you wanted to know about your family, or some of it at least," he told Turnbull.

"Okay."

Deeds paused, considering how to pass on the information.

"Your nephew is doing well. He's being fostered by a family in Modesto. They check out – no record, foster father has a good job. They go to church."

"Is he a he again?"

Deeds nodded.

"What about my asshole brother and that miserable sister-in-law of mine?"

"I don't know, Kelly. There's no record of them after they were taken. Nothing."

"Missing," Turnbull said coldly, attending to the sizzling meat.

"There are several hundred thousand people unaccounted for," Deeds said. "Maybe refugees, maybe..."

His voice trailed off.

"Maybe dead," Turnbull said.

"The blues killed a lot of people. Then there were the people killed in the fighting. Then the provisionals took their revenge."

"Payback is a bitch," Turnbull said. "How can anyone expect it all just to go back to the way it had been before the Split after all that blood?"

"I would tell you to find a professional and share your feelings, but that is not in the cards," Deeds said.

"Assuming I have feelings, what should I feel?" Turnbull asked, and it seemed to Deeds he was really wondering.

"I don't know, Kelly," said Deeds.

"What the blues did to our country was unforgivable," Turnbull continued. "What people like my brother and sister-in-law did was horrible too. There has to be some accountability, doesn't there? Hell, I've been accountability for a lot of those bastards, and I don't regret it. I don't have any doubts about what I've done. I do know my side did not start this. I don't know how they can expect me to be broken because it did not end the way they thought it would."

"When you throw open the Overton Window to violence and death, you might just find yourself thrown out of it," Deeds said.

"They broke our country, Clay. Broke it. Drove it to madness. I've seen it. And the people they hurt are going to demand that they pay."

"And that's how you get guys like General Scott," Deeds said.

"An American Caesar. And a lot of people are so hurt and angry, with justification, that a Caesar seems like a viable option."

"What do you think?"

"I think America had a good thing going, and stupid people screwed it up," Turnbull said. "There's a whole generation that doesn't even remember what America was like before the Split. But I can't forget. I don't want to."

Turnbull flipped a chop and it sent up an eruption of flames. The light flicked across the .45 on his hip and the FAL rifle leaning against the wall. He said nothing.

"Tomorrow's the sentencing," Deeds said. "Are you planning on watching?"

"They didn't want me at the trial, and I guess my tape was not particularly useful."

"What your phone picked up of Scott's speech was damning, but it also recorded a lot of you killing people," Deeds observed.

"I'm not interested in what happens to him as long as he hangs."

"He will," Deeds said.

"How do you know?"

"I always know these things."

"They didn't even prosecute him for any of his real plot, Clay. Not the murders, not the bomb plot. Just for corruption and being overzealous as a military governor."

"It was better that way," Deeds said.

"I never really saw him as corrupt – not in the sense that he wanted money."

Deeds smiled. "It was necessary to tarnish his brass, so to speak."

"So they framed him for that?"

Deeds shrugged. "Well, at least he was overzealous, wasn't he?"

"A lot of people don't think so. A lot of people think he was just doing what had to be done when he let the provisionals loose on the worst of the blues."

"What do you think, Kelly?"

"I think war is hell," Turnbull said. "I think what goes around comes around, and if you expect any tears from me for the MAPs and the butchers, don't bother. And I think our government may end up making General Karl Martin Smith a martyr."

"If it helps, I recommended that they prosecute him for everything. Well, almost everything. It probably would not do to announce that we lost track of a nuclear warhead twice." Deeds had personally seen to it that the nuclear weapon was disposed of properly this time.

"I hate politics," Turnbull said, gesturing with a spatula.

"It would have saved us all a lot of trouble if you had gone full Kelly Turnbull on him and not taken him alive."

"Like you talked me out of?"

Deeds shrugged.

"Scott suggested that too," Turnbull continued. "But I thought we were supposed to have due process and all that. Fair trials and so forth. I was informed that's the kind of thing we've been fighting for over the last couple decades."

"It is," Deeds replied.

"Except when it's inconvenient."

"True. Our world is not black and white, Kelly."

"Gray is my least favorite color."

"And yet you chose to live in the gray area."

"It's quite the conundrum." Turnbull flipped another chop and another fireball rose out of the Weber.

"The Constitution over the clarity of your big Wilson .45."

"Nothing is clear anymore. Thankfully, I'm done."

Deeds smiled coldly.

"Kelly, things will get worse before they get better. Scott had a lot of supporters. They won't be happy to see their boy swing."

"It was a lot less complicated when we were hunting down jihadist nutballs in Baghdad, Clay. And when I was fighting the blues back here in America."

"Human nature, Kelly. Greed, the lust for power, flat-out badness. Those things do not just vanish when the red, white, and blue flies from the flagpole."

"I kind of hoped they would."

"Hope is not a plan. We have got the Chinese probing up into Mexico. The blues in the northeast and northwest are still at it. The world is still an inferno."

"Speaking of infernos, these are ready." Turnbull picked up a plate and used the tongs to pull off the three medium rare cuts. He would roll the dice on trichinosis before he served a dried-out boar chop.

"Time to go inside," Deeds said. "I guess that concludes our secret squirrel discussion for now. Except for one little thing."

"Don't," Turnbull said.

"It's an easy job, Kelly," Clay Deeds promised. "A walk in the park."

"It's time to eat, so walk in the house," Turnbull said. "And stop talking."

AUTHOR'S NOTE

Human nature doesn't change. That's the lesson. Power corrupts, so watch the powerful. And let's try really hard to make sure this book's predictions don't come true. The other six are already too damn close to reality.

KAS, October 2022

Kelly Turnbull will return

in a new adventure in

2023

ABOUT THE AUTHOR

Kurt Schlichter is a senior columnist for *Townhall*. He is also a Los Angeles trial lawyer admitted in California, Texas, and Washington, DC, and a retired Army Infantry colonel.

A Twitter activist (@KurtSchlichter) with over 450,000 followers, Kurt was personally recruited by his friend Andrew Breitbart to write for his Breitbart sites. His writings on political and cultural issues have also been published in *IJ Review*, *The Federalist*, the *New York Post*, the *Washington Examiner*, the *Los Angeles Times*, the *Boston Globe*, the *Washington Times*, *Army Times*, the *San Francisco Examiner*, and elsewhere.

Kurt serves as a news source, an on-screen commentator, and a guest host on TV and on nationally syndicated radio programs regarding political, military, and legal issues, at outlets including Fox News, Fox Business News, CNN, NewsMax, One America Network, and on shows hosted by Hugh Hewitt, Larry O'Connor, Cam Edwards, Chris Stigall, Seb Gorka, Dennis Prager, Tony Katz, Dana Loesch, and Derek Hunter, among others.

Kurt was a stand-up comic for several years, which led him to write three e-books that each reached number one on the Amazon Kindle "Political Humor" bestsellers list: *I Am a Conservative: Uncensored, Undiluted, and Absolutely Un-PC*, *I Am a Liberal: A Conservative's Guide to Dealing with Nature's Most Irritating Mistake*, and *Fetch My Latte: Sharing Feelings with Stupid People*.

In 2014, his book *Conservative Insurgency: The Struggle to Take America Back 2013-2041* was published by Post Hill Press.

His 2016 novel *People's Republic* and its 2017 prequel *Indian Country* reached No. 1 and No. 2 on the Amazon Kindle "Political Thriller" bestsellers list. *Wildfire*, the third book in the series, hit No. 1 on the Amazon "Thrillers – Espionage" bestsellers list and No. 122 in all Amazon Kindle books. *Collapse*, the fourth book, hit 121, while *Crisis* hit 29. His previous novel, *The Split*, hit at least 43.

His non-fiction book *Militant Normals: How Regular Americans Are Rebelling Against the Elite to Reclaim Our Democracy* was published by Center Street Books in October 2018. It made the USA Today Bestsellers List.

His Regnery book *The 21 Biggest Lies About Donald Trump (and You)* was released in 2020 and hit Number 1 on an Amazon list.

His Regnery book *We'll Be Back: The Fall and Rise of America* was released in July 2022 and hit Number 1 on an Amazon list.

Kurt is a successful trial lawyer and name partner in a Los Angeles law firm representing Fortune 500 companies and individuals in matters ranging from routine business cases to confidential Hollywood disputes and political controversies. A member of the Million Dollar Advocates Forum, which recognizes attorneys who have won trial verdicts in excess of $1 million, his litigation strategy and legal analysis articles have been published in legal publications such as the *Los Angeles Daily Journal* and *California Lawyer*.

He is frequently engaged by noted conservatives in need of legal representation, and he was counsel for political commentator and author Ben Shapiro in the widely publicized "Clock Boy" defamation lawsuit, which resulted in the case being dismissed and the victory being upheld on appeal.

Kurt is a 1994 graduate of Loyola Law School, where he was a law review editor. He majored in communications and political science as an undergraduate at the University of California, San

Diego, co-editing the conservative student paper *California Review* while also writing a regular column in the student humor paper *The Koala*.

Kurt served as a US Army infantry officer on active duty and in the California Army National Guard, retiring at the rank of full colonel. He wears the silver "jump wings" of a paratrooper and commanded the 1st Squadron, 18th Cavalry Regiment (Reconnaissance-Surveillance-Target Acquisition). A veteran of both the Persian Gulf War and Operation Enduring Freedom (Kosovo), he is a graduate of the Army's Combined Arms and Services Staff School, the Command and General Staff College, and the United States Army War College, where he received a master's degree in strategic studies.

He lives with his wife Irina and their monstrous dogs Bitey and Barkey in the Los Angeles area, and he enjoys sarcasm and red meat.

His favorite caliber is .45.

The Kelly Turnbull Novels

People's Republic (2016)

Indian Country (2017)

Wildfire (2018)

Collapse (2019)

Crisis (2020)

The Split (2021)

Inferno (2022)

Also By Kurt Schlichter

Conservative Insurgency: The Struggle to Take America Back 2013-2041 (Post Hill Press, 2014)

Militant Normals: How Regular Americans Are Rebelling Against the Elite to Reclaim Our Democracy (Center Street Books, 2018)

The 21 Biggest Lies About Donald Trump (and You) (Regnery, 2020)

We'll Be Back: The Fall and Rise of America (Regnery, 2022)